THE DIAMOND SCAM

♦

JOHN DOWSE

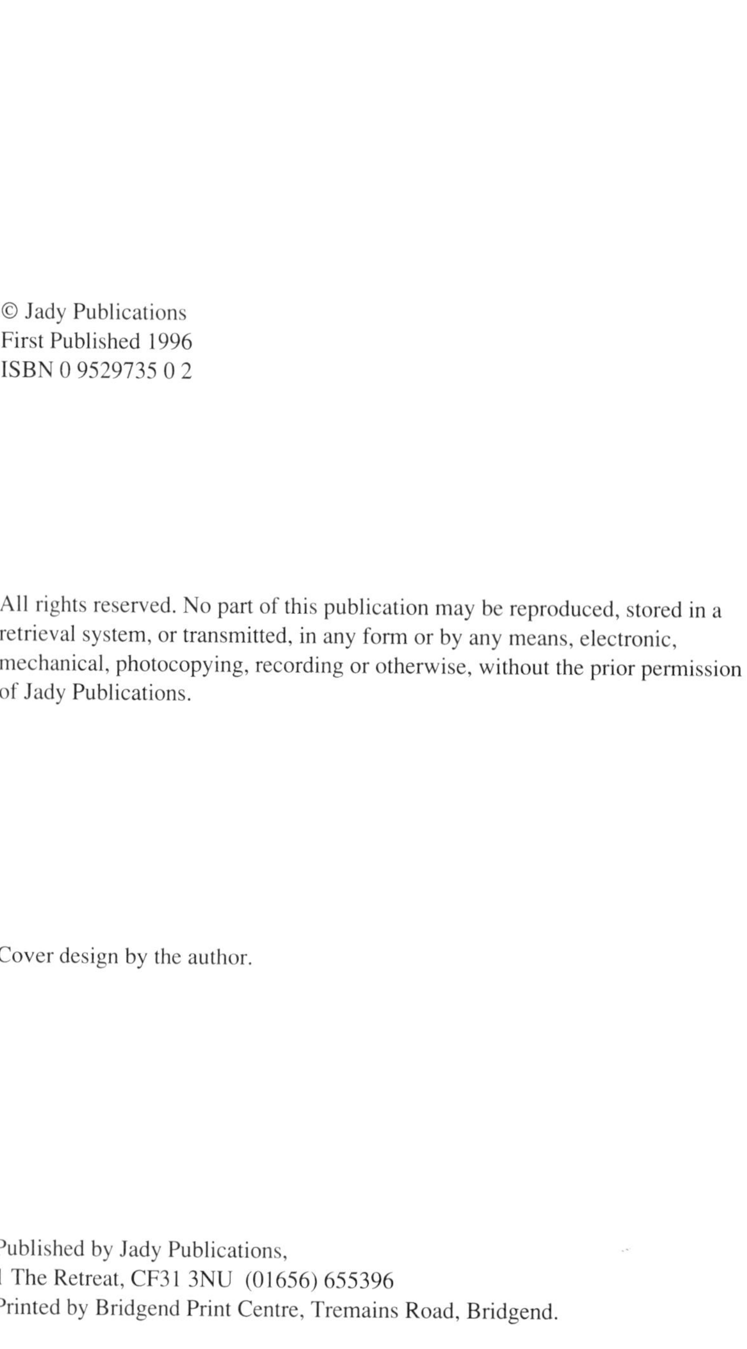

First Published 1996
ISBN 0 9529735 0 2

Cover design by the author.

Published by Jady Publications,
1 The Retreat, CF31 3NU (01656) 655396
Printed by Bridgend Print Centre, Tremains Road, Bridgend.

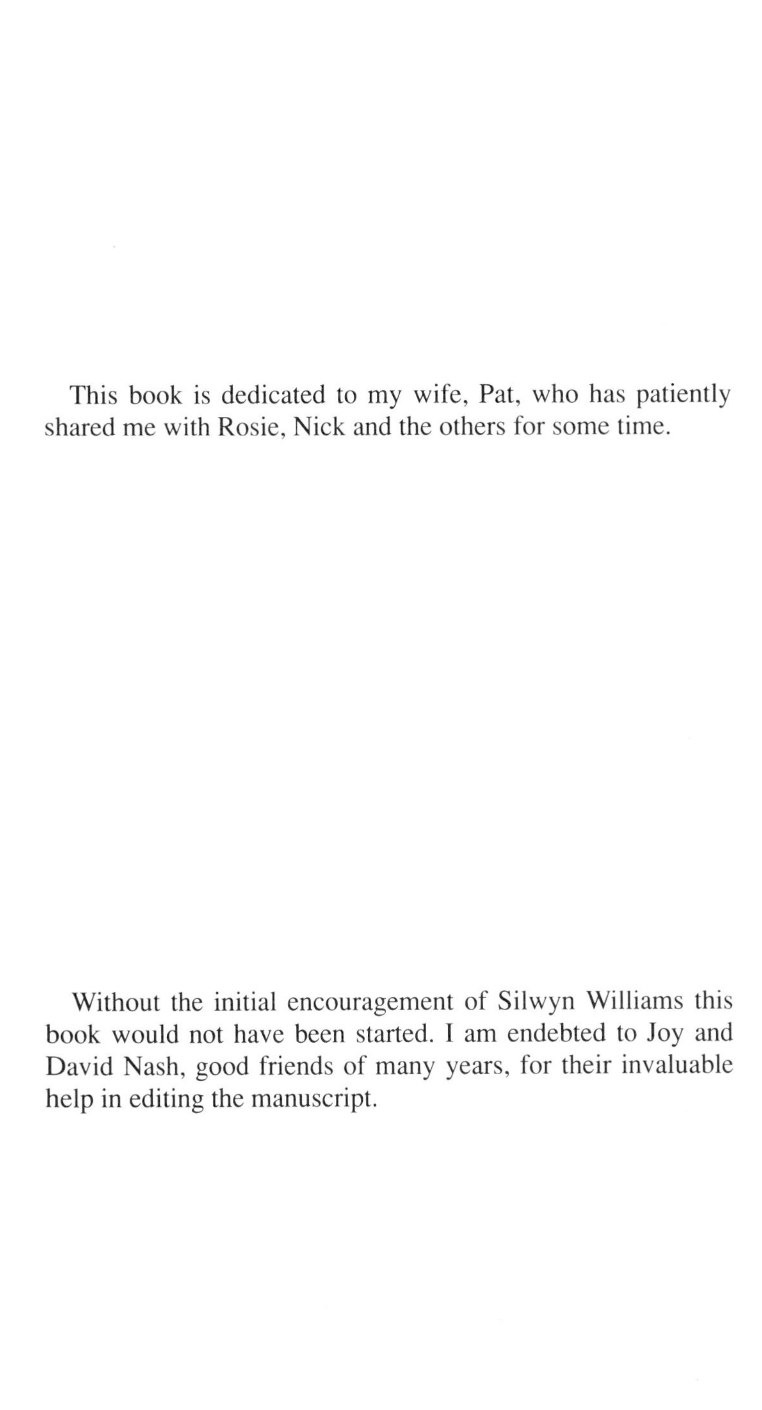

This book is dedicated to my wife, Pat, who has patiently shared me with Rosie, Nick and the others for some time.

Without the initial encouragement of Silwyn Williams this book would not have been started. I am endebted to Joy and David Nash, good friends of many years, for their invaluable help in editing the manuscript.

CHAPTER ONE

Nick awakened instantly. His years in the bush had trained in him an inbuilt awareness of time so that he no longer needed to rely on an alarm for an early call. Lying there, his mind focussed clearly on his diary for the day; his flight to New York with the diamonds he would declare and those he wouldn't, and his meeting with Sammy Goldstein with whom he knew he'd strike a profitable deal later today. He thought what he might say in praise of the quality of the stones he was carrying, though they were so perfect they needed no flattery from him; and the likely put down and banter he'd get back from Sammy. All in all, it was going to be an exciting day and a tiring one too if he flew back to London tonight as he had planned.
'I think I'll stay over a day or so and do the Big Apple as they say,' he thought. 'I've never found time for sightseeing before; a break wouldn't be a bad idea; might do me a power of good.'

He rolled back the sheets, stretching all six feet two of him and padded across the hall to the spare room he had converted to a mini-gym. On one corner of the uncarpeted floor stood an exercise bicycle; in the other, a small compact rowing machine and along the far wall Nick had arranged the weights. He cycled for ten miles in a high gear, rowed for ten minutes at a cracking pace, grunted with the weights for another ten minutes and finished with fifty press-ups in the centre of the room. Now he ran with sweat and he stepped quickly beneath the shower. Cruel jets of almost scalding water changed his skin to the colour of freshly boiled lobster. Adjusting the controls, he moaned as the near ice-cold needles of pain revived him. He rubbed himself down, his circulation restored. He ran the water into the washbasin and shaved his dark stubble, especially carefully around the deep cleft on his chin; he grinned as he remembered his mother's saying, 'a dimple on the chin, the devil within.'
'There must be one hell of a devil lurking inside you chum with a dimple that size,' he thought. He combed his damp hair, as jet black as it had been in schooldays; no sign of silver yet, nor should it be.
'I'm thirty years old and in the peak of condition.'

He breakfasted on fresh orange juice and crisp wholemeal toast plastered with marmalade and washed down with Kenyan blend coffee, freshly brewed. As he catered for himself, he made the starting and the ending of each day as easy as possible, especially as most of his daytime meals were eaten in hotels or restaurants. He had lived so long on his own it came naturally to him to clear up. Because he kept to this routine there never was very much to do and his daily kept the place spotless. She had been with him for years, ever since he had found this apartment. She would let herself in some time during the morning while he was away, get on with whatever needed doing and then let herself out, locking up behind her. He knew she was entirely reliable and for her part, she enjoyed looking after her young man.

Nick selected a dark grey pinstripe suit, hand stitched lapels from Savile Row, knowing his American counterpart would be wearing something loud and flashy; 'someone has to maintain the tone.' His shirt was crisp and white and he chose a grey silk tie with a thin white stripe which matched the suit perfectly. He looked what he was, a gentleman.

The diamonds he was taking to New York had been kept in his safe overnight for their protection. In the corner of the lounge there appeared to be a drinks cabinet. Made of walnut, it seemed to be a very charming piece of antique furniture. He turned the key in the right-hand door and opened it up, glasses sparkling in the room lights and decanters glowing with their amber contents. When he opened the left sided door the solid front of a safe could be seen, the lock presenting in the centre. Nick bent low, concentrating on the combination he dialled. He touched the handle and the door swung open. Inside, there were two soft leather pouches on the shelf of the safe. Nick picked up the larger of the two bags and taking it across to the table, he tipped the contents out on to a fine white linen cloth. Under a bright table lamp the stones were fired with all the colours of the rainbow, patterns dispersing across the white cloth; even he gasped at their beauty. Carefully, he picked up each gem with his tweezers and dropped them into the sac. He tightened the drawstring and placed the bag into his brief case. Returning to the safe he took out the other pouch which was much smaller than the first. With considerable care he emptied the diamonds it held on to the table. The others had been wonderful to look at but these three stones made the others look dull. These were brilliant blue-whites and they were flawless, without any blemish and rare. These three diamonds were worth more than a million pounds and they were kept separate from the others. These were not for the customs to find; Nick didn't plan to declare these. He held each one up to the light before he replaced them into the sack, watching the spectrum diffract from the edges of the diamond. These were perfect; he knew it would be a long time before he would own stones like these again; these were special.

He took the smaller of the pouches containing the three stones and placed it in his inside breast pocket on the left, adjusting it to lie smoothly with as litle disturbance seen on the outside of his suit as possible. He looked at himself in the mirror; only the faintest suggestion there was anything in the pocket. It would do.

- - - - - -

As Rosie watched her taxi weaving its way through the traffic back to the city, she felt very lonely. She had been planning her trip to the States for some weeks and now that time had arrived and it was all about to happen, there was no going back. When she had closed the door of her Maida Vale flat earlier this morning, it had been for the last time; tomorrow was to be the beginning of her new life in America.

After her graduation nearly two years ago, she had moved to London and joined some college friends she knew in a progressive art gallery in a small side street off Bond Street. She audited their finances and at the same time, gained insight into the current vogue in art investment. It was at this gallery she had met the agent of a New York casino, who had come over to London to buy pictures for the casino itself and also as private investments for the casino manager. During their business meetings together, he had, over many months, tried to persuade Rosie to leave Britain and join the casino as its accountant, something she would never have dreamed of doing. Eventually the offer he made was so generous, she felt she couldn't posssibly turn it down; now she was on her way.

Rosie now twenty-three, was tall and slim, green-eyed and auburn haired and looked outstandingly elegant in her Gucci suit bought especially for the occasion; she was eye-catchingly beautiful. The cab driver, smitten with her good looks, had readily helped her obtain a trolley from the bay and loaded her luggage on to it, but with a wave of his hand and a cheery cockney "Good luck luv," he had gone, out of Rosie's life; she was alone.

Well, not really alone. How could she be alone at London's Heathrow? Earlier she had felt the thrill of planning her trip but now she realised there were hundreds of others that must have been feeling exactly the same, probably experiencing the same anxieties, and now all jostling in the concourse of terminal 4, each seeking their exit to another world. Lights everywhere, signs, noise and people, most pushing trolleys just like Rosie's, advancing crab-wise, not always going where their present owners wanted them to go; bumping, struggling, apologising; a kaleidoscope of colour which dazzled and confused in this strange environment.

Rosie found the desk for British Airways to Kennedy, New York quickly. It was staffed with its smart young ladies in the navy, red and silver uniform of the company and as she had arrived early for the flight, there was only a few people around. The girls greeted Rosie cheerily, accepted her luggage for loading and issued her boarding pass, guiding her with a wave of the hand to the waiting area.

Rosie had chosen club class and she had booked into her flight about two hours before departure time, deliberately presenting herself early as she needed to get past the desk clerks before the next part of her plan could begin. As she walked through the passport control she gave a friendly smile to the officer on duty. She recovered her handbag from the X-Ray screen and as she did so, recognised the entrance to the speedwing lounge on the right. Without hesitation, she walked towards the door, at the same time as a dark-haired young man was about to enter the lounge.

- - - - - -

Nick's hand reached the handle of the door of the speedwing lounge a moment before Rosie's; they almost touched.

"Here, let me," he said, opening the door for Rosie.

"Thank you," she replied, blushing slightly. There was a group of people already there talking noisily in the centre of the room, the women seated and the men standing in a semicircle in front of them. When Rosie and Nick came in, they paused in their conversation, but only for a moment, opening their little ring to observe the intruders; but then they carried on with their talk almost without interruption, the men taking longer to take their eyes off Rosie before returning to their group.

"I'm travelling alone; may I join you?" Nick asked diffidently.

"I'd like that; please do," Rosie replied. "I'm on my way to New York. There'll probably be at least another hour to wait even if there are no delays. It always seems endless when travelling alone doesn't it?" Extending her hand she said, "I'm Rosie Haynes."

He took her hand gently but firmly. "I'm Nicholas Royle. I have to be in New York for a few days too. Are you on business Miss Haynes?"

"Not strictly, but I have been offered some work to do while I'm there." Should she tell him the sort of business she was going to join? Perhaps later, not now.

They found a seat in the corner of the room near the window. Fortunately the hostess checked Nick's ticket only, welcoming them both to the first class lounge. The barman approached them silently over the red carpeted floor.
"Would you like something to drink?" Nick asked.
"I'd like a white wine with soda please. You're not very busy today," she added to the barman. Saying that increased her confidence; it made her sound a regular and experienced traveller through the lounge though this was her first transatlantic flight.
"I'll have a tonic only, ice and lemon please," was Nick's order.
The barman brought their drinks and Nick laid a five pound note on his tray. He made to say there was no charge but Nick waved him away; that was his tip. He smiled his thanks as he withdrew to his bar; Rosie knew from the look he gave, he wished all his customers were so generous.

As Nick had walked into the lounge with her, Rosie had felt her interest stir within. He was the sort of consort any young woman would be pleased to be seen with; he was decidedly handsome. She noticed he was carrying a thin black leather brief case, so fine and light, Rosie wondered what could possibly be inside it. He wore a Rolex on his left wrist and gold cufflinks glistened at his sleeves' end.

As they talked, Rosie observed Nick closely; she had noticed he had an accent but just couldn't place it. His suit was businesslike and expensively smart and there were two faint bulges on either side in his breast pockets; one would have been his wallet. She wondered what the other could be. She noticed his hands were smooth and pale, his fingers long and strong like a musicians' and he wore no rings; they were hands which had never toiled at hard manual labour. All the time they sat together, he kept his case between his feet, never losing contact with it. Rosie felt that whatever was in it must have been extremely valuable. His hair, jet black, was surely the darkest she had ever seen; it was parted on the left and shaved high at the temples. He was such an incredibly handsome man, Rosie couldn't help be fascinated and attracted by him.

While they chatted away the time waiting for the flight to be called, Nick was becoming aware of her presence. It was more than just the fact she was a very beautiful woman, her skin flawless and her manicure and make-up expertly applied, but her crowning glory literally was her hair. The chestnut waves gleamed as if they were oiled silk, yet they hung freely on her shoulders, bouncing as she moved her head. Her slim figure was accentuated by the stylish cut of her suit and her shapely stockinged legs were tucked backwards, crossed at the ankle, coyly revealing as little thigh as possible, yet just enough to stir any man's interest.

"I hope you won't mind my asking, but are you a model Miss Haynes?"

"Good gracious me no; you flatter me Mr. Royle. I'm just a business girl; in fact I have been asked to join a casino in New york as their accountant."

"Good lord," he said, a chauvinistic chuckle in his voice, "I've never met a lady casino accountant before; in fact, I've never met anyone who worked in a casino before; you must be a very clever young woman."

"Not really."

"I still think you ought to be a model Miss Haynes. I'm sure you must have been told before many times, you are a very attractive young lady. You have such wonderful hair, quite remarkable. I would think the modelling agencies would be more than happy to snap you up. I'd be pleased to be your agent any time."

"You're sure you're not trying to turn a young woman's head Mr. Royle? What do you do?"

"Oh, I buy and sell at a profit; may I get you another drink?"

"No thanks; I think I had better try and keep a clear head with all these compliments flying about."

The director of cabin services entered the lounge to let the passengers know that they would be boarding in about ten minutes. Most of the travellers wandered off to the hospitality bar for another drink; it was free after all but Nick and Rosie remained seated in the corner. Rosie turned to Nick, blushing slightly.

"I'm afraid I shall have to say goodbye in just a few minutes. You see I'm a fraud Mr. Royle. I'm not supposed to be in here. This lounge is for passengers travelling first class. I'm not; I'm flying club class; I walked in here because I wanted to find out how the other half lived. Now it's time to go back where I should have gone in the first place. It was nice meeting you Nicholas Royle. You never know, perhaps we'll see each other in New York; they say it's a big city, but it's a small world." She got up to walk towards the door.

"Hey, just a moment Miss Haynes, don't go. I feel I was just getting to know you; perhaps I can fix up something." Rosie hesitated. "All the

first class seats may not be taken. If there are any that are empty, perhaps I can persuade the steward to let you travel as my guest, you never know. I've enjoyed meeting you so much, I'd be pleased to have you join me for the flight; that's if you'd like to of course." The director reappeared asking passengers to start boarding. Nick approached him.
"I say; are all the first class seats occupied on this flight? If not, I'd very much like this lady who was in club class to be my guest." He took a twenty-pound note from his wallet; the steward looked at it but didn't make a move to touch it. Nick brought out another; the steward still didn't move. A third note appeared. With a quick movement of the hand, the notes vanished and they were both invited to follow.
"There you are; it's all arranged. Come on, you'll really enjoy it and you'll make me very happy."
"Oh, that would be lovely."
"You'll love it. There's so much more room; it is really grand. Flowers on the table, free champagne and there's usually a superb menu to choose from. Come on, you'll have a super time." Nick overwhelmed her as he carried her forward with his own apparent enthusiasm. He held the door open for her and as she passed closely to him through to the walkway, she picked his pocket, something she hadn't done for ages. It was done so very gently. Together they entered the plane, the steward guiding them to their seats in the front. As Nick had said the difference was wonderful.

CHAPTER TWO

'Why on earth wasn't I satisfied? He's been so nice to me; why didn't I curb my curiosity? Why did I do it; why oh why?'

"Well," murmured Nick as they were seated and alone again, "that was a sweet little trick you pulled back there Miss Haynes. You're good, I'll say that for you; you're damned good."
"What are you talking about" Rosie squeaked. Her hand rose in front of her face; her voice had almost gone, a sudden tightness constricting her throat. Her mouth had dried and her heart raced noisily in her chest; she felt sure he must be able to hear it too as the pounding continued in her ears. She knew she had flushed a deep red, the blood pumping into her neck and face and a heaviness lay sickly beneath her ribs.
"Oh come on Rosie," Nick answered; "I've told you you were good but we both know you dipped my inside breast pocket as we moved through the doorway of the lounge." He tapped the left side of his

chest, indicating which pocket had been picked. "I knew straight away you had lifted that pouch." He hesitated. More urgently he asked, "You have brought it with you and not left it lying around anywhere? That would have been extremely silly of you and very awkward too. No, you wouldn't have had time to do that. That pouch is worth a lot of money young lady."

Rosie didn't know whether to slap him hard or to scream at his accusation, though that wouldn't be wise should they decide to search her. Hiding or running away now, 30,000 feet above the ocean wasn't on; she knew she was trapped, caught; for the first time in her life it looked as if she wouldn't be able to wriggle her way out of this.
'Why, oh why didn't I leave it alone?' she thought again. As Nick had come into the lounge, with her first glance she had noticed the slight bulge over his left breast; it wasn't his wallet which she had recognised on the other side. As he had held the door open for her to pass through it had been so easy to lift the soft leather pouch she found in his inside breast pocket. Now as she turned to him she knew the only thing she could do was to bluff it out. It would be tricky to try to return the pouch, now tucked in the cleavage beneath her bra, to his pocket inside or out; but Rosie knew she was going to have to try.

The stewardess passing among the passengers distracted Nick's attention for a few moments as she enquired whether they would like champagne.
"Yes, we'll both have some please" he answered. During those few moments Rosie palmed the pouch from its hiding place. As she reached across Nick for her drink, fate helped as some air turbulence rocked the plane slightly and some drops of wine were spilled over Nick. The stewardess was embarrassed and apologetic and in the time it took to dry the few spots, Rosie had put the pouch back into Nick's inside pocket.
He murmured to her, "Good girl; you're a real pro Rosie. I'm glad I didn't have to make any fuss. You see, there are three diamonds in that bag; they're perfect brilliant blue-whites; flawless; worth a million, pounds of course. So you see I couldn't let you get away with stealing them."

He knew she had taken the pouch and put it back; Rosie realised she was beaten. This man had to be a pro too. Only someone who knew how to pick a pocket as she had done would appreciate the sensations of it happening; and yet why hadn't he broadcast to all around that she was a thief?

She thought to herself, ‘Nicholas Royle, perhaps you’ve got something to hide; perhaps the diamonds don’t belong to you at all.’
“How did you know what had happened, that I had picked your pocket I mean. I was very careful?” asked Rosie.
“Well, many years ago I was trained by my country to steal, to pick pockets and break open safes.”
“You mean you were a spy?” Rosie had never met anyone like this.
“No, no Rosie; I was a soldier; a special sort of soldier, sometimes I worked on my own, other times with the platoon I commanded.”
“You were told to steal?” Rosie couldn’t understand that he could have been ordered to steal.
“Yes and how to. I’m probably as good as you. Well I used to be; fingers a bit stiff now I expect. It’s not something I have to do in civilian life. But I remember how it’s done and what it feels like to have it done to me; you brought back a lot of memories. That’s how I felt your fingers in my pocket, gentle though you were.” He paused as if reminiscing over past days. Rosie stirred beside him bringing him back to the present.
“Would you like to see what you had?”
“Yes, please; you said they were diamonds.”

Nick emptied the contents of the pouch on to Rosie’s palm. Three matching diamonds, each the size of a sparrow’s egg; all the colours of the rainbow flashed in the brilliant sunlight streaming through the cabin window from the multiple facets of the stones, the colours changing instantly as the movement of the pulse in Rosie’s hand changed their positions so slightly.
“I’ve never seen anything so beautiful; are they stolen?” whispered Rosie.
“Good Lord no Rosie; that’s my business buying, selling, cutting, mounting precious stones. I have offices in London and Amsterdam dealing mainly in diamonds which I buy usually in South Africa.” Rosie thought, ‘that’s where he gets his accent.’
“I expect to sell these later today.” He paused. “I had been thinking I’d take a few days break. I haven’t had a holiday for ages so maybe I’ll stay on in New York. Perhaps, if you’re free you’d be able to have dinner with me this evening?”
“You must tell me first why you haven’t had me arrested or something? I’m surprised you haven’t had the stewards lock me up somewhere though I suppose there aren’t that many places they could use. Are you a crook too?”
“No Rosie; I promise, I’m not a crook; just an ordinary business man. Come on, now you must tell me about yourself. New York is more than

seven hours away. I want to know everything about you, especially how you became a professional pickpocket and how a pickpocket becomes the accountant to a casino."

The time just flew. Two complete strangers a few hours ago, now had some sort of rapport between them. What had started as a polite conversation in a waiting lounge, developed when Rosie picked his pocket. Nick was clearly attracted to this beautiful young woman who was intrigued by this handsome young man who had not cried thief. Rosie couldn't think why unless he too was a crook which he had denied. In those few hours Rosie told him of those things she remembered of her childhood and her entry into the world of petty crime.

"I was brought up by my Mum. My father ran off before I was born when he knew I was on the way, so she had a tough time raising me in a small room over a cafe where she worked."

"That was hard for her."

"Yes it was; we had a lot of regulars who came in and I got to know them, even when I was quite small. I remember there was one man whom we all called 'The Gent' because he always dressed well and was so well mannered. I remember his hands were soft, not like the others. One day I watched him as he picked the back pocket of one of the rowdies we used to have. He knew that I had seen him. He slid his finger over his lips hoping I wouldn't say anything and went out to the toilet. He was only a moment; the wallet was back in this chap's pocket and he had no idea it had gone. He was good, the best; he taught me all I know."

"Sounds as if he taught you all the wrong things."

"Maybe. He taught me to play cards; he made me learn the suits and the numbers even before I went to school. Later I used to watch him play poker with the others and he'd usually win. He would make me think where the cards were likely to be and he explained how to work out the odds. He taught me how to shuffle cards and how to watch the eyes of your opponent and the importance of the sweat appearing on his brow; oh, so many things I owe to 'The Gent.'"

"Bit of a psychologist."

"Yes, I suppose so. Then I did well in school and got an entrance to university to read accountancy so you see I more or less left home then. Mum never really wanted me to join her in the cafe anyway. There seemed to be so many more exciting things to do with one's life."

"Do you have a police record Rosie? Are they looking for you?"

"No" said Rosie. "Then, when I left university I was asked if I'd like to work with some old college friends in an art gallery they had started off Bond Street. One of the guys' father had put up the money to finance them and I was to be their accountant. I enjoyed it a lot. I learned a lot about contemporary art and while I was there, I met an agent for an American gambling club, buying pictures for the casino. A month ago, I received a letter from the solicitors to the manager, whom I have never met, saying that as a vacancy had occurred, I was being invited to take over as the accountant in his New York casino. The salary I was offered was extravagant, one I couldn't refuse. Apparently, they had arranged the work permits. All I had to do was step into someone else's shoes. So this old lady is going to work in a casino in New York for someone I've never met."

Nick smiled. "Old lady? Not much more than twenty if a day; just in your prime of life. By the way, have you heard of any other women casino accountants? I would have thought it was very much a male dominated world."

"Do you know, I've never questioned it."

"It does seem a little strange to me." Nick hesitated for a moment. "I've been in business for quite a few years Rosie. I'm a respectable diamond dealer, yet I have in my mind a confidence trick which could bring in more than ten million pounds. It would take a lot of planning of course and I would need the assistance of a very beautiful woman, just like you. And d'you know, if we got away with it, the con may never be known about, ever, by anybody. Does that interest you young lady?"

"Nicholas Royle, you are a villain. You're leading me astray. But seriously, I've only been a small time crook; I'm good at it but you're talking a different league now. I've no experience at that level. But I must say you've whetted my appetite now so, speak on."

"Well I can't tell you the details now but if you agree to have dinner with me tonight I'll fill you in with the rough idea."

"What can a girl say other than yes; thank you; I'd love to have dinner with you Mr. Nicholas Royle."

"Perhaps you'd better get used to calling me Nick, all my friends do."

They talked for an hour or so and then lunch was served; eight unrushed courses, thought out and planned by Willi Elsener with all the same care and attention as those at the Dorchester; after all, British Airways is a member of La Confrerie de la Chaine des Rotisseurs. The prelude of Sevruga caviar was followed by a saute of fresh seafood in a basil cream sauce between lasagna pasta and baby vegetables.

The fillet of beef with roesti potato cakes and courgettes and carrots was so tender and mouthwatering and the apple cider vinaigrette dressing with the salad provided the contrasting tartness, cleaning the palate. The dessert they both chose was the poached pear with cinnamon and raisins in light filo pastry served with vanilla custard; it was delicious. After their coffee, they relaxed as they watched the in-flight film 'Pretty Woman'."

"She's a very pretty woman that Julia Roberts," murmured Rosie.

"Nowhere near as pretty as the young lady I had lunch with today."

"Thank you sir," she said, a blush rising to her cheeks.

"I think you'd better get some rest," Nick said. "Though we took off from Heathrow at eleven and it takes a little over seven hours to cross the Atlantic, we'll be landing at Kennedy at half past one, local time. So it's going to be a long day. And remember, you agreed to have dinner with me. Slip on the eye shades and have a little shut-eye. I won't disturb you; in fact I think I'll probably have a rest too."

"You're getting tired of me already Nick Royle," Rosie pouted with a grin spreading across her face. "That friendship didn't last very long did it?"

"Go to sleep" Nick said, pretending to throw the pillow at her. "Just rest."

Both Rosie and Nick found it strange to adjust to the blinding light and the noise inside the aircraft at 35,000 feet and rest was difficult. They both kicked off their shoes and put on the slippers provided, adjusted their seats so that they were reclining as much as was possible and plumped up the pillows, but even wearing the eyeshades, neither found it easy to relax; but they did try. As Nick had said 'It's going to be a long day.'

"This is your captain speaking." The intercom wasn't that clear with the sound of the engines and the wind rushing past at several hundred miles an hour. "We are approaching our descent path for John F Kennedy airport. They have had some recent rain but it's dry now; the air temperature is 20 Celsius, a pleasant 68 Fahrenheit. There's a slight breeze so humidity today is low. Please put your seats in the upright position, extinguish any lighted cigarettes and fasten your safety belts. Thank you."

"I hate landing and take off" said Rosie.

"Me too" said Nick, sliding his hand so very gently over hers in a protective sort of way. "Me too."

As the plane banked, the starboard wing dipped slightly and Rosie had a distant view of the eastern tip of Manhattan, towering skyscrapers, their heads in the low cloud. The Hudson River on the left of Manhattan island joined the East River there but wispy clouds prevented her seeing the details of the spectacular skyline. And once again on level flight, there was nothing to see until the plane landed, Nick's hand still holding Rosie's, so gently, he wondered if she was aware of it.

"I did enjoy being with you Rosie."

"I shall never forget this journey. It's been one of the most exciting days of my life. I do want to thank you for having me with you."

"It was all my pleasure; we'll have to get our things together; we'll be away first from here, before the rest."

So it was that Rosie who left Heathrow in the morning, not knowing anyone in America, was preparing to land with a new friend, Nick, who was almost certainly going to change her life.

CHAPTER THREE

Nick and Rosie and the other first class passengers left the plane before the three hundred and seventy or so world travellers crowded through the narrow exit to the crush of the grey bureaucracy of immigration and customs. A tall, grey-haired, tight-skirted, British Airways, time-expired stewardess controlled them in the snake-like queue, with her "Wait there," and "Next," and always they were under the watchful eyes of the New York police, guns swinging on their hips. Fortunately for Nick and Rosie, their passage through immigration was easy and rapid though the queue for the rest seemed endless and its progress snail-like. But nobody crossed the white line between 'us and them', not even the first class passengers before their turn and should they try to do so, the bossy woman would snarl harshly, "Stand on line," and push the offender back.

"Good afternoon Miss Haynes," the unsmiling immigration officer said as he looked at Rosie's passport and visa and then at her. The fact that she was a very attractive young lady seemed to have no effect on his boredom.

"Hallo," said Rosie.

"Can you tell me why it is you've come to New York?" His accent grated.

"I'm on a visit and I may take up an offer of work here. I believe my visa and work permits are all correct."

"What is your type of work Miss Haynes?"

"I'm an accountant. I have been asked to join a company on Park Avenue."

"Is that so Miss Haynes? A lady accountant? I've no experience of

them," a sneer in his voice. "Are you carrying any drugs or contraband itemised on this card?" he said, waving the list in front of Rosie. Glancing at it, Rosie denied she had anything. Stamping her passport with an overloud thump, he handed it back to her.
"Have a good day," he said without any enthusiasm.

Nick too had to pass through customs and immigration and he was asked the same questions as Rosie. As he was carrying the case of trade diamonds he needed to declare these to the official in charge. Their value was a million pounds and the bill of sale confirmed this. There were no problems and once the documentation was completed he joined Rosie in the concourse outside. No one questioned him about the other three stones in his pocket, another million pounds worth.

As they met again they both became aware of the paging announcement for Nick.
"Would Mr Nicholas Royle arriving from London Heathrow on flight BA 175 please call at the British Airways desk in the main assembly area."
"Did you hear that Nick? Is anything wrong?"
"No; it's probably Sammy come to collect us. Let's go check it out."
Struggling through the crowds, their cases now piled high on a single trolley, equally as wayward as the one Rosie had had at Heathrow, they made their way to the information desk in the main assembly area.

Sammy was as Jewish as bagels. He was short, about five feet four inches tall. Nick could tuck him and his delicately embroidered silver yarmulke under his chin easily. But he weighed about 15 stones; he was as close to being Mr Five by Five, five feet tall and five feet wide as you can imagine. He gave the impression of immense strength; an ox of a man. His nose was large and hooked with greying bristles sprouting from his flaring nostrils. Coarse tufts of hair shaded his cheekbones, which even at his age carried still the scars of pubertal acne. Above his dark purple-framed glasses and their powerful pebble lenses, his bushy eyebrows separated his face from his brow, which appeared to have no end as it passed backwards over his cranium circled with a friar's tonsure. His jowls shook as he spoke and wobbled as he laughed and he seemed to be a man who laughed often. The suit he wore was a shade of lilac, his shirt a pale green and his tie, a slash of bright yellow down the front. "Sammy, Sammy Goldstein, you old villain. It's good to see you again."
They embraced, patting each other on the shoulders as old friends do

and it was some moments before they separated, still holding on as they looked each other over.
"Hi Nick; it's nice to see you too; it's been quite a while. You look just the same though; as skinny as ever. Never mind, my Elizabeth will soon fatten you up."
"You're looking well Sammy; too well perhaps; put on a bit of weight eh?" said Nick, prodding his midriff.
Sammy grinned; clearly he had something of a weight problem.

"I'd like you to meet Miss Rosie Haynes; she kept me company on the flight. I said it would be no problem dropping her off at her apartment; is that okay?"
Sammy took her hand into his huge hairy paw, holding on to it rather longer than was really necessary.
"Sure thing." His rasping New York accent jarred. "Nice to meet you Miss Haynes. How did you enjoy your trip with this big hunk?"
"Hallo Mr Goldstein. I think he's nice. I'm sure we have both enjoyed each other's company."
Pausing, he said with just a little quiver in his voice, "Nick's been an old friend for more years than I care to remember Miss Haynes and meeting him always brings back old memories of times together. Where're you staying?"
"I've got an apartment at 812 5th Avenue, East 63rd Street; it belongs to the company. It's good of you to take me with you; it'll be a great help."
"It's no problem. That's a swell address Miss Haynes; by the way, call me Sammy; everyone does."
"Thanks; and I'm Rosie."
"Hi Rosie." Sammy had his car, a big silver-grey stretched Lincoln parked close outside; to Rosie it seemed enormous. His chauffeur jumped out when he saw them coming and helped lift the cases into the boot. Rosie noticed it was the first time Nick had let his brief case out of his control. Clearly, it had arrived; he didn't have to care for it any more; it was safe.
"Shalom aleichem Mr Royle; keeping well I guess?" He shook Nick's outstretched hand.
"Shalom Abe; your pa still giving you a tough time? How's the family? This is Miss Haynes."
"Hi Miss Haynes. Had a nice flight?"
"It was fine Abe. That's some car you're driving; it's huge. Tell me, is everyone always so friendly and helpful in New York?"
"Not always Ma'am," he chuckled.
"How long will it take to get to the city centre?" Rosie asked.

"About three quarters of an hour I guess. It depends a bit on the traffic; it should be okay now."

They moved off into the stream of traffic, westbound towards the city. No one was racing but all the cars seemed to be intent on getting there without holdup. Abe weaved his way through the lanes, overtaking, undertaking, pulling over, watching behind in his mirror all the time while Sammy, Nick and Rosie talked away in the back of the car. Abe interrupted.

"Excuse me Pa; don't look around, but do you know any reason why we should be followed? There're two guys in a black sedan which pulled out after us at Kennedy; they're still a couple of cars behind us, though I've passed quite a few and they could have passed us. D'you want me to lose them?"

"No Abe; don't do anything different for the moment; let's think it through; you may have got it wrong. Quite a few cars will have left the airport at that time and most will be going this way."

"Yeah, I'd thought of that but this one's on our tail, I'm pretty sure. He's had the chance to pass us on a number of occasions but he's still there."

"Okay; let's say you're right; then he's after me or Nick."

"Or perhaps Rosie," Nick said.

"Hey, why me?" piped up Rosie."

"Oh come on Nick; surely Rosie's clean."

"So are we for that matter," Nick replied. "But someone is following one of us in this car; could he be after you Abe?"

Abe grinned wickedly. "Not unless he's some chick's husband."

"So it has to be one of us; as this is Rosie's first visit to New York, I can't think why they should be trailing her," said Sammy.

"I agree," added Rosie.

"Maybe; but for the moment let's assume it's possibly all three of us. Would one of your lot want to follow you or me Sammy?"

"No of course not; and don't talk about my lot Nick," Sammy retorted crossly, "not in front of Rosie; she doesn't need to know. In any case, what about your guys keeping an eye on you?" It was Nick's turn to look cross.

"Okay, Okay; Let's not fall out over what may still be a perfectly ordinary occurrence. In any case, as we've been talking, I've been thinking. I believe it's likely our shepherd is keeping an eye on Rosie not us."

Rosie interrupted; "Why on earth do you say that? I would have thought I'd be the last person they would be following, not knowing anybody here."

"Well Rosie," Nick started. "I didn't say anything before when you told me you were head-hunted for the casino here, but didn't you ever think it strange, that you, an English woman was being invited into the American scene, into a man's world and not just an ordinary world but the world of syndicates, gangs and mobsters? Didn't you realise the casinos and clubs in the States, especially those in the big cities are controlled by the Mafia? They're linked with gambling, drugs, extortion, prostitution. Surely it must have crossed your mind?"

"Nick Royle, I've never heard such nonsense. I thought I was offered this work because I'm good at my job. And I knew the chaps I worked with at the gallery; we were in university together. I'm sure there were no drugs there. Surely you don't think there's any connection between the gallery and the sort of organised crime you are describing? No, that's just ridiculous,"

"Well maybe not Rosie; but here in New York things are very different. Protectionism makes it impossible for small legitimate club owners to survive unless they join the big boys and they are the Mafia. I must say I couldn't understand how it was you were offered this job in the first place, but I can understand their keeping tabs on you once you're here in the States. Like it or not Rosie, you've entered the big time with a vengeance and methinks you won't like it, not one little bit."

"You're frightening me Nick; I've told you I'm only a small time crook."

"They may know it too; now you're joining them in the big time. Maybe they know something about you that even you don't know."

"Nick, do shut up."

"Tell me Rosie; what's the name of the club you're going to work for?"

"The Green Baize on Park Avenue." Sammy picked up the car phone and dialled a number quickly; it was answered immediately.

"Hi, this is the diamond man; give me a quick low down on the Green Baize club on Park Avenue?" He cradled the phone as he waited the few moments for the reply. He spoke the words he heard on the telephone. "It's Mafia controlled, one of a chain, all with the same name, US and Europe, headman Celleri, thought to be from England. Been here a little over twenty years. Into coke and heroin. Bookkeeper found recently in the river, face down; known police informer; want any more?"

"No; thanks."

"Sorry Rosie; seems you've inherited a whole heap of trouble. Nick's right, now we can guess who's behind us. It's almost certainly the mob; and now they know about us. What d'you think Nick?"

Nick paused while he thought for a few moments. "Well, all they can report at the moment is that Rosie came out of the airport with a man,

me, and that you gave us both a lift into the city. There's nothing much in that. If you start to race to lose them now they'll know they've been rumbled and it will assume an important significance; at the moment it's just your giving a lift to an attractive young lady, who had met up with your friend. What's more important is what do you think Rosie now you've heard what Sammy's computer has to say?"
"I'm a bit scared. I'm not sure what to believe. I knew the people I worked with in the gallery in England; I'm sure there was no question of drugs there. I took this job because I was offered it; I never questioned how or why it was me; I felt I was good at my work; now I'm not so sure. I'm frightened."
They all fell silent; this was a problem no one had thought about.

The car sped onwards through the rutted Van Wyck Expressway, the bumps in the road smoothed by the soft suspension of the Lincoln. They passed the many clapboard buildings along the highway, disfigured by the multicoloured graffiti, through Flushing Meadow and Elmhurst, turning left on to Queens Boulevard through Long Island City towards the Queensboro Bridge and the centre of Manhattan. Sammy, who had been quiet for a while suddenly seemed as if a weight had been lifted off his shoulders.
"D'you know what I think? I don't think we have anything to worry about; this a hired car through one of my companies it is true, but I can't see them finding out anything about us that way. As for you Nick; you're just a guy she met on the plane; I would think Rosie could explain you away quite easily. We'll keep our ears to the ground for the next couple of days. If anything's brewing, we'll get to hear; I shouldn't worry. But I do think it's important you forget what you've heard Rosie, especially the bit about the Mafia, otherwise we may all be in the cart."

As they approached, the city still some distance off, Rosie became aware yet again of the impressive New York skyline, the skyscrapers towering into the blue afternoon sky, now clear of cloud. She had seen them first on the eastern tip of Manhattan Island when the aircraft banked as it approached the runway at John F Kennedy airport earlier, but now the mass of buildings, all laid out in geometrical patterns seemed overpowering; it appeared to Rosie that once she entered that concrete jungle she would be lost, like an ant in the garden back home.
"There you are Rosie, Manhattan. They tell me it cost only 24 bucks," Sammy chuckled; the others waited for Sammy to continue. "Yeah, that's the value the Dutch settlers paid in bartered goods to the Manhattan Indians for all you can see in front of you; pretty good real estate deal? And now, it's priceless."

Sammy and Nick tried to point out the various notable buildings they could make out as they got closer to the city. To the left, towering over the East River, was the spectacular United Nations complex and way back from that, many blocks inland she could see the tower of the Chrysler building.
"That used to be the tallest skyscraper in the world when it was built in 1930 Rosie, but it didn't stay like that for long; within months, the Empire State Building had overtaken it; that's it over there," he said, pointing out a slender pinnacle to the west. "Now of course there are several taller."
"It's got a strange shape to its top," Rosie said.
"It's made out of stainless steel; said to be the same as the radiator cap on a 1929 Chrysler though I've never seen one. There are lots of other motifs from their automobiles built into the facade too," said Sammy, pleased to be the fount of information. Rosie found the names of all the buildings so confusing and the busy crush of traffic all around rather frightening. So much so, later, the only names she could remember were the Chrysler building and the Rockefeller center. But it was all so exciting it was easy to put out of her mind those distressing things she had heard only a short while ago and concentrate on the present.

The car turned into 1st Avenue as it crossed over the Queensboro Bridge, and passed the Cornell University Medical Center on the right. The traffic lights into East 63rd Street were red and it was a few minutes before Abe could make the turn towards Rosie's new home, an apartment on 5th Avenue, probably the most wealthy, well-kept part of the city. Rosie's new home was quite impressive.

CHAPTER FOUR

The car pulled up along the vacant kerb outside the awning in front of Rosie's new home and Abe started to unload her luggage from the trunk. Nick went into the apartment entrance and persuaded the doorman to give a hand with the luggage.
"I'll come up with you if you'd like me to," he said; "I can find out your phone number so that I can keep in touch and I'll know where to come later this evening when I pick you up for dinner. Do you know what floor you're on?"
"No, I don't actually; I was told the keys would all be ready for me with the doorman; I have a letter of introduction to show him."
He had been listening to the conversation and when he passed

them with the cases ready to put them in the lift, he took the letter that Rosie had taken out of her bag and said, "The lady's on the 14th, suite 140, right on the front, overlooking 5th Avenue; it's some apartment, lady."
Sammy, who had got out of the car less quickly than the others, had walked in, just in time to hear the doorman's remark.
"You got a guardian angel up there Rosie? It takes a bundle to live here. You've gotta be dragging in loot to stay here. Would you mind if I came up too? I'd sure like to take a look around; see how the other half lives."
"Of course, do come up; I don't know what it will be like."
"I'll tell you now Rosie, sight unseen, it will be absolutely super."

The lift whisked them all to the fourteenth floor in a matter of moments. The doors opened automatically on to the corridor, brightly lit with crystal chandeliers suspended in front of the pink-tinted mirrors which lined the walls. The door to suite 140 was in front of the elevator and Rosie, who had been given the key by the janitor turned it gingerly in the lock. She opened the door into an airy room, brightly lit with the afternoon sun; it smelled fresh from the flowers on the entrance table. There was a card attached to the bouquet; across the centre, someone had written, 'To Miss Rosie Haynes; Welcome, from the Green Baize.'

"Say, this is real cool. Who's a lucky girl then? Are you sure you don't own this company, rather than just work for it?" Sammy voiced all their thoughts. It was all too good to be true; even Rosie was overwhelmed.
"I don't understand it either; it all looks so frightfully expensive; I'll never be able to afford this on my salary. I suppose there can't have been some awful mistake?" The doorman who had been struggling with the bags appeared again just at the right time.
"No ma'am; no mistake; this is your apartment."

Nick paid off the doorman and the three of them strolled around the place, touching everything and praising and generally admiring the decor and extolling the view from the window which overlooked 5th Avenue and which was spectacular. Rosie opened the door on to the balcony outside the apartment as they all wanted to have a closer and even better view. Though still fairly early in the afternoon, there were many people in the avenue below especially in the part of Central Park which was right opposite the apartment entrance. The landaus, those awaiting fares, stood around a freshly gilded statue of a horseman and an angel, the horses patiently scraping the ground. Others, their folded tops down in the spring sunshine, quietly journeyed around the park, showing the sights of New York to the vast throng of visitors to the city; everything constantly moving; a gigantic life force, throbbing away floors below; and the traffic, stopping, starting, yet almost silent, all that way away; everything disembodied; they were looking at it but seemed not to be part of it.

"Well Rosie. You should be happy enough here. You won't get a better apartment than this in the whole of New York and that's a fact," said Sammy. "Phew, I just wish I could afford to live here; this is some place."

The telephone rang in the hall; Rosie walked over to pick it up. "Hallo; who is that?"

"Ah, Miss Haynes; you have arrived. Did you have a good flight?" The voice was clear and not American.

"Yes, it was wonderful. Who is that please?"

"This is the manager of the Green Baize; I would like to meet you as soon as possible. Perhaps when you've unpacked your things, you'd care to come across and have a chat with me? My car will pick you up at say, six?"

"Yes; I'd be delighted to meet you; that would be fine. I shall look forward to that. I have to be back here in time to dress for dinner."

"So soon to have made friends; I congratulate him. Until six."

"That was my new boss," Rosie said to all the inquisitive faces looking at her as she put the phone down. "He wants to meet me this evening. I've just got in and he wants to talk to me tonight about my work at the casino; it's all go isn't it? I read somewhere that New York is described as the frenetic city; seems that's right."

"Well, we'd better go then and leave you in peace. I'll be back at eight; will that give you enough time d'you think?" Nick asked.

"Yes, I should think so; I'll see you then. Thanks Sammy for being so kind and helpful; and thank Abe too for me won't you?"

"Sure thing Rosie; it was a pleasure meeting you. Nick's staying with Elizabeth and me; I'll leave my number should you want to get in touch." He wrote his telephone number out as Rosie walked with Nick towards the door. No one saw him undo the mouthpiece of the receiver and introduce a small bean sized transmitter and replace the phone in its cradle. It was all done so quickly and professionally. But the bug was there.

Going down in the lift all they could do was talk about Rosie and her new apartment. Sammy, knowing the cost of living in New York found it most difficult to understand.

"Christ. That's going to take mucho gelt. You can bet your ass on it. Accountants may earn too much but not that much. There's something fishy going on here; you mark my words. Either Rosie's crook or her employer is; it just ain't right." Nick was considering what Sammy was saying; he knew Rosie had some crooked tendencies but she wouldn't be involved with the mob knowingly; he was sure of that. But this Green Baize casino; that was another matter. They knew it was part of the Mafia; that was certain. Sammy's computer, linked with Mossad intelligence had said so. What on earth was the girl letting herself in for? Nick suddenly felt very protective towards Rosie. Strange. He'd never felt like this about any girl before and he was aware his feelings for her were different; he couldn't wait 'till eight when they'd meet again.

CHAPTER FIVE

Sammy's car was still at the kerbside. As they approached they could see Abe sitting upright in the driver's seat. Nick thought it strange he didn't look across to them as they approached and stranger still he didn't get out of the car to open the door for his father. It was only as they opened it that his body fell forwards, slumped across the wheel. Then Nick could see the small puncture wound beneath the left temple where the bullet had entered Abe's skull and the scorch marks, where the muzzle of a gun had been pushed close to his head. A small trickle of blood was drying in front of his ear. The larger exit wound where the slug had forced the brain out through the smashed bone had been concealed from them; yet his little cap still remained on the back of his head. The inside of the front of the car was covered in blood. Abe had been murdered in the seat of the car listening to the radio while waiting for his father and Nick to return. Sammy groaned. He was grey and sweaty as he retched at the side of the road, his glasses all askew; he clutched his chest as the angina roared through him, his legs buckling beneath him; Abe was his firstborn.

"Nick, call the cops; they have to be told despite my connections with the organisation. If I don't, whoever did this will know they've made a score. It's got to be the mob; there's no one else right now; they're warning us, not me but us. I helped you so they hit at me. Take care Nick. I think we may be in big trouble. I will let my people know later; but first, we must call the police."

"I'll do that."

"By the way, check the trunk. See whether they've taken the diamonds. If they have, they'll have made a mistake and be in even bigger

trouble. My lot won't allow that; and if they haven't, perhaps it would be a good idea if Rosie looked after them for a while."
Nick felt this wasn't the right time to tell Sammy what had happened earlier today. He went around to the boot and opened it up. Now it was his turn to feel faint; the case containing the diamonds had gone.

The police were there within minutes. They learned that Sammy had met Nick, an old friend at Kennedy airport earlier that afternoon and that they had brought Rosie, whom Nick had met on the flight, to her new apartment on 5th Avenue. While taking Rosie up, someone had shot Abe, who had stayed in the car. Neither Sammy nor Nick could throw any light on why this could have happened.
"Looks like a gangland killing to me. They must have used a silencer," snarled the coloured police officer as he looked at Abe's body still lying on the steering wheel of the car. "Must have been risky with all these folk about. You stay cool man 'till the lieutenant gets here; he'll want to talk to you."
Sammy sat in the police car, slowly recovering from the shock seeing his son dead. The pains in his chest had stopped, his heart was now in control again. How was he going to tell Elizabeth what had happened? What would she say and what would she do? New York, where the crime rate was high, had the reputation of violence, but who could have guessed that this day, which was to have been such a happy one with the reunion with Nick after such a long time, should have ended like this? When the police lieutenant arrived he needed to hear it all over again but there was no progress. There were no witnesses, nobody had seen or heard anything. There seemed to be no obvious reason for Abe to be murdered; why should anyone want to kill him? It was all unbelievable. Sammy and Nick were taken home to downtown Manhattan in a police car, exhausted, just a little frightened and sick at heart. Telling Elizabeth was going to be the most difficult thing Sammy had ever had to do in his life; he was filled with dread.

Elizabeth knew something was wrong as soon as the police car drew up outside; it was as if she had had some sort of premonition. One look at Sammy's face and she screamed as only distressed Jewish women can scream. "Where's Abe?"
She listened tearfully as Sammy told her what had happened and then she started sobbing, her head on Sammy's shoulder.
"Oh Govuld, oh Govuld." She kept repeating the same phrase, over and over again. The women in the house, the wives of Sammy's three sons joined in the wailing, taking Elizabeth with them, apart from the men.

Sammy turned to his youngest son, Ben; "Go get the Rabbi and let him know what has happened? Ask him if he can find time to call this evening with the elders.We must say Kaddish together and we shall have to make the preparations for the funeral; tonight, we must read the law."
Ben left at once, not questioning his father's request while Sammy sat gently crooning backwards and forwards in his chair; his heart was heavy. Nick sat quietly on one side, not talking, not wishing to intrude into Sammy's grief.

Though Sammy and Elizabeth could not truly be called orthodox, their faith and traditions were all-important to them; their lives circulated around their prayers and their habits were based on Jewish customs. Later, in the privacy of their room on the evening of Abe's killing, they wept as they talked together.
"Why Sammy? Why did they have to kill Abe?"
"Beats me Liz; who the hell knows? I suppose just because they're killers. To them, life must be cheap. I can't think of any other reason. But they will pay for what they've done; I swear it. Abe's killers will die for sure."
"What will you do?"
"Firstly I must talk with the Elders in the synagogue, they must know. They will plan what needs to be done when Abe is released to us. Ben has gone to the Rabbi now and he will inform the three Gaba-im; they will prepare for the funeral; they will surely come tonight."
"Will any others come?" Elizabeth's expression was worried.
"Yes; those from the organisation will come as well. They will decide what will be the punishment of the scum who killed Abe, for punishment there must be. You would not disagree with that would you?"
"No Sammy, but it is a shame the killing must go on; where will it end?"
"You've been a good wife to me Elizabeth, the best a man could wish for. We've had three wonderful sons; but our first born has been taken away from us brutally, by evil people. There can be no forgiveness for that."
"No, no forgiveness for that." She paused, reminiscing over past times. "Do you remember his B'rith M'ilah? You were so proud when the Rabbi named him; Abraham ben Samuel. I thought you were going to burst with pride. Then you hoped he would have so many grandchildren for you; Abraham, the father of a multitude."

"Well not a multitude perhaps but he and Becci have given us two lovely grandchildren; and you are just as proud of your grandsons as I am."
"I sure am." Liz started to sob again, her heart heavy. "The Talmud says whoever leaves a son after him, studying the Torah is as if he never died." Sammy patted her arm affectionately, carressing her gently, yielding her love and respect.
"Abe will never die in our hearts."

Soon Ben returned with the Rabbi and the other senior members of the synagogue, the Chevrah Kedisha. With them too came younger men with bright eyes and with hate in their hearts.
Sammy turned slowly to Nick. "I've been a bum host, old buddy. It was to have been such a happy reunion, just the two of us after all these years. And I come up with a wet blanket." He paused; "You will want to catch a little shut-eye before you get ready to meet Rosie this evening."
"Damn," said Nick, "it had quite slipped my mind about Rosie. I'll ring her to say I can't make it; she'll understand I'm sure."
"No my friend, don't do that. You'll scare the living shit out of her. Trust me, I know. Nick, we have shared much in the past and our bonds of friendship are truly strong, but tonight I must pray with those of my faith and talk with those of the organisation too. No matter what happens, Celleri will be made to pay. Tonight you must try to put Abe's death out of your mind and go out and enjoy yourself with Rosie. She's a lovely girl Nick and she'll probably be dying to tell you of her meeting with Celleri this evening. You must let me know what she says about him. There's no doubt our paths will cross again soon; I have a gut feeling."

Despite his protestations, Nick was led up to his room. He wanted to help Sammy by being with him, but he knew his Jewish friends would be more able to help. He bathed and shaved the shadow already darkening his face and dressed ready for his meeting with Rosie. He returned to the living room just after seven but the door was shut and Ben sat on a hard upright chair outside.
"I guess you'd better give the minyan a miss Mr Royle; I think Pa would rather you stayed away tonight."
"Okay Ben, I understand; tell your father I'll be back about twelve."
"I'll do that. Goodnight Mr Royle. I wouldn't rush," said Ben.

CHAPTER SIX

Michael Celleri was agitated. He was a caporegime to one of the most influential dons in New York. Someone who, though he had never used it, had the power of life and death over any that opposed the Mafia. Yet he was afraid what the next few minutes might bring.

It had been more than twenty-two years since he had first left his home in England; he had been in a hurry then. Rosie's mother had telephoned him, letting him know that she was pregnant. Frightened, he had run away to one of the big towns where he could hide. He thought he would be able to make some sort of living for himself. He had always been a gambler; he was just naturally lucky. But unfortunately, Lady Luck hadn't stayed with him long and very soon young Michael was up to his eyes in debt. The people he owed money to wanted payment not promises, so when he couldn't pay, he had been picked up by the local button men and was about to be punished severely. Then someone realised his surname was Celleri. That had saved him; with a name like Celleri he had to be one of them. "Who's your papa?; Where do you come from, which part of Italy? How long have you lived here?" He couldn't remember his answers but they must have been all right; he was pardoned. He was told that provided he did as he was ordered in the future, his slate would be wiped clean. He couldn't believe his luck and after this reprieve, Michael fought his way up the ladder, obeying and carrying out the orders of the bosses, often committing acts for which, deep down, he loathed himself. But once you were in debt to the brotherhood, there was no easy way out. Much later, when things had got out of hand in Britain, he had been ordered to leave for the States. Now he was a capo, a voice with some authority in the court of one of the most powerful of the New York dons. But right now, he was scared.

He paced around the room anxiously, looking at his watch, an act he had repeated frequently during the last quarter of an hour. Every now and then, he would look through the louvred blinds at the window towards the wide avenue below, hoping that would make the time go more quickly. He started when the muted tones of the phone rang on his desk. He hesitated before answering it and it continued to ring, softly but insistently. "Yes." A muffled voice could be heard speaking rapidly at the other end of the line. He replaced the phone and for a moment he continued his restless walking. When he approached his desk he leaned on it gently as if receiving strength from it. Then, when the faint noise of the lift door outside could be heard closing, he sat down, now completely under control.

The express lift took only seconds to whisk Rosie to the penthouse at the top of the building. As the door opened she recognised the soft hum of the air conditioning and she was aware that the atmosphere was more pleasant than it had been at street level. She walked forward and was immediately conscious of the thick pile of the carpet. Her feet sank silently into the soft luxury of the floor covering. Her mind flirted with the idea of how soft it would be to make love on. Now however, she had to concentrate. She was about to meet the reason she was there. The man who had hired her and brought her all this way from the other side of the Atlantic to work for him and despite the things that Rosie had heard about the club she had come to, she couldn't hide her excitement. She wanted to meet him to find out what he was like; she wanted to ask why it was she who had been given this job, while there were so many others out there in the world who would have been even better able than she to do the work; why therefore was she chosen?

The man who had brought her knocked gently on the door in front of them and opened it slowly, though Rosie had heard no reply. Inside, the room was dimly lit and in the far part of the room near the window which overlooked Park Avenue, someone sat behind the large desk. Rosie heard a voice ask her to come in and she walked into the centre of the room. She could not make out the features of the man who stood up as she went towards him but he was tall and slim and she could make out his hair was dark and appeared to be receding at the temples. The hand he offered was cool and strong.

"Good evening Miss Haynes. It was very good of you to come at such short notice."
"Good evening."
"I thought we should meet as soon as possible so that I could explain your duties to the club. Forgive me; please do sit down, somewhere I can see you; can I get you something?"
"No thank you."
He guided her to a chair which was in an area of brighter light while his face remained in the shadow. "You will know that the Green Baize is a casino and that I manage a number of them both here and in Europe, all with the same name."
"Yes, I did know that."
"My agent in England informed me that you were extremely efficient at your work as the accountant to the gallery and had helped

him quite considerably. In fact, your choice of pictures has been just what I would have preferred. Really quite remarkable; I was very pleased with your selection." He waved his arms around the room with an expansive gesture. Rosie now had time to see a number of the pictures bought from the gallery on the walls, tastefully lit by concealed lighting above the frames. "I thought that as there was a vacancy here, I would invite you to come and join us. I wanted to see what you were like."
"Thank you; I wondered why I had been offered this appointment."
"Here, you will have the sole control of finance, reporting to me. If you find any problems you will speak to me and only to me about them. You see Miss Haynes, New York is a hard city, with a lot of crime around every corner but the casinos I run are honest. If you find evidence of dishonesty, I want to know; it will not be allowed. I hope I make myself perfectly clear?"
"Yes indeed." How could she tell him that she already knew he was part of the Mafia; that he was a part of the distribution of the pain and suffering of cocaine and heroin; that all he was saying was untrue.
"Perfectly clear Mr. err; do you know, as all the arrangements were made through solicitors, I don't even know your name."
"Forgive me Miss Haynes; I am Michael Chaney."
So, he wanted to be known as Chaney. "You don't have an American accent Mr Chaney."
A faint smile dragged at the corners of his mouth. "No Miss Haynes, I was born in Britain but I came here many years ago and now I am an American citizen. But now, if you have time, I would like you to tell me about yourself. Your background, where you were born, who were your parents?"

Rosie repeated the story she had told earlier that day to Nick more or less as she had told him. But Michael Celleri needed to know more, in detail. He expressed an interest in all the many and trivial things that had happened, things Rosie had long since put out of her mind.
"Tell me Miss Haynes, are your parents still alive?"
"I never knew my father Mr Chaney. He left my mother as soon as he found out I was on the way. My mum always told me how nice a young man he was and I'm sure she never stopped loving him; for her there could be no other man. I think she always hoped he'd come back home and they would marry, but he never did. We lived over the cafe where she worked. They were long tiring hours but we were happy; she developed it a lot when it was left to her and she still lives there. I used to go home and visit as often as I could while I was in university and I hope she'll be able to visit me here in New York when I've settled in."

"But of course."

A quiet descended over them both; Celleri recalled his last few weeks in school when he had recognised for the first time what a pretty young woman Meryl Haynes had grown into, though they had both been in the same school since childhood. He had fallen head over heels in love with her. He remembered seeing for the first time the shape of her tiny nipples showing through the thin material of her blouse, the slimness of her waist and her tight little bottom; a yearning stirred deeply within him still, after all these years. They had gone to the cinema at the weekends and she had allowed him a kiss and a cuddle in the back row; once when he had tried to go further, she had slapped him hard, right across the face and rushed out of the place. "You stop that Michael Celleri," she had shouted, "I don't like it and I don't want you to do it." She had hurt his pride and he hadn't tried it again, not until the last night of school, on the way home from the ball. That night Meryl had let his hands stray across the front of her. She had responded in a different way and he had been instantly aware of it. When he touched her she seemed to be more sensitive; she squirmed, as if a tingle ran within her, leaving her with a deep throbbing sensation where she had felt nothing like that before.

"Michael, we shouldn't be doing this," she had said, relaxing her body against his. His hands continued to search gently, carefully allowing her to love every moment of these new feelings.

"Michael, we must stop now before it's too late," she had murmured as his hand slipped beneath the arms of her dress and he touched her with nothing between his finger tips and her soft yielding breast. He remembered she turned her face upwards towards him, kissing him hotly and urgently; he pressed further until he could cup her breast in his hand. Gently he touched her nipple, now erect and loving and she squirmed with longing. It was too late then for second thoughts; where they should make love was the only thing on their minds at that moment.

Michael's father had lent him his car for the evening and he recalled driving to the riverside where courting couples frequently met. Secretly and tenderly, Michael took Meryl along pathways she had never been before and where he too was a stranger; two youngsters, so much in love, sampling the forbidden delights; virgins no more.

Just the one time it happened but it was enough; her usual regular cycle was interrupted and Meryl knew she was pregnant. Michael remembered her call as if it were yesterday.

"Michael. We've got to talk; I'm going to have a baby." He felt the chill come over him again all these years later as he recalled his fear. Having a child and settling down wasn't part of his plan for life just then. When she told him, he knew the time to leave town had arrived. He had not planned where he was going but he knew he had to go and quickly. That night he had packed his few belongings in an old beat-up suitcase and caught the early morning bus away, the first one to leave; anywhere, without telling a soul; he wanted to get lost.

Rosie was surprised at the long pause; it seemed an age since either of them spoke last.

"Are you all right Mr Chaney? Can I get you something?" She started to get up. A shadow moved near the door; all the time they had been talking, he had been protected by a bodyguard, standing silently, unseen.

"No Miss Haynes, thank you. What you were saying brought back memories of my young life. Tell me, how did your mother manage to bring you up? Did your grandparents help her?"

"No, they didn't, not one little bit. When I was born, Mum's stepfather made life hell for her, so she had to find a home for us elsewhere. Susan who owned the cafe, liked her a lot and kept her on. It was Susan's flat over the cafe which was home for us both until I left for university." Rosie couldn't help finding it strange he was asking all these rather intimate questions about her past.

'Why on earth does he want to know all these things about my childhood and about Mum?'

"Did your mother hate your father for what he had done? It wouldn't really be surprising."

"No; I can never recall her saying a bad word about him; I think she is still very much in love with him."

Again there was a pause as if Michael was absorbing all the information he had received, though most he already knew. Though he hadn't helped with Rosie's upbringing he had kept a watching brief from afar. He knew how well she had done in school and in university but he had never been able to get to know the real Rosie; he couldn't have known what Rosie's Mum would have said about him; whether she would have made Rosie hate him. He knew she had every reason to have despised him; in her hour of need, he had deserted her; left. He got up from his chair and prowled around the room in the shadows as if wrestling with a problem. Here, in front of him was his daughter, who had never known him, who didn't even know of his existence other than stories she had heard from her mother. And what hurt him more at that moment was that he didn't know her. Could there be any going back? Could all those years be forgiven? No; it would be asking too much; yet; would it be possible? No; of course it couldn't. Though he had told Rosie the business was legitimate and he had made damned sure she would only find out that part, he knew his involvement with the syndicate made any return to respectable life quite impossible. But he couldn't stop some part of his mind thinking, probing, seeking a way out of this way of life. If only he could put the clock back; if only; how many times had he whispered that to himself when only he could hear?

"Your mother sounds as if she is a very lovely lady. She must be I suppose to have such a lovely daughter; perhaps I will be able to meet her some time when she visits you here." Now was not the time to tell Rosie that he was her father; perhaps that time would come; perhaps not.
"I think for the moment Miss Haynes, I would prefer you not to tell anyone for whom you work; do not discuss me with anyone. I have always kept a rather low profile; do you mind?"
"No, of course not if that's what you want, but I know my mother would like to know a little about you. She was rather worried about her daughter coming all this way not knowing her employer."
"You must put her mind at ease of course. Now I expect you would like to be taken back to your apartment? I hope you will be comfortable there."
"I meant to thank you; it's simply wonderful, but you know Mr Chaney, I'll never be able to afford it. But it's so convenient for the casino. I'll be able to walk there quite easily."
"No Miss Haynes," he said rather brusquely. "Never walk to or from the casino; for your protection, there will always be a car available for your use. And don't worry about paying for the apartment, regard it as a company perk for you."
"That's very generous of you Mr Chaney. Before I go, please tell me again how it was that I was appointed to this job; it all seems too good to be true?"
"From what my agent told me I knew you were good at your job. I thought you might like the change Miss Haynes."

He stood up, extending his hand again. The interview was over. The shadow near the door moved forward to open it; outside, the escort waited.
"Good night Miss Haynes."
"Good bye Mr Chaney."
The lift shuttled her to the basement garage in moments. Her car

and chauffeur were all ready and waiting; in a quarter of an hour, Rosie was back in her apartment getting ready for her date with Nick; she couldn't wait.

CHAPTER SEVEN

The bell in the hallway rang at eight o'clock exactly. Nick had been spot-on with his timing and Rosie was ready for him. She must have looked at herself in the mirror half a dozen times, smoothing the figure-hugging dress she had chosen for the evening, not vainly, but she did want to look her best for her date with Nick. It was a simple black model she had bought in London on one of her shopping sprees before she left for America. It was smart if only for its simplicity. A broad silver belt was drawn tightly around her slim waist and the ankle length skirt was slashed to the mid-thigh, revealing a long black-stockinged leg; a small pearl pendant filled the V-neckline. Her chestnut hair was brushed upwards and held in position with a large-toothed comb, decorated with mother of pearl; no wayward strand escaped. The greenness of her eyes had been delicately exaggerated with shadow and the kohl liner was thinly and accurately drawn. Her cheeks were slightly flushed, partly excitement and partly blusher, so expertly applied, her appearance was breath taking.

His admiration on seeing her was apparent. He stood back and then taking her hand he said, "Rosie, you look wonderful; absolutely stunning."
"Thank you, sir," she said coyly, one finger under her chin as she bobbed gently. "I am ready. You were quite right Nick; it has been a tiring day."
"I won't keep you out too late Rosie; not tonight anyway. I've booked a table at the Top of the Sixes."
"That's a strange name for a restaurant; where's that?"
"On the top floor of 666 Fifth Avenue; it looks out over all of mid-town Manhattan. I called there earlier. I've arranged the table for half past eight; I know you'll love it there."
"I'm sure I will, it sounds super; I'm starving."
Wearing a white cashmere stole to protect her from the coolness of the evening air, Rosie left the apartment with Nick for their first dinner date together.

Rosie started to tell Nick of her meeting that afternoon with Celleri at the Green Baize casino. "He said his name was Chaney."

"He did, did he? Now I wonder why he said that?"
She described his particular interest in her parents and her home, and how he had asked her all sorts of questions about her childhood, some things she had forgotten about years ago.
"How odd."
"I told him the apartment was absolutely wonderful but much too expensive for me to keep; he said it was a company perk for me." Nick listened without comment. It was strange behaviour for any employer, let alone a Mafia capo in vice ridden New York.

Though the Top of the Sixes was almost across the road from Rosie's new home, Nick had arranged a car for them. Within minutes they had been dropped on the sidewalk outside, the forty or so floors towering above them and Fifth Avenue as they continued to talk about Rosie's meeting this afternoon.
"The pictures we had sold him from the gallery were arranged around his room. He had them beautifully lit with hidden lighting. I should think he must know quite a lot about art; he certainly was showing them off well."
"All very peculiar behaviour for a capo I must say," said Nick.

The arcade on the ground floor of the building was brightly lit and the entrance to the escalator was a little way inside. A few seconds later, the lift door opened into the foyer for them to be greeted by the maitre d'hote, a pleasant bespectacled young man.
"Good evening Mr Royle; nice to meet you again." Turning to Rosie, he said, "welcome to New York; I hope you will enjoy your stay here."
"Thank you," said Rosie, "I hope so too."
"Would you care for an aperitif before your meal?" the maitre d' said to Nick. He looked at Rosie enquiringly. "I'd rather not for the moment thank you," she answered.
"Then I'll have you taken to your table."
A hostess advanced, guiding them across the room to their window seat.

The inside of the restaurant was dimly lit in comparison with the brightness of the foyer outside and they paused for a moment as Rosie's stole was handed to the powder-room girl; it allowed their eyes to become acclimatised to the low lighting before they were led to their table just laid for the two of them. Through the toughened glass, the lights of Manhattan were spread out around and below them and some of the higher buildings glowed in the black night sky; the effect was magical. In the blackness, the lights of the helicopters winked as they ferried their passengers around the city, taking in the sights from even higher in the sky. And in the distance, many miles away, the coloured lanterns of the George Washington bridge could be seen dancing on the skyline. It was with difficulty that Rosie turned her attention to the menu from the many attractions outside the window.

The length of the day was beginning to be felt by both of them and Rosie was tiring despite Nick's attention. It was now nearly twenty hours since she had got up out of bed this morning and back home in England, it would have been nearly two in the morning; she would have been tucked up in bed hours ago. But the excitement was keeping them both going; after all, this was Rosie's first visit to New York. And as for Nick, he was dining with the most beautiful vision he could ever have dreamed of.

The waitress who came for their order was a vivacious dark-haired young lady with a glowing smile revealing perfect teeth. "I'm Rita," she said." Are you ready to order?"

"Well Rita, we've both decided to have the grilled salmon followed by the white chocolate and mocha marquise; how does that sound?"

"Sounds a swell choice to me," she said. "Have you chosen a wine?"

"We'll have the Chardonnay, 1988."

"Thank you sir; I'll bring the wine straight away."

She returned in a few minutes with the wine in an ice bucket. Deftly she cut off the foil and opened the bottle. She wiped the neck and poured a little into Nick's glass. Though the wine was Californian, it's bouquet reminded him of times spent in the gabled mansion house in the vineyard back home in Constantia, east of Cape Town in South Africa, where he had grown up as a young boy. The wine was cold and crisp and rich on the palate; it was delicious.

"That's fine," Nick smiled approvingly. She proceeded to fill Rosie's glass and then his. The golden colour reflected every light in the place despite its dimness. It caught it and sent it out in shafts of pale amber across the white table cloth, gleaming on the cutlery and in the dark windows looking out over the city.

"This is delightful," whispered Rosie. "The setting, the company, the wine and now this super meal. Oh, I'm so glad you met me and I met you today Nick; you've made my introduction to America so exciting."

"We must do it again sometime; soon perhaps?" Rosie looked at him. He was still gazing at her. She could see he meant it by the expression on his face.

During the meal there was a cabaret. There was a grand piano on a low dais only feet from their table and a young brunette, Shelley

Shields both played and sang a medley of songs for the diners. After a while she asked for requests, turning to Rosie first as she was closer than anyone else.

Flustered, she asked, "Do you know any songs from England?"

Shelley surprised them all with a collection of British melodies which had them all tapping their feet and snapping their fingers; the applause when she had finished from everyone present showed how much her performance had been appreciated.

"The evening gets better and better. I wish it would never end," said Rosie"

"Well young lady, I think it ought to now fairly soon or you'll be jet-lagged for a long time. You won't enjoy your stay here then."

The car that Nick had arranged took them firstly in the opposite direction from the way they wanted to go as Fifth Avenue is a one way street to the east; but it was only a few moments before the driver turned left into East 53rd and left again into Madison Avenue; another left turn into East 83rd Street and they were home, outside Rosie's new apartment."

"I'll come up with you; make sure you're safe," said Nick as he paid off the driver. The night porter opened up the plate glass door as soon as he saw Rosie on the step.

"Evening Miss Haynes; getting to know New York already I see. Evening sir," he said, turning to Nick.

"I'll take Miss Haynes up to her apartment," he said. "Won't be long." The doorman looked suggestively at Nick who walked Rosie quickly towards the lift. "Good night."

At the apartment door Rosie turned to Nick. "I've had such a wonderful time and it's all due to you. Thank you so much." She stood on tiptoe and holding lightly to his arm, she brushed his cheek with a kiss. "When can I see you again?" she asked.

"Would tomorrow be too soon? You see, I too have really enjoyed being with you; what say we see the sights together?"

"That would be super Nick."

"Okay, I'll collect you for beakfast at Pierre's at nine unless you think that's too early for a young lady who'll be so very tired in the morning?"

"Nine o'clock it is: I'll be waiting."

"Goodnight Rosie."

Nick found he was whistling in the elevator, tunes the singer had sung during their dinner together; what a day. He would never have believed when he started out this morning that all this would have happened to him. His mood changed as he recalled Abe's murder this afternoon, something he had been able to obliterate from his mind while he had been with Rosie. Now he began feeling guilty having left Sammy in his time of need, even though he knew Sammy would want to be with those of his faith right now. Why should anyone want to kill Abe? It didn't make sense. A cab took him back to Sammy's home, through the still-busy streets of Manhattan. Sammy was up, waiting for Nick's return. The minyan of his Jewish friends had gone.

"How'd it go Nick? You had a swell time I guess? Rosie okay?"

"The 'Top of the Sixes' is a super place to take a young lady. Rosie was very impressed. I felt very guilty leaving you this evening Sammy. I should have stayed with you."

"Don't give it another thought Nick. I had to talk with my people tonight; only they could give me the right advice. Now I know what I have to do. Tell me how did Rosie get on with Celleri this afternoon?"

"He told her his name was Chaney; all he seems to have done is ask her a lot of questions about her home and her parents. She was quite surprised at the detail he seemed to want to know."

"Strange. The whole thing stinks Nick. Capos don't behave like Celleri. They're ruthless enforcers for the Godfathers. Take that guy Sammy the bull Gravano, capo to Gotti who's just been sent down. He'd kill his own grandmother as soon as look at her. This guy Celleri seems too good to be true. Still, I'll find out a bit more tomorrow. I'm calling on him in the morning. The plans are all made."

"Are you going to tell me what you're going to do," asked Nick.

"No Nick; what you don't know, you won't have to explain; to anyone."

"You mean to Rosie?"

"Yeah, especially Rosie. What're you doing tomorrow? Seeing Rosie?"

"Yes; I thought we'd breakfast at Pierre's and then see the sights. D'you know Sammy, I've never been around New York as a sightseer before? We're meeting at nine."

"You never were one to let the grass grow under your feet. Have a good day."

CHAPTER EIGHT

"Where would you like to start?" asked Nick. "We could walk down Fifth Avenue to get the atmosphere; or we could start with a ride around Central Park; that would give us time to decide what we want to

do next. Yes, I think that's the way we'll do it; what d'you think Rosie?"
"It's all so exciting, I don't mind." Linking his arm lightly through Rosie's, they turned outside Pierre's, passing the red brick Knickerbocker Club to the corner and crossed to the eastern end of the park. Though it was still fairly early in the morning, the horses were all lined up, their carriages cleaned and gleaming, fresh flowers in their containers on the rail. The drivers were cajoling the passers by, encouraging them to choose them rather than one of the others. Some carriages looked nicer than others and Rosie was taken with a beautiful highly-polished black landau, pulled by a pure white horse.
"Sure would you be wanting to take a ride with Chauncey?" the driver asked in a deep Irish brogue. "Just jump in," he said. "There's a nip in the air still, so I'd wrap yourselves in the blanket." It was cold still. Winter had hung around longer this year than usual and the buds on the trees were only now beginning to burst; it would be some time still before Central Park would be green.
"I'm Arty," the driver said. "Now over there," he said, swinging his left arm in an arc towards the the west of the park, "they call that the Strawberry Fields; given by the widow of John Lennon, Yoko Ono, after he was shot. And in that building, they filmed some of the horror movies; you know, them, with 'orrible gargoyles on the roof." He continued in this vein and was a fount of information as they passed through the park, and he enjoyed filling them in with snippets of local knowledge. Rosie and Nick listened to what he was saying and took in all they were seeing; they watched the squirrels being fed by the visitors; they seemed so tame, some feeding from the people's hands.
"You can just see the apartment through the trees," said Rosie, pointing towards the block on the far side of the Avenue.
"So you can," said Nick. "Did you see that sign back there? Skaters and cyclists; speed limit 15 mph." They both laughed, when, whoosh, a skater shot past them, much faster than a car would have, completely ignoring the warning.
"Gosh," said Rosie, "he's in a hurry."
"Yes," said the driver. "You've got to watch out for them. They've been known to snatch ladies' handbags though most of them are just out for the exercise; still, you never know." All too soon the ride was over and Nick and Rosie, now arm in arm, walked down Fifth Avenue, taking in the sights of New York. They stopped first outside the Trump Tower, a bronze needle climbing into the sky.

"It seems, you always walk with a permanent crick in your neck in New York," Rosie observed.

"I know what you mean. Let's go inside; I've been told it's quite spectacular," said Nick.

They entered the atrium, a huge area inside the base of the tower lined with orange Breccia Perniche marble. On the side opposite the entrance, a waterfall cascaded over the ledges, skirted with tropical plants and through the dramatic glass skylight in the roof, they could see the tower standing high above them. Escalators took them upwards for five or six floors to landings housing international boutiques and galleries, selling to the rich and famous of the world.

"It's fantastic," Rosie whispered as she peered enviously through the window of Cache's, filled with the most expensive fashions of today.

"It's that all right." said Nick, thinking that Rosie had been speaking about the skyscraper, "and this isn't the tallest of their buildings by a long shot." They dawdled window shopping on all the floors as they took the escalators slowly down to the ground floor to mingle once again with the crowd in the street.

Back on the pavement, they were caught up in the hectic pace of life; people of all races and nationalities, some smartly dressed and affluent, while others, clearly not the winners in life's struggle, all hurried about their business in the Avenue. The ladies, still wearing their fur coats, mink and long, just above the ankles, surprised Rosie, as in England, the activities of the animal protection societies made people afraid to wear animal fur; but they did look very smart. Rosie and Nick, keeping on the same side of the road as Trumps walking eastwards, came to St. Patrick's cathedral, set gloriously amidst the modern high rise buildings in Fifth Avenue.

"Oh, we must go inside," said Rosie. The interior was dark, little light coming in from outside through the stained glass windows screened by the high skyscrapers which surrounded the cathedral. She walked to the stoup containing Holy Water, close to the bronze of Pope John Paul II who visited there in 1979 and genuflected as she crossed herself. The air was heavy with the smoky smell of hundreds of candles burning in the many small chapels around the nave and the myriads which had been burned before; in fact, most of the light inside the church came from these burning candles. Rosie bought one and lit it, placing it with the others in the black iron stand. For a moment, she stood in silent prayer, Nick close to her side.

"You are a Catholic Rosie?" he asked.

"Yes I am, though I've not been to church for a long long time. Lapsed for quite a while I'm afraid; always said I didn't have the time. I must try and make a real effort now." They walked around the aisles silently, side by side, very aware of each other. It seemed to Nick that Rosie had rediscovered her Catholicism and was happy; for his part, an agnostic, all he wanted to do was to be with her.

Outside, on the pavement again, the daylight was so very bright after the darkness inside the church.

"How about a coffee Rosie?"

"I'd like that; where can we get one near here?"

"Come with me," Nick said. They crossed the road and entered a side street. In the windows of the Nikkon building which bordered the street, some of the most beautiful colour photographs ever taken were on display, the best of a world competition. In front of them stood the massive golden figure of Prometheus overseeing the skaters on the rink in the middle of the Rockefeller Center. A little girl, her pink tights covering her spindly legs, staggered around the rink, almost, but never quite falling; the watchers gasped in unison as each time she changed direction, she nearly went down.

"They knew you were coming Rosie; they've put the flags out." All around the centre, were the many flags of the United Nations of the world.

"Fancy finding this in the centre of New York city," enthused Rosie.

"In a few weeks it will all be gone and they'll have an out-of-doors restaurant here. It's only like this as long as the weather is still rather cool. I thought you'd like to see that."

"See it; I'd like to be on it."

"You're a skater Rosie? You can hire skates from there in the corner if you'd like to. Go on; show me what you can do; I'd love to see."

"You come with me too."

"I can't skate Rosie. I've never had skates on before in my life," he chuckled. "I'll watch."

"No, not on my own. Let's have the coffee instead; I'd rather that." They entered the glass oval on the pavement which included the lift which took them beneath the road to the restaurant alongside the rink. Sitting in a window seat, they watched the skaters gliding on the ice outside through the black-tinted window overlooking the rink. They laughed as some of them, using the windows as mirrors, contorted themselves, grimacing, acting a role, just as if they were on a stage before an audience; it was a show for Nick and Rosie.

"I did enjoy that; what's next on the plan?" asked Rosie as they stood on the pavement once again.

"Well, a visit to the Empire State Building is a must; the Yanks call it the eighth wonder of the world. I've forgotten how high it is, but it's

pretty tall; it towers over most of New York. We can take a lift to the top and see what it's like from up there; pretty super I would have thought."
Rosie murmured her approval. They joined a short queue waiting for the elevator which would take them almost non-stop to the top.
"Step smartly," said the voice controlling the queue. They all crammed into this vast space which held forty or more people on its journey upwards. With a slight bowing of the knees as the lift started they hurtled into space, their ears popping with the change of altitude. In seconds, they were at the 80th floor where they changed lifts which took them to the 102nd floor, to the observation platform over a thousand feet above the street level. The spectacle was fantastic; Nick and Rosie enjoyed sorting out the sights for nearly 40 miles around.
" No place to come if it's raining," said Rosie; " wouldn't see a thing."
"Yes; lost in the clouds; it's said to move in the wind, quite a bit, I believe," Nick said.
"Let's go now before the weather changes," joked Rosie.

The journey down was equally exciting and within moments they were out on the pavement.
"Now where?" asked Rosie, a police car racing past, sirens screaming.
"There's so much to see but I think we should take a break now and have some lunch. There are any number of eating places around here." Pointing to a small Italian restaurant, Nick said, "What say we see what's on the menu?"
"Okay by me, I'm always starving," Rosie laughed.
Unhurriedly, they lunched on lasagna verdi refreshed with a light sparkling wine, which like the wine they had had the night before, had started its life in the hot Californian sunshine.
"Ummm, I did enjoy that," murmured Rosie. "When I met Mr Chaney yesterday he didn't say when I should start at the casino, but I expect it'll be on Monday next. What are your plans Nick?"
"I can give you my undivided attention until next week, if that's what you'd like; I'll have to return to London one day then. Until I have to go or until you want me to go, I'd be delighted to see the sights of New York with you Rosie. I can't think of anything I'd like better."
"Oh, that would be lovely Nick."

After lunch, back on the busy pavement of Fifth Avenue, Nick hailed a taxi.
"The World Trade Center please."
"Okay man. Where d'ya say that is?" his black face grinning at them in the mirror.

Nick couldn't believe his ears. "Surely you know how to get there?"
"No man. I only drive this thing. Got off the boat from Haiti yesterday man. Got this job staight away; ain't you heard? They're short of cab drivers here. Ain't had time to find my way about yet." He laughed. "Any time you want a job man, you be a cab driver; it's easy."
Pointing out the way to go, Nick smiled. "Yes, I must remember that."
Outside the center they, like all other visitors craned their necks looking upwards. It seemed impossible to go anywhere in New York without looking up into the sky. Everything was so enormous, towering majestically, climbing above the sidewalks and the Trade Center was even bigger and more impressive than the others. The thousands of windows from its 110 floors reflected the blueness of the sky so that the whole appeared to be a shining wall of steel, graceful yet manifestly enormously strong; beautiful but overwhelming.
"It's fantastic isn't it? We must go to the top." Nick was as excited as a young boy on a school outing. "There's an observation platform on the top, rather like that on the Empire State building. It's the highest building in New York. You look down on everything from there; you can see for miles."
"Race you you to the top," Rosie laughed as they joined yet another queue in the white marble hall, as large as a cathedral nave might be in the twenty-first century. "Why doesn't one lift take us right to the top rather than having to change?
"Apparently, there is sufficient movement in the lift shafts in bad weather to bend them, especially in the upper part. If the whole length of the shaft from the top to the bottom bent, the lift wouldn't be able to move inside; it would jam. So they break the run into sections. Frightening to think such a giant building can move in that way." Rosie was impressed that Nick knew the answer though it worried her to comprehend what he was saying. Through the toughened plate glass windows on the 107th floor, they looked down on the world more than a thousand feet below. People looked like insects forming colourful whirling groups which thinned out and then tailed away, following their leader. The geometrical layout of Manhattan was impressive, separated from the Bronx and Brooklyn and Queens by the East river, spanned by the huge bridges, beneath which, large ships passed freely on their way to the ocean. And from the other side of the building, they looked out over the Hudson towards New Jersey and Staten Island and countless miles away on the horizon, mountains painted blue by distant haze. From the south facing windows, the Statue of Liberty extended her welcoming arm to visitors arriving from the sea and close by, Ellis Island, the doorway to the States for so many immigrants, now looked disused and empty. They circled the viewing area many times,

spending time examining the stencils on the windows of the landscape in front of them, trying to understand the labels which pointed out the various features of the city far below them.
"Have you got your bearings Rosie? It's quite spectacular isn't it?"
"I've never experienced anything like this before. I wouldn't have missed this for anything. Thank you for bringing me with you."
"I've told you Rosie, I'm enjoying myself too seeing the sights. What's the matter?" Nick had noticed Rosie suddenly appeared flustered, looking around anxiously.

"My handbag; I haven't got it."
"Where d'you remember having it last?" Nick enquired.
"I know I had it in the ladies' room at the restaurant. I can't remember holding it since then."
"You probably put it down somewhere there; don't worry. Is there anything important inside?"
"The apartment keys are inside and a little money. Nothing else except the letters from the solicitor about the flat."
"So if anyone found it they'll be able to work out what the keys are for?" Nick said. "I think we'd better get back to the restaurant as quickly as we can just to see if it's still there." Speed was essential now. They took the next lift down and as luck would have it, a taxi was at the entrance discharging its load. Nick, not knowing the name of the restaurant could only guide the driver by giving the street number, but it was enough and in only a few minutes, they were standing outside. While Nick spoke to the waiter, Rosie went to the powder room but there was nothing to find. The bag wasn't there.
"They've been very busy since we left; they say they haven't seen it. I think we'll get back to the apartment, just in case; what d'you think Rosie?"

It was a silent journey back to Rosie's new home. The excitement of only a short while ago had been forgotten in the worries of the moment. There was little Nick could say to reassure Rosie. They just had to get there as quickly as they could. On the pavement, Rosie noticed that the doorman, who was usually hovering just inside, waiting to open the door, was nowhere to be seen. As they entered the foyer, a muffled banging could be heard inside the doorman's little office. Nick opened the door to find him on the floor behind his desk, bound hand and foot with tape, and gagged so that he could hardly breathe. Freeing him quickly, Nick learnt that two Hispanic types had arrived about twenty minutes earlier, apparently to deliver something to one of the tenants. He'd let them in but they had

jumped him and quickly overpowered him, bundling him into his room. Where they were now he didn't know, but both Nick and Rosie had a good idea.
"Miss Haynes has had her bag taken. Her keys were inside. Can you let us have your master key while you telephone the police?"
"Sure thing. Go get 'em bub."

On leaving the lift, they could see the door to Rosie's apartment was wide open and they could hear movement inside.
"You stay here," whispered Nick. "I'll take a look."
"Be careful Nick."
In the centre of the room there was a pile of those things that could be carried away fairly easily. There were several pictures, the video and television and a small jewel box, probably belonging to Rosie. The thieves were going through the place noisily, looking for money, though Nick couldn't see them. He was considering what to do next when the police arrived. Guns drawn, they advanced on the door, the one protecting the other.
"Freeze," they shouted. "On your face, arms outstretched, legs wide apart." As one of the thieves moved, one of the police growled, "make my day, punk," his gun close to his head.

Keeping their firearms ready, they handcuffed them, their hands behind their backs. It was only then they relaxed and holstered their guns.
"Thank you officers," Rosie said. "You certainly didn't waste any time getting here." Rosie explained how she had mislaid her handbag.
"All in a day's work ma'am. We'll need a statement from you later." Picking up her bag, now on the table near the door, the policeman joked, "You'd better keep an eye on it now. New York's no place to lose your keys in."

"What a way to end our first day; still all's well that ends well I suppose," Nick said. "I'll give you a hand putting these things back."
"Let's have a coffee first," Rosie suggested. While Rosie went out to the kitchen, Nick began replacing the pictures on the walls and the television and the video back on their stands. It didn't take long before the apartment was as it was before the burglary.
"Will you have dinner with me again tonight?" Nick asked.
"I'd love to Nick, but shouldn't you be spending some time with Sammy?"
"Yes, perhaps I should, but I know he's got a lot on his mind at the moment. I'll go back to his place now and I'll be here at eight if that's

okay. We could try one of the places around here."
"And it's on me this time," Rosie said.
"We'll see," Nick replied. "I'll see you later."
Once more, Rosie stood tall, kissing Nick gently on the cheek.

As Nick was being taken back to Sammy's home he had time to think about the happenings of the day. Certainly, there hadn't been a dull moment while he was with Rosie. He had known her for less than two days but already she had made a mark on his life and he was enjoying himself as he had never done before. He no longer felt lonely and he was looking forward to his next meeting with her. Their tour around New York had finished earlier than he had planned today but there were several days more he could be with her and so many more exciting things to do. He just couldn't wait for it all to happen.

CHAPTER NINE

Sammy paid off the cab and stood on the sidewalk outside the club. His younger son, Josh was by his side and as Abe had done, he towered over his father. Side by side, they approached the solid dark door of the casino. At eye-level, an iron grill protected a small wooden window which opened almost at once when they pressed the bell push. All the time, a security camera had watched their every movement, slowly moving to and fro, keeping them both in view, humming quietly as the electronic controls kept them in focus. Nothing they had said or done since they climbed out of the taxi had been missed.

"Yeah?" A gruff voice emerged from the other side of the grill. Sammy looked upwards to see the doorman, his pock-marked sallow face shaded by a dark fedora; the brim cast a shadow so that his eyes couldn't be seen at all.
"I want to see Mr Celleri."
"Who's asking?"
"Sammy Goldstein; just tell him I'm here."
There was a pause as the message was relayed somewhere in the building and after a while, the locks opened and the heavy door swung inwards. Inside, the hall was large, much more spacious than could have been guessed from the outside. Surveillance cameras twisted on their mounts on the walls and ceiling, so that every movement within the room was recorded; nothing escaped these multiple electronic eyes. The wide stairway on the right, which led upwards to the casino was blocked by a large aggressive man, his right hand

tucked into his lapel and at the top, there was another similarly threatening guard.

As soon as they were inside, the front door slammed shut noisily, the locks fired into place and the doorman advanced quickly on to Sammy and Josh, motioning them to adopt a 'be searched' position. This he did quickly and professionally and once done, they were herded along the hall towards the lift which took them upwards. No one had said anything. The lift opened automatically and two of Celleri's men came forward, guiding them to a pair of solid mahogany doors. One of them knocked gently and opened them into Celleri's office. Banks of video screens around the room, most of them blank at the moment, were ready to record the images from all the cameras in and around the building. A tall figure stood up behind his desk.

"Good morning. I am Michael Celleri; you asked to see me." His voice was precise, very English, so unlike Sammy's nasal New York accent. "May I ask who you are and why you should want to meet me?"

"Cut the crap Celleri; I'm Sammy Goldstein." Not a flicker of acknowledgement passed across Michael Celleri's face. "I came to tell you your hoods made a big mistake yesterday." Still Celleri made no movement. "Shall I explain?"

"Please do."

"We met a friend at Kennedy yesterday afternoon. He asked us to give a young lady he'd met on the flight a lift into the city. As we took her up to her apartment, some of your men shot and killed my son while he was waiting in the car. Then they stole a brief case containing nearly two million bucks of diamonds from the trunk. Now they didn't belong to me and I want them back. The police may have trouble pinning it on you and the mob but my organisation has found it much easier."

"That's a serious allegation Mr Goldstein. I hope you can back it up because I can truly say I know nothing at all about this; but I'll make my enquiries."

"You do that," said Sammy, "and do it quickly," he threatened. "I read from the Torah last evening with my people. You know the Torah Mr Celleri? It's our Jewish law. It advises us Jews how to deal with those who hurt us; you know, 'vengeance is mine, saith the Lord; an eye for an eye, a tooth for a tooth'; all that jazz. D'you get the message? According to our law, because you have caused me hurt, I can now hurt you."

"I get the message as you say Mr Goldstein, but I repeat I know nothing of your son's death nor of the stolen gems."

"Well, one thing my organisation is certain of. It was your men who

did the killing. Because you've killed my son, the Talmud says I can kill your children to avenge his death."
"But I don't have any children Mr Goldstein."
"Not even Miss Rosie Haynes?" murmured Sammy quietly. Celleri blanched as he leaned heavily against his desk. He looked as if he were about to faint.
"Don't panic Celleri; it doesn't suit me to kill your daughter. You see, my friend's kinda hot for her. To kill her would destroy him and the friendship of years we have for one another; so she will live. But there is a price. I want the men who killed my son delivered alive to me tomorrow morning at nine. I'll be waiting on the corner of 4th and 14th. They must bring the case of diamonds with them and two million bucks; that's for my son's family. You do understand me I hope," said Sammy.
"I understand you well enough Mr Goldstein, but perhaps I may not be able to deliver."
"You'll deliver Celleri. Talk it over with your top man. It's not my job to threaten you but I can trash your casinos anytime in the States or in Europe or wherever. Get the picture? You'd better consider what I've said very carefully. Warfare between the mob and my organisation won't profit anyone; but it will happen if you don't come up with the goods. Until nine tomorrow morning then."

As Sammy and his son turned towards the doors, Celleri's men moved to open it and chaperone them to the ground floor and out of the building onto the sidewalk. Michael Celleri had remained silent throughout.

Josh whistled up a cab. "Phew, you pushed your luck there Pa," he said as they settled back.
"Not really son. I think we've got him over a barrel. I believe him when he says he doesn't know anything about the killing or the theft of the stones, but he'll find out and sort it out, you wait and see. All it does really is value your brother Abe at two million bucks, that's all. It'll help rear his kids and look after Becci. The filth who'll make the delivery tomorrow are just that, scumbags, expendable. Make the arrangements Josh and make sure none of our guys get hurt."
"Sure thing Pa."

While the cab was ferrying Sammy and Josh back home, Celleri was summoning his lieutenants to an urgently called meeting in his office. Within a half hour they were all standing quietly in a semicircle around Celleri's desk.

"Yesterday, my daughter arrived from England." He walked backwards and forwards behind the desk, as if talking to himself rather than to them. "I asked two of you to keep tabs on her and bring her to her apartment in the city. You, Enrico and you, Albert were instructed to carry out my orders. However, I understand she had a lift into the city from someone else. Today, I heard that one of you stupid clowns killed the driver of the car which gave her a lift, while he was waiting outside. Then you foolishly stole a brief case from the trunk of the car. Is that so?" He barked the last question at them. The two hoods shuffled their feet guiltily, the one looking at the other, their hands perilously close to their holsters.

"Yeah, we did knock him off; he'd been watching us; he knew who we were all right so we blew him away. When we looked in the trunk there were all these cases and this thin brief case on the top of the luggage. It looked interesting so we took it. It was locked and we haven't had time to look at it yet; it's still in the car, unopened."

"Then leave it that way; unopened. I want you to deliver it tomorrow morning at nine to its rightful owner. Someone will be on the corner of 4th and 14th to collect. Don't mess this up or there'll be trouble. Do you understand? When you get back I want you to tell me exactly what happened." The meeting was over.

As soon as the doors closed behind the Mafia lieutenants, Celleri reached for his private phone.

"Papa; may I call on you straight away? I have a problem and I need advice. Within the hour; okay?" He replaced the telephone and strolled towards the window.

"Hell; what a mess." To his aides he murmured, "Get the car round; I need to leave; now."

The car weaved its way through the early morning traffic, hurrying Celleri to the don who controlled all the Mafia activity in the west part of Manhattan. It pulled up in front of a pair of large cast-iron gates which blocked the entrance to one of the elegant mansions on the foreshore of Staten Island. The chauffeur climbed out and facing the control camera, he turned to speak into the house phone. The gates opened silently.

The wheels of the limo crunched their way up the drive to the impressive front doors of the mansion. Pulling up outside, the chauffeur opened the car door for Celleri. Standing on the driveway, he fingered his tie nervously and brushed imaginary dust from his suit. The main door opened at once and a powerfully built major-domo ushered him inside, looking him over carefully. He led the way silently along the panelled hall as the two men approached the don's office and he opened the thick doors in front of him.

Celleri advanced deferentially, exchanging the bacio with his don.
"Hi there Michael; come in. It's good to see you; how're ya keeping?"
" I'm fine papa."
"Sit down, sit down; what can I do for you?"
His desk was in the corner of the room and his seat was in the window; it was well placed; the don's face remained in shadow but Celleri's expressions were clear for him to see. Behind him, Celleri could see the waves of the Atlantic crashing against the shoreline.
"It is good of you to see me so quickly papa but I need your counsel."
"You know I will do anything I can to help Michael; anything." His hands spread expansively.
"Yesterday, my daughter arrived from England; she doesn't know about me at all; doesn't know I exist even."
"Yeah? How is that?"
"Well, I left my home town in England before she was born. I asked two of the boys to meet her at Kennedy but I suppose she must have made a friend on the flight and she had a lift from someone who was waiting for him."
"So she had a lift from someone else; what's the problem?"
"This guy who gave her a lift; he's called Sammy Goldstein. I'd fixed an apartment at 812 Fifth Avenue for her; the guys followed them there."
"A nice address Michael."
"Yes; nothing but the best for my daughter, papa. While she went up with her new friends, the fools shot the driver. God only knows why. Just because he had been watching them they say."
"So they whacked him; so what?"
"It so happens, he was the eldest son of Goldstein. To make things worse, they stole a brief case containing nearly two million dollars worth of diamonds from the trunk of the car which belonged to the other guy, the one on the flight."
"Two million bucks worth of diamonds? Worth stealing."
"Maybe, but Goldstein came around this morning. He knew it was our goons who had made the hit. He says he's spoken to his organisation, whatever that may mean, and he wants the killers delivered to him tomorrow morning."
"What about the diamonds?"
"He wants the diamonds returned and two million dollars. He knew all about our connection with the casinos both here in the States and in

Europe. He said that I should talk with the top man as no one would want warfare between the mob and his organisation. I don't know, but I think he meant it."
"You said his name was Goldstein?"
"Yes, Sammy Goldstein."

The don turned to a computer concealed in a cabinet in the corner of the room. Entering the file he needed, he typed in "Goldstein, Sammy." The screen cleared, then rapidly filled with all that the syndicate knew about him; where he lived and worked; that he was a dealer in bullion and precious stones; the names of his family and all his business conections and ended with the ominous statement, 'has definite international connections, maybe a member of Mossad.'
" That's how he knows so much about us. If that is the case, he sure has the potential to cause us massive loss internationally. They could ruin us; shut us down. Tell me what you plan to do?"
"Seeing your computer data has confirmed my original intention. I guess I'll comply with what he says as far as sending those fools who did the killing; they deserve what's coming to them."
"Yeah," murmured the don. "What about the diamonds?"
"The contents of the brief case have not yet been examined so no one knows whether he's telling the truth or not right now; but I'm inclined to believe him. If that's so. I think I'll send it back to him unopened. I will find the two million dollars he wants from my account, I can't expect the firm to pay that sort of money. But I'd like your blessing on my decision; I've only until nine tomorrow morning."
"I don't like being leaned on by anyone, least of all by the Goldsteins of this world. But like you, I think we could just bite off more than we can chew if he has got those connections."
"That's true."
"He's only got to plant some dope in the clubs, give the cops a tip-off and we'd be shut down; permanently. Since the Gotti investigation has started and with the election coming up, I've heard the city hall is just dying to pin something on us. They want us all caught. We'd all be in the slammer for a long time then. Yeah; I think you should do as he says, this time anyway. Keep me informed."

Celleri shook the Godfather's hand respectfully and left the room. Once back inside the car he could relax. Now that his plan had received approval from the top he knew he could proceed without having to worry what the outcome would be. His only problem now was to raise the two million dollars demanded by Goldstein. He was going to have difficulty with that; he didn't have that sort of money in ready cash. He needed to sell something and quickly, unless he could persuade Goldstein to wait for it and if he could do that, maybe he'd get away with not paying at all. Was it worth the risk? If he failed and the casino was prejudiced in any way, he knew he'd be for the high jump; there was no sentiment in this business. Be successful and you were looked up to; fail, and you were dead meat; literally.

He found Sammy Goldstein's number and phoned from the car. "Mr Goldstein; this is Michael Celleri; I was ringing to confirm the delivery of the goods tomorrow morning at the time suggested but I'm afraid the cash transfer will have to be delayed for a while." He paused; there was no sound from the other end of the line. "Mr Goldstein, are you there?"
"Sure I'm here; have you finished?"
"Well, yes."
"Now pin back your ears; get this straight. Either you settle in full at nine tomorrow morning or my organisation will act. I've told you about the Torah; I've warned you what will happen. If that's what you want, that's fine. But be sure, these are not empty threats; they will be carried out, to the letter."
"Perhaps I can pay you half now and the rest later?"
"You haven't been listening Celleri." The line went dead.
Replacing the phone, he said to his driver, "Take me to Chase Manhattan."

CHAPTER TEN

The journey downtown took some time. "Wait for me," he said to his driver. At the plaza of the bank, Celleri had no time to observe the modern statues of Noguchi and Dubuffet; he was preoccupied with his problems. The towering 65 storeys of shining glass and aluminium were passed by unnoticed. He walked up to the toughened plate glass doors, which opened automatically as he approached, controlled by the infra-red sensor above.
"May I see the manager urgently please?"
"Who shall I say is calling?"
"My name is Michael Celleri."
He was taken to a small interview room on the side of the foyer by a young executive.
"Please take a seat sir; would you care to read the Journal while you're waiting?" he said, handing the Wall Street Journal to Celleri; "I'll see if the manager is free."

Celleri did not have to wait long. "Good afternoon Mr Celleri; we don't see you often at the bank; how may we help you?"
"I need to raise a large sum of money quickly. Something's happened and I've got to have two million dollars by nine tomorrow morning. You keep all my securities at the bank and using them as collateral I think there should be enough to find the money."
"Well let's see shall we?" He turned to a video screen on the desk and typing in Celleri's details, the pattern of his investments appeared, every last item.
"There's not as much as perhaps you thought you know; following the crash in 1987 some of your stock hasn't recovered as well as others." It took him more than a quarter of an hour with his calculator before he looked up again.
"If these are all your assets Mr Celleri, the bank could advance you a little over one and a half million; one million, five hundred and seventy five thousand, five hundred dollars to be exact, a shortfall of four hundred and twenty-four thousand, five hundred dollars. I'm sorry." He stopped in mid sentence; he had looked up to see Celleri's face. It was ashen; his eyes were glazed; he looked as if he were dead.
"I'm sorry it's been such a shock Mr Celleri; can I get you anything?" Celleri nodded his head.
"Is there any way I can obtain the difference before tomorrow morning?"
"I guess not, anyway not from the bank I'm afraid."
"Then I don't know what I'm going to do. Thank you for seeing me." He felt in the depths of despair.

His thoughts were in a turmoil; so many possible solutions flashed through his mind and all the possible sequelae too and they worried him. He was glad he had met with the Godfather. At least he knew the problem he had been forced to solve, forced into by those incompetent fools who had bungled such a simple order. If only they had done what they had been asked to do; if only they hadn't decided to kill Goldstein's son; here we go again; if only. But the germ of an idea had been circulating around his mind while in the car returning to the casino. He knew the club carried many hundreds of thousands of dollars in the safe in the office, perhaps more than a million. It had to, just in case there was a heavy run on the bank any night. Now, if he could borrow enough to make up the difference between his own money from the bank and the million he required just for a couple of weeks, he knew he could realise that from property deals he would make before anybody would recognise what he had done. All he

would have to do is put his signed IOU in the safe for a half a million dollars and take that much from the reserve.
“I wonder what the Godfather would say if he knew? Perhaps right now is not the time to find out.” He tapped on the window which separated him from the driver. “Take me back to the bank.” The die was cast.

Back at the bank he asked for the manager again but this time he had to wait a while. When he came into the room Celleri rose to face him.
“I’ve had time to think and if you can arrange for an advance of one and a half million dollars, in cash which I may have straight away, that will have to do. Somehow or other, I’ll have to raise the extra money elsewhere; can you do that?”
“If you give us a few moments, we’ll have it all ready for you.” True to his word, within ten minutes, two tellers brought a document case into the room. They counted out one million, five hundred thousand dollars in hundred dollar bills in front of him; it took fifteen minutes. Signing the transfer, he left for his car, the bank employees carrying the case between them. Once in the trunk, he thanked them for their efforts and returned to the casino.

His man carried the case up to his private rooms on the top floor of the building. Now he would have to see what funds there were in the safe; hopefully there’d be more than enough for his plan. Carefully he wrote his receipt for a half a million dollars and descended to the floor below. Dialling in the code, the door swung open and he carefully removed the money he needed; now he had it all. Hopefully, there’d be no comeback.

He went upstairs again to his rooms above the club where he had met Rosie the day before. It seemed an age since she had been there and so much had happened in the meantime.
“I wonder if she’s been told what happened to Goldstein’s son. Perhaps now she knows all about my connection with the mob. She’ll loathe and despise me if that’s the case; she sure won’t want to work here now. Damn those murdering fools. All they can do is kill. To Hell with them.” He kicked off his shoes relaxing in his favourite chair; the pressures of the evening had yet to begin.

Celleri descended the stairs to the club looking tall and every inch a gentleman in his tuxedo, but still smarting inside because of the problems his men had caused killing Goldstein’s son. But tonight he had a club to run and glancing at the people milling around, it was going to be a busy night; profitable too it would seem as the early receipts were shown to him. He circulated around the tables taking in all the action. There were some high rollers in; some were known to him but there seemed to be many new faces around. 'Let's hope they're all losers.'

It was two in the morning when there was a slight disturbance in the foyer of the club. A doorman approached him announcing the arrival of the sheikh of an emirate in the Gulf, someone who would expect personal attention. Celleri descended the stairs to greet his new guest.
" Salaam, Your Excellency; welcome to The Green Baize. What would you care to visit this evening?"
"Good evening." His English was like Celleri's, perfect, in his case the result of an education in a famous public school. "We'll start on the wheel; what are the house limits?"
"The limit is usually ten thousand dollars; will that suit your Excellency?"
"Raise it to a hundred thousand."
"As your Excellency pleases." He made the necessary arrangements with the croupiers and continued his tour of the tables. If he had stayed at the roulette wheel he would have realised that high rollers do win some of the time and when the stakes are so high, the demands for cash can be huge.

At four in the morning His Excellency had had enough and made to cash his chips. His underling presented the pile of counters at the bank. The sheikh had won more than eight hundred thousand dollars. Within the safe there were five hundred and fifty thousand dollars and an IOU for a half a million more; Celleri's IOU.
"Get the boss; now."

Celleri was in his apartment, enjoying a brandy at the end of what had been a most stimulating day, but certainly not an enjoyable one. The knock on his door was heavier and louder than was usual and the man who entered was more than a little excited; he was sure frightened.
"Boss; the sheikh's broken the bank. There's not enough to pay him out. The cashier wants to know whether you can settle this now." He put the IOU in front of Celleri. Once more Celleri broke out into a sweat; disaster beckoned.
"I'll have the money for the cashier in two minutes" he said, turning to his own safe in the wall. Paying the cashier meant that there'd be not

enough for Goldstein in the morning; but there was nothing else he could do. The casino just had to settle its debts there and then; there could be no backsliding.
"I'm sorry you had to wait," he said to the sheikh as the whole of the money was handed over. "Luck was with you tonight; perhaps we may be able to entertain you again on another occasion. Good night your Excellency."

The faint rays of early dawn were lancing the shadows over the tops of the high sky-scrapers towering above the still dark city streets, as Celleri climbed the stairs to his flat. The excitement of the last twenty-four hours had made him feel very tired. He knew the diamonds would be delivered shortly to Goldstein but not all the money demanded; hopefully he'd still have a few hours grace. It was nearly all that had been asked for; only a half a million dollars short. Celleri must have dropped off to sleep as the 'phone was ringing incessantly beside his ear; he fumbled for it, the room still in darkness, the blinds drawn.
"Hello."
"You disappoint me Celleri. Still you were warned, you can never say you weren't told what will happen."
"Just a minute," Celleri cried out, rousing himself immediately. "I had all the money you asked for last night. Unfortunately, there was a run on the bank; I've had to make it up. You'll get your money; you'll just have to wait a few more days."
"Sorry, can't do that, you've pushed your luck too far; even now it's too late. You'll just have to hope the top man understands when one of his clubs is put out of commission. Such a pity; it could all have been settled so easily."
"Easily; you think finding two million dollars in less than twenty four hours is easy? I can get the rest of the money for you in about three days, but it will take me at least that time."
"Good morning Celleri. By the way, I wouldn't go looking for the goons, the ones who you sent along today. They're already polluting the Hudson."
The line went dead; Goldstein had hung up on him. There was to be no further discussion; that was it.

CHAPTER ELEVEN

After his murder, the police had removed Abe's body to the mortuary for autopsy and the Lincoln was taken for forensic examination. Checking it for finger prints, comparing them to known villains on the police file proved useless as most were too blurred for use. Inside, the car was a mess with blood and brain tissue all over the front. Death had been instantaneous as the 38 slug had blown the right side of Abe's head completely away; he hadn't known a thing. The bullet had probably exited through the other front window which had been open, as there was no trace of it inside the car, something ballistics regretted as the markings on the bullet might have helped identify the gun and therefore the killers. The autopsy found nothing other than homicide by shooting and Abe's body was released to the family on the day after the run on the casino bank, the day Celleri couldn't raise the money.

CHAPTER TWELVE

There were five distinct groups of people who visited the casino that night. Firstly, there were the punters who regularly came to gamble on something or other; those with more money than sense and those who thought they had more sense than they really had. Those with systems which should beat the odds but never did; they were the people who kept the club financially sound. Secondly, there was a group of gamblers who had arrived in their ones and twos, who didn't gamble a lot but seemed to be waiting for something to happen. There were twenty or so of them and while they seemed not to know each other, somehow they all seemed to have something in common. Then, in the early hours of the morning, Sammy Goldstein turned up with Josh. He appeared to be somewhat drunk but those who knew Sammy were aware that he was a damned good actor. Sammy created quite a disturbance. In the foyer, he asked for Celleri by name, demanding he came down to see him and when he did, Sammy brought a hand grenade out from his pocket. With a theatrical flourish he made as if he were going to pull out the pin and detonate the grenade there and then in the hall; the guards really thought that was going to happen and they quickly hit the dirt, though Celleri maintained his dignified position in front of Sammy.

"All I wanted to do is indicate how easy it would be for me to destroy you and your casino; you'd rather that not happen I'm sure. What a shame you couldn't find the necessary cash; still, you were warned."

When he had finished speaking, Sammy turned around, apparently rapidly sober and walked out with Josh.

Celleri mopped his brow and looked with disgust on his cringeing henchmen.

"You? Guards? You're nothing but cowards".

Of course Sammy's outburst had been quite deliberate, a part of his plan to destroy the casino. Those unusual visitors to the casino that evening were also carrying the means of destruction in their pockets. Each of them had a small packet which once contained cigarettes but which now contained an incendiary device, and all were designed to go off at six in the morning, a time when the staff would have retired to bed, exhausted from the work of the day before and when everyone's resistance would be low. While the attention of the casino staff had been diverted by Sammy's noisy show, his friends had deposited these little fire bombs behind curtains and couches, down the sides of chairs and in numerous other places where they were unlikely to be recognised but likely to do most harm. Sammy was going to destroy the casino by fire and the final visitors to the club, essential to the plan, were yet to arrive; they were to come quietly and secretly, not to the front door as the others had, but to the outside of the casino, in the dark.

Sometime about five thirty in the morning, two dark-clad men drew up in their car alongside the small electricity substation which controlled the supply to the Green Baize. They were equipped with the necessary key to gain entry and expertly bolted an explosive charge on to the main cable as it came into the box. It too had a time switch planned to go off at five minutes to six, a short while before the fire bombs inside the casino were due to explode. As they moved away, the last group of visitors arrived in an unmarked truck which parked around the back of the club. The occupants of the truck did not get out straight away as there was no rush now; nearly all of the plans had been carried out. As the small charge exploded in the substation and the area was plunged into complete darkness as the electricity supply to the Green Baize and the whole of the district was disrupted, one of the men removed from the truck a long angled key which he used to turn off the water supply to the building. While he was doing that, his buddy attached one end of a strong steel chain to the fire hydrant and the other end to the tow-bar of the truck. They both climbed back into the cab and at six exactly, they drove away, dragging the hydrant off the water main.With a tremendous hiss a fountain of water pumped out of the torn pipe. The driver stopped the truck and quickly slipped the chain from the tow-bar and drove off towards the east of the city to get lost in the myriads of side turnings, slowly and carefully, not bringing attention to himself, just getting away from the luckless casino.

At six, the fire bombs all went off. As the power had been cut off, the smoke alarms didn't work and the loss of pressure prevented the water sprinklers in the ceiling supplying enough water to put out the fires which had been started. When the extent of the fire had been recognised, the destruction of the hydrant outside the building in the roadway, slowed down the efforts of the fire service. By seven in the morning, the Green Baize was little more than a charred brown shell. Nothing much was left. As Sammy had said, 'You had been warned.'

By the time the rescue services got to Celleri, his condition was critical. Smoke had gradually entered his room from the hallway outside and the fumes had overcome him such that he was unable to make sufficient effort to escape. He gasped for breath, taking in the hot corrosive and toxic fumes into his lungs and the heat seared the skin of his face and his arms and scorched his hair. He was alive but his life hung by a thread. The ambulance rushed him to the Bellevue Medical Center on First, sirens wailing, dispersing the early morning rush of traffic, while the paramedics set up the transfusions which poured the fluid he needed into him and gave him shots of morphia to dull the pain which now racked his body. Celleri was admitted to intensive care immediately; the fight for his life had begun.

CHAPTER THIRTEEN

Abe was buried on the morning of the fire and of Celleri's admission to Bellevue hospital.

Traditional Jewish Law, the Halachah, demands that burial occurs before the second sunrise, something that was not possible for Abe because of the delay caused by the nature of his death and the subsequent autopsy. But Elizabeth, once the initial shock had passed, had maintained the rigid conformity and tradition of the law within the home. To her, as to all Jewish women, was entrusted the religious practice of the family; it was she who removed the pictures of Abe from the apartment and covered the mirrors as is the custom and it was Elizabeth who lit the candles of remembrance in the house. Each day, the Minyan of Sammy's male friends called at the home and together they recited the Kaddish, a touching and moving service of prayers for Abe.

'Yis-gad-dal v'yis- kadash sh'may Rab-bo'. 'Magnified and sanctified be his great name.'

The symbolism which follows death in a Jewish family began when the undertaker brought Abe from the mortuary to Sammy's home and the three heads of the synagogue proceeded with the Tahorith, the ritual cleansing and purifying of the body after death. His Arba Kanfoth was placed over his head as it is the custom in Jewish families to inter the deceased in his Tallith, the same Tallith presented to Abe by Sammy and Elizabeth at his Bar Mitzvah when he was thirteen, to remind him always of God; while they intoned

'Baruch Atoh Adonoy Elohenu B'mitzvosor V' tzi-vanu L'hit-a-tafe Ba-tzitzith.'

'Blessed art though, Oh lord our God, King of the universe, who hath sanctified us by thy commandments and hast commanded us to enwrap ourselves in this fringed garment.' When all was complete the Gaba-im folded Abe in the Tachrichin to clothe him beyond the grave to Olam Ha-ba, the world to come. Shards of broken glass were placed over his closed eyes to symbolise the frailty of life and in his hands, small wooden sticks, to help him from his grave on his way to the homeland of Palestine.

On the day of the funeral, the casket was carried on the Mittah from the home to the hearse and from the hearse into the synagogue. The service was short and simple. The Rabbi in his eulogy, referred to Abe's many virtues linking his name with Sammy's and all the time there was the chanting of the 'El Molay Rachamim.' The bearers lifted the black-cloth covered coffin and proceeded from the west door to the cemetery. Three times the coffin was lowered to the ground, as if to delay the interment and each time, those that were there prayed "Yoshave B'sayser," loudly. The head of the grave faced Jerusalem and a small bag of sand lay inside at that end. The women cried, making heart-rending noises as the coffin was lowered into the grave and with the back of the spade, the first shovels of earth fell on to the casket; all stayed around the grave, family and friends until it had been filled completely; then and only then could they return home to begin the seven days of mourning following the interment, the Abeluth.

At that time, no one could have foreseen the changes that would proceed from Abe's death; changes that would alter so many people's lives.

CHAPTER FOURTEEN

The interns worked for hours resuscitating Celleri; his airway was scorched by the heat and the toxic fumes he had inhaled from the fire in the casino and he had great difficulty drawing each breath. His face was dreadfully blistered beneath the oxygen mask and the hair over the front part of his head had been burned away. His hands and arms were raw and bleeding where the skin had been damaged during his recovery from the fire. Intravenous drips of plasma and blood had been started and an airway into his trachea had made the supply of oxygen easier. Gradually, over some hours, his colour improved and his blood pressure recovered sufficiently for him to be taken to theatre to treat his burns. The burns were extensive but fortunately not deep. The initial surgery removed the dead skin and some split skin from the unburnt parts of his body, was used to correct the skin defects. Everything they did was carried out under strict aseptic conditions; any infection would undoubtedly prejudice his survival; Celleri was seriously ill.

Some hours later, Celleri was rushed back from the operating room to the intensive care unit which was to be his home for a number of days yet. His pain relief was of major importance, as without opiates, he would have been in agony and without the added assistance of the ventilator which was breathing for him, he would have been unable to survive. Monitors flashed as his blood pressure was recorded regularly; the QRS of his cardiogram peaked on the oscillator screen as every pulse of his heart was observed. The ventilator hissed rhythmically and the snake-like tubes connecting it to Celleri, coiled and uncoiled with the changes of pressure inside them. Wires, leads, plastic tubes, drips, everything, led to the machines controlling Celleri's very existence; without them and the skilled nurses who watched them, he could not live.

Rosie heard about the fire at the casino several days later. She was with Nick having morning coffee. He was reading the New York Times and noticed the entry about the destruction of the Green Baize casino three days earlier and the injury to the manager, Mr Michael Celleri, who had been admitted to the Bellevue Medical Center, critically ill with severe burns. It said he was now off the danger list, but would be in hospital for some time. It went on to say that enquiries were proceeding as the police had indicated there was some evidence the fire was started deliberately.

"Arson?" Nick murmured. "Now I wonder who could have done that?"

"You mean the fire was started deliberately? Surely not? Oh, the poor man; and to think it was only the other day I was with him. I know it may sound selfish Nick, but I wonder what will happen to my job now the club has been destroyed? I shouldn't think I'll be able to stay at the apartment indefinitely either; it just wouldn't seem right."

"No," said Nick absent mindedly, still reading the article.

"Lord, what a mess. Did you say the police thought it might be arson?"

"Yes; I was just wondering who could possibly be responsible if the fire was started deliberately. I suppose if the Green Baize were a Mafia casino, there'd be plenty of people who'd wish to get rid of it, even the other Mafia mobs. There's no love lost between them; perhaps that's what happened."

"I think I'd like to visit him if and when he can have visitors; do you think he'd like that? Would you come with me Nick?"

"Sure I will. We'll have to find out first if he's well enough. We'll both go together; I'd like to meet him."

Over the phone, it took them some time to find the ward Celleri had been admitted to, but the staff were all very helpful. Visitors would be allowed in provided they didn't stay too long as he was still a very ill man. Nick and Rosie arrived at the ward reception area at two o'clock.

"I asked if I could visit Mr Celleri; I was told it would be all right."

"You a relative?" The ward sister was a tall imperious woman in her stiff starched white uniform who would brook no argument; she was the boss.

"No, Mr Celleri is my employer."

"Don't you go worrying him about work now. He's only just well enough to see anyone; and don't stay more than ten minutes, d'you hear me?"

"Thank you sister; we won't tire him."

"Room 201; there'll be a nurse there; she'll have to stay." Nick, hand in hand with Rosie found room 201 just along the corridor. He tapped gently on the door and they both went in. The room was shaded by blinds drawn almost completely across the window but the artificial ceiling light was harsh and bright. Celleri was still attached to many machines, metering and monitoring his progress and his special nurse was occupied with her records. She looked up unsmilingly from her notes only for a moment, motioning them towards the bedside. Celleri appeared to be asleep but his eyes opened at once as they approached him; it was almost as if he sensed they were there. His face and arms were now swathed in bandages so it was not possible to know his reactions but Rosie could see that his eyes had smiled. He couldn't speak, a tracheostomy tube prevented it, but Rosie knew instinctively it had been right to come.

"Don't try to speak," she said. "I just wanted to come to see how you are. I only read about the accident today. If you would like me to, I'll come again when you're feeling stronger."

He nodded his head gently; he wanted Rosie to call and see him.

"This is Nicholas Royle. I met him on the flight over here; he's been very kind to me since I've been in New York. I don't know what I would have done without him; he's been a great help."

"Hallo Mr Celleri. I'm sorry to meet you like this. Don't worry about Rosie; I'll look after her."
"We won't stay now; just rest and get your strength back. Nick and I will be in to see you again in a little while. Bye."

"He looks dreadful doesn't he? I wonder how scarred he'll be when those bandages come off. I suppose he's lucky to be alive. "
"He's been badly burned, that's for sure," said Nick. "I just wonder how that fire started; the newspaper seems to think the place was torched."
"How dreadful; how could anyone do that to another man? It's not human."
"Maybe no one knew he was going to be there. There can't be many bosses who live over the shop. I'm sure it was only the casino that was supposed to go up in flames; he was just unfortunate to be inside still."
"Yes, wasn't he. What do you plan to do for the rest of the day Nick?"
"Well, I should do some business while I'm still here in New York. If you'd like to do some shopping for an hour or two, I'll pick you up at the apartment and we'll have dinner together later; how does that sound?"
"I'd like that; you have been absolutely wonderful Nick. I would have been awfully lonely without you; in fact, I don't know what I would have done on my own. "
"You'd have managed. You know I've enjoyed every minute I've been with you Rosie. I've been dreading the fact that I will have to be going back to England shortly; you know, I've got a business I have to run over there. "
"I shan't like that one little bit; but you will be coming to the States again soon won't you? I'd hate to think I wouldn't be seeing you again. "
"Me too; I'm getting to like you too much, young lady" he said, kissing her lightly on the cheek. "Now don't go off the beaten track and go and shop for a while and I'll meet you at seven."

Rosie made her way down Fifth Avenue, window shopping. After all, here reputedly were the best shops in the world and though she'd done a little gazing through the windows, she had not had that much time to enjoy herself. She had found out that within walking distance of the apartment, there was the world renowned Tiffany's at 56th, and a few blocks further on, Saks on 49th; Macy's, now a victim of the recession, was yet further on 34th street. Then there was Bloomingdales on 3rd and on Madison, every designer name in the book was there. For a woman, a few hours of absolute bliss; and no real need to spend a cent.

Nick flagged a cab which took him back to Sammy's home in downtown Manhattan. He wanted to talk to Sammy badly; to ask a few questions, like how the fire started in the casino? He wasn't sure but he had a sneaking feeling that Sammy and his friends were behind it. He had to ask; he knew Sammy wouldn't lie to him. If he had had anything to do with it, he would say. Nick couldn't help hoping deep down that he hadn't.

"Sammy, I'm glad I've caught you."

"Didn't know you were looking for me Nick." His face was unusually serious as if he guessed what Nick was going to ask.

"I was reading in the Times that the police think the casino was torched." He paused as if waiting for Sammy to intervene. As Sammy said nothing, he went on, "It seems as if Celleri was in the penthouse above the casino; he's badly burned. Rosie and I went to see him in Bellevue this afternoon. He's going to make it but he'll probably be dreadfully scarred."

"Yeah, I read it in the newspaper too; I wonder how it happened?"

"It must have been a hit. The power had been destroyed and the water cut off deliberately; someone wanted to burn that place down badly."

"Yeah; I guess a club like that makes a lot of enemies."

"I've got to ask Sammy; did it have anything to do with Abe's killing?"

Sammy hesitated, thinking before he replied. "Yeah; he was warned his club would be knocked off. No one expected him to be in the apartment over the casino when the fire started. We didn't plan for him to get hurt, that's the honest truth. We just wanted to teach him a lesson. "

"Why Sammy; why did you have to do it?"

"We found out it was his men who killed Abe."

"Oh no Sammy, surely not."

"I'm afraid so, Nick; I think you should know what else we found out about him. He lived in the same town in England that Rosie was born in; he left there a little over twenty-two years ago."

"Did he?"

"Yeah; and did you know Rosie had her twenty-third birthday ten days ago, just before her trip to the States?"

"No, I didn't."

"Now you've heard her say her father left as soon as he knew her mother was pregnant. We believe Celleri is Rosie's father." He waited while Nick considered what he was saying. "We think he has kept his eye on her throughout her life and when she qualified as an accountant, he offered her this job in his club here. You've got to admit, it all adds up; after all, you asked the question 'just how was it she got the job'?"

Nick's mind was sorting through the facts Sammy had told him. It seemed to be a long shot but it was possible. It would explain too why Celleri had asked Rosie all those searching questions about her mother back in England. Nick wondered how she would react if she knew? And was this connection going to involve her in any risk from Sammy's men or from the Mafia or both? Was she going to be at any risk at all?

"Thanks for telling me Sammy. I had a feeling that there had to be a reason for her getting that job, but I'm sure she knows nothing about this. Anyway, I'll have to give a lot of thought as to what I'm going to have to do or say."

"Yeah, do that." Sammy grinned. "And I've got new instructions to order another million pounds worth of merchandise; the quality of this last lot was superb and we'll need some more shortly."

"I've been meaning to ask what you do with them all. That'll be nearly ten million pounds in the last six months."

"They're used to grease palms Nick; to buy information, to pay off killers but particularly to find out what the Islamic world is planning to do to Israel. We know that Saddam Hussain is funding the Algerians to make a nuclear weapon, the so called 'Moslem bomb'."

"Yes, I've read about it."

"What we have to learn is exactly where they're making it and just how far they've got. When we know that, our guys will just go along and blow it all to kingdom come; they'll have to start all over again somewhere else."

"A sort of Entebbe?"

"Something like that. Unfortunately, these Islamic punks all over the world are becoming more militant, more fanatic. So, if we find someone who will give us information, we encourage them and pay them well. Then, when they have any more to tell us, they don't hesitate to line their pockets and talk some more. It's costly but it works."

"And what about the three diamonds; they were superb, the best I've seen on the market for quite a while. "

"They're already being set in platinum; a pair of earrings which will look absolutely fabulous when they're finished and a matching pendant. Now Nick; is there anything else you want to ask me? You

know I'll never lie to you but you know too there are some things I cannot tell even you."
"Thanks for talking to me Sammy." Nick thrust out his hand to shake Sammy's; they would always be friends.

CHAPTER FIFTEEN

As Rosie opened the door to her apartment, the phone began to ring.
"Hallo. "
"Is that Miss Rosie Haynes?" It was a jarring Brooklyn accent.
"Yes it is; who is that please?"
"Now that the Green Baize has been burned down there's no need for you to remain in New York is there? I expect you'll be leaving for home shortly; say not later than next week."
The phone went dead; whoever it was had rung off. It wasn't a request not even a command; just a statement. Suddenly, Rosie felt very frightened. Nick wasn't there and wouldn't be for another hour and she was scared; perhaps he was still at Sammy's. She rang the number Sammy had given her on the first day, when she had arrived at the apartment. The phone was answered immediately.
"Yeah?"
"May I speak to Mr Sammy Goldstein please?"
"Hi there Rosie. This is Sammy; how're ya doing? Y'okay?"
"Oh Sammy; is Nick there please?" Sammy recognised the fear in her voice.
"He's on his way to you Rosie. He left about fifteen minutes ago; he should be there any minute. Is there something wrong?"
"Someone has been on the phone saying, that as the casino had been burned down, I should return to England; I just got scared."
"I understand kid. Now don't get all worked up; nothing's going to happen to you, I promise. When Nick comes, ask him to give me a call. Don't worry."
"Thanks Sammy; it's probably nothing; he didn't threaten me at all. It was just that whoever he was, he knew I was here."
"Okay: you just ask Nick to ring."
"I will. Bye Sammy."

By the time Nick arrived, Rosie had regained some of her composure, but when she opened the door to him, her relief at his coming was obvious. For the first time since they had met, she threw her arms around his neck and hugged him to her.
"Oh, am I glad to see you?"

"Hey; what's up?"
She told him about the phone call, her talk with Sammy and his suggestion Nick should ring him.
"Hi Sammy," he said when Sammy answered the phone. "What d'you make of this; is it important?"
"Probably not but I thought I'd say that if you're worried about Rosie staying there on her own, Elizabeth and I'd be happy if she came here. By the way, we tapped the call she had; yeah, I forgot to tell you, I bugged Rosie's phone just in case. The call came from a Staten Island number; we're checking it out right now. We know that's where Celleri's don hangs out. It's likely to be him; God only knows why he should make the call."
"Doesn't make sense."
"Well, maybe the don thinks Celleri may talk following the fire bombing and if he is aware of the family relationship between Rosie and Celleri, he may think she knows something and might talk too. There's no way we can guess the way his mind is working right now, but I'll bet he's worried."
"We were just going out to dinner; okay if we ring when we get back? Maybe you'll have more news."
"Why don't you come back here tonight? I'll get the guys to keep an eye on the apartment just in case."
"Is that wise Sammy, to come back I mean?"
"Yeah, I believe so; I think maybe it's time to talk openly to Rosie."
"Okay and thanks Sammy."

Delmonico's, where Nick and Rosie dined was only a short distance from Sammy's home, so rather than call a cab after their meal, they strolled arm in arm the few blocks. This was not the most salubrious part of the city and there weren't many people about. Rosie held on tightly to Nick's arm. It gave her comfort. Two ragged men stepped out of a doorway a few yards ahead, their eyes still glazed, high on drugs. One of them, slightly taller than the other, blocked their way, a knife in his outstretched hand. Nick reacted quickly, all his old instincts for survival blotting out any fear he may have had. He pushed Rosie hard against the wall, protecting her, and crouched awaiting the attack. The man with the knife was fast but not fast enough. Nick caught his arm in a vice like grip and jerked it upwards, bending the elbow backwards. The knife clattered away into the gutter as the man screamed out in pain, his arm hanging crookedly by his side; it took only moments. Nick turned quickly to face the other mugger.
"Take him away unless you want the same treatment too." They limped away, mouthing oaths and swearing, the one acting as a crutch

for the other. Nick was completely unruffled, almost as if nothing had happened.
"Just as well it was a knife he had rather than a gun, otherwise we'd both be an addition to the New York crime statistics. You okay? Sammy's place isn't very far away now," he said.
"Wow, where did you learn to do that?"
"Remember? I told you Rosie, I was in the army. I was trained in the skills of self defence. Here's Sammy's. You'll love his wife, Elizabeth. She's a gem; been like a second mother to me. But let me warn you, you'll find her a bit sad at the moment."

Sammy welcomed them warmly, introducing Rosie to all the family. "Where's Abe?" said Rosie. Elizabeth let out a wail, pent up emotions racking her body as she sobbed in front of Rosie. Sammy put his arm around her gently, guiding her to a comfortable chair.
"We didn't tell you before Rosie because we didn't want you to be upset. When we came down from your apartment on the day you arrived, we found that someone had shot Abe while he was waiting for us."
"Oh no."
"He was dead in the car; he was buried two days ago."
Turning to Nick, Rosie said, "That's where you were the other morning. Why didn't you say something?"
"Sammy thought not to worry you," Nick replied.
"The police are still investigating the murder." said Sammy.
"How terrible for you; but why?"
"It seems as if it was probably done in error by the mob. You remember we were followed from the airport? Well Abe was killed by those guys."
"But you thought they were from the Mafia, from The Green Baize; from Mr Celleri."
"Yeah, we were right. He's more or less admitted it."
"You don't mean that Mr Celleri ordered Abe's killing? Surely that's not possible. He couldn't have done that."
"No; he didn't order the murder, but they were his men who did it."
"Is that why the casino has been attacked and burned? Why Mr Celleri is now seriously ill in hospital? Is this your way of seeking revenge Sammy?" Turning to Nick, she said quietly, "And did you know of all this too?"
Sammy took Rosie by the arm gently. "Nick knew nothing about this, not until he asked this afternoon."
Rosie continued to look at Nick. "It's true Rosie; when we read in the paper this morning that the police thought it might be arson, I

wondered then whether Sammy's lot were involved. That's why I came along here this afternoon to ask him."

"We didn't mean for Celleri to get hurt; just the casino."

"But he was."

Sammy hesitated. "Rosie; I think I should tell you something else we found out about your Mr Celleri. It may make you dislike me more than you do right now, but I have to let you know. You remember he comes from England; in fact, he comes from your home town in England, the town where you were born?" Sammy paused, waiting for each part of what he was going to say to sink in. "He left for some reason or other about twenty-two years ago; must have been a short while before you were born." Again Sammy lingered. "You remember too he wanted to be known as Chaney, Michael Chaney?"

"Yes, he told me his name was Chaney; I did think it was strange at the time."

"Perhaps he thought that when you talked to your mother back home it would be better if she thought that you worked for a man called Chaney rather than Celleri." There was another long pause.

"What are you suggesting," insight slowly dawning in Rosie's mind. "Surely you're not telling me that Michael Celleri is my father, are you?"

"We really don't know Rosie," said Sammy, "but you've gotta admit, it kinda adds up." She was silent; the eyes of all of them were on her, as her tears began to come.

Elizabeth broke the tension. Putting her arm around Rosie, she said, "Don't upset yourself my love. Sammy doesn't know for sure if he's right about Mr Celleri being your father. It's just a pity he was in the building when the fire began."

Rosie turned, her head resting on the older woman's shoulder, receiving the warmth and affection from the caress. There was no need for anything more to be said right now.

The phone in the corner of the room rang, startling everyone from their thoughts. Sammy answered gruffly.

"Yeah?" The sibilants of the voice speaking rapidly on the other end of the line could be heard vaguely. Sammy listened with interest before replacing the telephone in its cradle.

"Well, Rosie, it seems as if you've had two visitors to your apartment this evening while you ve been away; they didn't stay but they left you a note. One of my guys is bringing it over; shouldn't be long." Sammy defused the anxiety of the moment, saying, "Liz, how about some coffee? Let's all sit down and be comfortable."

Rosie sought to sit close to Nick; she needed his counsel right now. She was sure he had been as surprised as she had been to hear what Sammy had said about Celleri. She wanted to know what he thought about it all.

"Nick; what did you know about what Sammy has told me?"

"Sammy told me this afternoon. I knew nothing before that, but I must say I had a suspicion something was not quite right when you told me how you were recruited for the job. It didn't seem the way things happened in the real world, especially in the world of casinos; not kosher, as Sammy would say."

"But what do I do now?"

"I don't really know but I would think there are three possible ways forward; you could ask your mother whether your father's name was Celleri."

"She would never talk about him other than to say he was a nice man. What else can I do?"

"You can ask him yourself when you see him next, whether he is your father. I've no doubt he knows all about you and has kept his eye on you over the years."

"What's the third?"

"You could forget all about the last few minutes and continue as you were."

Rosie's thoughts were interrupted by the arrival of one of Sammy's men from the apartment. He brought a grubby brown manilla envelope, the sort commonly used for cheap mail. It was addressed to Miss R. Haynes. She tore it open. The note it contained was written on expensive handmade paper; it read,

"No casino; no job; no stay. Till next week." Nothing else.

"They're sure leaning on you Rosie," was Sammy's comment. "Whatever you think now about the attack on the casino, the rights and wrongs of what occurred, I think you should stay here for the time being; it'd be safer."

"Thanks Sammy and you too Elizabeth. You've been so kind to me; I'd feel much happier with you."

"I think you've got to stay too." said Nick. It was nearly midnight before they made their way to bed. None of them that morning could have remotely guessed what was going to have happened that day; it was all too bizarre.

CHAPTER SIXTEEN

When they returned to the hospital the following morning, there was a police guard at the ward entrance. "Where d'you think you're you going?" he said curtly,

"We're going to visit Mr Celleri."

"Celleri? Stay there." He spoke into his microphone. "Sarge; there's a couple just come in to visit Celleri. Yeah. Okay, I'll keep 'em." He turned to face them; "Wait here; the sergeant wants to talk to you."

"Why? What's happened?"

"He'll explain it all to you in a minute; just stay here." Nick and Rosie stood together in the waiting area of reception until the police sergeant came from the direction of Celleri's room.

"You want to see Mr Celleri?"

"Yes," said Rosie. "We called yesterday and said we'd come again today. The ward sister said it would be all right; what's wrong?"

"What's your name miss?"

"Rosalie Haynes. I arrived in New York a few days ago to work as an accountant for Mr Celleri at the Green Baize casino."

"So, you're Miss Rosalie Haynes?" He sounded relieved. "We were wondering how we would find you."

"I don't understand; why should you want to find me?"

"Are you related to Mr Celleri? Your name is in his records as next of kin." Rosie felt faint. It would seem as if Sammy's reasoning was correct: Michael Celleri was her father.

"I am not sure," whispered Rosie, "but I believe Mr Celleri is my father."

"Well Miss Haynes, last evening the special nurse recognised an intruder in his room, dressed as a doctor. He was trying to inject something into your father's IV drip. "

"But why, why would anyone want to do that?"

"To kill him. She was able to stop most of whatever it was going into him, but some did. The doctors here believe it was insulin. They caught the guy just in time. Another few minutes and Celleri'd have been dead. They might've got away with his murder too, because he's been so ill. Still, he's better now. You can go in to see him but don't stay long. Nice meeting you Miss Haynes."

"Nick, he is my father. Why didn't he tell me?"

"I don't know Rosie. You go and see him; I'll be with you in a few minutes.

Nick found the sergeant talking with the policeman at the doorway. "Sergeant; may I have a word with you?"

"Yeah; what can I do for you?"
"Do you know who tried to kill Mr Celleri?"
"Not yet, but the guy we caught is one of the mob all right. Who are you?"
"My name is Nicholas Royle," he said presenting his passport. "I'm on business here. I met Miss Haynes on the flight and I've been showing her the sights in New York. She wasn't certain Celleri was her father until you told her now, though she was beginning to work it out. She had been planning to ask him this morning. Another thing you should know; since the fire, she has had a threatening phone call and a note saying 'No casino, no job, go home.' She's getting scared."
"Do you have any ideas who would have tried to kill him?" said the cop.
"We figured he'd be Mafia. They're getting very jittery now with all the in-fighting. Perhaps his don's afraid he'll talk. Omerta is nowhere near the powerful force it was since the recent trials."
"How come you know so much about the mob?"
"I don't; only what I read in the papers, but I guessed the casino fire was a Mafia gangland fight."
"Maybe, maybe not."
Nick wished he hadn't talked so much. But there was nothing to connect the fire with Sammy; if anything, he'd sown the seeds elsewhere.
"What I'm really worried about now sergeant, is whether, as they haven't succeeded in killing Mr Celleri, they'll try again. Is there any way the hospital could release the news that he'd died as a result of the accident? If the mob thought he was dead, it'd take the heat off. If they try again, maybe they'll be successful the next time."
"We'll put a guard on him now but yeah, maybe you're right; I'll have a word with the captain; see what he thinks. He's the boss."

"They let me in because they said your next of kin was Rosalie Haynes; I wasn't sure but you are my father aren't you?" Though the tracheostomy tube had been taken out, speech was difficult; his voice was weak and there was a hiss through the recent hole in his airway. Breathlessly, he whispered,
"Yes; your mother, Meryl was my first and only love. You were the result of our one episode of love making all those years ago."
"Why did you run away and leave her? She did love you so."
"We were so young. I was a street-wise kid, without any career; no future to offer her. I just panicked and ran. I was scared; scared of poverty and failure." He paused, gasping; every word he had said had been an effort. "Since you were born, I have made it my business to

know everything about you. I have known of your vices and your virtues, your likes and dislikes. When you graduated, I wanted you to come to America so that I could have you near me for a while; that's why you were invited to join the casino. You see, I've regretted every one of those wasted years. So many times I've wished 'if only' I could have put the clock back." Rosie touched his bandaged arm so gently.
"When you're well again, why don't you come back to England with me? I know at least two people who'd love that."
"We'll see. Go now but do come again. I am rather tired. Go and find Nick. He seems a nice young man."
"He is, very nice. Bye-bye for now." There was nowhere she could kiss him; he was still covered with bandages. But now she had a father, she felt wonderful; she'd never had one before, that she knew.

Rosie turned at the sound of footsteps hurrying behind her; a slightly balding middle-aged man wearing a camel-coloured trench coat was trying to catch up with her before she left the ward. His tie was only loosely knotted and the upper button of his shirt was undone; he looked hot and sweaty, harrassed by the pressure of his work.
"Miss Haynes; I'm Captain Stryker," he said, waving his ID in front of her. "May I have a word with you? I'm in charge of police investigations in this precinct. Perhaps we can use Doctor Paul's room. I know he wants to speak to you too." He dabbed his moist brow as he opened the door into the doctor's office. Dr Paul was inside waiting for them.

"Do come in Miss Haynes," he said, drawing up a chair in front of his desk for Rosie to sit on, signalling to Nick to pull up another. "I see you have met the captain of police. We both feel that now is the time to talk to you about your father, Mr Celleri."
"He's coming on all right isn't he? I thought he seemed to be a little better today."
"Oh yes, he's doing fine. It's not that. I believe you've been told that someone came into his room last night and tried to kill him. Fortunately, the nurse came back in time to stop anything serious happening but it was a close shave; a few minutes more and he'd have died."
"How dreadful; who would want to do that?" Rosie asked.
Captain Stryker interrupted. "Well the man who's been caught is one of the mob without any doubt."
"Has he said why he did it?"
"No, he's much too frightened to say anything at all at the moment. We

may be able to break him but he'll probably keep silent. He knows, that should he forget the Mafia's law of silence, he will surely die. Omerta is a good reason for keeping your mouth shut."

"God, it all sounds so horrid," said Rosie

"Yeah, but that's made us afraid for your father's safety. It's near impossible for us to maintain absolute security in a hospital like this one with such an acute intake in all the wards every hour of the day," said the police captain. "We can keep a guard here on Celleri but even he'll have to have some breaks. We feel you ought to know that if someone is determined enough to kill your father, he'll succeed at some time."

"Would it be an advantage if Nick and I helped to look after him?"

"Not really Miss Haynes but thanks for the offer. But we do have a suggestion to make however and we'd like you to think it over fairly quickly, because if you agree, we'd have to move straight away." The captain of police turned to the doctor who had been listening to his conversation with Rosie.

"You're very pleased with Celleri's progress I believe doctor?"

"Indeed, he's done remarkably well. When he was admitted, he had extensive burns and they had caused the severe shock he was in. "

"How's he doing now?"

"He has been fortunate in two respects. The burns, though widespread are not deep. Scarring will be minimal and he will not require the skin grafting we originally thought was going to be necessary. He has responded to the treatment of his shocked state very rapidly. The major problem at the moment and for the next few days will be the damage the hot and poisonous gases have done to his lungs, but even that seems to be going along quite nicely. "

"So what you are saying is that it may not be absolutely necessary for Celleri to stay in hospital as long as you first thought?" interjected the captain.

"That's right," replied the doctor.

"You do realise Miss Haynes, that if this attempt on your father's life had been successful, he'd be dead; he'd be leaving the hospital this morning in a casket. You do understand the seriousness of the problem?" Stryker said. Rosie shuddered at the thought.

"I say," said Nick, "Cut it out. Miss Haynes has gone through a great deal of stress over the last few days."

"Yeah, I'm sorry," agreed the policeman. "But don't you see, if we could make the mob think they'd been lucky and killed Celleri, then the heat would be off for a while; maybe for good. None of you would have any need to keep looking over your shoulders all the time just waiting for someone to rub him out. Can you see what I'm getting at?"

"You mean ..." said Rosie.
"Yeah; the hospital would announce to the papers he'd died; that he'd failed to recover from his burns. It happens all the time, they win some, they lose some. We'll get him out of hospital discreetly without anyone knowing he's still alive and you can fix a fake funeral for him, one that you can attend and mourn as a daughter would be expected to. With a bit of luck, most of your worries would then be over. Don't you see, it's perfect."
"Why would you be willing to do all that?" said Nick.
"Ah well, I'm glad you asked; we'd expect Celleri to talk."
"How could he do that? He's supposed to be dead."
"Clearly he wouldn't be able to take the stand like Sammy the bull did against John Gotti, but he could give us some incriminating information to make an investigation stick. If he did that, we'd have another Mafia family all locked up and put away for a long time. Maybe some youngsters wouldn't have to die unnecessarily from heroin or coke peddled by these hoods, or some young women may find something other than prostitution to live for. The Mafia has controlled the rackets long enough. It's time to get rid of them once and for all time."
"What has my father got to say about all this?" asked Rosie.
"What say we go and find out?" said the captain.

The four of them returned to Celleri's room. They dismissed the special nurse who had been attending to him and the captain drew up a chair for Rosie to sit beside the bed, where Celleri could see her without having to move his head. Nick stood behind Rosie so that he too could see his reactions. The doctor was on the other side and the captain of police at the foot of the bed, obviously where he knew he would appear most threatening.
"Celleri; I've been talking to your daughter. I've explained to her that it was probably the mob who hit you at the casino and they probably wanted to make it permanent last night when they tried to fill you with insulin, enough to kill a bull elephant I'm told."
"What makes you think it was the mob?" Celleri whispered with difficulty.
"The guy we caught is one of your hoods all right. So now we're worried about your safety. We can't keep this place secure all the time so they can't get at you again; understand?"
The tortured voice whispered, "I understand officer. Get to the point."
Rosie felt a sort of pride the way he responded to the bullying tone of the captain, despite the frailty of his reply.
"Okay then, I'll make it clear. We'll guarantee to get you away from

the hospital to a safe place, where you can have time to recover properly from your burns, maybe even give you a new identity, provided you supply evidence that'll put your boss and his gangsters away for long time."

"You want me to inform against those who have given me help and backing all my life; to give you information against my friends." Each word was an effort.

"It was those guys who tried to kill you last night."

"Maybe it was, maybe it wasn't, but I can't do as you ask even if there is a risk to my life." Looking at Rosie he said, "I'm sorry. I can't betray them; they're my brothers." Tears ran down Rosie's face; she had only found her father today and now it seemed as if he was going to be taken away from her before she had got to know him. Nick's hand found hers as he placed it gently on her shoulder and she rested her head against him.

The doctor who had been looking after Celleri said, "You are probably well enough to leave hospital now provided you're looked after. You'll be able to leave the dressings off within the next few days and your chest is getting better all the time."

"So you want to get rid of me too?" Celleri whispered.

"No, it's not that." The doctor was flustered. "It's just that we don't want you to be killed here. The publicity wouldn't do the hospital any good."

"I'll think about it," Celleri whispered almost inaudibly. "I'd like you all to go now. Nick, perhaps you could stay for a few minutes." Rosie made to stay too but Celleri murmured softly to her, "My dear, I'd just like to have a word with Nick alone. I won't keep him."

"I'll be along in a moment Rosie. Go with the doctor; I'll meet you in his office in a few minutes." Rosie was supported on her way to the doctor's room, her face red and blotchy from her crying, tears still running down her cheeks. To anyone watching, she'd had a deep shock.

"Tell Goldstein to get me out of here and find somewhere to hide me till I can get about again. Tell him he got me in here; now I'm well enough to be moved, it's his job to get me out somehow or other."

"I'll tell him. I don't know what he'll say; maybe he can do it. Do you want me to tell Rosie about this?"

"No, definitely no. Her tears will be all the more real if she doesn't know. Go now and see what he can do."

"What did he want to say to you he couldn't say in front of me?"
"I guess he realises how much I like you and he wanted to be sure I'd be around to give you help if you needed it. I said I would." Rosie squeezed his hand affectionately, fresh tears appearing in her eyes. "Let's get out of here. Thank you Dr. Paul for all your help to my father; I'm eternally grateful." To Captain Stryker she admitted, "I had hoped he would have agreed with what you suggested; perhaps he'll change his mind."
"Maybe he will. We'll keep in touch Miss Haynes."

Rosie and Nick took the elevator to the ground floor of the hospital. Anyone watching could not have avoided noticing and recording Rosie's puffy face; that she had gone through a period of stress and anguish was clearly apparent. In fact, the report the don got that evening gave him every reason to assume Celleri had died or would die soon following his man's attack. Even though he had been caught in the act, a good lawyer would work something out for him. And with Celleri dead, his branch of the cosa nostra would sleep more soundly, that's for certain; there'd be no backsliding there.

Rosie went off with Elizabeth when they got back to Sammy's home, the women comforting each other, while Nick went to find Sammy in his workshops.
"Sammy, I saw Celleri this afternoon."
"Yeah? How's he doing?"
"He's doing okay. The doctor says he's almost good enough to leave hospital now. The police offered him protection if he gave the Mafia the kiss of death by informing on them."
"What'd he say?"
"He turned them down. But he got me on one side before I came away and said to tell you, you got him in there, you get him out. What d'you think? Is it possible?"
"All things are possible Nick with time, but is it practical? I don't want to cross the police at all right now. I'll give it some thought though." Sammy wandered away, his mind already turning over a plan he and his organisation had been considering should it've been necessary to get Celleri out of hospital quickly, for any reason.

At four o'clock that afternoon, two hospital orderlies appeared on Celleri's ward with a request form, signed apparently by one of the staff and a trolley to take Celleri to the X-Ray department. The nurse on duty took only a perfunctory look at the form and then with a lot of grumbling, helped the porters lift Celleri on to the trolley.

"We'll use the service lift," the one porter said to the nurse. "The others aren't working properly." She couldn't have cared less. The ward was busy and as always, they were short staffed. They could have used any lift as far as she was concerned. Once in the lift, one of the men took a small screwdriver from his pocket and unscrewed the lid of the control box. Very quickly, he lifted out the fuse and the lift came to an abrupt stop. Meanwhile his colleague had spoken to Celleri.
"We've been sent by Sammy Goldstein. Can you get out of bed?"
"I can try," said Celleri and he pulled himself upright on the trolley. He felt light-headed as his legs swung over the side, but he was strong enough to cooperate as they slid a pair of trousers over his hospital gown. There were no drips to clutter up his arms now so it was fairly easy to slide an anorak over his shoulders and zip it up. With the hood covering his head and face, most of the bandaging was concealed and on quick inspection now, he looked just like any worker might look. The two porters abandoned their white clothing in among the covers and now they too looked as normal visitors to the hospital. The fuse was put back into the box and the lever pointed to the underground car parks. It took ten minutes thirty-five seconds from the time the orderlies arrived on the ward to Celleri climbing into the back of the getaway car.
Huskily, Celleri said, "It seems you've done this before."

"Miss Perry; would you get me Mr Schuster of the legal department?"
"Yes Dr Paul." There was a few minutes delay as his secretary tried to find the hospital attorney. "You're through," she said.
"Marvin, this is David Paul; how are you?"
"I'm fine. Don't tell me, you've got a problem. You only get in touch when there's something wrong. I can guess, your wife's run off at last with the junior intern; can't say I blame her, having to put up with you."
"No, nothing so simple," he said with a chuckle. "Don't tell her I said that; I'll deny it anyway. No, this is serious. We've lost a patient."
"You've had patients die on you before; what's new?"
"Lost, not died. We've never lost a patient before. Can you come along to my office and I'll explain?"
"Sure; give me fifteen minutes."

"We admitted this guy, a capo called Celleri, with burns. He was pretty ill when we got him in but he improved quickly, so that by the third day he was not too bad. Last night, someone comes into his room and tries to fill him full of insulin."

"You mean an outsider tried to kill him?"
"Yes. The nurse stopped him of course and the security caught him before he could leave the building."
"Where is he now?"
"The police have been questioning him down at the station but he's not saying anything. They say he's a known Mafia hitman, probably with a contract to kill this capo before he talks. It seems this guy Celleri is one of their top men. He knows too much for his own good."
"So they tried to knock him off in the hospital?"
"Yes. Anyway, the police talked to Celleri and his daughter earlier this afternoon, suggesting they'd get him out of the place and give him protection provided he gives evidence against the mob. They'd even give him a new identity to get him off the hook."
"What'd he say?"
"He turned them down; said he'd think about it."
"So, where do I come in? D'you want me to persuade him?"
"No, what I've told you is just the background. About an hour ago, two men dressed as orderlies came on to the ward with a trolley and an order to take Celleri to the X-Ray department. "
"The nurse checked the request?"
"No, she was busy and didn't think anything about it; didn't think at all really. She only took a glance at the request and in fact, she even helped to get him on the trolley. The cop on the ward didn't even see them go. Celleri's just disappeared."
"He's been kidnapped not lost. We've got problems if the family sue."
"Yes, I thought as much. Somehow or other they got him out of the building. There's no trace of him anywhere inside. We've searched everywhere."
"I suppose the police are involved in looking for him too?"
"Yes, but they haven't a clue where to start. Nobody seems to have seen a thing. The nurse can't even give them a reliable description of the fake orderlies."
"Well, all we can do is wait. I'd organise a search of the hospital again just in case something was missed and then I'd leave the rest to the police."
"I suppose so. I can't say I'm looking forward to meeting the family."
"No, I don't think I'd like to be in your shoes either. Still, if my office can help, you'll let us know."
"I sure will. Thanks for coming over." The two men shook hands; both knew of the problems the next few days might bring.

CHAPTER SEVENTEEN

Sammy found Rosie and Nick talking in the sitting room.
"I've been thinking. Perhaps I ought to go and see your pa Rosie and talk things over with him. After all, I suppose I am responsible for his being there. What say we go across and have a chat?"
"Okay, that's real nice of you Sammy," Nick said, slipping into Sammy's way of speaking."Shall we go now?"
"Yeah, why not."
Josh brought Sammy's car round and chauffeured them to Bellevue. They sat in the back and talked about all the many things that had happened since Rosie had arrived in New York, still less than a week ago; there hadn't been a dull moment. When they arrived on the floor, the ward receptionist recognising Rosie, asked them to come along with her to the office. She said she knew the director of surgery wanted to speak with her.
"Miss Haynes, I'm sorry to say we have some bad news to tell you."
"Oh no, surely nothing has happened to my father since we were here earlier?"
"Well; we don't know. He's been abducted somehow by two men dressed as fake orderlies since you were here this afternoon. The police are looking into it now but we haven't a clue where he could be."
"This is awful. What on earth can we do?; there must be something?"
"How the devil can a sick man like Mr Celleri be taken out of hospital without anyone seeing him go?" Nick said."Surely someone must have seen something? They'd have needed an ambulance to get him away wouldn't they?"
"Maybe; we just don't know. Everything is being done that can be done."
"Would it be better if we stayed? Is there anything we can do to help?" asked Rosie.
"Not now," said the director of surgery. "There's nothing much any of us can do right now. We'll get in touch if there's any progress."

Within minutes of Sammy's departure with the others for the hospital, the car containing the pseudo orderlies and Celleri drove into Sammy's underground car park space at his apartment block. Fortunately no one was about and the transfer of Celleri from his hospital bed to Sammy's home was complete and no one was any the wiser. Elizabeth who knew about Sammy's plan had been preparing the room for Celleri's coming. As she closed the door behind her, she saw him on the landing coming towards her with the two 'orderlies'. She turned away, not wanting to meet him, the

man who had killed her son, Abe.
"Mrs. Goldstein." His words were whispered. "I can't tell you how sorry I am that your son was killed."
She turned back to face him. She paused. "No, I guess it wasn't your idea." Tears welled up in her eyes. "I've heard a lot about you lately. Not all good I must say but I suppose not all bad either."
"Yes, I suppose you have."
"I'm sorry you got burned in the fire. I hear you'll mend okay though."
"Yes, I hope so."
"Sammy says I'm to tell you that no one knows you are here, not even Nick or Rosie."
"No?"
"He thinks this place will be kept under observation by the Mafia and the police and he figures that if either Nick or Rosie knows you're here, they're likely to give you away."
"Yes, I agree."
"Not deliberately, sure, but he thinks they won't be able to keep it secret. So if you hear anyone around, keep quiet."
"Okay."
"When you're better will be soon enough for anyone to know. Then we'll have to think of getting you away, perhaps back to England with a new identity. Yeah, I guess you could easily become Michael Chaney. I hear that's what you call yourself."
"I'm most grateful for Mr Goldstein's and your help." Speech was getting more and more difficult for Celleri. "I'll try to be as little trouble as possible. I'm a bit concerned about the burns though; they'll still need some looking after."
"Don't worry about them. Our son-in-law is a doctor and his wife is a nurse, so we should be able to look after you well enough. I was told to ask you if you needed anything for the pain when you came?"
"No, thank you. I feel a bit shaken and a bit weak but I'm okay really. I'm not in much pain. Perhaps I'll take a little rest for a while."
"Yeah, do that. There's a phone you can use to ring us downstairs but Sammy wants you to use it only as a last resort. It doesn't ring out."
"I understand and thanks again."

Ten days later, a body was recovered from the Hudson river. It was male, Caucasian and had been badly burned before death. It had been in the water for some time and what with the effect of the burns, the maceration from being in the water and the damage caused by passing shipping, especially to the face, accurate identification was impossible. As it was of the same height and build as Celleri and fortuitously the same blood group and showed the presence of burning, and the remnants of his hospital clothing and the hospital identity bracelet were still attached, it was assumed the corpse was that of Celleri. Tissue typing wasn't considered necessary. An inquest was held and after the medical details had been given, it seemed only reasonable to assume that these were the last natural remains of Michael Celleri. The death certificate was issued and the body released to the mortician for burial.

The body had been of that of a wino, found dead in the grounds of one of Sammy's factories. Hopelessly drunk, he had fallen on to a fire he had built to keep himself warm and he had died a horrible and painful death. He had been dead for some time before Sammy's men found him but when he was told, Sammy realised the potential of the discovery; this was to be Celleri's body.

All they had to do was dress the body in Celleri's hospital gown, slide the plastic name tag over the wrist and now the final chapter of Celleri's life could start; the burial of these remains would allow the arrival of the new Michael Chaney.

CHAPTER EIGHTEEN

"Morgen Baas." It had been years since they had lived and worked in South Africa, yet Sly always greeted Nick in that way when they met in the morning. When they first knew each other, Nick had commanded a platoon of special troops of the Ossewa Brandwag, the undercover Africaner force employed by the government to crush the Swartgevaar, the tide of emerging black nationalism; Sly had been his sergeant. In hidden camps, known to only a very few in high places, young men, the select few, the cream of the graduates from the major universities, were sworn to secrecy and trained in the skills of counter-espionage and subversion. They learned how to steal and to kill, to destroy and to survive and later they were to serve the fatherland with distinction on active service.

On one occasion, Nick had led a raid deep into the bush against the umkhonto we sizwe, the military wing of the African National Congress. It had been sunset when he and his troops were dropped by helicopter about twenty miles from the enemy camp of thatched cottages which surrounded the central radio transmitter. They had made a forced march overnight through jungle pathways to encircle the compound just before dawn. They were invisible as they lay still in their camouflaged tunics, large patches of sweat soaking through their uniforms. As the sun tinged the sky, the quavering bird call echoed around the camp, the signal for the attack to begin. Resistance had been much stronger than they had expected but eventually, with the complete destruction of the opposition forces, the firing from the camp ceased. As they advanced, a single shot had caught Sly in the thigh and he fell to the ground. Luckily the bone had not been shattered but the bleeding was brisk, bright arterial blood pumping his life away into the dirt. Nick had responded at once using his lanyard as a tourniquet to stop the blood loss; had he not acted so quickly, Sly would have bled to death on the spot within minutes. Later, when mopping up had been finished and the base razed to the ground, Nick called in the helicopters to ferry his men back to base; no long trek back. Sly had kept his life and his leg but the tourniquet had been on for a long time causing some death of the muscle which had left him with a permanent limp.

After this mission had been completed they had both been honoured by their country and soon they returned to civilian life. Nick, who had graduated as a mining engineer from Stellenbosch joined de Beers, the diamond conglomerate and Sly trained with them too as a cutter. They remained close friends, often working together late into the night with especially valuable gems, discussing the many ways a stone might be cut to produce the least waste and create the greatest possible brilliance and fire and its ultimate beauty. Sly had a natural gift; a flair that could transform the uncut pebble, unlocking its fiery heart, shaping the gem, so that all the light it absorbed was reflected through its many facets and it became a living scintillating force. It seemed a natural step for Sly to join Nick when later he set up as an independent dealer in London and Amsterdam.

As Nick came into the workroom, Sly stood up awkwardly, sliding his stool away from the bench where he was working. The noise of the whirring lathes made easy conversation difficult and the brightness of the spotlights was hard on the eyes. Though Sly was the only one working there, clearly there was a lot going on the room. Before Sly followed Nick through to the quiet of the office he limped over to one of the machines, made a fine adjustment, added a little paste to the tip of the grinding wheel and stood back to see whether all was well. On the bench alongside the rotating wheel were his tools. There was a multitude of fine discs of all sizes and pots of diamond dust paste used to produce the polish, releasing the fire of the gem; small tweezers were needed to hold the stone while it was set in the correct position to grind and polish the 58 facets of the finished diamond, all lying on a clean white cloth which covered the bare area of the working surface, littered with brilliantly flashing, partially cut diamonds, in all shapes and sizes.

"Welcome back. I got your telegram. Abe getting shot must have been an awful shock for Sammy and Liz. Have the police sorted it out yet?" He noticed Nick hesitated. "D'you want to talk about it?" Sly said.

"It's a long story Sly; so many things have happened. The police seem to know nothing; said it was a gangland killing, but Sammy's lot found out it was the mob almost straight away."

"Yeah, they would. They won't take it lying down either. What did Sammy think of those three stones?" asked Sly. "I can't help thinking it was a pity we had to get rid of those; they were the best we've had for a while. Still that's what we're in business for I guess."

"Yes Sly, and I got the asking price; no quibbling and beating about the bush with Sammy. I think he knew how good they were and he'll make his profit, naturally. He told me he had his market all lined up ready for them."

"What had he planned?"

"They're being mounted in platinum as matching earrings and a pendant."

"Sounds great. Perhaps we ought to have a retail outlet; there'd be more profit for us."

"Yes, that's true, but a lot of other problems too I guess. I think it's better we stick to what we're good at."

"You're probably right."

"By the way Sly; I forgot to tell you; I had a most unusual experience on the way to New York. I had my pocket picked."

"You didn't."

"Yes; the pouch which I had those stones in was lifted from inside my breast pocket and by the most beautiful girl you've ever seen. She was absolutely stunning, you would never guess she was a pickpocket and such an expert too."

"Really? Trust you to get all the luck."

"If it hadn't been for the training back in the home country years ago I wouldn't have felt her lifting it. I told her I knew what she had done and blow me down if she didn't put it back equally well. There's no doubt about it, she's a pro."

"They were good days."

"It started me thinking again about that con we've talked about so often in the past. Now's perhaps the time to start perfecting it; she'd be just the right woman for the job."

"Yeah, she sounds like it."
"I'd like you to meet her; see what you think."
"What d'you mean, what do I think? You've already decided," Sly said, grinning from ear to ear."
"You're right. But seriously, if you agree, we can start finding out the details of what's being held round the world at the moment. Keep your ear to the ground. Find out what's being moved about and to which companies; find out what's being made and by whom. Check what's coming up in the auction rooms. You've got your contacts, just be discreet. The less people know enquiries are being made the better."
"I thought you looked in a good mood as you walked through the door. You must have had a good time," Sly said, giving Nick a leering grin.
"It wasn't like that at all, but it was a very interesting time. Mind you, it's just as well I've come away from New York for a while. I think I could be falling for her; she's a very lovely girl."

During the morning Nick filled Sly in with all the excitement of the week, starting with the trip from the airport which led up to Abe's killing, the subsequent burning of the Green Baize casino and the injury to Celleri, who was probably Rosie's father and his abduction from the hospital. Nick explained that Rosie would be coming back to England when her father had been found and that she would probably bring him here too, to meet Rosie's mother who still lived in this country. It was all a bit confusing but Sly seemed to get the gist of it.
"What say they never find Celleri? What then?"
"I really don't know," Nick answered. "I expect Rosie'll stay for a while, just in case he turns up, but if she isn't earning anything, she'll have to come back to England, unless she is able to find a job there. At the moment she's staying with Sammy but she won't be able to do that indefinitely. Perhaps we can get the scam planned ready for her return; what d'you think?"
"It's not a bad idea. It'll need a lot of planning and rehearsing. There's a lot at stake, like ten years each including Rosie." Nick shuddered at the thought of someone as lovely as Rosie being incarcerated for such a long time.
"Yes, we must get it right; there'll be no room for mistakes. I thought we'd go for five carat stones, brilliant blue-whites of course. What do you feel is the right size?"
"I think five is probably large enough. But you could be more ambitious and go for larger gems, maybe ten or even twenty carats, perhaps even larger."
"That is reaching high. But I suppose we wouldn't have to carry out the con so often. It would minimise the risks."

"It might and there again, it might not. It's going to be pretty difficult to switch such a large stone. There'll be so many video cameras on you, it'll feel like being in a movie. But I suppose with practice, it'll all fall into shape. A lot depends how good your Rosie is."
"You wait and see. I think she's designed for it. Tell me, what do we have in zircon at the moment? We don't want to start buying any quantity just now."
"Just the best; don't worry about that, that's all under control. The more I think about it Baas, we might consider switching a single very large stone should one become available," Sly said.
"You appreciate we must possess an identical diamond for the plan to work?"
"Yes of course; if not, then the substitution can't be made."
"Well, that's the first problem. I suppose I could order something special from the jeweller. I could say I want a perfect, flawless, brilliant blue-white, round cut, ten carats, mounted in a four-clawed platinum ring, size fourteen, cost, about a quarter of a million."
"At least that, nearer half a million if the stone is anything like as good as those we sold Sammy."
"If we ordered from Cartier's and Garrards here in London and Tiffanys and Cartier's in New York and all the famous jewellers in Paris, Amsterdam, Berlin; everwhere in fact, we ought to make a killing in a few days."
"Ummm; but there's a flaw in your reasoning Baas."
"Tell me."
"It's possible but unlikely any company will have the perfect diamonds of the size you're seeking in stock. The buyers'll all be on the market looking for stones. If that's the case, it's certain they'll get to know that a large number of gems of such a sort is being looked for and very soon someone may put two and two together. I think that's very risky on the scale we are planning. One or two maybe; but ten or twelve or even more; that's bound to go wrong."
"You could be right Sly. Have you had any ideas?"
"You asked me to keep my ear to the ground. Well, I heard a close relative of one of the sheikhs of an emirate in the Gulf is hard pressed for cash; some scandal about gambling and drinking I believe; and women, of course. His family is not prepared to support him any longer. It is said he has a fantastic collection of both cut and uncut diamonds, some of them known to have been obtained illicitly. My informant says he is about to put some on the market, perhaps ten million pounds worth. If we could get an introduction to the sale, it would be a piece of cake to substitute the apparent for the real."
"Now that is interesting. I'd much rather steal from those money

grabbing Middle Eastern gentlemen than from a hard working jeweller, albeit the big names, whose mark-up defies belief."
"I thought you'd like to know that. I'm told he wants to get rid of some of the best diamonds from his collection. I've traced some of the gems he's bought over the last ten years. The best were bought through Sotheby's and Christie's here in London. We've probably got all the details of those. They may never have left the country and have lain in some strong box somewhere all the time."
"Why doesn't he sell them through the auction houses in the same way as he bought them? Would be easier I would have thought."
"It all has to be discreet. His countrymen don't need to know."
"How long would it take to make the copies if you shelved all the other work?"
"Working sixteen hours a day it'll take between two and three weeks to cover most of his collection. Mind you, nothing else will get done; all the machines will be in constant use."
"Come on then Sly; stop talking; get on with it."Slapping Sly on the back in a friendly way, Nick left him to his beloved machines.

Sly's plan had been a much better one than Nick had thought of; to start with, he'd had a lot of misgivings, planning to steal from his own breed, from the trade, from those who made their living dealing in precious stones. It would be much easier taking from the greedy wealthy of the world, those who gave least but took most. Yes, that would be a much better thing to do; he'd have no qualms about that at all.

'Good,' he thought. 'Now all I have to do urgently is select the next million pounds worth of diamonds for Sammy. He's going through them pretty quickly and I'll bet he'll want more in another few months. Still, we shouldn't worry.'

Rosie's telephone call that evening dismissed further thoughts of the scam from his mind. He knew he had to get back to New York as quickly as he could; she needed him now.

CHAPTER NINETEEN

The funeral was a grand affair as befits a caporegime. Rosie was the chief mourner, attended by Nick. The coffin was of gleaming black ebony and expensive looking, with large stainless steel handles, but despite its huge size, it was lifted with apparent ease by the bearers as it was lowered into the grave. There were many men there in dark grey and black, hats low down on their faces, defying recognition and in the background, plain clothed and uniformed police mingled with the feds, all seeking any information they could learn about the Mafia, America's dreaded enemy. Cameras were directed at the big men, cataloguing their every contact as they strolled back to their black-glassed limousines. This meeting of the brotherhood was recorded in detail.

Rosie had remained in New York after the disappearance of her father, but no information had come to light. He had disappeared from the hospital with two fake medical orderlies and apparently from the face of the earth; no one had seen him since, that is, until the body was recovered from the river. Rosie was not asked to identify the remains. The changes caused by immersion in water for such a long time were too advanced, but she had been brave attending the inquest, longing for it all to be over. The police were apologetic and apprehensive. After all, he had been under their protection, while the hospital awaited the inevitable litigation which they knew might run to massive damages and enormous legal fees. But Rosie had for that brief moment met the father she had never known; that fleeting fragile period of time she would remember for ever.

Nick had flown back as soon as Celleri's body had been found. Rosie had met him at Kennedy. Absence makes the heart grow fonder but the passion of their embrace took them both by surprise and neither could have expected the hunger of their kiss. These were not now just friends meeting again; these friends were in love.

The journey back into the city from JFK seemed endless to Rosie. The taxi found each rut in the road, jerking them ever closer together as they sat arm in arm, snug in the back, still savouring the unexpected passion of their meeting at the airport. It was as if neither of them wanted to be separated from one another ever again.
"Let's go back to the apartment Nick," Rosie whispered, so quietly, that Nick hardly heard it; so quietly, that no one would have guessed her meaning.
"Sure," Nick whispered, "I'd like that a lot." He too was in something of a turmoil. He had never felt this way before about any woman and he recognised, deep down, sensations he normally supressed and kept dormant, were now surfacing gradually.

During the journey, Rosie filled him in with the trivia of life in NewYork without him in the few days he'd been away, while Nick told her something of his talks with Sly.

"You must tell me more about the scam you mentioned and the part you want me to play," said Rosie. "Up to now, you've only explained the briefest of outlines."

"Well Rosie Haynes, your teaching is about to begin," he laughed. "Tell me, why are diamonds so expensive, especially the blue-whites and why are they called blue-whites? Why are large diamonds relatively much more valuable than smaller stones? And why are diamonds usually the main stone used in engagement rings and why are they worn on the third finger of the left hand?"

"I don't think I know anything about diamonds other than they come from South Africa," Rosie replied hesitantly.

"You're almost right. South Africa used to mine the most and the best diamonds recovered in the world, though Australia, Zaire and Russia produce more than it does now. Because of South Africa's importance in the past, it used to control the market price."

"How does it do that?" asked Rosie?

"De Beers, for whom I worked at one time and where I learned all I know about the practical side of diamond production, leads a world cartel in diamond sales; what de Beers says, goes."

"That doesn't sound fair," piped up Rosie, always ready to defend the underdog.

"Well, maybe. But if de Beers flooded the market with all its reserves of diamonds, the market price would drop overnight. The economies of many other countries would go under, rapidly. So you see, it's important that new stones are released in a controlled way."

"But it could be argued, the cartel maintains an artificially high price for diamonds throughout the world, so it's the customer who has to pay," Rosie countered.

"True," Nick agreed, "but were it not so, many economies would just not survive. The international arguments outweigh any fairness to the individual."

"I see. You said de Beers used to control the market."

"That's right. New countries emerging from the old USSR who mine diamonds in quantity, now want hard currency urgently to maintain their development, so they have produced a black market, selling stones outside the cartel."

"Is that a problem?" asked Rosie.

"It sure could be. Producing diamonds costs a lot of money," Nick continued.

"But I've read somewhere that people had found diamonds on the beach; just picked them up like pebbles on the sand."

"That's true as well," Nick said. "Those stones had been washed down by rivers in flood over centuries. They had been dropped at the mouth of the river, well away from where they were released to the surface of the earth and moved around by the tides. Part of diamond production consists of sucking up vast amounts of sand and passing it through screens to separate out the stones, but huge quantities have to be dredged to find one diamond of importance."

"Is that why diamonds are so expensive?" asked Rosie.

"That and the capital cost of equipment and the increasing cost of labour. A large quantity of rock, 250 tons to be precise has to be blasted, brought to the surface and crushed to produce just one carat of diamond. It's a huge enterprise."

"What does the word carat mean?"

"It is the unit of weight used to measure diamonds. Thousands of years ago, the ancients noticed the seeds of the carob tree were constant in size. The word carat originated from the natural unit of weight, the seeds of the carob. When measurement became more important, the system was standardised so that one carat equalled one fifth of a gram."

"You were going to tell me why blue-whites are so called?"

"You will have read probably that diamonds are pure crystals of carbon formed miles down, deep in the earth. As molten rock empties on to the surface through faults or volcanoes, the enormous heat and pressures on the carbon atoms changes them from the black amorphous carbon into the crystalline shape of diamond. If the diamond is pure, containing no other material, it is a brilliant blue-white. There is nothing more beautiful. When you see it with the naked eye, it flashes all the colours of the rainbow, brilliantly. Examine it with a loupe and it is free from faults and blemishes. Those are the types of stones we are after; flawless. Inclusions within the diamond are the finger print of the stone making it unique and so the fewer inclusions present, the more difficult it will be to identify the stone subsequently. But this sort of stone is rare."

"I see," said Rosie.

"And of course, large stones are much more uncommon than smaller stones. Large carat perfect brilliant blue-whites are very scarce and almost priceless. Those I was taking to Sammy were the best stones I have been able to find for a long time."

"They did look wonderful."

"Yes, they did. But did you know that diamonds can be yellow or green or blue and even orange? They're called Fancies and they're very rare too. Their colour depends on the amount and type of chemical contaminating the diamond. They are as a rule not as valuable as blue-whites, though there is the priceless Blue Hope, now in the

Smithsonian and a peach coloured stone, the Hortensia, part of the French Crown Jewels. And then there are some stones which are brownish even to the naked eye. That's because of the unchanged carbon inclusions they contain; they are not nearly so worthwhile. Shall I go on or am I boring you?"

"I'm fascinated by it all; don't stop now," Rosie replied.

"Diamonds are very hard, one of nature's hardest materials. Crude diamonds containing many inclusions and flaws which prevent their use as jewelry and small stones are used in industry because of their extreme hardness. Drills which are used to go through rock are tipped with diamond bits which can penetrate the earth's crust in the search for oil and minerals."

"Go on," prompted Rosie.

"Well, there are crystalline stuctures which resemble diamond in appearance, but because they are found more commonly in the perfect state and can be worked and shaped much more easily than diamonds because they are not so hard, the end result is much cheaper yet it looks just as good as the real thing."

"Why don't we all have this substitute if it looks as good as diamond?" asked Rosie.

"It is used, widely. But being softer than diamond, with each day of wear, there is a minute amount of scratching, even from the clothing it rubs on. After a period of time, the brilliance is lost; the stone appears hazy."

"So what is it you plan to do?" queried Rosie.

"All Sly and I need to know is the weight and the cut of a stone. All cut diamonds have 58 facets basically, in distinct shapes, round, oval, marquise and so on. If we know the details, Sly can cut an identical stone in zircon within a few days, whereas it would take months or even years to cut a similar gem in diamond. Once finished, the zircon stone would look as good as a brilliant blue-white."

"I see," mused Rosie.

"An expert wouldn't know the difference on a superficial examination and even then he may need to check whether it scratched a piece of glass before being certain. So you see, if we have an identical stone in zircon, all we have to is to substitute it for the real one and walk away."

The taxi had arrived at the apartment and Nick and Rosie took the elevator to the 14th floor.

"One thing we'll have to do is to change your appearance," said Nick.

"And what's the matter with the way I look now?" Rosie asked quickly.

"Nothing Rosie, nothing." Nick raised his hands playfully, as if to defend himself. "You are the most beautiful thing I've ever seen. But just imagine you're going somewhere, it doesn't matter how or why. Don't you think any bystander would remember a beauty like you, with hair the colour of gold sovereigns and eyes so green, they would have bored a hole into his heart?"
"And have they bored a hole into your heart Nick?"
"I'll give you but one guess," he replied laughingly.
"So what do I have to do?" Rosie asked as she opened the door to the apartment.
"Firstly, I'd like you to kiss me again as you did at the airport," Nick said. She turned to him, blushing slightly and looking at him carefully, she took his face in her hands, lifted her head and kissed him. As his arms held her, pulling her closer to him, her body relaxed. Both Nick's and Rosie's lips parted and after a tentative advance by Nick, both tongues moved together. The pressure of their bodies made both aware of the hardness growing in Nick and they knew that unless they stopped now, inevitably they soon would be lovers. But Rosie didn't want it to end. The kiss lasted for what seemed an age and when they both surfaced breathlessly, it had been so enjoyable, they clung to each other to start again.

"Oh Rosie, I've missed you so much; I never thought I could ever feel for anyone the way I feel for you," whispered Nick, gently kissing the side of Rosie's arched neck.

"Nick, I've been so lonely without you; it's been dreadful. We did have some lovely times together before my father was hurt, didn't we? You were so kind and supportive when I needed help most. I can't tell you how much I looked forward to seeing you all the time. I'm sure he liked you too, Nick."
"Yes, I think he did. I must say he seemed to be a really nice guy despite his mob conections. It's such a pity neither of us had time to get to know him better."
"I'd like to get to know you better Nick," Rosie said seductively.
"And how d'you think we'll go about that," said Nick, guiding her gently to the long settee in the centre of the room.
"I've a better idea than that," said Rosie, changing direction, pulling Nick towards the bedroom.
"Are you sure you want to Rosie?" Nick asked her quietly.
"I'm sure Nick; very sure," she answered.

Shyly, hesitantly, both feeling their way, they slowly undressed each other. Nick stood back to look at Rosie, a blush spreading all over her body, who stood tall and proud of her appearance. Her breasts were smooth as white satin and beneath her dimple, a mound of hair which matched her crowning glory, shaded her flat belly. Nick's muscled body looked pale in contrast to his jet black hair. They came together, their naked bodies moulded into one, breathlessly kissing and fondling and examining each other, gradually reaching a stage of excitement which took them to the bed. Rosie eased herself slowly beneath Nick who moved so gently. He propped himself up looking at Rosie. Her head was arched slightly backwards, her eyes closed and a slight frown furrowed her brow. Nick remained still. It seemed an age but could only have been a few seconds before Rosie's body moved forwards as if driven by some unseen power. Gradually, a rhythmic movement began, her head moving from side to side as if some wild force was urging her on and muted groans of pleasure encouraged Nick to join in the climax. When it came, they were joined together as one.

Lying side by side afterwards, Rosie cradled in Nick's arm, both of them damp and tired but so full of love for each other.
"Oh, it was wonderful Nick; surely we both were meant for each other," said Rosie, propping herself up on one elbow, the sheet falling back revealing her pale shapely breasts. Nick looked at her adoringly, fondling the soft smooth skin, bending to kiss her nipples softly.
"I do hope so," he murmured. "That day, when I spoke to you at Heathrow, I couldn't believe my good luck when you said I may join you."
"You were a handsome man and I was quite lonely just then. I was exchanging all the past at home for a doubtful future in America; and then you came along. I thought it was Christmas all over again."
"Saint Nick, you mean," he joked.

"So how would you want to change me Nick?" Rosie asked after they had relaxed for some time in each others' arms."
"Only to change your appearance, not the real Rosie Haynes. She's much too nice to want to change. First, we'll visit an optician and fix you up with some blue eyes."
"How'll you do that?"
"Pale blue contact lenses."
"But I don't wear spectacles."
"Pale blue contact lenses of plain glass. Pale blue eyes are more noticeable than just blue eyes; they're more piercing; people remember them more certainly. Then, when you've got used to wearing them, we'll get you a wig; a blond one; one that has been made for you and

looks real, not a fake. We'll pad you out so you become a bigger woman and we'll change the style of your clothes. We'll coarsen your make-up, use a cheaper perfume and lots of it, change your lipstick colour and the shape of your lips, lengthen your nails and alter the colour to a gaudy bright nail varnish and you'll become a different person."

"And what about you? You'll have to change too won't you?"
"Of course. I'll become light brown haired, perhaps sandy coloured and I'll need green-brown lenses as well, so my appearance will be very changed. Then a brown suit, tailored over a padded waistcoat so it would seem I'm a forty-four chest, brown shoes, one blocked so I will have a natural limp and a flashy tie that everyone could remember. When everything has been done, we'll look a very different couple from now."
"You've got it all worked out haven't you?" Rosie said.
"Nearly everything I believe. We'll have plenty of time for dummy runs, first here and then in London, when we know we've got it right, we'll try it on Sly. If we pass him, we're there, home and dry."
"It sounds awfully tiring Nick. Perhaps before we start practising for the scam, we can practice something else right now," Rosie laughed cheekily. "After all, we have to get it absolutely right, don't we?"
"You little hussy," Nick laughed, caressing her lovingly, raising them both emotionally once again to heights neither had known before tonight.
"I do love you," murmured Rosie.
"And I'm so in love with you Rosie," Nick replied.

Nick sat up suddenly: "I forgot to telephone Sammy," he cried. Rosie cuddled up to him lovingly. "Don't worry about Sammy tonight," she said. "Didn't I tell you? I told Elizabeth I would ask you back here to the apartment. She had that knowing look in her eye; she knows where we are."
"And probably what we've been up to," Nick groaned.
"Now sir. Perhaps you'd like to explain the importance of the use of diamonds in engagement rings and why are they worn on a special finger?" Rosie asked cocquettishly.
Nick became serious. His whole character seemed to change. He was no longer talking factually about diamond production that he knew so well; now he was to embark on talk of romance, of love, an experience until now he had never known.
"The ancient Greeks thought diamonds were splinters of stars fallen from the heaven; some said they were the tears of the Gods. Cupid was

said to have tipped his arrows with diamonds giving them magical powers."
"He did, did he?" joked Rosie.
"The word diamond comes from the Greek 'adamus', meaning the eternity of love and they thought the fire in the diamond reflected the constant flame of love." Rosie watched Nick intently, listening to his every word.
"Romantic lot, those Greeks," she said.
"And the Egyptians believed the vein of love ran directly from the heart to the top of the third finger of the left hand; that's why an engagement ring is worn on that finger."

Rosie's head rested on Nick's shoulder as they lay very close together, his fingers gently smoothing the skin of her breast. "What d'you plan to do with the diamonds you steal in the scam?"
"That's a good question. Probably nothing, just keep them for a rainy day. Maybe sell them and give the proceeds to charity. I don't know Rosie; I can't say I've given it much thought. It's not their value that counts, it's the skill in carrying out the scam."
"Will you sell them to Sammy?"
"Well, if anyone could dispose of them successfully, he could. His contacts in Israel would probably find little difficulty in getting rid of them, though the stones we shall be stealing will be unusually rare and expensive, not diamonds you could buy in any old jeweller."
"Why Israel? I thought Holland was the leading diamond selling country."
"You see; you do know something about diamonds. Antwerp is the diamond capital of the world, but now, Israel is one of the world's most important cutting centres. Two billion dollars worth of diamonds pass through the hands of many thousands of cutters in Tel Aviv and Jerusalem and I've done a lot of business there over the last few years; they know me."
"Where are the diamonds you plan to switch? In famous jewellers I suppose."
"Maybe, but probably not. Before I came away, Sly had heard a relative of a Middle Eastern sheikh was in financial trouble. He was going to have to get rid of a superb collection of stones shortly to cover debts his family would no longer pay for him. If that's so, he would be the ideal target."
"Watch out Mr. Sheikh. You ain't seen nothing yet. Nick and Rosie have you in their sights; what a team."

CHAPTER TWENTY

The day following her father's burial, Rosie, received a letter from Celleri's attorneys, Greystoke, Harper and Smith.

> *Dear Miss Haynes,*
> *May I on behalf of the parters of the firm, express our deepest sympathy to you following the tragic and untimely death of your father, Mr. Michael Celleri, who had been a valued client for many years. As you are the major beneficiary in his will, I think we should meet as soon as possible, to discuss the legal steps that have to be taken.*
> *I should add, that I and one other partner in the firm, are the executors of your late father's estate. We have made an appointment for 11 tomorrow morning, Wednesday, May 20 at this office. I would be most pleased if you would confirm the time is suitable.*
> *Yours sincerely.*

The signature was indecipherable but beneath, the secretary had typed the name, Maurice Webster.

"I hadn't thought about there being a will Nick. Do you think you'd be able to find time to come with me?"
"Of course I will if you'd like me to. You may turn out to be a wealthy heiress."
"I would much rather he'd lived and I had got to know him properly, perhaps even have taken him back to England perhaps to meet Mum again."
"Play Cupid?"
"I don't think there'd be any need to do that. He had never married; I think it was highly likely he still loved her and I know she has always carried the torch for him. It was purely a question of getting them together again."
"It does seem a shame I must say, but there's nothing anyone can do about it now; it's all too late. Remember to telephone the solicitor to say you'll be there."

His office was in one of the large trendy buildings on the south side of New York's Central Park. It was ugly and box-like; its walls were large mirrors of golden glass, in which the scudding clouds and the blue sky were reflected unnaturally. His rooms were, like the building as a whole, starkly modern. The lighting was artificial. The furniture was in black ash and the chairs chrome, covered with black leather. The occasional table which occupied a large space in the centre of the room, was made of smoked glass, thick and bevelled, standing on chrome legs, like slender girders, spanning beneath the dimly transparent top. It all matched his library around the room, black shelves, crammed with books behind sliding black tinted plate-glass doors, the whole designed to create the impression of affluence. He wore a dark suit and was much younger than Rosie had imagined. He spoke with a drawl as heard in the southern states rather than the harsh New York accent to which Rosie was becoming accustomed and while he was nowhere near as tall as Nick, he was incredibly handsome; the snag was, he knew it.

"Good morning Miss Haynes, I'm Maurice Webster. It was good of you to reply so promptly. Do come in. Your stay in New York has been quite an upsetting time for you." The hand he offered was limp, reminding Rosie of a wet fish.

He placed his other arm around her waist, as he guided her to a chair in front of his desk.

"Yes, it has. This is Mr Nicholas Royle who's come with me today. He's been a very good friend to me and has been so kind and helpful over the last few weeks. I don't know what I would have done without him." They shook hands; was there some feeling of antagonism in the air? Was his first impression of Nick that of a money grubbing gold-digger, just dying to get in on Rosie's inheritance? Did Nick feel at all threatened by this smart-assed slick city shyster, already planning how to spend his exorbitant legal fees? There was no doubt about the tension in the air as Maurice Webster smarmed his way around Rosie while Nick looked on.

"It is good to have someone to rely on at times like these," he said. "Can I get you a coffee?"

"No, thank you. I was really quite surprised to receive your letter Mr Webster. I suppose I hadn't thought about there being any estate. You see, I didn't know anything about my father until a few days ago, only a short while before he died in fact."

"I see; well Miss Haynes, if you can prove your connection with the deceased, and I believe there'll be no difficulty doing that, you, as sole beneficiary, will become a very wealthy woman. Mind you, all of your father's wealth was in property, rather than in assets which can be converted into cash rapidly. Property which has, since he bought it over the years, increased in value quite considerably; it includes the apartment you are now staying at."

"It is a very beautiful apartment."

"Yes, it is a smart address. For some reason that we don't know about, Mr Celleri sold all his shares about two weeks ago and withdrew a large sum of money from his bank, removing all the liquidity from his estate. However, as I said, other than some small bequests, you are the only one to benefit greatly from his will." He slid a folder of papers across the dark leather inlay on the top of the desk. "Here are the documents you will need to sign to enable us to act for you. I'm sure you'd like to take them away and read through them at your leisure first."
"Yes of course; thank you."
"I may add, that all the funeral expenses have been taken care of by a business colleague I believe."
"Really, how generous of him. I wonder who that could be?"
"I don't know but I can probably find out."
"Please do. Would you be kind enough to write and thank whoever it was on my behalf?"
"I certainly will try. Perhaps when you have signed the papers you'd send them back to us so we can proceed."
"Of course. I'll have them back to you within a day or two."
"One other thing, Miss Haynes. We have been approached by the hospital solicitors. The hospital has never had a patient abducted from their wards before nor has there ever been a death subsequent upon abduction as has happened to your father. They feel they are in deep trouble without any precedent they can refer to. They are awaiting your legal action against them for negligence. If you can prove that, and I must say there seems to be no defence against it, then you can probably claim almost unlimited damages from their insurers, running into millions."
"Gracious, I had no idea. I hadn't given it a thought. I must say I had no intention of suing the hospital. I'm sure they did all that could be expected of them."
"That may be so Miss Haynes, but no one would expect a serious attempt to be made on the life of a relative while in hospital, nor a relative to be taken from a busy ward while under treatment, disappear and then when found again, be found dead. You must take action. I would advise you to go away and think about it. Talk it over with your friends."
"I'll do that; and thank you again for your help."

As they left the solicitor's office and descended in the elevator, Rosie turned to Nick. "What d'you think about that?"
"I see what he's getting at. In a way, it does seem rather slipshod of the hospital to allow it to happen."

"But I don't need any more money Nick. I will inherit a vast sum I had no idea about when my father's estate is proved. I don't need any more."
"No. Why don't you let Webster proceed and sue the hospital for as much as he thinks he'll get and then donate the money to them to build a Celleri wing for burns. You won't gain anything financially and the hospital will benefit from the insurance pay out. Furthermore, your father's name will be remembered in New York for good. The more I think about it, I think that's a super idea."
"Yes, I'm quite taken with that. We'll discuss it again, perhaps with Sammy and Elizabeth. They'll have more insight into the American way of life too."

When Nick and Rosie left the office, they took a cab to Sammy's home.
"Well Rosie, it looks like you're going to have to hang around in New York for quite a while now getting all your problems worked out," Nick said. "I suppose it's possible you might even want to stay and live here, though I had hoped we'd have been able to plan our life together."
"We can and still plan the scam Nick. Remember, you've only told me the outline up to now. We're going to have to practise a lot getting it ready and that's going to take quite a while."
"But I had hoped we'd return to England."
"We will Nick, we will. But I will have to sort this out first. I can't just leave it as it is can I?"
"No, I suppose not," he agreed grudgingly. Both of them recognised the change of mood which had descended over them. Perhaps, now that Rosie was an heiress to a large fortune, things would never really be the same again. They sat silently as the taxi took them downtown to Sammy's.

"How's our lucky lady then?" chuckled Sammy as he welcomed them in. "Will you be talking to a poor little fat guy like me from now on?"
"Yip, I sure will," Rosie quipped, entering into the spirit of Sammy's remark. "Oh Sammy, you and Liz have been so kind to me especially as you've gone through so much sadness recently. I hope we shall always be friends."
"Of course we will Rosie. Come on, tell us all about your new fortune."
Rosie recounted the morning's meeting with the attorney. Sammy was amazed at all he heard. He, as a New Yorker was aware of the inflated value of city real estate and as Rosie itemised the property listed in the

documents she had received from the lawyers, he could only gasp at her good fortune.
"At a rough guess Rosie, I'd say you're worth about eight or nine million bucks give or take a few hundred grand. Hell Rosie, you're rich."
"Let's hope the mob don't want a share," Nick said when all the gaiety had settled.
"Yeah, that's true," said Sammy. "As an heiress, you'd be a likely kidnapping victim, though to whom they'd send the ransom demand other than to you, I can't really think."
"Can't you?" said Nick. "Perhaps it could come to me or even you Sammy. They've enough reason to pick either of us."
"Hell, what a fart you are. But you've got a point. Have to put you under house arrest Rosie; can't let you ramble around on your own now." He grinned from ear to ear at his joke, lightening the tension, but he knew he was going to have to try to provide some sort of protection for Rosie as long as she remained in New York. She wasn't going to be able to walk the streets any longer as if nothing had happened; not with Celleri's Godfather still around.

"While we were with him, Mr Webster suggested I should sue the hospital for negligence, in as much as Mr Celleri was abducted from the hospital while under their care and that subsequently he was found dead. He thinks they can have little defence against such a charge. I don't want the money but Nick thinks if the insurers were sued to pay damages, the money could be donated to the hospital to fund a Celleri wing for burns. What do you think I should do Sammy? I'd like to know your views."
"Gee; I had wondered whether there'd be an action against the hospital board. They certainly would be expecting one. And of course the damages would be horrendous. It would be considered extremely generous of you Rosie. It's a super idea. Your father's name would be remembered in New York for a hell of a long time to come. I like it."
"I'll instruct the solicitors to proceed along those lines," agreed Rosie.

Within a few days, Rosie had returned the documents to the solicitors with a request that they continued to act for her. Nick had had to return to London and Rosie was already missing him dreadfully. They had spent so much time together and had so much love to share. Now she was alone she felt she had been cooped up in Sammy's home for long enough, that she was an embarrassment to them, though they didn't show it at all. But she had an apartment to go to and a very lovely apartment at that and she wanted to be able to go and live there; she wanted to be freer than she felt.

"Sammy, Liz, I've been thinking. I'm sure it would be okay to go and live in the apartment now don't you? I've hardly stayed there at all since I arrived in New York." Neither of them said anything. In a coaxing voice she said, "You've been real friends letting me be with you this long but I think you all need a break now; you deserve it." There was still no response. "Oh come on. Once I've settled in, perhaps you'd come and have dinner with me. I'm really quite a good cook you know."

"We can guess how you're feeling Rosie, but we've loved having you and there's really no need to think like that."

"Thanks, but I know I'd like to make a go of it."

"Okay Rosie, I'll run you round in the morning. If you're worried about anything, you just let me know. Nick would never forgive me if something happened to you." Rosie blushed shyly.

"Oh, I'm going to miss you both such a lot; good night," she said, tears slowly rolling down her face, "thanks for everything."

CHAPTER TWENTY-ONE

Sammy drove Rosie to her apartment first thing in the morning. Once she was installed in the flat, he left her to settle in on her own. The place had been locked up for some time and there was a certain staleness in the air despite the air conditioning. She opened the vents of the windows and felt the breeze blowing the past away; the apartment now was hers. She revelled in her new-found freedom and in the simple things around her. She had great difficulty tearing herself from the views from the lounge window. It fascinated her to see the soundless activity going on in the long straight avenue stretching away below her and in the park across the way; she had never experienced anything as magical as this before. Perhaps Nick had been right; maybe she wouldn't want to return to England quickly. Maybe she would even want to stay.

She rang Nick or he'd ring her every day. He hadn't been at all pleased to hear she'd left Sammy's to live on her own in the apartment but he could guess how she had been feeling. He knew he was going to be worried as long as she remained in New York alone, but for the time being, he had a business to run in London and Rosie had to sort out her problems there. As much as he wanted to be with Rosie, there was nothing else that could be done at this time. The Goldsteins phoned her quite often as well, but they too knew she had to find her own feet and start living again without their protection.

"Sammy, it's Nick."
"Hi there Nick, how goes it?"
"Sammy I'm fine. Is Rosie with you? I haven't been able to get in touch with her for three days now."
"No, she's not been here for a while. We spoke on the phone last week sometime but she hasn't been around. If you like, I'll call in later today."
"Please Sammy, would you do that? To tell you the truth, I'm worried."
"Okay Nick, I'll go now and call you back."

When Sammy got to the apartment he questioned the doorman first but he said he hadn't seen Rosie for a couple of days.
"Think man; when did you see her last? It's important."
"Well, it's Tuesday today. I guess it must have been Friday or Saturday I saw her. Yeah, it was on Saturday morning. That's right, there was a game over in Bronx park in the afternoon and I planned to get away soon after lunch. Yeah, it must have been about eleven. She was going out then, I remember. She said Hallo to me. She always sounded kinda strange with her Limey accent, you know, most people around here just say Hi."
"Did you think to tell anyone she hadn't been around?"
"Hell nope. Since she arrived she hasn't stayed here very long. I didn't think anything about it."
"Anyone been snooping around lately?"
"Haven't seen anyone," he said quickly. "Come to think about it though, there has been a strange car parked around here last week. One of those black stretched Cadillacs, dark glass windows. Ya couldn't see who's inside. It hasn't been around this week."
"Hell. Can you let me into the apartment? I'm worried about her."
"No, I can't do that; it's more than my job's worth." A large dollar bill appeared in Sammy's hand and it disappeared into the doorman's pocket like lightning.
"I'll have to come with you," he said "just to keep an eye on you."
"That's okay; let's go."

They took the lift to Rosie's apartment and the doorman let Sammy in with his spare set of keys. Beneath the door was an envelope, brown and grubby, just like the one that had contained the somewhat threatening note Rosie had had once before. 'Goldstein' had been

scribbled across the front in pencil. Sammy bent down to recover it. He showed it to his escort.
"It's addressed to me," he said. "I was expected. Now I wonder why anyone should do that?"
"Aren't you going to open it?" the doorman said.
"Yeah, but let's take a look around first, just in case there's something else to find."
They went into the bedroom together. The wardrobe doors were wide open and the cupboards were empty. All of Rosie's clothes had disappeared.
"Are you sure no one else has been in here?" asked Sammy, turning to face the janitor, watching his every movement.
"No, honest," he said, but Sammy knew he was lying. He had started to sweat and his hands shook holding the keys.
"Well yeah. Some guys came to collect her clothes. Said she was staying with friends for a couple of days."
"Why didn't you tell me that when I asked?"
"I hadn't thought anything about it. They seemed okay."
"Were those guys the ones in the car outside?"
"Like I told you, I couldn't see who was in the car." Sammy glared at him.
"Honest, I couldn't." he said.

Sammy returned to his car, clutching the letter in a screwed up ball in his hand. Inside the car, he looked at the writing again. It was similar to the scrawl on the other note sent to Rosie some time ago. 'Goldstein'; nothing else was on the outside of the envelope. He tore it open. Inside was a piece of fine quality paper, the sort Sammy had seen once before. The letters were printed crudely.
'MISS HAYNES IS STAYING WITH FRIENDS FOR A WHILE. I AM SURE SHE WILL GET IN TOUCH SHOULD SHE WISH TO SEE YOU.' That was it; no signature, no address; nothing. Sammy knew straight away she was in trouble and big trouble at that. Whoever was holding Rosie was holding her against her will and couldn't care a damn what happened to her. Her life was definitely at risk and he hadn't got a clue what he could do to help. He couldn't go to the police. There was no evidence that anything had happened to Rosie. He knew what he needed to do right now was think.

When Rosie had said she wanted to return to her apartment, Sammy had spoken to his friends in the organisation who had agreed to keep an eye on the place. As they told Sammy when he got to them, they too had been aware of the big Cadillac hanging around and they had made a note of the licence number. Rosie had never been near it as far as they could say. They had recognised the car hadn't been there since Saturday morning but they hadn't seen it leaving. The fact that Rosie hadn't been around for a couple of days hadn't worried them particularly. Sammy knew that all he could do for the time being was to check the car registration. If he could find out the owner, perhaps he'd be able to find Rosie's kidnappers. He knew a few people in the City Hall who owed him one, who'd do that for him, so that shouldn't present a problem. And then, he'd have to think whether he'd let Nick know now or whether he'd try to work it out first?

Sammy's contacts soon found out the owner of the Cadillac lived on Staten Island. It was registered through intermediaries to the don who Sammy knew had controlled Celleri. The phone number had been included in the information supplied and it was the same number Sammy'd identified from the phone tap and which had threatened Rosie some time ago. It was all beginning to tie up. But why? Celleri was dead to the rest of the world. Why would anyone want to threaten Rosie now, unless they had doubts about Celleri's death? Perhaps because the casino had been destroyed they blamed the fire on Rosie's being in the States. If so, perhaps they were planning to take it out on her. Somehow, Sammy was going to have to get her away from them. The best way in Sammy's view was always the direct approach; but how?

On the day of the kidnapping, Rosie hadn't really known much about what was going on until it was all over. That Saturday morning, she had left the block as usual through the door on to 5th Avenue. She noticed a thin band of red and white tape fluttering in the breeze, the sort used to shut off areas where work was going on, stretching from the apartment entrance to a hydrant near the kerb and then along the roadside. Pedestrians were being guided to a small strip of pavement near the edge. She was not aware of the Cadillac, stationary alongside the kerb. As she was about to pass the back end of the car, the near-side front door opened widely so her progress was stopped. The driver jumped out and as he did so, the rear door opened and the man inside leaned across, grabbing her arm. The other man bundled her into the car unceremoniously and the car moved away from the kerb, slowly and deliberately without any squealing tyres, creating no fuss. Its departure was unnoticed. It took just five seconds. Rosie's head was pushed down between her knees so she had no idea whether she was going north or south, east or west and when she tried to scream, they jerked her head upwards cruelly and with a deft movement, her mouth and eyes were covered with sticky tape. Her hands were wrenched around her back and tape used to fasten them as well. Once that had been finished, her head was again forcibly pushed down in front of her. Her disorientation was complete.

Sammy's watchers had not seen her leaving the apartment block and as she was a prisoner within the car in less than twenty seconds from her leaving the apartment, they had missed her abduction. All they had noted later was the absence of the Cadillac.

The car taking Rosie out of the city travelled in an easterly direction, turning right into 39th Street before entering the Lincoln Tunnel under the Hudson River and onwards through Hoboken, heading towards the sea. The car turned and twisted and Rosie was thrown about between her two captors. They handled her roughly as they pulled and pushed her to keep her on the seat in that crouched position. Rosie was confused and bruised. It took more than thirty minutes to arrive at the gates of the large mansion which opened as the car approached and they drove straight into the garage. The door shut behind them. Rosie was now trapped in the home of the don, but for all she knew, she could have been anywhere.

Inside the house, she was taken by her captors to a small suite of rooms; there the blindfold was taken off, the tape over her mouth ripped away and her hands freed. Her lips were sore from the adhesive gag and her fingers tingled as the circulation was restored. Her legs and arms were bruised and scratched and she ached all over. As she slowly recovered from her ordeal, she looked around her. She noticed the windows were shuttered on the outside so that no natural light came through. The lights were in the ceiling and as she found out later, they were controlled from elsewhere. There were no switches inside the room to turn them off. There was a bedroom, a bathroom and a small sitting area; comfortable but basic. There were magazines on the table for her; it looked as if her stay might be a prolonged one. She went to try the door but the door had no handle on the inside. This was a prison; there was to be no getting out.

The lights had dimmed and a small spotlight illuminated a chair near the centre of the room. The door opened and the Godfather walked in, flanked by his henchmen.
"Sit down Miss Haynes, in the light where I can see you. Now then, I

would have thought you'd have been on your way back home to England by this time. You've no job now the Green Baize has been destroyed and your boss Celleri has died, so what's keeping you in New York?"

Rosie hesitated. She was reluctant to confide in anyone, certainly not him. It was his men who'd kidnapped her; who was he anyway? It sounded from what he was saying that he was the one who had been threatening her.

Proudly, she looked at the don and said, "Mr Celleri was my father and I am to inherit his estate. I shall stay here until the will is proved."

"I see; it's as I expected. Well then, as your presence here in the States has caused me so much hassle and cost me a lot of money, I think I may have to make sure your father's estate comes my way. He must have salted away quite a pile I should think over the years. Getting my hands on that may help me rebuild the Green Baize. Yes, I think I'll let your Mr Goldstein stew for a while before telling him what I want and what he'll have to supply. It'll be good to watch him squirm for a while."

"I don't think there is much in my father's estate. Apparently, he withdrew a large sum of money a few weeks ago and that has disappeared."

The don laughed. "The money has disappeared has it? You'll have to ask Goldstein where it's gone then won't you?" He continued to laugh loudly.

"I don't understand; why should Mr Goldstein know anything?"

"Oh he knows my dear. Mr Goldstein has your father's money but it wasn't enough for him so he burned down the casino. It was because of Mr Goldstein your father was injured. If he'd been satisfied with whatever your father had been able to get for him, there would have been no fire, no burning and no death. Your Mr Goldstein has a lot to answer for."

"He didn't mean for my father to get burned in the fire. The fire was to get back at you. He believed it was your men who murdered his son; is that true?"

"Yes, the fools did kill him, but they've paid the penalty too for their stupidity."

"But that won't bring Mr Goldstein's son back, will it? Nothing will do that. It's no wonder he hates you so."

"Yes, I suppose you're right. But now I have you and I think both he and your Mr Royle will pay well for your safe return."

"I hope that what you're doing will cause no further killing. I've got a feeling you might live to regret what you've done."

"You're not threatening me I hope." The don looked anxious. For the first time he had doubts about his actions. In the beginning it had all seemed straight forward. With the girl he'd be able to extort a ransom, probably enough to replace the casino. But now, he wasn't so sure. 'Goldstein's a hard nut; let's hope I can crack it,' he thought.

CHAPTER TWENTY-TWO

Sammy only became aware of the kidnapping on the Tuesday after Rosie's abduction on the Saturday. What he couldn't understand was why there had been no contact between the kidnappers and either him or Nick in England. The silence frightened Sammy. No news was bad news in this sort of case. If there was to be a ransom why had nothing been heard? Maybe Rosie had been killed already? Perhaps if he waited another few hours until the morning, something would turn up. But he'd promised to tell Nick something.

"Nick, Hi. I'm sorry to be a long time getting back to you. To tell the truth, I can't find Rosie at the moment. She's not at the apartment. It seems strange, but could she have gone off on a holiday for a day or so without letting any of us know?"
"No Sammy, of course not; that's not like Rosie."
"No, well anyway, I'll try again later and keep in touch."
"Sammy, you're not hiding anything from me are you?"
"Would I do that? Honestly, I don't know anything else. I'll give you a bell this evening, early, so I don't get you out of bed."
"Okay Sammy; you won't forget will you?"

After Celleri was taken from the hospital, he had been well looked after in Sammy's home. Sammy's doctor son-in-law had cared for his medical needs and Liz and her daughter had dressed his burns and nursed him back to full strength. In fact, now he was out of bed all day and his wounds had healed almost completely. He was particularly fortunate, as the scarring produced by the burns was minimal. His face was still reddened but as each day passed, the skin was becoming more natural. His hair was growing back where it had been scorched and a small dark beard, flecked with grey had started shading the lower part of his face. His hands were slowly getting better and they too would be fairly well within a short while. He knew that soon he would have to start thinking about his new life, well away from New York where, if it were known he was alive, there'd be a contract to kill him, one it would be difficult to escape for ever. Perhaps this was now the time to assume a new identity, Michael

Chaney, and return to England. Who knows, maybe to see Meryl again and fall in love.

Each day Celleri had been staying at Sammy's, the two men had met. During this time, a sort of friendship had developed between them, developed by need. Sammy, because it was his plan and his organisation which had caused the fire and Celleri's accident, he had felt the need to assist now in Celleri's recovery. His was a guilt reaction, made worse by his friendship with Nick who had brought him close to Rosie, Celleri's daughter and who he now loved as he loved Nick. Celleri's need was more practical. He knew he had to hide somewhere while he recovered from his injuries to avoid the revenge of the mob, angered by the casino fire and which they attributed to his mismanagement. As he had failed in their eyes, even though he couldn't have stopped it, he was expendable, of no further use to them.

Celleri had agreed with Sammy's substitution of a body for his and had been told of his funeral. They had laughed together at the ceremony of the occasion. With luck, Celleri knew the contract on his life would have been removed and the search to kill him, probably called off. He too had been aware that if he were considered dead, his estate would be inherited by Rosie and he would be left penniless. That had concerned him when he had discussed it with Sammy.
"I've got one and a half million dollars of yours in my safe downstairs," said Sammy. "It's yours. When your hoods hit Abe, my son, I wanted the money to help bring up his kids and look after Becci, his wife. But they're family; we'll take care of our own. You can have your money back."
"That's good of you; it will help to have some of my own now that I've given all the rest away," Celleri chuckled. "Can't say I ever planned it this way."
"There's something else I should talk to you about. Rosie's missing from the apartment; she's just disappeared."
"What d'you mean? There's nowhere she can go." Celleri sounded anxious.
"I'm not sure. There was a Cadillac hanging around outside the apartment, but since she's not been seen, the car has gone. My guys were keeping a stakeout on the place but somehow, they missed it go."
"Do you think those in the car have got Rosie?"
"I guess so. I had the car traced to your don out at Staten. I think he's got her. I don't know why, unless he thinks you're still alive."
"Maybe, but I think it's more likely he wants to get his hands on

Rosie's inheritance. With the casino gone, he's looking for cash. Has he got in touch?"
"No; that's what's worrying me." said Sammy. "I feel he might do something silly."
"I shouldn't think he will, not yet anyway. He'll want to make something out of it if he can."
"You got any ideas what we can do?"
"What you must do is threaten him before he can start levering you. Firstly, can you get your hands on a small amount of heroin or cocaine? Not a lot, just enough to worry him. You'll have to get this dope smuggled inside one of his brothels and perhaps inside one of his working men's clubs near the docks; that shouldn't be too difficult. Then you ring him and tell him. He'll get the message. When he knows you can finger him any time you want, he'll panic. He's afraid the cops will put him down for a long time given half a chance."
"Hey, that's a swell idea."
"When you ring, tell him, unless he releases Rosie pretty quickly, the next time the dope will be in his house and the police there shortly afterwards. I should start preparing a welcome home party for her. I'm just sorry I can't join in."
"I'll get started straight away."

"Hey, Godfather; nice to talk to you. How'r'ya doing? Can't talk too freely, I hear the feds have got a tap on your phone. Thought I'd tell you about the white stuff; you know, the snow in the business over on the Wharf club. I'd find it before the fuzz do if I were you."
"Who's that?" blustered the don.
"You don't want to know really. Thought I'd warn you this time. The next time it'll be closer to home."
"Who is that; what d'you want?" A fine sweat was breaking out over his brow.
"Just release Mis Haynes, that's all. Let's say she'll be home in her apartment in an hour. Not a moment longer y'understand? Otherwise?" The line went dead.
"Damn him; Goldstein. Damn him, damn him. Damn him to hell."

The door into Rosie's room banged open. The don strode in, his face was livid.
"It seems your Goldstein is going to have the last laugh."
"What d'you mean?" asked Rosie, startled by his sudden entrance.
"The bum's planted dope in one of my places and threatens to let the police know if you're not freed soon. The interfering bastard; I'll get

him yet. Get your things together, you're going home now."
With that, he turned on his foot and was gone.

"Sammy, I'm home, back in the apartment. I don't know exactly how you've done it but he's let me go."
"Nice to hear from you Rosie."
"Take care of yourself Sammy, he's really mad. He's got it in for you."
"Thanks for the warning Rosie. Ring Nick straight away. He's been chewing his finger nails up to the knuckles, worrying about you. Both of us think you'd be better off in England now. Safer anyway? Give it a thought."
"I do too. I'll call him now. Thanks again for everything Sammy."

"Nick, darling; I'm all right. I'm back in the apartment. I've got so much to tell you."
"Thank God you're safe Rosie. I've been so worried. Where on earth have you been?"
"The godfather kidnapped me on Saturday. Sammy's just got me out; said he'd frame the don if he didn't release me straight away. Oh, it's so wonderful to be free again."
"I'm sure it is Rosie. Oh, Rosie, I have been worried."
"Poor Nick. When I was a prisoner there I thought I wasn't going to see you again. You'll never guess how I felt."
"I think I can Rosie. I haven't been able to concentrate on anything since I heard you were missing. I'll get a flight across as soon as I can fix it."
"No, Nick. Don't come over here; I'm coming home to England. I'd like you to meet Mum. If I mean as much to you as you do to me, you'll want to meet her too."
"I can't wait Rosie. You see, I love you."
"I love you too Nick; see you in the next day or so. Bye."
"Bye Rosie."

CHAPTER TWENTY-THREE

Rosie's departure from New York was not to happen as quickly as she or Nick had wished for. Now that she had inherited such a large estate, it was taking longer to get things organised than she ever imagined. The solicitors seemed to be dragging their feet and delays were occurring all the time. She had lost count of the number of times she had had to call at Maurice Webster's office during the last week, to sign this or to confirm that and every time she squirmed inside as she shook his limp, wet outstretched hand.

"How nice to meet you again Miss Haynes. Today I want you to cast your eyes over this." It was always the same; 'cast your eyes over this'. Oh, how she longed for Nick's powerful embrace again. Goose pimples arose along her spine as she remembered their being together, their companionship and their love making. Every day they would speak to each other on the phone but it wasn't enough.
She needed to be with Nick; now; all the time.

Sammy and Liz had been so very kind to her. Following her disastrous attempt to stay alone at the apartment ending with her kidnapping, they had insisted she remained with them for as long as she had to be in New York. They were like parents to her, looking after her every need, caring for her and protecting her, worrying about her, just as they did about the members of their own family. In fact, Sammy had complained loudly to those in the organisation who had earlier tried to keep a watch on Rosie, trying to protect her, giving them a severe reprimand for not preventing the kidnapping. They were still smarting from his strongly worded reproof so they now never let Rosie out of their sight. She was not aware of it, but every time she left Sammy's home, she had a tail, someone ordinary looking who blended in with his surroundings, but who was now much more watchful than before.

One morning as she was returning from her attorney, window-shopping on Fifth Avenue, she stopped outside an opticians, the sign in the window advertising soft contact lenses catching her eye. She remembered Nick telling her she would have to change her appearance and this, he had suggested, was to have been the start. To Rosie, now seemed an excellent time to begin, on her own, without anyone knowing. She knew that Nick would be pleased she had got on with things and she chuckled wickedly inside, as she thought how she would fool Sammy; yes, she'd start right this minute.

"Good morning," she said gaily, a large smile directed at the male assistant who came forward to serve her. "I noticed your sign outside and I wondered whether I could buy coloured plain glass contact lenses so my eyes would be a different colour. You see, I want to go to a fancy dress ball as a blonde bombshell and I'm told all blondes have pale blue eyes."
"Of course madam; let me show you what we have in stock, though why you should want to change those lovely green eyes you've got,

I'll never know." He was a handsome but much older man and he enjoyed flattering her.
Rosie blushed shyly. "But Marilyn Monroe had lovely blue eyes didn't she? And I want to go to the party as Miss Monroe; I want to try and turn my boyfriend's head."
The shop assistant chuckled. "Strangely enough, I don't think she did have blue eyes." Continuing to flirt with Rosie, he said, "I wish I were twenty years younger, I'd give your guy a run for his money." He showed her the latest in soft lenses, ones that could be worn for long periods without causing the wearer any trouble. "I think these are the best suited for what you need" he said. They were of the palest blue and Rosie knew Nick was right, they would change her whole appearance.
"Do I need any tests; will they be all right?"
"Here, try them now." He showed Rosie how to lean forward, place the lens on the finger tip and flick the lid down so the lens lay comfortably on the front of the eye. The first time she tried, she dropped the lens on the counter top, but within a few minutes, she became happy to do it repeatedly and accurately. When she had both lenses in position, she looked in the mirror. Who was this woman looking back at her? It sure wasn't Rosie Haynes. She was thrilled; she had already overcome her first hurdle. The assistant taught her how to look after the lenses and how to keep them clean and scratch free, advising Rosie that if she needed any further help, all she had to do was call in.
"I'd be happy to see you at any time, madam." The way he said it, Rosie knew he meant it.
Now for the other changes. Macy's; that would be her next stop. The shop with the sign that said, 'If you haven't seen Macy`s, you haven't seen NewYork.' No time like the present. "Taxi."

She took the lift to the third floor, 'Ladies' fashions.' She looked around the rails, largely taking note of the staff rather than the stock. She felt she would get more help from someone her own age rather than an overweight middle-aged woman, the sort of person she wanted to become. She caught the eye of an assistant in her mid twenties who wasn't wearing a wedding ring, someone she felt she could confide in.
"I wonder if you could help me. I'm thinking of going to a fancy dress ball, looking something like Barbara Bush. She is such a lot heavier than I am but I wondered whether I could find a wardrobe in Macy's to make me look as matronly as she does. What d'you think?"
"Have to start at the basics I guess. She'd be a 16 or 18 I should think. You'd need a lot of padding to make you a 40 C, but I suppose it could be done. You'd get that from a theatrical costumier I would

think. There's a place just around the corner from here. Then she goes in for skirts and blouses a lot so there's no problem there. We've got plenty of stock for the woman with the fuller figure. Stockings, well perhaps a darker shade and thicker denier than you're wearing right now. And shoes; she wears a more practical heel than those of yours. You'd have to get your hair fixed. Our beauty salon would get it the right shade of blue-grey for you; would you like me to arrange an appointment?"
"Not at the moment, but I'd like you to organise the rest if you would. If I call at the theatrical shop first, I'll call back directly. Okay? Then you can kit me out."

Rosie was longer than she expected collecting an inflatable, busty chest piece usually worn by drag artists rather than slim beauties like Rosie. It was soft with a cotton backing that moulded itself to Rosie's figure and a pink coloured latex front which, when inflated, swelled to a buxom shape, many sizes larger than Rosie really was. As Macy's was not overflush with shoppers at the moment and customers like Rosie were few and far between, with commission falling every month, Rosie had the assistant's complete and undivided attention. When she saw the new foundation garment, she chuckled.
"Jees. You're sure gonna be different. I'm sure you'd like to try things on; get the feel of it. It'll be very uncomfortable for you; a bit hot too I guess beneath that contraption."
One at a time, the items were brought for Rosie to see and to try on. Putting on the new figure she had acquired from the costumiers, Rosie tried on the new bra. The cup was large enough to put a plum pudding in but the inflated breast fitted snugly. The assistant entered into the spirit of the dressing up, all the time murmuring 'Up the Democrats,' interspersed with 'I can't think why on earth you want to hide that,' referring to. Rosie's figure. When all was complete, wearing the enormous brassiere, a blouse and skirt over her padded hips, thicker stockings and sensible shoes, Rosie began to look the part and strangely, began to feel the part. She walked differently, stood with a slight stoop and she could see how her whole appearance was changing and how with a change of make-up, she could quite easily be Mrs Joe Public.
"Pack them for me please. I'll call back in an hour or so."
"Yes ma'am," the shop assistant replied, full of enthusiasm. Now for the wig.

On a number occasions since she had been living in New York Rosie had had her hair done in a small salon in one of the side streets off Fifth Avenue. It was a quiet and select establishment run by an ebullient overweight Italian who greeted each client so effusively, it was as if he was meeting a long-lost friend after a long period apart. His hair was thick and long and dark, his curls tied back with a black invisible band into a pony tail, and his hands moved constantly, imparting their own welcome. He recognised Rosie instantly as she entered the door.

"Signorina; where have you been? I am desolate; I have missed you so; we have all missed you, haven't we?" he said to his staff of three younger Italian boys as he took her hand, kissing her finger tips. "My sons were only saying to their mama the other day, the nice lady with the beautiful hair hadn't been in to see them recently."

"Hallo Gino; I know you say that to all of your ladies. I've been so dreadfully busy lately I haven't had time for my hair. Can you fix me in now?"

"For you signorina, Gino can arrange anything," he said, twirling a chair for Rosie to sit in and snapping his fingers, organising his helpers.

"I want you to do something else for me rather quickly. I need a blonde wig. Can you make it? It has to be unrecognisable from the real thing with dark roots especially, so it looks natural."

"Si signorina it can be done, but it is a wicked thing to hide your wonderful hair. No, no; I cannot do it."

"Well, I guess I'll have to go to another salon then; it's a pity."

"No, I cannot let you go elsewhere. You want the best, Gino will make it for you; Gino will make you the best. Come, sit down. I will make some measurements; it will take me three days."

"Make it for the day after tomorrow Gino." He hesitated. "Please Gino; just for me." She pouted. "I have to go back to England urgently for a while. I'll need it for the trip."

"For you, I will have it ready signorina, but you should never cover that gorgeous hair of yours; it's much too wonderful"

"Thank you Gino. I'll call this time on Thursday. Ciao."

As Rosie continued her stroll along Fifth Avenue she knew she had already accomplished her part of the plan. Was Nick going to get a surprise when he met her at Heathrow? She couldn't wait; damn the solicitor Webster. Why didn't he get a move on? The decision was made; then. Webster would have it all tied up by the weekend or the whole thing would have to wait until Rosie came back to the States later; and who knew when that would be. She was going back home to England on Monday.

CHAPTER TWENTY-FOUR

Sammy took Rosie to Kennedy airport for her flight home to England and Elizabeth went along too, to keep her company. The women sat in the back of the limo, quiet, without much conversation, all eyes moist with sadness at her departure. Every now and then, Elizabeth would sigh and murmur tearfully, "Oh Rosie; we are going to miss you so."
Rosie would take her hand and whisper, "and I'm going miss you too. You've both been so kind to me; someone you didn't even know a few weeks ago. But don't be upset, both Nick and I will be back soon and maybe, you never know, you'll be coming across to visit us in England shortly."
Elizabeth visibly brightened. "I do hope so. I know it will be such a lovely wedding."
"Well Nick hasn't asked me to marry him yet, though I think he will. I do love him such a lot."
"I'm sure your mother will like him. Has she met him yet?"
"No, but I know she'll fall in love with him, just as I have."
"What d'you think your papa would've thought?" asked Sammy who'd been concentrating on the driving while listening to the conversation.
"Mr Celleri? I think he liked Nick well enough though they didn't really have any time to get to know one another. Yes, I think he would. approve."
"Me too. I think he would. And I think Nick's a lucky guy finding you. If it doesn't work out Rosie, you and Nick I mean, you let me know. I'll dump Elizabeth and we'll make a go of it someplace," Sammy chuckled wickedly.
"You mind what you're saying Sammy Goldstein and concentrate on your driving. What makes you think anyone would want to look at a fat old Jewish bagel like you any more?"
"You do old thing. I'm only kidding." He chuckled; "But it's a smart idea. Nick'd be a fool if he didn't recognise what a super girl he's got. I'm pretty certain he does."
"I can't wait to introduce him to Mum. I do hope they get on well together," said Rosie.
"Sure they will; he's a nice guy."

The car weaved its way along the rutted freeway that took them back to the airport and the British Airways departure terminal, arriving in a cloud of dust from the unfinished roadway. Sammy helped Rosie with her cases and as she approached the ticket desk, he put them all on the scales.

"No, not that one Sammy," Rosie said quickly, recovering a small holdall, about to pass on the conveyor belt. "I'll take that one in the plane with me." She held on to it as the girls proceeded to book her into her flight.

"Yes, non-smoking please; executive." Though Rosie could well have afforded to travel first class now she had inherited her father's estate, old habits were difficult to break, though she had made a concession to her improved financial circumstances, travelling executive class instead of tourist.

"Thanks for bringing me to the airport, Sammy. I've loved being with you both so much. And don't be upset; we'll soon be seing each other again. I'd rather you didn't wait any longer. I hate goodbyes."

"Me too," said Sammy. They embraced each other as firm friends and the women kissed their tear-stained cheeks. Picking up the holdall she was to take with her, Rosie turned towards the stairway to the departure lounge. She waved to them as she climbed the stairs, wiping away a tear at the same time and she was gone. She made her way through passport and customs controls and her bag passed through the X-Ray detector without any problems. Nor should it appear in any way abnormal; after all, it only contained those clothes Rosie would need later; in England.

When Rosie had got back to her apartment with her purchases from Macy's, she had tried on everything again several times, making mental notes of the problems she might face. She even carried out the change of clothes in the broom cupboard, the smallness of the space simulating the cramped space in the toilet where the change at Heathrow was going to have to be made. By repeating the manoeuvre several times, she was able to get out of the clothes she would be travelling in, dress in the new outfit bought from Macy's and repack her other clothes, all in five minutes. Then, once she combed up her hair and had adjusted the wig so that it felt and looked the real thing, she was able to stand in front of the vanity mirror and put on her make-up. She practised drawing a cupid's bow mouth with a brush, filling it in with a gaudy cherry-red lipstick. She rouged her cheeks and darkened her eyebrows to hide their copper colour and lined her eyes with pencil. She blued her eyelids and finally, she inserted the contact lenses. She could easily have been her old blue-eyed headmistress. Yet, when she looked at herself in the mirror, there was something not quite right. It was almost right but something was missing; what could it be? That was it; the character she was to become needed a hat. She was to be the sort of woman now who would never be seen without one. Tomorrow, she would go back to that nice assistant who would find her one that matched, perhaps a straw with a flower on it. Anyway, she certainly knew she had to have one to complete the disguise.

The steward put the grip in the overhead locker and after Rosie had taken her coat off, he folded it neatly and placed it alongside the bag. Rosie sat in her window seat, watching the frantic last minute activity outside as the ground staff prepared for takeoff. As she relaxed she reminisced about the flight out when she had met Nick for the first time, and smiled as she thought of the surprise Nick was going to get when she arrived at Heathrow. He would be there expecting to meet his very attractive young lady friend, not the middle-aged crone who would turn up in her place.

The flight, east to west is always more tiring than the journey west to east and this one was no exception. After her meal, Rosie tilted her seat as far back as it would go and, covering her eyes with the shades, she tried to rest. But her brain was so active, sleep was impossible. At least she avoided the eye-strain of the bright light coming through the cabin windows. She recalled the three brilliant blue-white diamonds Nick had shown her on the flight to America and how they had reflected and diffused all the colours of the rainbow as she held them on the palm of her hand. Following that brief encounter with diamonds she could now understand Nick's warm affection for them. Like others with a need for drugs, Rosie recognised within her an urge to possess and own them. The scam was something she looked forward to now, a thrill she could hardly wait for.

Her eyes closed, she felt comfortable as she rehearsed in her mind the personality change that was to take place in her when she arrived at Heathrow. She had planned things very well. Her luggage. was new and she had replacement labels in her handbag. Once she had passed through customs she would remove the ones on the cases now which indicated the luggage was hers, Miss Rosie Haynes' and slide in the new ones which belonged to a Mrs Ruth Havers. She had even bought an old wedding ring in a pawn shop on the east side to wear to complete the change. She knew Nick would never be able to recognise her or her new luggage; well, hopefully he wouldn't. The middle-aged bent dame she would become wouldn't get a second look.

"This is your captain speaking. We are flying at 35,000 feet in the jet stream. Our air speed is 450 knots but we're in luck today. We have a tail wind of 150 knots so our speed over the ground is about 600 knots. Our arrival time at Heathrow will be an hour earlier than planned." A murmur of appreciation rustled around the aircraft, everyone pleased to hear that the flight time would be less; but there was still a long way to go. Rosie must have dropped off to sleep as the intercom crackled again, rousing her to hear the captain announce that they were now on their descent on the flight-path for Heathrow. Only a short time longer and she was to carry out her own scam and change her whole appearance. Watch out Nick; you're about to meet Mrs Ruth Havers.

CHAPTER TWENTY-FIVE

Now, on the other side of the customs and immigration officials, Rosie sought out the toilet where the metamorphosis would take place. Unlike the change that takes place between the ugly caterpillar as it weaves its silk cocoon, hiding away from everything that goes on around it until the time arrives for it to become the delicate butterfly, this was the transition of the very beautiful Rosie into the dowdy middle-aged frumpish woman. Somebody who was nobody; somebody at whom no one would look twice, not even once. And as the transformation took place, Rosie became even more thrilled at her success; she giggled with glee. Youth and beauty in the shape of Miss Rosie Haynes had entered the cloakroom. Leaving, was a mature, shabby, unobserved Mrs Ruth Havers.
'Now Nick Royle; let's be seeing you.'

Though her change had taken her some time, she joined the main throng of passengers which was still winding its way towards the exit and the large number of people waiting for their friends and family on the other side of the barrier. Rosie strained her eyes for her first view of Nick. She wanted to see him so that she could judge his reactions. She wondered whether he would see through her disguise or, as she hoped, he would never give her a second glance. But hard as she looked at the many people there, she couldn't see him anywhere. She pushed her trolley to one side of the hall and looked again at the mass of faces, but there was no sign of him. Perhaps he'd been delayed Rosie thought, after all the flight had arrived earlier than expected. That was probably it; perhaps there'd be time for a cup of tea, then she'd look again.

When Rosie returned from her visit to the restaurant the mass of travellers had thinned and only a few, those held up by custom searches were still in the hall and they were surrounded by their friends. Alone, on the far side of the room there was an old man, probably in his sixties, sitting hunched over his walking stick. He looked tired and

worried. Every now and then he'd stand up and crane his neck, looking back into the exit as if he was expecting someone to come, probably a friend or relative still held up in customs.
He would walk up to the barrier, look and listen and then return to his seat, shoulders drooped; resigned. Rosie had noticed him but Nick's absence was on her mind and now causing her concern. If there had been an accident, hanging around in Heathrow wasn't doing any good; she had to go.

Approaching the exit from inside the airport the automatic doors opened and Rosie walked towards the only taxi waiting outside. She felt absolutely desolate. The taxi man made no effort to help the middle-aged Mrs Ruth Havers, unlike those in New York that fell over themselves to assist Miss Rosie Haynes, the gorgeous auburn headed young woman. Struggling to push her wayward trolley towards the cab she was aware that the elderly man who had been in the arrival hall was now there at her elbow, ready to help her.
"Perhaps I could help you with your cases and if you're going into London, maybe you'd allow me to share your taxi," he suggested. She hesitated. The last thing Rosie wanted right now was the company of a strange old man. She wanted to think; she didn't want to share a cab with a complete stranger for the half hour or so the journey to Nick's flat would take.
"I'd rather not," she said.
"It's the only taxi here," he said. "I'll pay the fare and you could be dropped off first. I'm really feeling quite anxious after waiting for my friend who wasn't on the flight. I must get back to telephone as quickly as I can."
"Oh all right," said Rosie, giving in, dejected at Nick's absence and suddenly too tired herself to offer any objection.

As Rosie climbed into the back he put her luggage in the front of the cab beside the driver before he joined her.
"Where shall I tell him to go?" Rosie's new friend asked,
"Holland Park Mews."
"That's strange," he said. "That's where I'm going too." She looked at him more carefully now. Clearly he was close to sixty, though his mousey hair showed little greying. His face was lined and his eyebrows were bushy, sticking upwards as the politician, Healey's eyebrows did; it gave him a startled expression. He held a stick in his hand and Rosie had noticed earlier he had walked with a slight limp. But when she looked at him more closely, his hands did not match the man. There were no blotches of age on the backs of the hands; no swelling of

arthritic joints; no callouses of hard labour. These were the hands of a much younger man; the fingers were long like musicians' fingers, something that Rosie remembered about Nick's hands when she first met him. A memory stirred inside her. There was something about this man that was unnerving; a feeling she knew him though she knew she had never met him before. She looked at him again, even more closely than before. Was there a twinkle in his eye? Was he laughing at her?
"Rosie, it's me." His hand took hers gently, holding on to it as she tried to take it away from him, suddenly a little frightened. "Rosie, it's me, Nick. We both had such super disguises. I would never have recognised you until you started to walk to the exit. It was when you straightened up and went to the exit, you changed from the old lady you had become. Then you looked younger; you walked more quickly than you had done; your character became visibly more youthful. But your get-up was absolutely first class. If you hadn't moved towards the door and had remained seated there, I'd still be waiting for my Rosie inside tbe airport."

Rosie hadn't spoken a word. She had been so overwhelmed by Nick's approach, she was stunned. Tears welled up blurring her vision. Suddenly, her legs felt weak; if she hadn't been sitting down she would have fainted and fallen.
"Nick, oh Nick. I couldn't understand why you weren't there to meet me. I felt so unhappy. I was worried. I thought you'd had an accident coming to Heathrow. I'd planned our meeting so much. How I was going to walk right up to you, hoping you wouldn't recognise me. I never thought that you too would be different. You look so much older, all those lines on your face; I'd never have noticed you. Oh Nick, I've missed you so."
He took her in his arms, kissing her gently on her eyes, cradling her as the taxi began its journey back to the city. Any outsider seeing them through the window would have thought, 'what a romantic old couple they are; I hope I'm like that when I'm their age.'

Once Rosie had regained her self-control, she began to tell Nick about the plans she had made in New York to change her appearance and of her shopping sprees in Macy's and of her practice in changing in the confined space of the toilet.
"I must say you did a super job with your costume. I really wouldn't have known it was you until you moved. It was then you forgot your age; you walked differently, as you usually do, upright. It was then I looked again and followed you to the door, but I still wasn't absolutely sure until I spoke to you."
"Your poor lined face; you really do look a wrinkly," laughed Rosie.

"Do you think we'll do?"
"I'm certain of it. I wouldn't think we'll have to make any changes. Your wig is super. You thought it out well. I believe the character you've become would be showing the roots a bit. I think we've both cracked our disguises."
"It was clever thinking about the roots wasn't it? It makes it much more natural. It's your hands that gave you away. They're too fine, too youthful; no blemishes of age. You'll have to do something about them."
"Mmm; I hadn't noticed that. You're right; they don't fit the man; Still, now you've told me, that shouldn't be too much of a problem."

During the journey back to the city they talked about the days spent apart, Rosie in New York and Nick in London.
"Have you thought any more about the scam," Rosie asked Nick.
"Not really," Nick replied." Sly has found out more about our target. Apparently, his family have abandoned him completely. They're not going to bail him out this time and he's up to his eyes in debt; to the big boys too. He's run up gambling bills of several million pounds with at least three syndicates. The interest alone is rising at hundreds of thousands every day. He hopes his relatives will put up the cash but they won't; they've made that very clear."
"How do you know all this?"
"Sly's had his ear to the ground for quite a while. The underworld is waiting for something to happen. You see, he can't be let off the hook; they'll want their money. They've suggested he solves his problems by selling his diamonds. That's how we know he's ready to do a deal."
"What will happen next?"
"Well, once we're certain he's going to go ahead, we'll make our moves. Sly has the contacts to get us introductions and he knows many of the gems that will come up for sale. Knowing that has allowed him to make some of the prime gems in zircon. For example, we know he has a diamond weighing 106 carats. He's only owned it a short while. He bought it in Geneva a few years ago. It's value is close to nine million pounds. That's the one we want to lift."
"Nine million pounds; phew, that must be some diamond."
"It's a beauty, nearly as big as a golf ball and perfect; flawless. It's a very rare and beautiful diamond. There's nothing quite like it. It'll be difficult to switch because of its size and it'll take a bit of practice, but I'm sure we can do it okay."
"Have you any plans, I mean exactly how it's to be done?"
"Not really."

"Did you notice the buttons on this coat Nick? They're quite large. When I chose it I wondered whether it would be possible to replace one of them with a hollow one, inside which the diamond could be hidden. But the size of this stone seems enormous."
"It sounds a super idea Rosie, but don't worry about that. I think Sly has developed another way of getting the stone away which seems to be first class too. We'll have to try them both out" She glowed inside knowing that the suggestion she had made had been a good one in Nick's eyes.

The taxi turned into Fortnum Mews pulling up outside Nick's flat.
"I forgot to ask Rosie. Perhaps you'd rather have gone to your hotel?"
Rosie blushed. "It's true I was only coming here to find out if you were all right. I think it would be best if I went there. Do you think we'd be able to have dinner together later?"
Redirecting the taxi, Nick replied, "Of course we can; I'm going to keep you as close as I can now you're here."
"But I plan to visit Mum tomorrow; will you be free to come?"
"I'm dying to meet her. If she's anything like her daughter, she must be a lovely lady."

That evening over dinner, once more as Nick and Rosie rather than Mrs Ruth Havers and her ageing friend, they recounted all their past outings together in New York, falling gradually more and more in love with each other. When the meal was over, though Rosie was extremely tired from the flight, she wanted Nick with an urgency she had not anticipated. There was a deep seated hunger for his touch; a feeling of warmth and a glow, a sensation of emptiness she knew only he could fill; a physical need to be satisfied soon.
"You must be exhausted Rosie and tomorrow is going to be another hectic day for you. I was hoping we could find time to call in at the office so that you can meet Sly. He's dying to see the woman I keep talking about. Then we can drive out to meet your Mum."
"But there's still tonight Nick. I am tired but not too tired to end the day happily. Mmmm."

CHAPTER TWENTY-SIX

While Nick and Rosie had been making the changes to their appearances by all forms of artifice, Celleri, still staying with Sammy, was undergoing changes, the result of his injuries. He had healed well and quickly, though he had been fortunate the burns had not been as deep as at first they had seemed. But the changes had been quite marked. Now his hair had stopped growing in the front leaving him with a high receding forehead and the growth of new hair had been rather patchy and streaked with silver. Whereas previously, he had been proud of his hair, jet black and until the fire, untinged with any grey hairs, he now had to comb the strands of hair of indeterminate colour with care to conceal the bare areas of scarred scalp. The scars on his face had made the skin over the nose tight, giving it a hooked appearance and the cheeks were taught and reddened and shiny. His hands had also been damaged in the fire and the scarring had made them bent. The joints seemed to be swollen, giving his hands an arthritic appearance. In fact, he now needed a stick to get about though each day there was some improvement and with luck, he'd soon be able to dispense with it. During his long recovery period, Celleri had had time to reflect on just how lucky he was to be alive.

He and Sammy had spent much of their time together in the evenings, talking about their lives, neither giving much away, both realising they had loyalties to others, friends and associates that prevented their speaking freely. Celleri had long forgiven Sammy's part in the arson attack on the club knowing that had it not been for the stupidity of his own men, Sammy's son, Abe, would still be alive now and the club would still be working; but that was now all in the past. Celleri knew he would have been considered a failure by the Mafia and would have been a wanted man had Sammy not engineered his apparent death and burial. On the day of the funeral the mob had all come to see Celleri's casket lowered into his grave and later, they had known that Rosie had inherited his fortune. The pressure was off him. All he needed to do as Rosie and Nick had done, was to assume a new identity and the changes in his physical appearance made that all the more easy to accomplish.

That evening, on the night of Rosie's departure for England, the two men had met as they had done on many times before in Sammy's apartment, Sammy enveloped in the clouds of blue smoke from his unbearable cigar and Celleri enjoying his end of day brandy.

"I'll have to be moving on shortly," Celleri said to Sammy. "I'm almost healed and when I look in the mirror now, I'm damned if I can recognise the chap who's looking back at me." Both men chuckled. It was true, Celleri was very different from the suave self assured manager of the Green Baize casino. This Celleri was an older man, stooped, shrunken, and arthritic, a shadow of his former self.

"Yeah," grunted Sammy. "But I'll be sorry when you have to go. I've enjoyed your company and the time we've spent talking together. I'd

like to think we've grown kinda friends; what d'you think?"
"Yes I do; I shall miss you too," answered Celleri.
"I've spoken to my people," Sammy said, "and they're happy to fix you up with an Israeli passport to get you out of the country, wherever you're going. In fact, they suggest you travel El Al. You look a bit Jewish now with that hooked nose," Sammy laughed, "and if you've got an Israeli passport it'll help to get you cleared."
"You've been a great help Sammy. I don't know what would have happened without you. Probably the mob would have got me by now. They blamed me for the fire in the casino even though I know I tried my hardest to prevent it happening."
"Yeah; if only we could put the clock back. Abe would be here; your club would be going strong and Rosie would be here too." There was a pause.
"If only."
"Have you heard from Rosie or Nick?" Celleri asked.
"Not yet. Rosie said she'd ring from her hotel when she arrived, but perhaps she'll forget when she meets Nick again." Both men looked at their watches automatically.
"Any moment now I guess," said Sammy.
"Yes. The thing I regret most is my not having had the time to get to know her. All those years I've kept an eye on her through agents. I've known about her growing up and how pretty she had grown and I've heard all about her success in university. But when we met, it was just as if I was meeting a stranger. I wasn't prepared for her beauty, her self control, all the things I would have wanted her to be; it was uncanny."

The telephone trilled, jerking them both from their sentimental thoughts.
"It'll be Rosie," Sammy said, moving quickly across to the phone.
"Yeah," he said expectantly, not his usual explosive grunt.
"Sammy; it's me, Rosie. I'm with Nick now. He was at Heathrow to meet me and we've just got in. Everything's okay. You've been so kind to me. You'll give my love to Elizabeth won't you?" Her words came quickly, giving Sammy no time to ask his own questions, getting in as much information as possible in the time available.
"Liz and I are both missing you like crazy already. You take care of yourself and tell that Nick he's to look after you or he'll have to answer to me."
"He will; he's listening over my shoulder. And thanks again. Take care. God bless."
"Lucky fella," chuckled Sammy. "Thanks for ringing Rosie; we'll talk

again, soon." The line went dead, both men silent with their own thoughts; Celleri was the first to react.
"At least you were able to talk to her," he sighed. "You never know, maybe with the passage of time we'll be able to get together once again. Maybe I'll even be able to assume the role of her father; I'd like that."
"Yeah; look on the bright side. I think Rosie would have wanted you to be part of her life if you'd not died; in fact she said as much many times. I believe she would have tried to be a match-maker between you and her ma too; she's a romantic is Rosie. She'd love to get you both together again."
"It would be nice; but so much has happened. I doubt whether Meryl would ever forgive me for running out on her; I don't think I could."
"Well, you'll never know if you don't try. What you've got to do now is get back to England and see how things are. Play the cards you've got; maybe your hand is stronger than you think. Rosie said her ma never stopped loving you. She sure didn't marry anyone else did she? I bet she's still got a thing for you after all these years. It's up to you to recharge it a bit. You can't lose anything by trying."
"No. I suppose you're right. I must say that's the way my mind's been working. Another week and I think I'll be ready to give it a go."
"Yeah, that's the way. Think positively and you'll win her."
"I'm sure going to give it a try. By the way; do you think Nick will ask Rosie to marry him?"
"He hasn't told me but I know he's in love with her. It's strange isn't it how people fall in love? For them it was a chance meeting on a flight out to the States and somehow the chemistry was just right."
"Yes, I suppose so. I can remember the time I became aware of Rosie's Mum as clearly as if it were yesterday. We'd just been kids in school together and suddenly, she had blossomed as a woman, all curves and warmth and sweet-smelling talcum powder. She was a lovely pretty girl; I was such a fool running off like that."
"That's all in the past; keep thinking positively."
"Yes, I must keep trying. I'm feeling rather tired Sammy; I think I'll say goodnight."
"Yeah, yeah; goodnight."

Celleri climbed the stairs back to his room. Tears were blurring his vision as he thought yet again of all those wasted years. He knew he had to accept the challenge. He had to meet Meryl and try and explain to her why he had behaved as he had. Maybe she would understand and forgive him; maybe, as would seem to be more likely, she wouldn't. He had to try. To him now there was sense of urgency; it had to be just as soon as it could all be arranged. Throwing his cane into the corner, he straightened and walked the rest of the way to his room without any aid. All it needed was an incentive and now he had one; to get home to England, to find Meryl and ask her forgiveness.

CHAPTER TWENTY-SEVEN

"Sly, this is Rosie."

"Well hallo Rosie," Sly responded, extending his hand towards her. "Gee, you're every bit as pretty as Nick said you were. Wouldn't you prefer a better looking guy like me though?" His voice had the same gutteral tones that Nick's had but they were much coarser and very obvious.

"Nick has told me so much about you Sly, I feel I've known you for a long time," Rosie laughed, "but I think I'll stick with him for the time being. You never know though; play your cards right and who knows; maybe I'll fall for you too."

They all joined in the laughter that followed, Nick adding, "I can see I'll have to keep my eye on you two."

"I should be so lucky," added Sly wickedly.

"Why do they call you Sly?" Rosie asked.

"I wish you hadn't asked," Sly replied. "My mother insisted I was to be a Sebastian; my father wanted a Laurence and my grandfather was Yacoub. So they gave me all those names and very soon my friends started shortening them to Sly; it's stuck ever since. Sly doesn't sound that nice but I prefer it to any of the others."

"I want you to explain to Rosie what you've been up to recently," Nick said, throwing his arm around Sly's shoulders. "I've told her about the part each of us will play but perhaps you can throw a bit more light on the practicalities you face particularly."

"Well Rosie. We know the sheikh's relative we plan to con is in big trouble. He's in real severe financial difficulties. We're not sure but we think he owes the syndicate maybe twelve million dollars, about nine million pounds." Rosie whistled quietly.

"How on earth has he got into that sort of debt?"

"Oh that's easy the way he lives. Most of his markers arise from the casino. Because of his background they let him run up enormous bills hoping his relatives would pay up rather than cause a scandal. Now they've publicly abandoned him, the vultures are closing in. Either he pays up or they'll break his legs before rubbing him out all together. And they'll do just that; they have to. They have to make an example of him to ensure no one else takes

them on. It's a hard world out there and he's up to his eyes in trouble."
"So what do we have to do?" asked Rosie.
"During the past few years, when the oil was flowing freely from the Middle East and he had no money troubles, we think he was buying as many of the best diamonds that came on the market as he could afford. As a result, over many years he has acquired some of the most wonderful gems ever mined. We know of one in particular he bought a while ago in Geneva. It weighs 21.2 grams, that's 106 carats and it's an oval shape, a little more than an inch by an inch; it's a magnificent stone and very rare. He paid nearly nine million pounds for it. We've copied it exactly, so well in fact, that put the two side by side and I'm sure no one would know the difference."
"The skill making the zircon copies is entirely Sly's," Nick said. "Show what you've made to Rosie."
"Okay, but no touching, neither of you; you can look only."
"Why can't I hold it Sly?" Rosie asked.
"Every time it's handled, even so gently, it's damaged; so minutely that it doesn't really matter, but cumulatively, it does; so no touching. Furthermore, I don't want your finger prints all over it."

Opening the safe in the corner of the room, Sly removed a small sac of soft brown suede leather tied tightly at its neck. He shut the safe behind him and walked towards the centre of the room to the long table covered with a white cloth. He tipped the sac upside down gently, releasing a single large gleaming stone. Immediately the rainbow freed within the bag was reflecting across the white table cloth and around the room. There was a clearly audible hiss as Rosie caught her breath.
"It's wonderful," she gasped. "Those you showed me were marvellous Nick but this is fantastic; quite unbelievable."
"Yes, even this copy is a beauty," whispered Nick." And all we have to do is swap this one for the real thing and it'll be worth a great deal of money to us."
"That's all we have to do," Rosie said mischievously. "When are we going to make the switch?"
"Well the replacement gem is ready. All we have to do now is wait for the meeting to be arranged."
"How will you pay for something as expensive as that?" asked Rosie.
"Well you must remember that we don't plan to buy it, just swap it. But you are right. We have to have letters of credit for that amount of money; that's in hand. We need new passports to explain who we are and they too are in the making. The sheikh's relative will still be at the

Ritz; there'll be little problem getting to meet him. We start our rehearsals this afternoon."
"I had hoped we'd be able to go and see Mum before we started work. I know she's dying to meet you."
"Yes, we will. We'll go to meet your mother this afternoon and we'll come back to start work in the morning. Fair?"
"Oh you're a darling Nick Royle. I'm such a lucky girl finding you."
"Aren't you too?" replied Nick, ducking under Rosie's swing, gripping her tightly around her waist, twisting her around, kissing her fiercely.
"Hey, who's a hungry boy then?" Rosie gasped cheekily.
"Sly; we'll call on Rosie's ma this afternoon but we'll be back tonight in time for an early start. We'll have to be ready at any time now. Fix up lights and cameras where you think they'll need to be."
"Cameras?"
"Videos. For this you're going to be absolutely perfect; our every move will be monitored by someone when we carry out the switch. If you're not absolutely spot on, it'll be a couple of years in gaol for you, my girl."
"In the nick you mean?" Rosie giggled.
Nick sighed. "Rosie, this is deadly serious. Maybe more deadly than you think; take it less frivolously. The people we're up against are hard nuts. They won't think twice whether it's necessary to kill or maim; they'll just do it."
"Stop it Nick; I do understand."
"Right then; let's go. See you tomorrow Sly."
"Okay Baas. You take care, especially of this lovely young lady of yours; and don't you worry, I'll have everything ready."

CHAPTER TWENTY-EIGHT

Nick opened the passenger door of the red Mercedes coupe parked outside the office so that Rosie could climb in. Decorously, she sat on the seat, swinging both legs in together, exposing only a hint of stockinged thigh before she was inside the car. Nick slammed the door shut, walking around the boot end of the car to gain the offside door. He looked around carefully as he usually did. On the other side of the road, he noticed a large stretched limo, a black Merc with darkened windows, so that no one could see who was inside. On the each wing, a small flag fluttered limply. Nick assumed, quite rightly that this was a diplomatic car.
'Now why should that be there?' he thought silently.

Moving out into the line of traffic he headed west out of London along the Great West Road at first and then along the M4 towards Maidenhead, where he knew he must turn north to the little town in Buckinghamshire, that Rosie called home. Through the rear mirror he watched the limo follow him out of the maze of side streets and on to the motorway.

'So what; it's a busy road', he thought, but when twenty minutes later he turned off the motorway on to the A308, and the limo followed, he knew it was unlikely this was a coincidence. He was being followed.

'Now why should that happen?' He knew the one thing he mustn't do was to direct those following him to Rosie's Mum's home; that could be disastrous.

"I'm going to pull in for a moment Rosie. Perhaps we can have a coffee or something," he said, turning sharply into the forecourt of a small hotel on the near side of the road.

"Why?" Rosie asked. "I'm sure Mum will have coffee ready and waiting for us when we get there."

"Yes I'm certain you're right Rosie, but I believe we've had a car on our tail since we left the office. I want to be quite sure they are following us and if so, why and I'm equally certain I don't want to lead them to your mother's home."

Sure enough, the limo followed them into the car park, drawing up alongside. The electrically operated car window lowered itself silently. From inside the car, a voice called out. The Engish was impeccable though very slightly accented; Nick could see no one.

"Mr Royle. I was about to call on you when I saw you leave your office. There was no easy way to stop you and as I wanted to speak with you urgently, I followed, hoping you would stop shortly as you have in fact done. You drive very quickly Mr Royle; it was difficult to keep up with you and stay within your country's speed limit."

Nick was still seated in his car. "Who may I ask is speaking? I'm afraid I cannot see you." Turning to Rosie he said, "keep looking straight ahead. Don't let them get too clear a view of you. Lock your door." The instructions were terse whispers and Rosie got the message from their urgency. An Arab face appeared at the window of the limousine.

"You are a dealer in diamonds Mr Royle." This was a statement; it didn't require confirmation or denial. "A close relative of mine is in financial difficulties. I have indicated I will not help him. Because of this, he has plans to sell his collection of diamonds. The collection has to remain intact within the family. I would like you to act as my agent to purchase them without my relative knowing. Naturally you would be paid a commission for your services. Will you do that for me?"

"I had heard there was a priceless collection coming on the market but I hadn't heard whose it was," Nick replied. "Do you have any limit on the amount to be spent? It's likely to be millions."
"The whole collection may well be many millions as you say. I expect you to do your best for me; otherwise, there is no limit."
"Is there anyone else interested?"
"Probably; others have been making enquiries."
"Can I think about it? I'd love to see and handle the collection but I've never been involved with anything so costly as this before. Where can I contact you?"
The Arab handed his card through the open window. Nick saw the cruel face of the wealthy Middle Eastern potentate and the powerful clawed hand which passed the card across. His relative would be saved from the hands of the mob killers. His legs would remain unbroken and his life intact, but the price would be the loss of his collection of diamonds to the head of the clan. But he wouldn't know it. Faces would be saved; honour kept.
"I'll get in touch within twenty-four hours," Nick said. The conversation over, the limousine window rose, the blackness hiding those inside and the car moved off. Once it was gone, Nick breathed a sigh of relief. "Phew; what d'you think about that?"
"Does that mean the scam is off?"
"Certainly not. We've put too much time and effort in to drop it. What it means is that probably we now have to move fast; very fast. We can carry out the scam as planned in our disguised role. Then I go along as myself, with no disguise, working as the agent of the sheikh, though no one else will know about that, with all the necessary bankers references and arrange to buy the lot. Probably I'll be able to buy them at a very good price I would think if I were buying the whole collection."
"Yes, but what if the zircon stone is recognised? The sheikh would be after your blood then."
"I'm only an agent for their purchase, not their authenticity. The provenance of all of those stones in this collection is well documented."
"But what if the con is found out?"
"Then I should think it would be good night Nick Royle."
"Be serious Nick."
"I am being serious Rosie, believe me, I'm being very serious." A silence fell over them as the magnitude of what might happen sunk in.
"I'll have to give this a lot of thought," Nick said after some time had elapsed. "A number of possibilities is coming to mind as I'm sitting here. I'll have to chew them over and we'll discuss them all tomorrow. Now let's forget all about it and go and meet your mother."

It took them another half hour or so before Nick pulled in to the 'transport cafe' where Rosie had grown up and where her mother still lived. It was quite different from what Nick had expected. In fact, the improvements Meryl had carried out over the years had developed the original restaurant for long-distance lorry drivers into something more like a motel and a very attractive one too. The eating place was now very much upmarket, with accommodation nearby, behind the carpark, for those who wished to stay, usually overnight. At the other end, now screened by trees, was an area for lorry parking, well away from the dormitory part and the original cafe remained for the truckers use. All in all, it was a place catering for everyone.
"Your mother has developed the place remarkably," said Nick. "It doesn't resemble what you described to me at all. Perhaps the end where the lorries are does, but the rest is very tastefully done."
"That's how it was when I was a girl," Rosie said, pointing towards the lorry parking area. "It was pretty grim then I can tell you; but mum has worked wonders with it over the years. Come and meet her," Rosie said, indicating the small neat bungalow, set aside in its own garden.
"You'll love her."

Nick parked the car and walked with Rosie up the red bricked path. Meryl had been looking out for them and when she saw them, she opened the door, rushing out to envelop Rosie in a loving hug.
She backed away and turning to Nick, she said, "And you must be Nick; I think I would have known you anywhere, Rosie's told me so much about you." She took his hand and pulling him towards her, gave him a big welcoming hug as well.
"Hello Mrs Haynes. I was just saying to Rosie how you have worked wonders here; it looks really very lovely."
"Call me Meryl. It doesn't look too bad does it? Taken a lot of time mind you and a fair bit of heartache too, but it's been worth it. Come along in; how long can you stay?"
"We have to be back in London tonight," said Rosie. "Nick has some business there tomorrow and I'm going to go along I believe, but we've got all of today free."
Meryl was disappointed they couldn't stay longer but she said lightly, "That's lovely; come and have some coffee; it's all ready."

Meryl, arm-in-arm with Rosie led the way into the lounge, closely followed by Nick; everywhere was designed for comfort. The furniture was soft and the pattern of the covering fabrics was pleasing to the eye, blending with the decor of the whole room; nothing clashed. Rosie's Mum may have had a lonely life but it was one protected by some of the luxuries which made it easier. Pleasing pictures hung on the walls and the photo frames flashed silver from the side tables. Nick bent to examine them, having seen one with Rosie in her degree ceremony robes. They were largely of Rosie during the developmental stages of her life but there was one of a young man, perhaps in his late teens. It was an old black and white photograph,with a crease running from side to side where it had been folded, perhaps illicitly obtained and the edges were now decidedly tattered. The lad was tall even then and his hair was jet black. The eyes in the photograph seemed to follow Nick as he moved. He felt he knew them and then he remembered; they were the eyes of the man he had visited in the hospital in New York. He had been so severely burned, his face had been swathed in bandages and it was only the eyes he had seen. Nick knew then it was a photograph of Michael Celleri, Rosie's father.

The day passed all too quickly for Meryl as the happenings of Rosie in the States during the last few months were unfolded. Though Rosie had told her mother of Michael Chaney's accident in the fire and his subsequent death, she had thought it wise not to mention the fact that Michael Chaney had admitted that he was really Michael Celleri and that he was her father; neither had she told her mother of her inheritance. There'd be plenty of time for that later. Nick joined in the talk but was somewhat preoccupied, thinking of the meeting earlier this day with the sheikh and the possible solutions to the problem he posed. He was obviously a hit with Meryl, both of them getting along very well straight away; clearly there was not going to be a problem there.

As they walked back towards the car at the end of the day, Meryl squeezed Rosie's hand as she confirmed she liked Nick, adding jokingly, "is he always as quiet as this?"

"No, not as a rule mum. He's got some business worry at the moment; he's been asked to act as agent to a very rich man who wants him to buy some very rare diamonds for him. It's a very responsible job; there's a lot of money at stake."

Hearing what Rosie had been saying to her mother, Nick said, "I'm sorry I've seemed so rude. It is true this deal has been rather worrying but I shouldn't have brought it with me this afternoon."

Nick helped Rosie into the car as he had that morning. Just for a moment, before the ignition had been switched on, as Nick walked around the back of the car, Rosie was unable to open the electric window. Quietly Meryl said to him, "Don't hurt her Nick."

"Don't worry I won't; I plan to marry her shortly, just as soon as she says yes. You see, I'm very much in love with her."

Meryl embraced Nick in a motherly way. "I'm so pleased for you both," she whispered. "Now you drive carefully," she said as the windows came down and they started to move off. "Come again soon."

"She's a nice lady, your mother. She will make me a good mother-in-law I think," Nick jested. "But seriously, I think we'll get along all right. Did she say whether she liked me?"

"You know she did; she was just like putty in your hands, especially when you put this morning behind you."

"Mmm; that did keep worrying me. Any way I care to look at it, I'm probably in big trouble. But we've put too much into the preparation for the scam to drop it just like that. I think we'll effect the swap before I present myself as agent to buy the lot. That way, I needn't touch the stones at all. But no one would buy without examining them very carefully first; it's difficult."

"But you said if you put them side by side, you couldn't tell the fake from the real thing. Surely, no one would ever know."

"Let's hope I'm right," Nick breathed quietly.

They drove silently back towards London, each in their own thoughts.

"Suppose we don't make the swap from the sheikh's relative's collection but carry out the scam once the sheikh owns it; wouldn't that be easier?" Rosie asked.

"I don't think we'd get a chance to do that. Once the collection has been handed over to the sheikh, it will be locked away probably, not to be seen by anyone, certainly not for some time. He doesn't want anyone in his family to know he's got it. There are no two ways about it, the switch will have to be made first."

They moved into an empty parking space outside Nick's apartment both knowing that for a little while anyway, they could forget the problems in store; they had a little living to do.

CHAPTER TWENTY-NINE

"I'm goin' to kinda miss you," grunted Sammy. It was late afternoon and the two men were sitting together in Sammy's living room, steaming cups of black coffee in front of them. "Like a brandy with it, just for old times' sake?" he asked.

"No, I don't think so, thanks. I'd better keep my wits about me, travelling with that new passport. I've gone as Michael Chaney before, but I've never had a passport in that name. It was good of your people to help with that."

"No problem," Sammy said; "pleased to be able to help. D'you know, I envy you meeting up with Rosie and Nick again?"
"Now just a minute. How am I going to be able to see them? Remember? I'm supposed to be dead. It's been on my mind quite a lot lately, but I can't say I really know what to do or what might happen at the moment."
"Mmm; It sure is difficult as hell."
"I had thought to call on Rosie's mum pretty soon somehow or other. If she can't stand the sight of me, I may as well disappear altogether. I don't think I'd want to go on living without her love now. I've got used to the idea of us getting back together. I know it sounds selfish; it probably is, but I'm going to try to make a come-back in her life."
"Yeah; get stuck in there. You never know your luck."
"I mustn't, be late now," Celleri said, looking at his wristwatch. "I can't rush as I used to. When I've finished the coffee, I must be on my way."
"Don't worry. A cab has been booked for six; it will take you from here to the Omni Berkshire in East 52th. Go into the foyer for half an hour or so. Have some tea or go into the gents or something. Leave, turn right into 5th Avenue and take another cab from there straight to the airport. We'll have someone watch you all the time to make sure you're not followed."
"You don't think that's likely do you?" a note of concern in Celleri's voice.
"Nah; just a precaution. The mob think you're six feet under now; worm bait."
"That sounds revolting," Celleri said, registering disgust.

With warm and affectionate embraces the two men separated as the taxi called to take Celleri on the first part of his journey to England. Sammy's massive horny hand engulfed the slimmer finer hand of Celleri and the firm handshake confirmed the bond of friendship which had sprung up between them.
"I'll call you," said Celleri, "when I've got something to tell you. Just to have a chat; tell you about my love life maybe."
"You should be so lucky," Sammy joked. "Take care of yourself."
A tear may have been forming in the 'hard as nails' Sammy's eye.

The cab moved away into the busy street, horns blowing as other cars had to slow down, letting it through. The plan had been made gradually over the last few days, discussing the pros and cons of the various options that had been thought through. Celleri's worry was that someone would recognise him, despite his considerably changed appearance. Sammy had tried to reassure him that he was as different as chalk from cheese following his accident and that there would be little risk that anyone would know him. But Celleri was frightened. He knew what the mob could and would do; if he was recognised, he was a dead man. That's why a complicated and devious route had been planned for his journey to the airport and his every move in New York would be monitored by Sammy's friends.

Booking in at Kennedy was routine. He travelled executive, giving him more space to stretch his long legs than the tourist class provided. Once aboard, he tried to rest but unsuccessfully; he was tense with excitement. The flight home, as he considered it to be, to England, was proving long and tiresome to him. To many, travelling eastward always affects their body clocks adversely and Celleri was beginning to feel the strain of his illness. His joints ached and the skin felt taut and unyielding over the bony points. His eyes were heavy with tiredness but his brain raced away, not allowing him any respite; the journey for Celleri couldn't end soon enough.

At Heathrow, the other passengers departing the plane outraced Celleri to the luggage carousel, but it made no difference; his was one of the first cases through. It was with considerable difficulty he managed to heave it on to a trolley and begin his slow passage through customs and to the outside world. The immigration officer merely glanced at him and his new passport as he entered a land he hadn't seen for more than twenty five years. Hesitantly, he searched the concourse for the Hertz car rental office where, by telephone some weeks earlier, he had arranged to hire a car; now he was here, he wanted to be mobile.

Inside the car the firm had included a map of the United Kingdom for tourists' use and Celleri checked the way he had to go. Motorways, only in the planning stages all those years ago were now blue lines spreading all over the place, like a spider's web, linking A to B and then on to C and so on, joining all the other letters of the alphabet. It was all so different. Adjusting the seat to suit his tall frame and tilting the mirror, he saw himself. He didn't like what he saw but he knew that Sammy was right; the injuries had made him almost unrecognisable. He needn't have worried; even he didn't recognise the face that looked back at him. He moved out of the airport car park slowly in the early morning sun, unused to driving on the left hand side of the road, looking for the signs which would take him westwards on to the M4. He had no plans to try to meet Meryl straightaway but he wanted to get closer to his home of years ago so he could spend some time getting to know the place better. He wanted to refresh his memories of his boyhood; they had been good days; alas, now so long ago.

Celleri drove along the motorway as far as exit 6 to Windsor, where he had arranged to stay at the Hilton. As far as he was concerned, it was central for all his needs, within a half an hour or so from Meryl's home and only a stone's throw from London. But all he wanted to do right now was to rest, as he had slept little overnight travelling the three and a half thousand miles, give or take a few, across the Atlantic. That was enough to tire most people, even when they were well. But after what he had been through, he was completely done in. He drove up to the main entrance and the doorman helped him unload his cases from the boot, taking them inside the hotel. Celleri parked his car himself, fairly near to the main entrance.

"How long do you plan to stay Mr Chaney?" asked the receptionist after she had looked at the card Celleri had filled in and checked it with his passport.

"I'm not very sure," he answered truthfully. "I'm almost certainly going to be here for a week or so, but I guess I'll be moving on then."

"Have you come sightseeing?"

"No, not exactly," he replied carefully. "I plan to look up my family tree. Look back into the past, see what I can find out."

"How interesting. Did your family come from hereabouts? Chaney doesn't sound a local name."

"I believe so. I've got a lot of work trying to find out."

"I hope you enjoy your stay Mr Chaney and good luck with your hunting. Room 147, on the first floor. Charlie," she called out to a youth standing near the doorway. "147; take Mr Chaney's cases; newspaper in the morning sir?"

"I'll have the Times please. Call me at seven thirty."

"Seven thirty it is sir, she replied gaily.

The young man summoned the minute lift and they both squeezed in with all the luggage as it started, only to stop almost at once as the gates opened automatically on the first floor.

"Just along here sir," the porter said, as he turned to the right along the corridor. By the time Celleri had caught up with him, he had unlocked the door and Celleri's suitcases had been lifted on to the stand ready for opening. The pound coin which Celleri presented him with was obviously all right.

"Thank you sir; any time. Just ask for Charlie; I'll be pleased to help."
"Thank you Charlie; I'll remember that."

All Celleri wanted to do once he had established himself in his room was to bathe away the tirednes of the journey and to lie down. His brain was a whirl and his arms and legs ached as if held in constrictive vices. He switched on the room television, catching the tail end of the news. 'The recession catches up with the oil producing states; as sales of oil have fallen dramatically over the last year, it is understood a businessman from the Middle East, (pictures appeared of an Arab dressed in a typical burnous), is planning to sell his portfolio of diamonds collected over many years. Considerable interest is reported to have been shown, including buyers from the United Kingdom.' Celleri watched the screen which changed, showing the outside of the Ritz Hotel, shoppers unaware of the cameras, passing by in the street. He looked again; that man leaving the hotel; 'Don't I know him? Yes, I thought I recognised him; it's Nick, Rosie's Nick. I wonder where she is?' Celleri continued to watch the screen, hoping she would come into view, but she didn't. 'I wonder if Nick is one of those interested in buying part of that collection?' The screen changed to another feature of the news and he was gone. 'I shouldn't be at all surprised to find out he would be keen to acquire those diamonds. He would have the contacts who would want them and who could get rid of them in the international market. I must remember to ask him.'

Celleri lay down partly dressed and within minutes was fast asleep. It wasn't until the early afternoon he awakened. He was hungry but refreshed from the jet-lagged feeling he had had when he arrived this morning. He rang the restaurant on the intercom and within a few minutes he had a snack of pizza and coffee brought up to him in his room. He ate it ravenously, not surprisingly really as he hadn't eaten much since he had left Sammy's place and that seemed ages ago. Once he'd eaten, he bathed and changed and prepared to drive towards Meryl's home, the other side of the M4. He had no plans to see her, but he wanted to recognise old haunts, to get the feel of things again; let nostalgia wash over him for a while after so long.

CHAPTER THIRTY

While Celleri had been travelling to Britain and getting to know again what being back in England was really like, Rosie and Nick were putting the finishing touches to the way they planned to carry out the scam. It had been Nick, Celleri had seen, picked up by the television cameras as he left the Ritz. He had made the first contact with the sheikh's relative's go-betweens, declaring his interest, showing his passport and banker's references, which by virtue of the sheikh's influence issued him with credits for twenty million pounds sterling. The vendors had been quite impressed and clearly considered Nick was the person to sell the collection to, though no one at this time had brought any of the items for sale out for viewing. That may happen on the next occasion or the next, but when dealing with Arabs, who knew when the trading would start? In between whiles, Rosie and Nick, in their other roles as Mr and Mrs Regale would have had to have carried out the switch. It was going to be a tight time table but given any luck at all, they could do it.

They had practised the scam a hundred times or so it seemed. They had worked in front of videos from all angles, wide-angled, close-ups, and lights so bright their make up had melted, something they hadn't thought about. The actual exchange of the zircon for the real diamond had proved easy for Rosie. That was no worry at all. The skills of her past had developed in her a sleight of hand which fooled Nick and Sly every time. The problem they faced now was how could they get the gem out of the room safely without getting caught, in the event of some guard or other having some funny ideas. They had to think of a way to escape detection, even if someone insisted on a body search. Neither Nick nor Rosie thought it likely, but Sly insisted they had a foolproof plan, just in case.

They had considered Rosie's suggestion that a button on her coat should be hollowed out, but the size of the stone made that difficult to do. Instead, Sly had come up with an idea the others couldn't find fault with. He had made Rosie a pendant out of paste, facetted like a large diamond itself. Though artificial, it was beautifully worked. At one end he had fitted a gold ring for its attachment to a chain and at the other end, there was another gold fitting, similar in appearance but it was able to rotate and in so doing, it allowed the pendant to separate into two identical halves, delicately hinged at that point. The inside of both halves had been shaped to form a space large enough to house the stolen diamond. It could then be closed and then locked by turning the gold fastener again. Inside the crystal pendant, the diamond would be quite invisible, even on close inspection. It was a delicate piece of engineering, typical of Sly's superb workmanship with gems; he had the feel for them. They had practised this manoeuvre on a number of occasions and now Rosie had it mastered, they were ready.

CHAPTER THIRTY-ONE

Celleri was confused by the multiplicity of road signs, signs and roads that hadn't been there all those years ago. He found driving in Britain now difficult. Back in the States, he had been ferried around by his men; rarely did he have to drive himself. But now, on his own and driving on the left-hand side of the road, something he had only just started to do when he had had to leave the country quickly nearly twenty-three years ago, he felt insecure, uncertain. Slowly, he made his way northwards towards his old home and to Meryl. Everything had changed. Nothing he thought he knew was anything like he remembered it. Villages were now large towns, sprawling urban developments, replacing the countryside he vaguely remembered. Blocks of flats towered over rows of housing, already shabby from neglect. But this had been his old home and now it had to be his new one.

His mind wandering, he had to brake sharply as he veered towards the wrong side of the road. Expletives from the other driver, the same ones as he had heard many years ago, shook him back into his new world.

'Concentrate Michael my boy,' he urged himself. 'That's if you want to remain all in one piece.'

He drove past Meryl's home. In a lay-by a little further along he stopped to look back at that which she had achieved. She had really made a success of her life, perhaps such a success she wouldn't be interested in seeing him again. But he'd never know that unless he tried. He knew he wanted to see her. Perhaps he could stop over for a coffee; maybe he'd see her in the hotel. She'd never recognise him, the way he looked now; perhaps, he wouldn't know her. But was he ready for that right now? Did he need more time to acclimatise? All these thoughts raced through his mind, leaving him with a sense of doom. Not today, but soon.

CHAPTER THIRTY-TWO

Nick and Rosie, now in their new guises as Mr and Mrs Mick Regale, using American addresses, had also made contact with the go-betweens, seeking plans to view the collection. After many telephone calls arranging visits which had then been cancelled by the Arabs, they were both doubtful whether they would ever have a chance to carry out the scam they had perfected. Each time the visit was called off, Sly had insisted they had carried out the switch, just as if it was the real thing. "Practice makes perfect," he said repeatedly. "You can't become too good."

They both would groan their disapproval but get on with the job until it was now so perfectly done, neither of them had any worries about the switch at all; it just came naturally.

With the morning post came a crisp white envelope, an impressed crest in the upper left hand corner. The design clearly indicated the origin was Middle Eastern.

"This is it," Nick exclaimed. "I bet it's our invitation to go and see those stones at last; sure took their time." He ripped open the letter. The notepaper was thick and hand woven, suggesting superlative quality. The letter was hand-written by a secretary indicating that as Mr Regale had shown an interest in the purchase of the diamonds, he was invited to call at the penthouse of the Ritz at noon tomorrow. That was all; polite but to the point.

"What did I tell you? We're in with a chance; tomorrow's the day." He reached for Rosie, holding her tightly around the waist. "Tomorrow, you'll do your stuff; tomorrow, we'll have it."

Punctual as was their custom, Nick and Rosie presented themselves at the Ritz hotel, this time fully disguised as Mr and Mrs Michael Regale from New York city. They had chosen Michael as the best name for Nick, just in case Rosie made the mistake of calling him Nick. It was felt that they would get away with correcting it to Mick if there were a need. Nick would not use Rosie's name at all, using an affectionate nickname and they had decided on Honey after the head of peroxide hair she would be sporting. In the foyer, the western-suited emissary of the sheikh's relative met them, bowing them effusively into the lift which would take them to the penthouse. There was no conversation on the way up, but they became aware of a distinct change in his behaviour. As they ascended quickly, he changed from being the obsequious servant and he began to behave as if he were a man of some importance. When the lift came to a halt, the doors opened smoothly. The exit of the lift was brightly lit, dazzling them. In front of the lift doors stood a guard, armed with an automatic weapon of some sort. Nick recognised it immediately as an Uzi, a gun he knew was commonly used by guards and protectors as well as terrorists and the underworld. Clearly, the meeting was to be well guarded.

They were ushered in to the vestibule at gun point, the barrel pressed cruelly into Regale's ribs; he knew it would be dangerous to make any fuss. All he could say was "Wadda ya'think you're doing?" remembering his fake American accent. Quickly and expertly, he was searched to ensure he was not carrying any weapon and it was all done before he could say anything else. His case was opened and the contents examined carefully before returning it to him. By that time Blondie had recovered her composure and the first words she uttered after their arrival in the penthouse were her squawked, "Hey, you get your hands off me," as she was pushed roughly after her husband.

"We can't be too careful can we?" replied the go-between, a slimy smile creasing his face. "It would be silly of us not to take all the precautions we think necessary, don't you agree?"

"Yeah, I guess so," said Regale. "But you keep your hands off my wife."

"I don't think we need to search her," the aide replied. "Will you follow me please?"

He walked from the hallway into the reception room, the doorways and windows protected by men dressed in Arab clothes, all standing alertly, ready for trouble should it arise.

In the centre of the room was a low table covered with a velvet cloth of royal purple. Around the table were four chairs and in between the chairs were four lamps, their spotlights directed on to the table top, where the light was brightest. The go-between waived his hand, inviting them to sit down, the two of them together, opposite him; the fourth chair remained empty. He clapped his hands and one of the Arab guards approached holding a casket of amboyna wood. He placed it almost reverentially on the table and retired.

"You have expressed an interest in the diamonds, particularly in the Geneva diamond as you have called it, the one acquired by my master a year ago at auction there."

"Yeah; he outbid me for it then."

"As you say. Well you know how much the stone cost then. What is it worth to you now I wonder? I might add, we've had a considerable

interest in this particular diamond."
"Yeah? Well the market's changing all the time. Let's take a gander at it again; maybe we can come to a deal." The go-between opened the box and took out the small chamois leather sack holding the diamond. Loosening the draw-string, he tipped the stone gently on to the velvet cloth. At once, under the bright lights, the loosened fire flashed around the table top. Honey was captivated at once by its beauty and Regale, who had considerable experience with stones of great value was equally overwhelmed with its exquisiteness. This was magic; this was what they had come to steal.

Regale reached into his brief case, withdrawing a small jeweller's scales, his loupe and a jeweller's callipers.
"It sure is a beautiful stone," he said as he pulled on a pair of fine cotton gloves. He took out his notebook, opening it at a page covered with figures, headed Geneva Diamond. Using the loupe, he examined its flawless appearance, but made no comment. Then using the callipers, he measured the maximum length of the stone and then its maximum width. Noting the measurements, he compared them with those already in the book. He frowned, checked the instrument and slowly made the assessment again. He erected the miniature jeweller's scales, adjusted the zero and weighed the stone. Again he readjusted the balance and repeated the measurement, noting the weight of the diamond to an accuracy of a fraction of a milligram.
"Pray; what are you doing?"
"I'm checking it out."
"But you know the provenance of the stone."
"That's true; but I'm damned if I'd pay a fortune for a stone without checking it out first against all the known facts. It's just as well I have. This is not the real thing. This is not what I call the Geneva Diamond."
The go-between rose quickly from his chair. "What do you mean it isn't the real thing? This is the diamond my master bought at the sale."
Remaining in his seat, Mick Regale said, "Well if it is, then he's been had. This is a good fake, but not good enough. You can see from my calculations it is more than a millimeter shorter and almost a millimeter less wide than the real stone is. Furthermore, it weighs 4.5 milligrams less than it should. It's a honey of a copy but I'm sorry, I'm not out to buy a fake. Any fool can have an imitation; it's the real McCoy that I'm after."
"But you can't be right. Since it was purchased it has been in the vault. No one has had access to it; even my master would have needed the second key from me before the safe can be opened."

"Perhaps the guy you bought it from pulled a fast one on you. Maybe he made a substitution after the sale; maybe this is the stone you bid for. I don't know, but it sure isn't the diamond I came to buy."
Michael Regale replaced the instruments of his trade in his case alongside his notebook of information. As far as he was concerned, the meeting was over.

While he had been talking, the owner of the diamond had come into the room quietly and unobserved. He had heard all that had been said. Controlling his feelings he approached the table on which the stone lay, now ignored.
"You are an expert?" he enquired of Regale. The go-between sprang to his feet, bowing towards the newcomer.
"I sure am when it comes to investing a lot of money on a stone I would like to own. 'Fraid this one's a phoney." said Regale, looking up at the Arab.
"What do you suggest I do about it now," the Arab asked him.
"I really don't know. That's your problem. You could approach the auctioneers and find out exactly how the stone came to the sale. They should be able to help, they'd have all the details. You might have to squeeze them a little; threaten them with adverse publicity or something. They'll tell you what you want to know. After all, their commission was nearly a million."
"Would you undertake to do that for me? Naturally I would pay for your services, provide you with all the necessary documents and authority to undertake the enquiry."
"That's real nice of you, but no, I'm sorry; that's not my kinda job. I can't find the time to hunt the diamond, so to speak. It may take months."
"For a hundred thousand dollars?"
"That sure is a lot of money. I'll need time to think about it."
"Yes, do. Ring me here when you've had time to consider my offer."
"Yeah, thanks. Well there's nothing to keep us now. Mrs Regale and I'll be on our way." Regale picked up his case and shaking the hand offered by the Arab, he and Honey left the penthouse suite.

"Well then; tell me what was wrong with it?" urged Rosie just as soon as they were inside the taxi taking them back to their base where they could change back to being Nick and Rosie again.
"It was a copy all right but not nearly as good as the one Sly made for us to swap. Clearly someone has changed it over before we had a chance to see it. Whether it's an inside job or whether he was sold a

pup in the first place, I can't say, but it's a dummy alright."
"What are you going to do? Will you work for him?"
"No, of course not. I'm no investigator. In any case, if I plan to swap the diamond, I need to work alone, not for him. But I know where we're going to start; with Sly. He knows everything about diamonds; he can smell them."

They changed taxis three times, walked through a large department store as well before getting back to their base and getting out of their disguises. Nick had thought it necessary to take all these precautions to minimise the possibility of avoiding detection. Just one slip up and they could be facing death. Nick had no illusions about it; he knew the enemy. Only by careful planning could they outwit the opposition; there was a lot at stake.

CHAPTER THIRTY-THREE

Once they were back, Sly demanded they told him all that had happened at the penthouse suite. Nick reported faithfully all that had occurred.
"So where d'you think the real stone is now?" asked Nick.
"I would guess it is in the safe of the guy who was selling it in the first place. He probably pulled a con on the Arab who bought it, switching the fake after the sale somehow or other. If it's not there, then it could be anywhere, especially if he got rid of it to somebody else."
"How are we going to find out?"
"What d'you mean, we? The best thing we can do now is forget all about it. Either that or you take up his offer and start trying to find out where it is legitimately."
"You mean give up after all our planning? No chance," Nick said. "If the diamond is still with the previous owner, then somehow I'm going to find it, make the switch and then we can forget all about it."
"You sure make life difficult," murmured Sly. "The ex-owner was a Spanish count; lives in Barcelona. I hear it gets rather hot there this time of year but it'd be a nice place for a holiday for you and Rosie. I'll come along too if Rosie needs a chaperone."
"No, I think I can manage some things without you. What d'you think Rosie? Like a holiday in Spain?"
"You try and keep me away," she blurted out; she'd been silent for a long time, listening to the old warriors working things out.

"Suppose Sly's right and the diamond is in this count's safe, somewhere in Barcelona, how on earth are we going to get it out and away?"
"With difficulty I'd say," replied Sly. "But everything can be done if planned properly. Find the guy, find the house, find the safe, know what sort of safe it is and what the alarm is and bingo; we'll have the diamond before you know it."
"Is that all?" enquired Rosie."I thought it might be difficult."
"And if we substitute the zircon for the real thing, no one, not even the owner will ever know the switch has been made, that I can guarantee. One other thing. If we're going to do it, we'd better get on with it quickly, just in case the Arab has any ideas about trying himself," Sly added.
"Yes, I hadn't thought about that. Don't know how he'd go about it though."
"In exactly the same way we will, though with less finesse. I would think he would be prepared to use force and someone may get killed, like the count maybe."
"I don't think we'll steal it," Nick said. "At least, we'll not break in and steal it as you suggested. I think we'll use a little psychology; make him worried; let him sweat a bit and then offer him a way out, one he'll probably jump at. I've just an idea flitting round my head but I'm sure it'll work. Where d'you think the count is right now?"
"He has the reputation of being something of a gambler. He's rarely at home; spends a lot of time visiting the casinos around Europe. I can make a few telephone calls; maybe someone will know where he is."
"Do that Sly. I think we'll go and have a chat with our count. Ask him a few pertinent questions like 'where is the diamond now?'"

Nick and Rosie were high with the tension of the planned visit to Spain and the scam, but she was unusually quiet in the taxi that took them back to Nick's apartment. She had noticed a small muscle around the left hand side of Nick's mouth was twitching, as if he were worrying about what was going to happen.
"What are you thinking Nick?"
"It's going to be tricky; a bit more difficult than we had planned. It would have been a piece of cake to have made the switch as we'd practised it, but I've got a gut feeling someone's going to get hurt. I don't know what I'd do if it were you Rosie. I think you should stay here, in London, Rosie; it'd be safer."
"Don't say things like that Nick; don't even think of it. We're in this together. Nothing's going to happen, you wait and see. Tell me how you think Sly will be able to help?"

"He's got lots of contacts, some of them legit and others on the fringes. He'll be able to get in touch with some of them quickly. You'd be surprised what information there is just for the asking. Someone will know whether the count is at home and if not, where he is and when he's due back."

He took Rosie in his arms, gently lifting her face to his. "Given the rest of our lives together, there's such a lot for you to find out about me and for me to know about you; that's why I think you should stay home."

"Nick; I do love you so. I don't know whether I would want to go on living without you."

"You will." He kissed her gently on the mouth, Rosie responding with a ferocity he hadn't expected.

"When Sly rings in the morning, he may well have all the gen we need."

"Well, we mustn't waste any time then must we?" Rosie said cheekily guiding Nick towards the bedroom.

"I think we should both have a clear head in the morning," Nick joked.

"I can't think of any better way of clearing the mind, can you?"

"You're a hopeless case Rosie; quite beyond recall, I'm pleased to say."

Nick and Rosie's flight with Iberian airways from Heathrow to the El Prat de Llobregat airport at Barcelona was quick and easy, taking less than two hours and their passage through customs was smooth without any hiccup. The cool marble floors reflected the bright sunlight outside and the airy hallways, still in pristine state following the major changes which took place prior to the Olympics held there a few years ago brought a gasp of surprise from Rosie.

"They must employ an army of cleaners to keep it looking so immaculate. No dirt or debris on the floors; no graffiti; it looks just like a palace," whispered Rosie. Only the Spanish police, with their funny hats and their grey, badly-fitting uniforms, which seemed to be held together only by the leather webbing of their Sam Browne's and their holster belts, looked out of place in such an attractive first impression. Nick made his way to the Hertz car rental, followed by Rosie, still gazing around open-mouthed at her surroundings.

"It really is a super airport Nick; it's so clean. I've never seen anywhere quite like this."

"They did a first class job for the Games. Let's hope they can keep it looking good. Bona tarda," he said smilingly to the young lady in charge of the office. Hesitantly he continued, "Quisiera alquilar un coche, hagael favor de incluir el seguro a todo riesgo, por favor."

"I didn't know you spoke Spanish," Rosie grinned, "even though it does sound a bit funny."
"Of course you can hire a car sir and congratulations on speaking in Catalan. Do you have any particular model in mind? We have everything from a small Seat to a Merc."
"Oh, it's such a relief you speak English," Nick sighed. "I learned that from a phrase book; after that I'm afraid I'm stumped. I'll take something from the middle of the range, say a Peugeot 405, something like that."
"For how long do you want the car?" the assistant asked. Nick hesitated. Looking at Rosie, he said, "What d'you think? Shall we have it for a week?"
"We could see the sights in that time; and after all, our work may not be completed before then. I should think, at least a week."
Settling the account, Nick asked, "Will there be a good road map in the car?"
The car hire lady reached beneath the desk and brought out a large map of Barcelona, opening it for him to see.
"I'll have the car brought round to the exit for you straight away."
She moved away into the back of the office, leaving Nick and Rosie to study the plan of the city together.

It took them some minutes to get orientated, but after a few moments Nick said, "there's the Diagonal. Do you remember Sly had found out the count's home was on the west end of the Avinguda Diagonal; it cuts right across the city. It must be over five miles long."
Further discussion was halted as the young lady arrived with the car keys and invited Nick to check things over with her.
"It seems fine," Nick said.
"I hope you enjoy your stay here; we think ours is a lovely city," she replied. "May I wish you a safe journey."

Slowly and carefully, Nick eased his way out of the airport, facing the confusion of road signs.
"I never find this driving on the right side of the road easy," he said.
"Why it can't all be standardised and everybody drive on the same side as we do I'll never know."
"You mean everyone should change for us Brits; I can see that happening."
"It's still a pity we're not all the same. Rosie, check the map; see if you can find the road the hotel Claris is in."
After some time Rosie muttered, "I do wish you'd keep this blessed car still. I've found it several times only to loose it when the car hits a

bump. There's a Carrer de Pau Claris which runs between the Diagonal and the GranVia. I expect it will be there; the only problem now will be the one-way street systems. It looks pretty straightforward otherwise."
"That's my girl; oozing confidence."

It took them nearly half an hour to find the hotel, which fortunately had a curved bay into which Nick could park the car. The doorkeeper advanced through the rotating door. He was huge, tall and fat and as black as the ace of spades. He summoned a bellboy to give Nick a hand with their cases and after registration, they were whisked up to their room on the third floor. The punched card which replaced the key opened the door. The room was floored with dark hardwood. There were no carpets or rugs and the tables and cupboards and fitted wardrobes were all made of this deep red-brown wood rather like mahogany; it was very impressive.
"We should be very comfortable here I think," Rosie heard Nick say.
"Now you remember what we've come to do; you concentrate on that Nick Royle."
"But not all the time surely," whispered Nick as he caught her around the waist.
"Well, not all the time," she replied, turning within his embrace. Kissing him lightly. "I'm sure we'll find time for something. What's the plan now?"
"We'll unpack first and then I thought, as we've had no exercise today sitting in a plane, we'd walk from here to the Plaça Catalunya, it's not that far. And if you're not too tired, we'll stroll down La Rambla towards the port."
"What's La Rambla?"
"It's the centre of Barcelona's life. When you walk in La Rambla you're aware of the whole character of Barcelona."
"How come you know so much about the place, never having been here before?"
"Sly and I had a job to do here many years ago. We didn't stay long; little more than a long weekend but we did have a chance to see some of the sights while we were here. I can remember some of them but it was a long time ago."
"What did you come for then?" asked Rosie.
"We were the escort to some of our political bigwigs. They'd come to meet an Israeli with atomic secrets he wanted to sell. My country wanted to buy, so we came along as protection."
"Is that how you got to know Sammy?"
"Not then; later. He was part of their security set up. He had to try to stop the meeting, but his outfit arrived too late. We got to know each

other when we were able to help them with something else they were concerned with here; that's when we became friends."
"Tell me more," Rosie asked.
Nick hesitated. "Sammy saved my life then." was all he said.

CHAPTER THIRTY-FOUR

As they walked along the Passeig de Gracia, gazing in the many boutiques, shops selling high class leather goods and other luxuries and the innumerable book shops, Nick pointed out the house on the other side of the road, painted an unusual shade of blue, extravagantly designed by Gaudi.
"Even these pink and turquoise odd-shaped tiles in the pavement you're walking on were planned by him," Nick indicated.
"How strange," Rosie commented. "I can't say I like the house. Look, those carvings are bones in the leg and there's a joint where the two come together. I don't like it at all. It's bizarre," she added.
"I agree. You either like his work or you hate it. I never thought it was up to much. In fact I find it strange that he had any support to start the building. You wait 'till you see the cathedral he began, La Sagrada Familia. You've never seen anything like that."
The fountains pulsed in the square, crowded with the young and the old, the scruffy and the chic, many sitting but most milling around, the women carrying red roses, all gradually making their way to La Rambla. From the heat of the square, they entered the cool shade of the tree lined boulevard, jostling with the crowds, all slowly making their way to the port. Bookshops, flower stalls and shops selling caged birds lined the street; it was all so different from any British town or city. Rosie walked in a sort of dream state, looking at everything, not wanting to miss anything.
"It's cruel the way they have all those tiny birds caged in such a small space. I'd like to come along and open all the doors and let them fly away," Rosie said. The birds were creating quite a din with their song, flying distressingly within the confines of their cages.
"Don't try it will you, otherwise you may end up in another sort of cage; a Spanish prison cell," Nick said. "The birds don't seem to be too upset."
"But look at those larger birds; those macaws and parakeets cramped in those tiny cages; that can't be right."
"Mmm. I must say they look pretty tatty. That one's got alopecia or what ever they call it when a bird's feathers drop out." The parrot really did look sick.

It seemed no time at all before they were on the front of Barcelona, gazing up at the statue of Columbus, his outstretched arm pointing the way to the New World.

"There's the cable car crossing the harbour," Nick pointed out to Rosie. "Must be a super view from there I should think. We must find time to do that."

"Yes, I'd like that. I wonder how you'd get up there?" Rosie asked.

"I'm not sure but it seems to start at that tall pylon over there. I believe they call that part Barcelonetta. It ends across the water on the mountainside at Montjuic. Yes, we certainly must give that a go."

They continued their walk along the sea's edge, looking at the menus in the doorways of the many restaurants along the promenade, one of which had a huge model lobster on the roof.

A small band played from a dais erected close to the sea wall and the plaintive melody, repeated over and over again was clearly of North African origin. In front of the band, a circle of children, boys as well as girls, all dressed in national costume and holding hands, danced the sardana, a slowly progressive dance that appeared to go on for ever. Clearly they were all enjoying themselves in the late afternoon sun, even the musicians, perspiring with their effort. The sea breeze ruffled their hair as they walked on, passing close to the harbour's edge, Nick looking longingly at the expensive yachts moored against the wall.

"I've always had a yen to own a boat," Nick said.

"One like this," Rosie said, pointing out a huge sleek motor yacht flying the Spanish flag at the stern.

"Why not? One can always dream. But no, not really. I'd like to have a sailing boat and not have to rely on an engine. We could cruise the Med, calling in at all the beauty spots, Cannes, Nice and all the exciting harbours in Italy, before the islands of the Adriatic and Greece; on to the Turkish coastline, down to Israel and then back along the North African coast. Now I'd really like to do that. It would take a year or more I expect."

"Well then Nick Royle, let's get this business finished and we can bear it in mind for the future."

"You mean, you'd like that too?"

"I sure would. I'd have you all to myself for months on end. I guess I would know you pretty well after that."

"You're some woman Rosie. Do y'know, I'm so glad I met you. When I saw your mother the other day, she said to me as I was getting into the car, 'Don't hurt her Nick.' I told her then I wanted to marry you. Once we get back to England, would you give it your consideration Rosie?"

Rosie stopped and turned to Nick, her arms lightly around his neck.
"I don't need to wait until we get back home Nick; the answer's yes. I want to marry you too. I'm very much in love with you."
Gently, yet passionately, the two sealed their love with a kiss for all the world to see; all the world in Barcelona that is.

The Restaurante Los Caracoles was heaving with the night life of Barcelona. It didn't look as if Nick and Rosie could possibly be fitted into the crowd of customers, but as soon as the patrone saw how beautiful Rosie looked, there was no hesitation; he found a table for the two of them in a quiet corner of the room. But the noise of the people in the cafe talking, together with waiters calling to each other and the wandering band of minstrels and singers strolling around made easy conversation difficult. But tonight there was no need for talk. They were a couple obviously so much in love, all they wanted to do was to hold each other's hands as they looked into each other's eyes. The minstrels noticed them quickly and were soon around their table, serenading them both. It took a high denomination note to get them to move on.

The meal was superb.
"I really did enjoy that Nick; had you been there before?"
"Yes; that was one of the good things I remember."
"What do you plan to do now we're here?" asked Rosie. "You will be careful Nick won't you? I don't know what I would do without you now. As the song goes, 'I've grown accustomed to your face'."
"Don't worry; I'll take care. I'm expecting a fax from Sly in the morning. It will give as much guidance as we need; well, I hope it will anyway."
"Is it safe to have a fax sent so that anyone can read it, especially if the contents may link you later to the diamond?"
"A good question Rosie. You must wait 'till you see the fax tomorrow; perhaps it will be quite unintelligible, even to you."
"I don't understand."
"It'll be in code. An easy to break code by experts but not by a hotel receptionist. You wait and see. It's a system Sly and I have used before. It's worked okay in the past; it should do here too."

The Claris was dead when they got back to the hotel. The restaurant was empty and the barman leaned lazily on his counter, shiny from the innumerable times he had run his cloth over the unmarked bar. The tapas remained uneaten; the ash trays were empty.
"Not many customers in tonight," Nick remarked.

The barman shrugged his shoulders as he wiped another imaginary speck of dust away. “Business very bad,” he replied. “Nobody has any money.”
“The recession?” Nick asked.
“Si; the recession.”
Nick shrugged his shoulders. “Bona nit.” The barman’s eyes brightened momentarily hearing Nick’s parting in Catalan.
“Bona nit, senor.”

As Nick and Rosie were about to sit down to breakfast one of the reception staff presented Nick with a sealed envelope.
“Excuse me sir, this fax arrived for you during the night,” she said.
“This is what I’ve been waiting for,” he said. “All the details that Sly has been able to find out about the count will be inside. Let’s hope there’s enough to proceed safely.” He put it on one side, unopened.
“Aren’t you going to look at it straight away?” Rosie asked.
Nick passed the fax to her. “Go on; open it,” he said. Rosie tore the envelope open and withdrew the sheet of paper. It was covered with a lot of letters which were quite unintelligible; it was gibberish.
“I told you it would be in code. It’ll take a while to translate it into something we can understand, so eat your breakfast up first; there’s plenty of time.” Reluctantly, Rosie continued her meal, but inside, she was dying to get to grips with the contents of the message.

They took the lift back to their room and Nick took out from his case a sheet of paper on which he wrote all the letters of the alphabet vertically on one side. About a centimetre to the side of this column of letters, he wrote the alphabet out again but this time he started at the bottom of the sheet, so that opposite Z he had written A, opposite Y was B and so on. Once he had completed that he looked at the fax again.

YZZH: SLFHV: XZHZ NLWVIMZ, XLIMVI WRZTLMZO/ HZIIZ,
MLIGS HRWV.
LDMVI ZDZB N. XZIOL: HVVM BVHGVIWZB DRGS TFZIWH
AG XZHRML: SLFHVPVVKWI LMOB:
HZUV: XSZGHDLIGS: XLNYRMZGRLM OLXP: MLG PLMDM:
ZOZIN: MLG PMLDM
HVXFIRGB: MLG PMLDM: YZXPFK 9089636
HLIIB: H.
Slowly and patiently, Nick translated the coded fax so that they both could understand what Sly had sent to them.
BAAS: HOUSE: CASA MODERNA, CORNER DIAGONAL/
SARRIA NORTH SIDE.

OWNER AWAY MONTE CARLO
SEEN YESTERDAY AT CASINO WITH GUARDS.
HOUSEKEEPER ONLY.
SAFE: CHATWORTH COMBINATION LOCK. NOT KNOWN.
ALARM NOT KNOWN.
SECURITY NOT KNOWN. BACKUP 3630191
SORRY
SLY

"Well that's the lot. We know the count's not there and his strong-arm men aren't there either." As he was speaking, Nick burned the fax and the translation and ground the charred remains into dust. Moving to the bathroom, he flushed the ash down the lavatory; the evidence had all gone.

"Let's go and see where the count lives and after that, I think we'll both take a trip to Monte Carlo. I quite fancy a turn on the wheel. You much of a gambler Rosie?"

"I think I can read the odds as well as the next. You know, I might just come in handy."

"D'you now? You might just do that," Nick joked.

They descended to the ground floor, crossed the marble floored hall, passed through the revolving doors to the street outside, where their car awaited them. Nick took the wheel and drove towards the Plaça de les Glories Catalanes, turning sharp left into the eastern end of the Avinguda Diagonal. This tree-lined avenue slices across the city blocks as far as the hills. The part that Nick had entered was the business district with many light industries, but as he drove along, the buildings changed to the luxury hotels and shops and expensive restaurants and discotheques, which provided the showcase for its modern architecture.

"Look at that wall of glass," Nick exclaimed.

"You can see the clouds reflected in it. Spectacular but not nearly as outstanding as those skyscrapers in New York," Rosie added.

"No, but it always worries me how they stay up."

They missed the Avenguda Sarria the first time they passed it, there were so many other things to see. Nick turned right into the Gran Via de Charles III, and rather to his surprise, within a hundred metres, the road they were seeking was on their right. Nick drove along the avenue slowly and where the road intersected with the Diagonal, he pulled in to the side.

"Let's have a walk around; find out which of these houses is the

Count's." Rosie joined him on the pavement and linking her arm through his, they strolled along the pavement.
"There it is," Rosie announced after a moment. "There, just as Sly's info said. Right on the corner."
"Well now we know where it is I think we'll forget all about it for the time being and find the quickest way to the casino. If the Count's still there we'll see if we can twitch his tail at the tables."

CHAPTER THIRTY-FIVE

Within an hour, Nick and Rosie, now as Mr and Mrs Regale, were ready for their trip to Monte Carlo. They looked the typical middle-aged brassy American couple with more money than manners; more bucks than taste.
"Just as well you brought something you could wear at the casino over that inflatable body suit of yours?" Nick said laughingly.
"Yes; I thought I might need a suitable cocktail dress."
"Fortunately, I brought a tuxedo. If we're to meet the Count at the casino it would be as well to look the part. If we're going to talk in millions, we should at least look as if we have that sort of money rather than look like a couple of country bumpkins."
"You said you were formulating some sort of plan; are you ready to talk it over yet?"
"Yes, I think so. We'll play the same tables as he does and I hope we'll be winning while he's having a losing streak. Sometime during the play, I will refer to the fact that he was the owner of the Geneva diamond as we shall call it. That should stir things up a bit and then we'll see how it goes afterwards. If we can keep him on edge we may be able to suggest something to him his greed won't be able to resist. We'll have to play it by ear a bit."
"It's a bit vague but I don't suppose one can plan anything more definite until we meet him and see what sort of man he is."
"No, I think you're right. I believe if somehow I mention the diamond to him, that's very likely to unnerve him, especially if he's having a bad night. Let's hope so."

Nick had calculated there'd likely be a direct flight to Nice and as luck would have it, there were seats on one leaving in a couple of hours. They booked in, checked their luggage and settled down to relax for a while. They had been on the go, without any break since breakfast and both were feeling hungry and slightly the worse for wear.

"Wake me up if I drop off Rosie, would you?"
"I will, if I'm awake," she smiled.

The flight was announced and shortly after, they were winging their way eastwards over the border to Nice, Less than an hour later they were hiring a car from the Hertz rental at the airport.
"I wonder, do you know where we'll be able to find a hotel in Monte Carlo," Regale was enquiring of the agent.
"This time of year it's all fairly crowded but there's nearly always some vacancies in the large hotels. Shall I try the Hotel de Paris for you Mr Regale?"
"That would be kind of you; do you mind?"
"Not at all; it's a pleasure to be of service sir."
It took only a few minutes and the Regales had their accommodation arranged for them.
"Enjoy your stay in Monaco," the agent added as they prepared to drive away.

Once established in their hotel they rested a while, as though the night was still young and they wanted to get along to the casino as soon as they could, they knew there was little object getting there before the Count arrived and they were going to need clear heads to accomplish their plan.
"I think we'll go about eleven," Nick suggested.
"That's okay by me," replied Rosie. "I think I'll have a bath; it'll wake me up."
"Oh, it will, will it," Nick said."Perhaps I'll come too. We can get aroused together."
"Awakened, I said, not aroused. But come to think of it, it's not a bad idea."

They made love, they bathed together and rested until the time came to prepare to leave for the casino. Mr and Mrs Regale in their evening wear were a different couple from those of the daytime. They were still dowdy and frumpish but at least they did appear to have a bit of life in them.
"You look swell Honey," Nick drawled in his ersatz American accent.
"Gee Mick, thanks; you don't look so bad yourself," Rosie drawled back, as she adjusted his bow tie. "I sure picked a swell guy when I chose you." In her normal voice she said, "It's awfully hot in this contraption," referring to her inflatable undergarment. "I hope the air conditioning is working in the casino or I'm going to boil."
"Remember Rosie. If you feel faint or anything wrong, don't stay

there; we'll have to leave. Our disguises are good but not that good."
"I understand all right. Remember, I've got more beneath my bodice to be discovered than you. Poor Count. I feel sorry for him really; he doesn't know what's going to happen to him."

As they entered the casino they were aware immediately of the myriad lights in the glittering chandeliers, the smell of cigar smoke wafting through the open doors and the noise of the one-armed bandits, chattering their benefits to a lucky winner. The murmur of voices, some raised in laughter, others worrying away their losses, were quietly blurred by the recurring, mesmeric, 'Rien ne va plus.'
Walking up to the caisse, Nick asked the cashier, "Dix Mille francs, s'il vous plait." He placed the ten thousand francs on the front of the grill and in return was given the chips.
"How much is that?" Rosie asked.
"Something over a thousand pounds sterling. Consider it an investment. Let's go and see where the man we're looking for is."
"D'you know what he looks like?" Rosie asked. "You know, I hadn't given it a thought. I've no idea who he could be."
From his inside pocket, Nick withdrew a photograph.
"Sly gave me that before we came away. It's a copy he got from somewhere. I don't know how old it is, he didn't either. But it's all we've got. I expect it'll do. If not, we'll just have to ask someone."

They made their way towards the roulette wheels on the far side of the casino, looking at those playing, while trying not to stare. Rosie stopped short, nudging Nick gently. He turned towards her.
"Isn't that him there?" she said under her breath, twisting slightly towards a table on her left.
"Good girl, Rosie; I believe you're right. Watch the play for a while and then start yourself. Try to get opposite him so he can see both of us but you especially."
"And less of the Rosie. I'm Honey or Blondie; remember?"
"You sure are Hon."
As a space came at the table, Rosie edged in, almost across the green from the count.
"Faites vos jeux."
All around the table, punters placed their bets. Those with systems had piles here, there and everywhere. Others had their stacks of chips on their lucky numbers and the conservative betted on the red or on the black. Within a few seconds the baize was covered with hundreds of thousands of francs of chips.
"Rien ne va plus," intoned the croupier as he twisted the wheel and

popped in the ball, which rotated in a contrary direction. Backs straightened, just for a moment while those who had bet waited for the ball to stop bouncing around, jumping from one number to the next and was still.
"Rouge; trente," the croupier called, at the same time scraping away all those chips not on or related to number thirty. The Count had lost that time, but not his nerve as he placed his bets for the next turn of the wheel. Rosie watched him as she placed her chip for a thousand francs on the next square. He looked across at her but for a moment only. He just wanted to know who was placing a bet close to his, even a small bet; his stake was for ten thousand francs. The wheel spun, the ball jumped about again, trying to find a place which would have it.
"Rouge, quatorze."
"Gee, I've won first time," Rosie cried.
"Well done Honey; I knew you could do it," drawled Nick. "Remember what you learned at the Green Baize. Use the system."
The croupier looked uncomfortable. He didn't like anyone to win, least of all someone who had just arrived at his table and was reputed to have a system. He looked up to see if his supervisor was near.
"Come on," snarled the Count. "Pay the woman and clear the table."
The croupier complied with his demand and prepared the table for the next round.

This time, the Count waited for Rosie to place her bet first and then he chose another number, nearby, as if he had been going to use the same square as Rosie but he wasn't going to be seen to follow anyone.
"Rouge, vingt-six."
"Yoohoo; it's my lucky night," Rosie cried. Most of those around the table congratulated Rosie, but the Count's face remained glowering. He did not share in the praise Rosie was getting.
"What d'you say Count, didn't she do well?" Nick admonished him from across the table from behind Rosie. "How about some blackjack? Now I'd like to challenge you on the cards. How about it?"
The Count hesitated. "My pleasure," he replied. "You're right, the wheel is not as friendly tonight as I would like." He proffered his cigar case to Nick who declined the offer with a polite shake of the head. He picked up his balloon of brandy and joined him around the table, extending his hand.
"You called me Count. Have we met before?"
"Not exactly. I'm Mick Regale." Nick shook the Count's outstretched hand.
"We both attended the auction of that beautiful diamond last year at

Geneva; a lovely gem that. I've always called it the Geneva diamond since then."

"I sold the stone at that auction, that's true, but I did not attend the sale, so we couldn't have met then."

"No? I can't say then. I guess someone must have pointed you out somewhere. What happened to that stone? I know I bid for it but it went for more than I wanted to pay."

"An Arab bought it. Someone related to a sheikh or something I believe."

"Is that so? That's strange. I was invited by an Arab to buy a stone just like the Geneva diamond last week. I went along to his hotel in London, but what he tried to sell me was a fake. What d'you think about that? He tried to sell Mick Regale a fake."

"Did you tell him it was a fake?"

"I sure did. He was a bit upset. He wanted to employ me to find the real thing. I told him I couldn't find the time to do that."

"Then what?"

"He asked where I thought the stone could be now?"

"And how did you answer him?" There was a hint of nervousness in the Count's voice as he brushed his handkerchief over his moist brow.

"I told him either the auctioneers had switched the diamond, which was unlikely, or someone in his pay had cheated him, or maybe you still had the real diamond."

"Me have the diamond? How could I possibly have it still? You must be crazy to have suggested that to him. What say he takes you seriously and comes after me. He might kill me." The count was clearly upset.

"He sure was mad enough to kill you when I left him. I told him it was extremely unlikely you still had the diamond."

"I should think so."

"Do you?"

"Do I what?"

"Still have the diamond."

"Don't be so stupid. And even if I did, do you think I'd tell you?"

"Well, I tell you what Count," Nick said quietly. "If you do, let me know. I'll give you six million pounds for it, all in untraceable small notes, no more questions asked."

"But it sold for nine million."

"But that sale was legitimate." The Count paused to consider Mick's proposition. "Do you mean if I sell the stone to you now for six million pounds, you'll get this guy off my back and then hopefully, there won't be any more problems?"

"I can't guarantee the result. I can put it about that I've heard someone else may have the diamond. But one thing I know, unless you do, you're in for a rough ride. Life is cheap in the Middle East. Think about it."

"I've thought all I need to. Six million you said; sterling? Yes, I do still have the diamond; it's at my home in Barcelona. If you can get across there tomorrow, maybe we can do business."

"We sure can," Nick replied.

"Here's my card; give me a ring when you arrive. I'll expect you some time tomorrow afternoon."

"You understand Count. I don't carry that sort of money around with me and as I've already been shown a dud diamond, I'll want to confirm what I'm buying is the real thing first. I'll bring my gear with me and check the stone against the provenance. If it's okay, then I'll have the money in Barcelona in twenty-four hours. How does that sound to you?"

"That sounds fair to me. Till we meet tomorrow then."

The two men shook hands and the Count left the gaming room.

Rosie who had been listening to their conversation without interruption now turned to Nick.

"Seems a nice enough guy," Nick said.

"But what if he's not such a nice guy. What if he gets you to his home and kidnaps or kills you? You're the only one who knows he still has the diamond; all he has to do is get rid of you and he keeps it. It's an awful risk Nick."

"Yes, there is a risk, but we'll just have to bluff it out. I'll have to persuade him I'm only part of a syndicate. Make sure he realises others will know where I am and what I'm about. But you are right; it is a bit risky."

"Perhaps we'd better go now and get some sleep. You're going to need your wits about you tomorrow," Rosie advised.

"Let's spend your winnings first. I'd prefer blackjack but we'll stick with roulette if you'd rather."

"I'd like to have a go at blackjack; isn't it rather like pontoon? I've played a fair amount of that in college. Come on, let's both have a fling."

The Count had gone; Nick's news had concerned him enough for him to leave rather quickly. Nick and Rosie walked over to the dealer and looked at a few hands being played before they took over the vacant chairs. Nick watched Rosie. She handled her cards professionally. Though he was sitting next to her, he was unaware of

the cards she held. She bet with certainty and to his surprise she began to win. At first, the bets she placed were small and the winnings were small, but as she continued, her betting became more confident and the larger her bet, the greater her winnings became. Within a short while, Rosie had accumulated a not inconsiderable pile of chips in front of her.
"We're supposed to be losing your winnings not making more," Nick commented. His pile of chips had diminished markedly and his next bet would probably be his last.
"I'll bail you out," Rosie said cheekily. "Any time you want some chips, you come to your Honey; she'll look after you."

Nick lost.
"Let's go Hon," he said loudly in his fake American accent.
"Oh gee, Mick; I'm winning. Can't we stay a little longer?" Rosie responded, also in her artificial accent. "You always wanna go just when I'm having a good time."
"We've a lot to do tomorrow. Pack it in now and go and cash your chips, there's a good girl."
The ten thousand francs Nick had changed when they came had now increased substantially. The cashier paid out twenty-two thousand, two hundred and fifty francs to Rosie. Nick leaned across and tossed the odd two hundred and fifty francs to him.
"Merci monsieur; bon soir."
"Bon soir. Nous nous sommes bien amuses."

They collected their car from the garage and returned to their hotel, a pair of tired but excited gamblers, still on a high.
"I did enjoy myself tonight," Rosie said. "Brought back memories of sessions of pontoon in the students' club; haven't played at all since then, but it all came back. I think that dealer was glad to see us go; well, me go. I was the only one winning."
"You played very well Rosie; you had the cards too mind you. You can't win without the cards."
"But you have to know what to do with them when you've got them," she said.
"True, and I must say you did. Our investment in meeting the Count paid off handsomely with a nice profit. Let's hope the rest of our business with him is equally profitable. We'll fly back to Barcelona in the morning."
"What if there isn't a convenient flight?" asked Rosie.
"Well, you've won enough tonight to hire a plane privately. I'm sure we'll be able to work something out."

"And do you have a plan when we get there?"
"No, but we will let the back-up team know what we're doing and when. That way we'll be covered should the Count turn nasty. I don't think he will though."
"But we can't afford to take any chances."
"You're absolutely right Rosie; we can't and we won't."
Sleep was a long time coming. Life together was exciting; never a dull moment.
"God, I'm in love with that girl," dreamed Nick.
"We made such a handsome couple even in our disguises. Just think what a pair we'll be when we're together normally," mused Rosie.

CHAPTER THIRTY-SIX

Nick was awake bright and early after only a few hours sleep, leaving Rosie mewing gently, still fast asleep, lightly rolled in the sheet on her side of the bed. Her auburn hair tumbled over the pillow and where the sheet had fallen away, the smooth waxy skin of her breast attracted his attention. He bathed and shaved and dressed and then sat quietly for a while, thinking carefully of the likely plan for the day. There was a risk and a not inconsiderable one, but with the back-up team he knew had been arranged, the risk seemed to be negligible. The one thing he knew he mustn't let happen was for them to become separated at all. Together, he felt sure he could bluff his way through anything, but if they were apart for any reason, the Count might just be able to exert tremendous pressures on Nick through threats of harm to Rosie. That would never do; he knew he wouldn't be able to stand it.

"There you are. What are you thinking?" Rosie disturbed his thoughts.
"You're awake at last. Oh, I was just thinking of the day ahead."
"And what did you work out?"
"Not a lot really. I was thinking that whatever happens, we must under no circumstances become separated. It might become awkward if somehow you were in one place and I was in another. The Count may then be able to influence us and we might lose the upper hand."
"That's okay; I'll stick with you. That shouldn't be a problem if we adhere to the switching plan. After all, I've a key part in that."
"That's absolutely right, but we must stick to the plan exactly. I think you should get yourself ready quickly now Rosie. I'll ring the airport to see what flights are available."

There were no scheduled passenger services to Barcelona from Monaco or Nice that would have got them there on time, but the airport was able to contact a private company which could lay on a flight for them, allowing them to arrive in Barcelona in the early afternoon in plenty of time to organise their visit to the count. All Mr and Mrs Regale had to do was to get to the airport at Nice and they'd be on their way.

A handsome young pilot met them at the arranged spot and after clearing customs, he walked them across the tarmac to the waiting executive aircraft. The door, which formed the stairway almost rested on the ground and Rosie and Nick climbed aboard the steps inside.

"We'll be off in about five minutes," the pilot said. Nick and Rosie fastened their safety belts while the pilot fixed the intercom around his shoulder and over his head, as he spoke to the control tower. Clearance was given and he taxied across the forecourt towards the runway. He applied the brakes and the aeroplane came to a standstill. The engine revved and when released, the plane lurched forwards, accelerating quickly, the white marks on the ground outside rushing past in a blur.

"Hold tight," Nick whispered to Rosie, holding her hand gently as he had when they first met on the transatlantic flight. Within moments, they were airborne, the airport buildings disappearing beneath them.

"It will only take an hour," the pilot said as he turned around from the controls, "unless we meet any trouble. You can undo your safety belts now."

"You keep a hand on the stick or whatever you have to keep hold of," Rosie called out cheekily.

"Don't worry; it's all on automatic now. See; I've set the course, set the speed and the plane just flies itself. Easy isn't it?"

As he had been invited to look at the controls, Nick released his belt and walked forwards to the cockpit. With one glance over the multitude of dials he took it all in and he knew instantly that something was wrong. What Rosie didn't know, nor the pilot hired to take them to Barcelona, was that Nick had a pilot's licence of his own. During his military service he had been trained to fly helicopters and though he would have found flying a fixed wing plane different, nevertheless, he knew all about the principles of navigation. One look at the compass on the plane's instrument panel showed Nick they were flying in quite the wrong direction. Thinking quickly, he judged they were heading inland, perhaps to Lyons or even Geneva. The count probably had his own back-up service arranged for them, unless they were to have the heave-ho, somewhere over the Pyrenees. Well, if that were the case, it would be up to Nick to get them to

Barcelona. When they turned up at the Count's front door, that would upset his plans.

He strolled back along the aisle and stood behind the pilot. He couldn't pretend he had a gun. They had all gone through the metal detector screen. And in any case, the pilot may have had his own concealed on board already. No; Nick knew he was going to have to rely on his army training again. A quick chop on the pilot's unsuspecting neck would render him unconscious, probably for the rest of the flight. Nick thought no more; a quick movement of his hand and the young man slumped forwards. Nick caught him and propped him up, avoiding his falling on the instruments.
"Nick, what on earth are you doing?" Rosie cried as soon as she realised he'd knocked the pilot out. "What has he done? Who's going to fly this for us now?"
"Don't worry Rosie; I'll fly it. It's better for us to fly where we want to go rather than end up somewhere else. I checked the course before I hit him. If we'd stayed as we were going we'd have ended up, goodness knows where."
"Do you mean he's one of the Count's men?"
"Could be, or in the Count's pay. If the Count knew there were no flights suitable he may have arranged something for us. As you said, if we were out of the way, he'd be able to sleep more easily. Now we have to show him we're still around."
"Can you really fly this plane?" Rosie sounded worried.
"Of course I can Rosie. You don't think I'd have hit him if I couldn't. It's another one of the things my training in the army taught me. First, I have to plot the proper route." He reached for the map in the pocket beside the pilot's seat and drew a few lines on the paper. Having found the correct flight plan, he switched off the auto-control and changed the plane's heading. The wing banked as the new course was adopted and as the plane was now flying over water, Rosie could see the blue Mediterranean sea five thousand feet below.
"It shouldn't be too long now we're on the right course," Nick said.

The pilot was recovering in the tailplane, his moans attracting their attention. Nick walked back towards him, stooping slightly over him.
"Sorry about that, but you weren't going where you said you were taking us. Why were you doing that?"
The glazed expression on the young man's face cleared. "You fool," he said. "You'll get us both killed."
"What was supposed to happen to us?" asked Nick.

"I was to land at Geneva. I presumed the Count had arranged for his men to pick you up there. I don't know what would have happened to you afterwards."
"And you didn't care either. How much was he paying you?"
The pilot remained silent.
"Perhaps we'll drop you out somewhere over the water. What d'you think?"
"You wouldn't dare."
"No? I wouldn't count on it. Now I'll have to concentrate on getting us there safely won't I?"
"You'll have to untie me so I can land the plane," the pilot sneered.
"Wrong again. I think I'll gag you too." Nick stuffed one of the linen seat backs into his mouth before he had a chance to resist.
"That's better," he murmured.

"You'll never cease to amaze me Nick," Rosie began.
"You mean Mick Regale can still mystify his wife after all these years together. It's all my army training coming back Honey. We'll get this thing down in one piece; don't you worry so much." Turning to the pilot he said," You see what you've done? You've upset Mrs Regale and I don't like anyone upsetting my wife." He looked angrily at his captive. "I've a good mind to drop you out somewhere. If you want to stay aboard I would advise you keep absolutely quiet. One squeak out of you and I might change my mind." An indistinct mumble came from the gagged pilot.

Picking up the headset, Nick spoke to Barcelona control. All the details of the plane were available on the documents clipped to the pilot's flight plan, so unhesitatingly, he asked permission to land and received their directions. Confidently, Nick released the auto control and guided the plane safely on to the landing strip at Barcelona airport.
"Nothing to it," he breathed. "I think we'll leave you there for the time being," he said to the pilot. "Cover him with that blanket Hon while I fix him to the seat. We don't want him running about just yet."
Rosie did as Nick had said.
As they left the aircraft Nick locked the entry door securely. He wanted to leave the plane just as it was. He had a feeling they may want to use it again.

They walked across to the customs control and met the senior officer in command. Nick extended his hand.
"Hi, you brought us in real well. Thanks."

"Where is the pilot?" the controller asked.

"I am the pilot," Nick said. "We hired the plane from Nice. I have a licence and after they checked it out they let me fly it here."

"That's most unusual," the official said. "May I see your licence?" Nick had been afraid he might do that; his licence was in the name of Nick Royle, not Mick Regale. He knew he was going to have to bluff it out. He made as if he was searching through his papers to no avail.

"Gee, I guess I must have left it with the company in Nice. Yeah, I remember I showed it to the guy there but I don't think he gave it back to me. I'll have to pick it up when we get back."

"When do you think you'll be using the plane again?" the flight controller asked Nick. "We'll try and confirm the information in the meanwhile."

"Yeah, you do that," Nick replied, thinking there goes the further use of the plane. "We plan to be leaving about seven tonight; maybe a little later."

"You'll report to me before you return," the officer demanded.

"But of course," Nick said, knowing that would be the last thing they'd be doing. "Until this evening then."

"Phew, that was close," Rosie whispered. "I thought he was going to call your bluff over your pilot's licence. And if he'd searched the plane and found the pilot, there would have been some awkward questions asked. I went cold all over."

"Yes, it was a bit close, but that's behind us now. Let's concentrate on the problem ahead of us. Our car is somewhere in the carpark. We need that first to get us to the Count's place and later to get away from here."

"You know Nick, that car is hired out to Nick Royle not Mick Regale. If it should be seen, someone may be able to draw a connection between Regale and Royle; that would be disastrous."

"Good thinking Rosie. We'll leave that car where it is and hire another in the name of Regale. Later, when we change our identities back again, we can pick up the other one and enjoy our stay in Barcelona."

"It does seem sensible doesn't it?"

"It sure does Honey. I don't know what I'd do without you. I mean it Rosie," Nick said reverting once more to his natural voice. "Let's get mobile again."

From a call box at the. airport, Nick phoned the back-up number Sly had given him in the faxed message they had received at the hotel. He told them quickly and briefly what had happened on the flight to Barcelona and that they planned to call on the Count at about four in the afternoon without telephoning him first. He asked that they would intervene should he not ring them again within the hour. They listened to him without interruption and agreed at the end of the conversation his plan was sound.

CHAPTER THIRTY-SEVEN

Using a car hired from a different agency, the middle-aged American couple Mr and Mrs Regale, drove out towards the south on the Diagonal, looking once again for the home of the Count they had come to swindle. It was precisely four o'clock when they parked the car outside his home and walked slowly up the drive to the front door. Nick stretched out his hand and tugged an old-fashioned bell pull. He listened for the bell ringing inside the house but he couldn't hear anything through the heavy wooden door. Within moments an elderly housekeeper opened the door, peering short-sightedly at the two of them.

"Bona tarda senora." Nick's Catalan stopped there. "We have an appointment with the Count this afternoon." The housekeeper's English was no better than Nick's Spanish.

"Wait there," she said, shutting the door in their faces.

"That's a good start," Rosie murmured under her breath. There was a sound of movement inside the door which opened once again.

"Good Lord, it's you," the Count said, clearly surprised they had arrived. But he recovered quickly saying, "I wondered whether there would be any suitable flights which would arrive in time."

"Oh, I just hired a plane and flew it here myself," Nick told the count. "If I have business I want to complete I get on with it as quickly as I can."

"You certainly do. Well you'd better come in," the Count replied.

He led them through the dark hall. It was perfumed with the wax polish of years and lined with oaken panels hung with ancient and tattered banners, part of the Count's heritage. They entered a sunny lounge at the back of the house. This room was as bright as the hall was dismal and dark. The furniture here was light in colour yet heavy and substantial and the soft furnishings were vivid and exotic, brightly-hued, almost garish, but completely in keeping with the sunny nature of the room. Rosie fell in love with it straight away.

"What a lovely room," Rosie said, quite spontaneously.

“Yes it is pleasant, isn’t it?” Turning to Nick he said, “I’ve thought over your proposition and if you can keep this Arab fellow off my back, I’ll sell you the Geneva diamond, as you call it for six million pounds sterling.”
“I can’t promise anything but if I suggest the stone is in somebody else’s collection, then I would think he’ll have no more interest in you and will concentrate his attention on them. All he wants is money at the moment; how he gets it is I’m sure unimportant to him.”
“As long as that’s understood.”
“As I say, I’ll do my best. Can I see the diamond now?” Nick said as he opened his case, revealing his instruments.

The Count moved a picture over the hearth to one side revealing the front of a safe and carefully he dialled in the combination so that neither Nick nor Rosie could see what he was doing exactly. He swung open the door and, putting his hand inside, he lifted out a small chamois leather sac, tied at its neck and returning once more to the safe he removed a blue velvet cloth. He spread the cloth on the table in the centre of the room and untying the sac, he tipped the diamond gently on to the cloth. On the brightly lit table, the fire within the stone was released from all its multiple facets, leaping around the room, the spectra of colour exploring every nook and cranny.
As Rosie saw the magic of the stone revealed for the first time, she gasped, “It’s beautiful,” in such an awed tone, it was hardly audible.
“You’re right my dear; it is beautiful. Perhaps you can understand why, when I had the chance to swap the fake for the real stone, I took it. If it wasn’t for the threat of discovery by the Arab, and the possibility of making more money, I’d be keeping it still. Just looking at it, knowing I still own it, thrills me.”
“Perhaps I can take a closer look at it,” Nick said, putting on his cotton gloves and bringing his instruments on to the table. As he had done before, he measured its longest length and breadth and checked them with the information in his book. Then he took out his scales and weighed it carefully and again compared the results with those he had brought with him. Finally, he examined the stone carefully through his loupe.
“This is the diamond,” he said. “The statistics are quite different from those of the fake stone the Arab had.” Turning to Rosie, he said, “Wanna take a look at it Honey? If you want it, this is worth six million pounds, unlike that Arab crap.” He passed the stone to Rosie; the rest was up to her. He turned to the Count as he said, “I guess this is the real thing. As I told you I don’t carry that sort

of money around with me, but arrangements have been made for the cash to be available at the Banco Espana in the Diagonal at opening time tomorrow. May I suggest you keep the diamond with you now and bring it when we shall meet at the bank at nine fifteen in the morning. How does that sound to you?"
As Nick was speaking, Rosie had switched the diamond and the fake now lay on the table. The real stone was already inside the glass locket around her neck. The change had been easier to carry out than expected as the Count, concentrating on what Nick was saying to him, wasn't watching Rosie at all. The scam was over.

"That sounds very fair; no fear, I shall be there. Some champagne I think is called for." He rang a bell close to the safe and the door was opened almost immediately by a tall powerfully built man; protection had not been far away.
"Some champagne for my guests Miguel."
The manservant left to reappear almost at once with a tray covered with a soft linen cloth on which stood a bottle of Moet Chandon and four flutes. The majordomo opened the bottle carefully and poured out the drinks for them all.
"Will there be anything else senor?" he asked deferentially.
"Not now Miguel. When my guests have left, tell Pedro I'll need him shortly with the car."
"Si Senor." He left, closing the door quietly behind him. Raising their glasses they clinked them gently together; the deal was sealed.

No sooner had they clinched the deal with champagne when there was a heavy knocking on the front door. The count appeared to be startled.
"Who on earth can that be?" he said.
"Let's hope it's not the Arab. If it is, then I'll have some explaining to do," Nick said quietly.
"You don't think it could be do you?" The fear was apparent on the Count's face, sweat dewing his upper lip. He moved quickly, putting the fake diamond into the safe and, twisting the dial, he replaced the picture in front of it. "Who is it Miguel?" he called out to his manservant.
There was a gentle knock on the door and Miguel appeared immediately, followed by two tall men in uniform, their peaked caps beneath their arms.
"Senor, there are two men from the immigration authority. Apparently they followed the Americans from the airport. They want to see them straightaway. There is some problem with permission to fly the aircraft.

It would seem they stole the plane. I told them you were busy but they insisted on coming in." The servant spoke quickly and was clearly not happy in the presence of authority which resembled police.
"What do you want with me or my guests?" the Count asked smoothly.
"We just want to ask the American how he obtained the plane he arrived in. The owners did not give him permission to fly it himself. They are talking of bringing a charge of piracy against him. We have to ask them both to come with us to the airport to answer some questions."
"Now just a minute. I'm sure there's some mistake. I showed my pilot's licence to the man at Nice and he checked it out. He said it was okay. When I got here, I found I'd left my licence behind, at Nice. I told the guy at the airport here and said I'd sort it out when I got back tonight."
"I'm afraid you'll have to come with us sir."
"Hell." Turning to the Count he said, "Well, we had completed our business, hadn't we and if I'm able, I'll be there to meet you in the morning. If not, then Mrs Regale will complete the deal."
"I hope it all turns out well for you," the Count said as they all departed from the front door. As he shut the door, he grinned to his manservant, still hovering close in the hall.
"Didn't Pedro and his brother look like real customs officers in their uniforms? That'll cook their goose. It always pays to have another plan ready Miguel, just in case the first one fails. But I still can't understand how they were able to hire another aircraft though. I thought they'd have to take the one I'd arranged for them. Never mind; I don't have to worry about them any more and the diamond is still mine."
"Si senor," he replied, grinning from ear to ear. "I thought they looked like the real thing too; uniforms always scare me."

As Nick and Rosie were bundled into the back of the car waiting outside, Rosie whispered into Nick's ear.
"How did they know we were at the Count's? We hadn't told anyone where we were going and they couldn't have followed us. Could this be another of the Count's surprises?"
"I believe it could well be. I had wondered about that. Keep your wits about you my girl and watch where we're going."

As they halted at the traffic lights, another car drew up closely alongside theirs and through the open window a silenced pistol was aimed directly at the driver's head.
"Pull over and stop." The command was terse and accompanied by a

threatening wave of the gun. Once the car had stopped at the kerb, the passenger of the second car, also armed, threw open the rear doors.
"Get out," he said to Nick and Rosie and when they hesitated, he growled, "Get out; now."
Nick and Rosie slid across the seat and were unceremoniously pushed into the car. With a quick shot at the rear tyre, which sounded no more than a car back-firing, the gunman jumped in beside them. The car sped off leaving the other stranded at the side of the road.

"We're your back-up team just in case you were getting upset. We arrived at the Count's shortly after you and waited to see what happened. We figured if he had tried to stop you getting to him permanently once, he might try again and have something else up his sleeve. When we saw those fake immigration and customs' officers appear from around the back of the house, we knew he was going to try. Even if they were the real thing we thought you'd rather not want to be investigated just now; so we set out to release you."
"And I'm jolly glad you did too, though we had worked out they weren't kosher."
"Yeah; well now you're free, where d'you want to go?"
"First, we have to get out of this fancy dress we're in and then we'd like to get back to the airport carpark. We have another car parked there."
"Okay; we'll take you somewhere you can change. Then you're on your own."
"That sounds just fine," Nick answered.

Nick and Rosie were taken to a small backstreet building and into a parking bay where they could leave the car without anyone seeing them. They were ushered upstairs to a windowless room over the back and there they were given jeans and sweat shirts to change into.
"What d'you want done with the fancy dress as you called it?" the senior man of the back-up team grinned. "Shall we burn it?"
"Yes, if you can. It's done its job and the sooner it's destroyed the better. Once that's gone, it'd be very difficult to connect either of us with the scam."
"Yeah, you're right," he replied as he saw Nick and then Rosie and her startling auburn hair. "Who'd have guessed you were the same people?"
The tension was lightened as they all joined in the laughter at the comparison of Nick and Rosie and the Regales.

"Would you like us to run you to the airport or would you rather go on your own?" they asked.
"I think we'll be all right on our own now thanks. You must know how indebted we are to your organisation."
"That's our job. We'll get you a cab and then you can be on your way."
"Thanks again," both Nick and Rosie said together.

Once in the taxi Nick and Rosie both breathed sighs of relief. "They've got an extremely efficient set-up," Nick said.
"Yes. I was really frightened when we were with the other people; it didn't seem right. And then when I saw that gun sticking in through the window, I really thought it might have been meant for us." Rosie replied.
"I'm glad no one got killed or injured. It could have happened so easily if anyone had done something silly. After all, the others may have been armed. Anyway, I shall be glad to get our own car back and into our own clothes. This gear we've got on is almost another disguise."
"Oh I don't know; it quite suits you," Rosie teased.
"By the way; where's the diamond?" Nick asked, an anxious expression on his face. "I haven't seen the necklace for a while."
"Underneath the shirt." Rosie indicated the lump beneath her clothes.
"I knew you wouldn't have left it behind," Nick said.

They found their car in the airport carpark and drove it out of town, seeking a lay-by or somewhere they could change their clothes with some degree of privacy. A few miles north of Barcelona they found just such a place and with a certain amount of laughter and teasing, they were soon in clothes much more suited to them. They rolled up the trousers and shirts they had been given by their rescuers and set them well alight, dropping them into a litter bin filled with dried paper and rubbish. As soon as they were sure the clothes would burn completely and all evidence would be destroyed, they got back into the car and drove back to their hotel. Now the scam was over and was successful. Now they could relax and enjoy themselves; now they could have fun and explore Barcelona.

CHAPTER THIRTY-EIGHT

For the next three days, Nick and Rosie enjoyed the sights of Barcelona. Nick thought they should visit La Sagrada Familia first, the partly finished cathedral, with its eight cigar-shaped spires, designed

and started by Gaudi at the end of the last century and still far from completion.
"It's ghastly," said Rosie. "I can't see anything beautiful in it at all."
"It's different, I must say," agreed Nick. "It will cost a bomb to finish it and I should think there's more than a hundred years work still to do. I can't understand how he was allowed to start such a monstrosity; it's so ugly." There was little or no work being done on the site, almost as if the workmen had no enthusiasm to see it finished.
"After that, I think we need a bit of excitement," said Nick. "I know; we'll go to Tibidabo."
"Tibbi who?" asked Rosie.
"Tibidabo; there's a restaurant, a church and a fun park, all on the top of the mountain."
"How do we get there?" Rosie asked.
"We'll take a taxi to the tram-car terminal and then the funicular to the top. I hear it's well worth the trip."

Their cab took them to the little blue wooden tram which wound its way slowly and jerkingly up the mountainside to the funicular.
"How on earth it climbs this gradient I'll never know," Nick said. "And those bends; well, I never would have believed it possible."
They climbed out of the tram and crossed the road to the funicular. The bell rang, the doors clanged shut and they began their noisy bone-shaking run to the top. From the observation platform, they had a magnificent panoramic view of the city stretched out below them and beyond, the shimmering Mediterranean Sea.
"The Olympic stadium is over there," Nick said as he pointed to the prominent land-mark produced by the television and radio aerials, gleaming white on the hillside across the city.
"And you can see the cathedral we've just been to," Rosie added, pointing to the spires of the Sagrada Familia, almost lost in the complexities of Barcelona. "And there's a cable car just starting out across the harbour; oh, it's absolutely marvellous up here, looking down on it all. I'm glad we didn't dash home." Rosie was so excited.
"Coffee I think," said Nick, guiding Rosie towards the restaurant.
"Before we ride that menace down there in the fun-fair," Rosie pointed out.
Nick groaned. "Oh no; not that. I'll be sick."
"Don't you dare," Rosie threatened.

It was two overgrown children who enjoyed the fun of the fair on the mountain top at Tibidabo and who, windblown and flushed with happiness, entered the small church of the Sagrat Corazon, which

incongruously shares the same place as the funfair and the tall television aerial which towered above them. It was cool and dark inside the church; little light entered by the small windows and the smoke of candles pervaded the atmosphere.
"Would you agree to be married in a Catholic church Nick?"
"I would if that would please you Rosie, but I wouldn't want to become a Catholic. I love you and as long as we're together, I don't mind in which church we are married; all I want to do is to make you happy."
"Oh, Nick, I'm such a lucky girl to have found you. I know we'll be happy together. I expect Mum would like us to be married in a Catholic church. I'd like to please her. When do you think we can go home Nick?"
"What say we try for a flight tomorrow."
"Oh Nick, that sounds super; you are such a darling."

CHAPTER THIRTY-NINE

Each day since he had been in England, Celleri had driven past the motel owned by Rosie's mother and parked in a lay-by a short distance beyond the entrance. There always seemed to be a regular coming and going of cars and people walking in and out throughout the day, but at no time had he seen anyone whom he could remotely have regarded as Meryl. He wanted to see her, in this rather clandestine way first, before he met her properly. He had felt that in this way he might have had some advantage when they did meet, but despite the fact that he stayed there for several hours at a time, he never caught a glimpse of her. He began to wonder whether he would recognise her after all these years. Perhaps he had seen her even but hadn't known her. He questioned how much longer would this very inefficient method of observation be even sensible? Perhaps the time had come when he should call in at the hotel, for coffee or afternoon tea or something. The chances of meeting Meryl straight away were remote. She was a busy woman running the hotel. She wouldn't be sitting around waiting for guests to appear and certainly not for him.
'Yes, that's it; that's what I'll do. Tomorrow, I'll call in the morning for coffee. I'll be able to look around probably with little chance of coming face to face with her and if I did, it would be extremely unlikely she would recognise me now, following the burns. Yes, that's what I'll do.'

He drove into the carpark in the front of the hotel the next morning and getting out, he stretched himself. Any distance in the car made him feel stiff and uncomfortable and locking the doors, he walked slowly towards the entrance. Once through the revolving doors, he turned towards reception.

"Good morning," he said to the young lady behind the desk. "I'd like to have coffee please; do you serve non-residents?"

"Of course sir. Would you like it in the lounge or at one of the tables in the garden?"

"In the garden, I think. It's such a lovely day; it really is quite warm."

"Just through those doors sir; we'll be with you in a few minutes."

Celleri walked slowly into the garden, selecting a table where the umbrella over the table produced some shade and where he could keep an eye on anyone moving about in the hotel foyer. Minutes passed. He could see the receptionist pointing him out to someone in the hallway, but he couldn't see the person with his tray. The door opened. His heart missed a beat. He had known her straight away. He had been aware that Meryl might appear at any time but he hadn't thought that she would have been the one to bring his coffee to him. She was a handsome woman now, a schoolgirl no longer; her complexion was clear and her colouring natural, just as he remembered her. Her hair was golden, perhaps carefully assisted with a rinse or something, but she had looked after herself. Her figure even after all these years was attractive and desirable. Deep within himself he was aware of feelings he hadn't known for years.

'You fool. Why on earth did you run away and leave such a wonderful woman? You could have worked something out; you would have done so well together. And Rosie; what a daughter to have sired. Any father would have been proud to have her for a daughter. You stupid, stupid fool.'

"Good morning sir; it was you for coffee wasn't it?" While Meryl had been walking towards him, Celleri had slowly stood up. It had seemed the right thing to do.

"Don't get up. It's just the morning to be having your coffee in the garden. Take full advantage of this gorgeous spell of weather; it's sure not to last."

"It is so very lovely today," Celleri replied. Meryl looked at him carefully, first his face, then his hands.

"Do I know you?" she asked.

"I shouldn't think so," Celleri answered. "I'm on holiday from the States, just getting over some burns I had recently."

"Yes, I noticed; I'm sorry I stared but there's something about you I

remember; I feel I've met you somewhere. Are you sure you haven't been to this hotel before?"
"I can assure you I've never been here before; this is my first time here. I was last in England about twenty-three years ago. I can hardly recognise any of it now; it's all changed so much."
When Meryl heard him say he had last been in England twenty-three years ago, she hesitated and looked at him again, searchingly, as if trying to see past the veneer of his injuries.
"You don't sound as if you're an American; you've no accent."
"No, I'm English by birth and though I've lived there all those years I never acquired their accent."
"Where were you born?" Meryl asked, her heart beating rather more quickly than usual, her woman's intuition working overtime. "I am sorry; I'm asking too many questions; please forgive me."
"I was born only a few miles from here I believe," Celleri replied. He too was becoming more anxious as the conversation progressed. "And don't apologise; I'm the one who should be saying I'm sorry."
"And why should you apologise to me?" Meryl ask hesitantly. It was Celleri's turn to pause.
"Well, it was all those years ago we saw each other last Meryl. Do you remember that summer's evening on the riverbank, the night Rosie was conceived? I remember it as if it were yesterday." Meryl gasped, her hand to her throat and sat down quickly, feeling faint, in the chair opposite Celleri.
"You?" she breathed.
"Do you remember telephoning me some weeks later when you knew Rosie was on the way? Like a coward, I disappeared and left you to the tongue lashing I knew you'd get from your mother and your stepfather?"
"Michael." She almost whispered his name. "You are Michael? I thought I recognised you but I didn't dare think it could be possible. I thought you had died in the fire at the casino."
"I didn't think Rosie would have told you about the fire."
"She didn't; she told me her boss was a man called Michael Chaney. She said you were English, which we both thought was rather surprising and that you had asked so many questions about her and her family, particularly about me."
"Yes, I did; I wanted to know as much as possible."
"Later, I had time to think and to wonder why anyone would behave like that. So one morning after she had telephoned me, I rang the club and asked for the manager. Whoever it was I spoke to said, Mr Celleri was not in. I knew then, at least I thought I knew then why things had happened in the way they had."

"I see; but you didn't do anything?"
"No, of course I didn't. I didn't think I should tell Rosie that I knew."
"She was so upset after the accident when she came to see me in the hospital and found she had been listed as my next of kin. It was then, when I thought I might die, I told her I was her father."
"I understand."
"Then I was abducted from the hospital by the people who had caused the fire and looked after by them until a week or so ago when I left the States for England for good."
"But she said she had been to your funeral."
"Yes, well she did in a way. There was a funeral but there was no Michael Celleri in the casket. You must understand. After the casino was destroyed by the fire, the mob blamed me, even though I had nothing to do with it. They put out a contract to kill me. They tried even while I was critically ill in hospital; they nearly got away with it, but luckily, they failed."
"So those people who tried to kill you now think you're dead?"
"That was the idea. I've been in hiding since I vanished from hospital and now with the changes in my appearance caused by the fire and a new identity, I've left the States for good as Michael Chaney."
"Does that mean that Rosie doesn't know you're still alive?"
"Neither Rosie nor Nick. It was thought best they shouldn't know in case they gave the game away. There was such a lot at stake. The mob would have killed me without any qualms and both of them as well. I hope with this new identity and different looks I can keep them away. Otherwise, I'm a dead man."
"Poor Michael. Where are you staying now?"
"At the Hilton in Windsor. I wanted to be near enough to try and see you, though I hadn't planned to meet you quite so quickly. I didn't know how you'd react when we met. Perhaps you'd hated me so much over the years, you wouldn't have wanted to meet me at all. I can't say I could have blamed you. What I did all those years ago was mean and despicable. I could only expect you'd still loathe me."
"At the time I was dreadfully upset. I just couldn't understand why you should have run. I felt let down. I thought it was the real thing between us; I know that's how it was for me."
"I think it was for me too Meryl, but I just wasn't ready to settle down. I was frightened. I had no job, no future to offer you; no home; nothing. I loved you then as I've always done but I just hadn't the courage to make a go of it."
"Did you ever marry?" Meryl asked.
"No. I have always been in love with the memory of you. In that

respect I was true." He paused. "It must have been extremely hard for you in those early years."

"It was. If it hadn't been for the friendliness of Susan who owned the cafe, I wouldn't have had a roof over my head nor a job. She was a gem. When she knew I was having a rough time at home, particularly from my stepfather, she took me in. And when Rosie arrived, she helped with baby-sitting and so many other things that made it possible for us to survive."

"She must have been a lovely woman."

"Yes, she was. And when she died, she left me the cafe and all this ground around it and enough capital to consider developing the place. Since then, it's gone on from strength to strength."

"You've done well Meryl."

"I've been lucky; hard work too mind you but I have been very lucky. You did well for yourself too Michael?"

"I suppose I succeeded in the way I had chosen, or more correctly, was chosen for me. But being a member of the Mafia brings few friends. Fortunately, I can truthfully say I was never called upon to make decisions of life and death. I mean, I never caused the killing of anyone directly. But I was part of the world of drugs and gambling and I suppose, indirectly, prostitution."

"How could you Michael?"

"Once I was trapped in the underworld it was impossible to get out; I was one of them. Obey or be punished and punishment was often death. And then I was promoted to a capo. Capos have tremendous power and can execute those who stand in the mob's way, but I never needed to take advantage of that. I succeeded somehow or other in a different way. But now all that is behind me. If the mob should recognise me, they would have me killed instantly; there'll be no second chance."

"Well, we'll have to make sure they never find you, won't we?"

"You're very kind to me Meryl. I must say I thought you'd show me the door pretty quickly."

"It was all a long time ago. I've had a lot of time to think things through. There was a time I'd have given you short shrift. You'd have been out on your ear PDQ. But I suppose I've mellowed over the years. And then, when I realised you were Rosie's boss, I must say I had started thinking how I would cope with meeting you, as we almost certainly would have met and fairly soon too. So, perhaps I've had a little more time than you to adjust."

"Maybe. But after meeting Rosie for the first time and hearing her speak about you, I couldn't help saying to myself 'if only' over and

over again and wondering whether we'd ever be able to get together again."
"It's a bit too soon to think like that, but we've met again and been able to talk to each other civilly; that's a wonderful start, don't you think?"
"It's more than I could have hoped for Meryl, I must say."
"What will you do now? Do you want to transfer to this hotel or would you rather stay as you are for the time being?"
"I hadn't thought that far ahead. I'd love to be nearer to you now we've met. Perhaps we can spend some time together and get to know each other again; there's so much to talk about. That's if you want to of course," he added quickly.
"Of course I do; it is lovely to see you and to know you are alive. You must remember Michael, I thought you had been killed in the fire. What say we both go and collect your things? In the car you can tell me more about yourself. We've got to catch up on, nearly twenty-three years."

Meryl left for a few moments, returning with a small wicker hamper. "We'll make it a picnic," she said.
Opening the passenger door for her, Celleri murmured, "You've made our meeting so easy Meryl. I had been dreading it, afraid of a scene, afraid of your hate and loathing. I didn't know how things would go."
"Well I don't hate or loathe you as you put it. Come on, let's get going. I'm simply dying to know all about those lost years."
"Telling you of my life will be pretty boring. All I did was run a casino. We entertained everyone; royalty and plebs and all sorts in between. The money we made was the property of the Don and what he said was law in the club. My part was purely administrative."
"What members of the Royal Family did you meet?"
"I don't think we ever had any British Royals, but we certainly had minor royals in from countries without monarchs on the throne."
"Go on."
"Well, there were many reasons for the fire in the casino. As you probably know, it was started deliberately, but what you won't know is, it was because I was unable to raise two million dollars that had been demanded of me. Well, I had all the money ready the afternoon before the fire, but an Arab sheikh had an amazing run of luck and won a lot of money that night. The money I had put aside had to be used to pay him off; gambling debts must be paid at once; there can be no welching. So, in the morning I was half a million dollars short. That wouldn't do, so the casino was torched. Unfortunately, I was inside and well and truly cooked."

"Poor Michael. Look at your poor face and hands. It must have been dreadful for you."
"They're a lot better now than they were and my doctor tells me that within a short while I should be pretty good. I had to have a stick at first but I've been able to throw that away. Now you tell me about yourself."
"Rosie's made a good job of that I should think, but I'll try to fill in some of the gaps."

The journey there and back was finished all too quickly. Meryl showed Celleri to his rooms; she had chosen the best for him.
"This is really very good of you Meryl."
"Not at all. Take a rest now. I have some work to catch up with and if you feel up to it, we'll have dinner together this evening."
"That would be fine. I must say I do feel a little tired now. I am really looking forward to seeing you later."

Now apart, Celleri had time to review the happenings of the day. He couldn't believe his good fortune.
'Maybe? Who knows?' His initial meeting with Meryl had been so much easier than he could have planned, he couldn't help thinking 'Well, maybe.'
And Meryl too was amazed at the way she had controlled the day, for it had been she who who had guided and led the actions of the day.
'He's become a very nice man and I know I am still in love with him. But can I put the clock back? Is it fair to him and especially to me? Can I forgive him for a frightened action all those years ago?'
She knew she could and would; but how exactly? She mustn't allow things to rush any faster than they had already; she would take things slowly, one step at a time.
'Poor Michael.'

CHAPTER FORTY

Sly met Nick and Rosie from Barcelona at Heathrow.
"How did it go?" he asked anxiously. Nick had told him part of the story over the telephone, but cryptically so that anyone who may have overheard would have found the conversation confusing and rather unintelligible.
"Well, we're both here, but for a short while, just before we were rescued, I did wonder what Spanish gaols were like. Their reputation doesn't come too high."

"Where's the diamond now?" Sly asked.
"In the safest place possible, around Rosie's neck in that glass hiding place you made. It's perfect."
"I didn't realise you'd be bringing it out that way; I'm glad it's held together."
"Well, I did pop a bit of super-glue around the edges to make sure," Nick teased. "We couldn't have it falling apart in front of the custom's man could we?"
"You rotter," Sly laughed. "It would withstand anything you could sensibly do to it."
"Of course it would. It was as I described, the safest place possible. Now we must put it in a safer place still. It's just on the cards some people may come and pay us a visit to see if we have it."
"I don't think so," Sly said.
"How come?" Nick asked
"Well, it's only a rumour of course, but apparently the sheikh's relative, the one who owns the fake stone, thought as you had done, that the Count probably still had the diamond and followed you to Barcelona. He called on him with some of his heavies."
"Then what?"
"He informed the Count that he'd been told the stone he bought at auction was a fake and as he was the vendor, what was he going to do about it?"
"That must have set the cat amongst the pigeons."
"The Count blustered, threatened to call the police and all that, but he must have folded. Perhaps some of his favourite possessions were broken, like an arm or a leg. Anyway, rumour has it that the Count parted with the diamond which is now in the Arab's safe."
"So the Arab thinks he's got the real thing now. That means he's almost certainly going to approach Regale again to buy it from him. Just as well we left no forwarding address. We must be sure the bank doesn't release anything."
"They can't. They don't know any permanent address anyway," Sly said.
"What if the sheikh himself comes back to ask you to buy the collection?" asked Rosie.
"I'd have to decline. There's nothing else I can do if I want to stay in one piece. He can't make me. I'll have to suggest somebody else."

The journey continued in silence for a while.
"I've got some more news for you Baas. While you've been gallivanting about on the continent, some of us have had to carry on with the work." He grinned; he loved to banter with Nick.

"Get on with it, you big oaf."
"I had a call from a Russki from one of those new Russian states. I know you don't really like dealing with them but he had a few stones which I think you'll like to see."
"Are they stolen?" Nick asked.
"No, they're all right. He had all the official documentation; I insisted on that before I met him."
"Okay; what's so special about these?"
"I think using the Yehuda treatment on some and the laser on the others, we can make a big profit, really big. This guy's government needs the hard currency pretty quickly to keep going. We needed a large down payment. Finance may be a problem but I figured you'd know how to get around that. I should say we'll make in excess of 100% profit easily on this deal."
"Where are the stones now?" Nick asked.
"In the safe in the office. I had to draw £100,000 from the petty cash, 1% of the cost as down payment," Sly replied.
"You mean you've contracted to buy ten million pounds worth of diamonds?" Nick cried out in amazement.
"Yes and I think you'll agree they're cheap at the price. As they are now, untreated, they're worth half as much again on the market. Treated, as I said, they're worth a lot more than double the price paid. Anyway you look at it, we'll make a good profit."
"We'll see," Nick said slowly

"What's this laser treatment for diamonds?" Rosie piped in.
"Well, you remember when you had your lecture about the formation of diamonds deep down in the earth, the product of heat and pressure?"
"Remembering where the lecture took place, it wouldn't be so surprising if I had forgotten everything you told me about diamond production," Rosie said coquettishly.
Nick blushed. He did remember. "The clarity of a stone depends on the absence of inclusions within. These are usually minute pieces of carbon which have not undergone the crystalline change during the conversion to diamond. A flawless stone, so called Fl is extremely rare and is therefore very much more costly than a stone which contains a number of flaws. If we could direct a laser beam at the defects accurately, the heat and pressure it produces within the stone can convert the carbon deposit which created the flaw into crystalline diamond. If that can be done, the stone then looks flawless and is worth perhaps three, four, five times the price of the flawed stone."
"Do you have the facilities to do that?" Rosie asked.

"Yes we do. The equipment was an expensive investment for enhancing the value of flawed diamonds. We have to take a great deal of care when we use the machine as lasers are very damaging to the eye; only a short period of exposure can cause permanent blindness."

"It sounds very dangerous," Rosie countered.

"Not really. The workroom is always locked when the laser is in use and there is an illuminated sign over the door, advising those outside that the instrument is on. Inside, we always take precautions and wear goggles all the time when the laser is working. If you're protected, it's quite safe."

"Is it legal?" Rosie asked.

"Pefectly legal. It is usual to advise other dealers of the change but even that isn't essential."

"And what was the other thing you said you could do?"

"The Yehuda treatment. Yehuda was the man who recognised that it was possible to fill the hair line fractures, which also devalue a stone, with a glass-like substitute. Even an expert using magnification may not be able to recognise the improvement carried out, though if you look hard enough, it can usually be seen. But the diamond-buying public would certainly not be aware of the fact that the stone had been treated. Sly is particularly adept at treating these diamonds and I have failed to spot a number he has dealt with."

"Is that legal too?" Rosie asked.

"Yes, both improvements are acceptable though it is usual to advise other dealers of the changes. But some people believe that once a stone is flawed, it is always flawed, despite anything done to it or how well it's been done. I can't say I subscribe to that entirely, though I am a little hesitant in treating large stones. You see, sometimes the value of a diamond can be advanced more than five-fold with laser treatment to destroy the carbon and the Yehuda treatment filling for a surface crack. There's a lot at stake."

"But if it's all legal, what's the problem?

Nick frowned at Rosie. "Are you sure you two haven't got together on a 'let's get Nick' attack? That's exactly what Sly says. I'm not so sure. Our customers have to have confidence in what we sell them; this way, maybe that confidence will be lost; we just can't afford for that to happen."

"Anyway, you wait till you've seen these Baas. We can always sell them as they are; we won't lose in any case, you'll see."

During the rest of the journey, all the exciting parts of the Barcelona trip were recalled for Sly.

"It was just as well we arranged with the agency to provide support if anything went wrong. We sure owe them one now," Sly added.
"They were efficient all right," Nick said. "Once inside the fake customs officer's car, I thought, 'Goodbye Nick Royle and goodbye to both of us and for a long time too'."
"I felt like that too," Rosie added.
"And then when the rescue car pulled up alongside with this chap waving a gun in our faces and I hadn't a clue who they were, I must say I got really worried then. You'll never know the relief I felt when they said they were the back-up team."
"Will you get in touch with Sammy? I did tell him you were safe but I'm sure he's looking forward to a call from you."
"Yes, of course I will; I hadn't forgotten."
"And give him my love too won't you and to Liz," Rosie added.
"I will," Nick said. "By the way, where would you like to be dropped now Rosie, at the flat or would you rather come along to the workshop while I have a look at Sly's new possessions? I must say I'm dying to see these stones."
"So am I Nick; I want to see what you've been talking about."

They drew up outside the office and as they climbed out of the car, Nick noticed the large black Mercedes parked across the road, the one he had seen some weeks ago and which at that time had followed them towards Rosie's mother's home. The car door opened and the chauffeur walked across the road to Nick. He indicated to Nick he should come towards the Mercedes. The window opened as it had before but the face that appeared was not that of the sheikh, but of another Arab.
"My master has bade me wait for you until you arrived; it has been a long wait Mr Royle. He told me to give you this letter and asked if you would reply as soon as you can. If you could read it now I can take your message back at once."
"I'll read it shortly and get in touch with the sheikh fairly soon. At the moment I must get back to the office; there is much that needs my urgent attention. I will reply shortly."
"As you say Mr Royle. I shall pass your communication on to my master." The window closed. The car moved off. Nick and his friends went into the office, locking the doors behind them securely; this was no time for surprise visits, not from anyone.

Sly opened the safe and brought out several soft leather sacs, each tied lightly at the neck. Gently, he opened one of them and tipped the contents on to a soft white cloth covering the workbench.

Nick picked up an eyepiece and under the bright anglepoise lamp, he carefully examined the first diamond, moving it firstly this way and then that and it was some minutes before he put the stone down.

"If it weren't for the superficial blemish on two of the facets, that would be a perfect diamond. I suspect it has been cut badly. If that is the case, that was an expensive error. Would it be possible to recut the stone differently, removing those flaws, without filling in and without losing much of its value?"

"I've thought about that," Sly replied. "I've drawn a plan of recutting but the stone would become considerably smaller. It wouldn't pay us to do that, but with the Yehuda treatment, the stone could be sold for three times the price paid for it and nobody would know."

"We would Sly; we would." Nick picked up the next diamond, a beautiful looking stone of about ten carats. He looked at it just as carefully as he had the other. "You have a look Rosie; tell me what you see," he said. Copying the moves Nick had made, she too examined the diamond.

"Well, on the table, it looks a brilliant white stone just as those you sold to Sammy. But through the loupe, there are brown particles; I can see several of them. I suppose those are the carbon deposits in the diamond."

"That's exactly right Rosie; well done. We'll make a gemologist of you yet."

She glowed with his praise. She wanted to know the things that he knew about and take an interest in those things that interested him. Nick continued. "So, if I can direct the laser beam at those carbon particles, one at a time, the intense heat it produces will change those inclusions into crystalline diamond. Then, the price of this diamond alone will be more than half a million pounds. As it is now, maybe £100,000 if we're lucky. Few people want to buy poor quality. Despite the high price, quality counts and people will always pay for the best."

Slowly, meticulously, Nick went through the individual examination of all the diamonds Sly had bought. Every now and then, he'd stop and ask Rosie to tell him what she had recognised. While she was obviously new to the exercise, she was clearly interested in learning the tricks of the trade which Nick was gradually teaching her. It was some hours and many cups of coffee later before Nick had completed his survey of the gems of which Sly had taken possession.

"You're right Sly. These stones are worth a lot of money just as they are and considerably more when treated. I think some of them should

be left alone but others could be enhanced with advantage. You bought well there Sly. I'll have to find the money tomorrow to pay for them, quite a lot too it would seem."
"I'm pleased you're not disappointed Baas."
"Far from it; I think you've made a marvellous buy. There's enough work there for quite a while, maybe a couple of years. I think we'll put them in the vault rather than in the safe. We can get them out a few at a time, as we work on them."
"Will that postpone our other plans?" Rosie asked shyly.
"No, of course not, but after our honeymoon, there'll be a lot of work for me to do while you set up our new home; that is unless you'd like to stay in the flat for a while."
"For a while perhaps, but that wouldn't be a place to bring up our children would it?"
Nick looked at Rosie knowingly. She blushed. "No I'm not," she blurted out.
Nick encircled her in his arms.
"I hope we have lots of kids, girls as pretty and as smart as you and boys as handsome and as smart as me. And I'll bet you, they'll all be carrot tops, just like their Mum." Rosie struggled in his grasp helplessly.
"Oh, you Nick Royle, I'm not a carrot top; you wait till I get my hands on you. Anyway, you always said you loved the colour of my hair."
"I do Rosie; it's your crowning glory; it's wonderful. But can you imagine a son of mine having reddish hair? I'll bet none of our children have my black hair; so very distinguished, don't you think?"
"You two having your first disagreement and over something neither of you can alter," Sly called out. "Perhaps they'll all be brunettes."
"Perhaps you're right. Come on young lady, it's time to be off. Leave you to lock up Sly. Probably see you in the morning, though I have promised Rosie I'd take her to see her mother some time soon."
"There's plenty for me to get on with now you've seen our new stock."
"Goodnight Sly."
"Goodnight Sly," added Rosie.

CHAPTER FORTY-ONE

In the morning, the post brought a number of letters, most of them for Nick, but there was one official looking envelope of fairly large size addressed to Rosie. It had an American stamp and had been franked with a New York postmark. It had been addressed to and then redirected from Rosie's Manhattan apartment. Rosie hurriedly opened it. Inside there was a legal document accompanied by a letter from the attorney, Maurice Webster.

Dear Miss Haynes,
Subsequent upon receiving your instuctions regarding the action to be taken against the hospital from which your father was abducted and later found dead, I approached the attorneys acting for the hospital board and their insurers. They are aware of the gravity of the situation and rather than be subjected to the prolonged and unfavourable publicity which would follow an action for damages, they are prepared to consider an out of court settlement of ten million dollars.

The partners have discussed this in your absence and believe the assignment to be fair and reasonable. We have little doubt that a larger sum could be gained by continued legal action, but should judgement not be in your favor, the agreement may be reduced by the court. It is our considered opinion you should accept this offer.

I enclose the documents you need to sign if you agree and would ask you to return them at your convenience.

"Nick, it's from the solicitors. The hospital has agreed to an out of court settlement of ten million dollars. Would you read it through for me please? What d'you think? It's an awful lot of money."

Nick read the letter quickly and then scanned it again. "As he says Rosie, it's possible you'd get more by continuing the litigation, but you would feel pretty silly if the court did for some reason reduce the award. I think I too would advise your accepting it."

"I think you're right. Do you think that's enough to build the wing for burns we talked about?"

"Very likely I should say. When you reply to Webster, hint that after the money has been deposited in your bank and only then, you'd consider making a sizeable donation to the hospital. I wouldn't say much more than that right now. Get the money in your bank first."

"Will you help me read through this document Nick? I'm finding it all a bit confusing."

"Sure. Give me a few minutes. I've got a bit of a problem of my own for a moment. Once this is done, I can give you my undivided attention."

Slowly, they waded through the legal jargon in the settlement document, rereading the tricky parts from time to time. Eventually, they reached the end.

"Well, it's clear enough when you take the time to read and understand it. I think you would sign that, don't you Rosie?"

"Yes I do." She took her pen from her handbag and signed the paper straightaway. Nick signed as a witness. It was done.

"I'll enclose the letter you suggested too; I think that's a first class idea."

While Rosie was writing her letter to Webster, Nick found the note from the sheikh he had received the day before and stuffed unread into his pocket. Nick looked at it quickly. It asked him whether he had considered the sheikh's request to act for him in the purchase of the diamond collection belonging to his relative. It pointed out that time was of the utmost importance, as in the event of his relative not being able to settle his debts, it was very likely his legs or his arms or even both might be broken and perhaps his life be sacrificed. The sheikh felt certain that Nick wouldn't want that on his conscience, nor would the sheikh like any blame be attached to Nick by anyone. He felt certain that Nick would be able to find the time to act on the sheikh's behalf and fairly soon. There was a thinly veiled threat in the letter, one that threatened Nick's livelihood. He went to his bureau and wrote his reply to the sheikh.

Your Excellency,

I am deeply flattered you should continue to want to use my services in the purchase of your relative's collection of diamonds. I regret I am not free at this time to be able to carry out your request as business pressures are too great.

May I suggest you ask one of the major diamond houses in London to do what you ask. They have some of the most skilled lapidaries in the world and I am sure they would be only too pleased to assist you.

Yours sincerely.

Nick reread his letter and signing it, he folded it and slotted it into an envelope. Addressing it to the sheikh staying in one of London's prestigious hotels, Nick stamped and put it with Rosie's, ready for posting.

"What did you say to him?" Rosie asked.

"I told him I was too busy and suggested he got in touch with one of

the main diamond houses. They'll be only too pleased to work for him."
"Let's hope he's not too upset by your turning him down."
"That's his problem. He can't expect me to drop everything just for him. There's all those stones Sly has bought recently. I've got to find the finance for those this morning and there's months of work to do on them before they can be sold. And then there's our visit to your Mum. I'd like to tell her what we plan to do as soon as we can. Then, we have to think about our wedding. I expect you'll want plenty of time for that, won't you? So you see, we're not going to have time to chase around for him."
"Would it take long?" Rosie asked. "It would help to finance the purchase of these new diamonds wouldn't it?"
"Rosie. I just don't want to buy the fake stone for him and let him think it's all right. In the long run, I'll be held to blame and I don't want that."
"I know. I thought if you bought the diamonds for him, you'd get him off your back, once and for all."
"No, Rosie. I don't want to work for him."

Rosie walked across to Nick and gently held him to her.
"I do love you Nick. I know we'll be so happy together. When do you think we'll be able to go and see Mum?"
"I thought we'd go today Rosie."
"That would be wonderful Nick; but there's so much to do in the business."
"Rosie, I want us to be married as soon as we can. I love you so much, I don't want to be without you even for a short while. So I think the sooner we meet your Mum again and get her approval, the better."
"Get her approval? You know she loves you, just as I do."
"Whatever; we'll go today."

In the autumn sun, they drove carefully out of London to Meryl's home, her hotel in the Home Counties. A little more than an hour later, they pulled up in the forecourt and strolled across to the bungalow, set back behind the hotel and surrounded by her colourful garden. Rosie rang the front door bell and stood back, looking across the flower beds, waiting for the door to open.

"Good God," whispered Nick. Rosie, who had been gazing the other way heard his faint words. She turned to look at the tall, slightly stooping man who opened the door.

Through quickly indrawn breath, she said, "Oh no, it can't be; you're dead." And with that, she fainted in a heap on the doorstep.
"Rosie," Nick cried out. "Here, give me a hand," he motioned to the other man. Together, they lifted Rosie into the bungalow and on to a setee in the living room. She was worryingly pale, a fine dewy sweat dampened her face. Nick kept rubbing her hand, gently calling her name.
"Rosie; it's all right. Rosie."
As soon as Rosie showed signs of recovering, Nick stood to face the other man.
"God, what a fright you gave us. You are Mr Celleri aren't you?"
"Yes, you're right. I'm sorry to have given you both such a scare, but I could have had no idea it was you ringing the bell. I was as frightened as you. Rosie will be all right won't she?"
"I expect so. She, like me thought we were seeing a ghost. You must have a fascinating story to tell. And to find you here, you must have met and made up with Rosie's Mum."
Rosie's murmurings indicated she was coming round, back into the world of the living. She looked around her and saw Celleri stooping low to look at her.
"I didn't dream it; it is really you. But we both thought you were dead; we went to your funeral. We saw you buried. The solicitors think you're dead and are handling your estate, passing it over to me."
"Shhh, Rosie; there's a perfectly ordinary explanation, albeit it's a bit complicated. All will be told to you; don't worry yourself."

The door opened again and this time Meryl walked in and she was equally taken aback by their being there."
"Why on earth didn't you phone and say you were coming? I could have prepared you for your meeting with Michael again. I don't suppose you've had time to think about it yet, but isn't it marvellous that he's still alive and here with us when we all thought he was dead?"
"I'm sorry to have created such a fuss," Rosie said. "It was a dreadful shock seeing you there."
"Of course it was," Meryl said. "Come on, let's have some coffee. We can sit around and Michael will explain the hows and whys and wherefores of the last few months."
All eyes turned towards Celleri.

"Well you all know the fire at the casino was started by Sammy Goldstein's friends. The Mafia hoods had killed his son, Abe and he came to the casino, demanding I turn in his son's killers and two million dollars to Sammy. I couldn't find that much money quickly enough; I could only get together one and a half million. So, though I pleaded, asking for more time, they wouldn't listen and the casino was torched. I lived in the apartment over the club, but they didn't know that and so I was caught in the fire and damned nearly died."

"I remember how ill you were in the hospital," Rosie whispered.

"Yes, I too remember your being there; it brought me such pleasure even in my pain to think you cared. You showed such affection and sorrow in your eyes and it was then, when you asked, I told you I was your father."

"I wanted to help so much, but I couldn't."

"While in hospital, the mob made an attempt on my life, injecting insulin into my drip. Fortunately, the nurse stopped it in time. But it frightened me and the hospital and it was they who suggested they should announce my death to take the heat off. You will remember Nick, I asked you to ask Sammy to get me out. Well, he did. I lived over you in Sammy's home until a week or so ago, when I left America for good to come here."

"He didn't say a thing to me; in fact, he behaved as if you were dead. I just assumed the mob had got you."

"He thought neither of you should know lest you gave the game away."

"But you were buried?"

"No, not me. A dead wino was found in Sammy's works. He was badly burned, having fallen into a fire, probably when drunk and so they put my hospital tags on him and floated him in the river. When the body was recovered with my name band on, the police thought it was me and after the inquest, the body was released for burial, It was his funeral you attended not mine."

"What a story. And who looked after you while you were getting better?"

"Sammy's doctor son-in-law and his wife took over my care; I couldn't have been looked after better. Now I have a new identity. My passport says I'm an Israeli subject named Michael Chaney; you will have met that name once before Rosie. I hope that and the change in my appearance will keep me safe from the mob. If they should get to know of my existence, without any doubt, they'll be after me again."

"It's unbelievable," said Rosie. "But what about all your possessions which the solicitors say I have inherited? They're not really mine."

"I shouldn't worry about that," Celleri chuckled. "Sammy Goldstein gave me my money back so I've plenty to get on with."

"And the solicitors have sued the hospital following your abduction and death. The hospital insurers have agreed to an out of court

settlement for ten million dollars. I have instructed them to build the Celleri wing for burns with the money."
"Good for you Rosie. What a thoughtful daughter you are."
"Well, it was Nick's idea really. I didn't need to profit from your death any more than I had. And Sammy thought it was a good idea too. He said you'd be remembered in New York for ever. People would say, 'who's this guy Celleri?'"
"Well, perhaps not for ever," Celleri laughed. "Though I'm not dead, I don't think you should change the plan in case someone starts asking questions and putting two and two together."
"What d'you mean?" interupted Meryl, who had been listening closely to the conversation between the others.
"I suppose that if the plan to call the new unit something other than the Celleri wing was proposed, someone may notice and wonder why. If the mob should get an incling that I'm still alive, they'll start looking again, and I'd rather that didn't happen, just in case."
"Would it be impolite to ask how you two are getting along," Rosie enquired.
Blushing slightly, Meryl replied, "Michael came to the hotel for morning coffee two days ago. I brought it to him. It was quite a surprise for me too I can assure you. Since then, we've been getting to know one another again. It's amazing how quickly all those missing years fall away." Meryl stretched out her hand affectionately to Celleri.
Taking her hand and moving to her side he said, "Your mother has been very kind to me and made it so very easy to get to know her again. All I can think of is, what a fool I've been all these years. I keep saying to myself, if only, if only."

During a lull in the conversation, Celleri said, "By the way, I saw you on television a few days ago Nick." Nick looked surprised.
"Yes, you were outside one of the London hotels. It was a news story about an Arab who had to sell his collection of diamonds. I thought you might have been interested in buying them."
"Oh yes, I was approached but I didn't make an offer."
"Were they worth a lot of money?" Celleri asked.
Nick hesitated. "Yes, they were. I was asked to buy the whole collection for a sheikh. It was his relative who had to sell because he's up to his eyes in debt with the syndicate. It was a matter of honour for him. The sheikh knew he had to help him, because he was his kinsman, but he couldn't be seen to be helping; he would have lost face. But fortunately I had had the opportunity of examining the collection beforehand. It was magnificent, but the one major stone was a fake and

because of that, I didn't want anything to do with it, so I opted out."

"You mean this fellow tried to sell you a dud? That was a bit silly of him knowing you were an expert," Celleri said.

"Yes, it did cause a few problems. Hopefully, I shan't be asked to buy them again."

"Where d'you think the real stone is now?" Celleri asked.

Again Nick paused.

"Don't say anything if it's confidential," Celleri said. Nick looked at Rosie; she shrugged her shoulders.

"I had to think, as you have, where the diamond was likely to be. We're talking of a stone bought recently for nine million pounds sterling. A remarkably beautiful diamond weighing 106 carats; a perfect flawless stone, very rare, very lovely, highly desirable. It seemed likely to me the previous owner had, somehow or other, changed the real stone at the time of the sale."

"The crook," Meryl said.

"When I thought about it, I knew if I were right, I too could swap a copy in zircon for the real thing without the owner knowing. So that's where Rosie and I have been for the last few days, carrying out the scam in Spain."

"You mean you've involved Rosie in a confidence trick?" Celleri asked.

"Don't worry Daddy," Rosie said, a huge smile splitting her face as she used his name, Daddy for the first time. She reached out to touch Celleri's arm. "Without me, the scam wouldn't have been possible."

"What have you two been up to?" Meryl asked. "Before you went away Nick, I asked you not to hurt her and now you've been involving her in some form of theft."

"It's not Nick's fault Mum; we did it together. And in any case, the Count who had the stone still, shouldn't have had it, because he was supposed to have sold it a year ago. And the beauty of it is, he doesn't even know it's gone. He thinks he still has the real thing in his safe."

"So what are you going to do with the real diamond now you've got it," Celleri asked.

"We have been giving that some thought," Nick answered. "You realise it's not the ownership of the diamond that was important to me, it was the scam getting it. We carried it out perfectly. The Count still has what he thinks is the diamond but we have something of incredible beauty and value."

"Will you be able to sell such a rare diamond on the open market? I thought most diamonds of that ilk are well catalogued and recognisable," Celleri asked.

"You're absolutely right; because of its rarity, it almost has a label on it. But I would be able to sell it for an enormous sum; less perhaps than it's really worth, but a lot of money just the same."

"Then what will you do with the money if, as you say, you don't really need it?" This time it was Meryl who asked the awkward question.

"We're both open to suggestions; that's why I've told you about it. If I had wanted to keep it quiet, I needn't have said anything. But we didn't want to profit from the scam; so, if you have any ideas, please say."

"Can't you give it to a charity?" Meryl enquired.

"Indeed we can; but which charity? Or shall we give it to a number of needy causes? Anything is possible at the moment. We just haven't had time to decide yet."

"I'm sure you'll make the right decision," Meryl added. "Now then what other news have you got to tell us?"

"It must be a mother's intuition," Rosie smiled. "There is something we want to tell you, though how you knew I'll never understand."

"Well it's something I have to ask you really," Nick said. "Would you mind very much if Rosie and I got married? We've known each other for many months now and have spent lots of time together. We get on well and are very happy in each other's company and we're very much in love. I've asked her and she has said yes, so now we'd like your approval."

"You've came to ask for our daughter's hand in marriage?" Celleri asked. "What a quaint and lovely idea. What d'you think Meryl? Alas, she's more your daughter than mine. I abdicated from those responsibilities years ago."

"Maybe you did, but right now your opinion has been asked for too. So do the caring father bit and find out what his prospects are or something," Meryl said jokingly.

"Well then young man. It would seem you live a life of crime, swindling crooked counts out of their ill-gotten goods. You keep our daughter out late and are teaching her bad ways. What do you have to say for yourself?"

"You're right sir. I have led her down a rocky path of wrong-doing but I promise once this is sorted out, I'll encourage her in a life of domesticity," Nick answered laughingly.

"That sounds all right Meryl, don't you think? What say we give him our whole-hearted approval?"

Meryl threw her arms around Rosie, hugging her closely, tears of joy running down her cheeks. "Oh Rosie, I'm so happy for you. I liked him from the very first time you brought him here. I knew that sooner or later he would want to marry you."

Celleri took Nick's hand in a man's grip, despite his burns.

"I'm delighted," he said. "I haven't had time to get to know either of you properly, but I remember how supportive you were to Rosie when I was in hospital in New York. I feel certain I couldn't have chosen a better man for her. I hope you'll be so happy together."

Meryl broke free from Rosie's embrace and hurried to Nick. "I couldn't be more pleased too. I know you'll be fine for one another. But you will look after her won't you? She's all I've got."
"And Mr Celleri?" murmured Nick. Meryl looked shyly at Nick.
"Maybe," she whispered.
And Celleri moved across to Rosie. "And may I wish you well too." He kissed her cheek. "Perhaps you'd let me be a proper father to you and give you away at the service? There I go; the story of my life. I found you only a short while ago and now I'm giving you away."
"I'd love that. I'm so happy I've found a father and oh I'm so glad you survived that awful fire and that you're now on the mend."
"Thank you my dear, so am I."
"And I hope you and Mum will continue to become friends again; very good friends."
"And I do too," Celleri added.

"This demands a celebration," called out Meryl."You two," she said to Rosie and Nick. "You don't have to dash away this time do you? You can stay to dinner this evening can't you? Say seven?"
"We'd love that," Rosie replied. "But Nick will have to be in London tomorrow. You've no idea how much work he has to get done. And I think I will be needed to give a hand as well. Then we'll have to make arrangements for the wedding. We don't want to wait a long time."
"Will you be married in church?" asked Meryl.
"If you'd like that Mum. Nick isn't a Catholic but we both want to do whatever would please you."
"That's thoughtful of you Rosie, but I'm very much a lapsed church-goer as I expect you are Michael, so though I would like you to be married in church, I wouldn't try to influence you, certainly if you would prefer somewhere else."
"I think you may find it difficult to persuade a priest to agree to marry you in church unless you promise to continue to go regularly. They can be very particular. And you will probably have to promise to bring all your children up in the Catholic faith too. What d'you think about that Nick?" asked Celleri.
"As I have said to Rosie. I'm in love with her and I want to marry her, in church, in a registrar's office. It doesn't matter to me as long as we can be together properly as man and wife. I don't approve of the

popular way nowadays of couples living together in trial relationships without a proper marriage."
"It's good to hear a young person speaking in this way," Celleri said.
"I hope Rosie and I have lots of children and I would want to bring them up in a secure and happy home based on a sound marriage, but they don't necessarily have to be Catholics."
"Nick Royle. I love you more and more when you talk like that," chimed in Rosie. "If there's any difficulty in getting married in church, then we'll use the registrar. How about that?"
"That sounds just fine Rosie." To Celleri, Meryl said, "would you like to give me a hand with these cups Michael?" They moved away to the kitchen, leaving the two lovebirds together.

Once away from Rosie and Nick, Meryl turned to Celleri and standing in front of him, slowly stroking his lapels, she said to him seductively, "Michael. You wouldn't like to make it a double ceremony would you?"
"Meryl, you don't mean it."
"I do. I've never stopped loving you Michael, even when you ran away all those years ago. Now you are back in England and you said you were planning to stay, why don't we get married? I'd like that, wouldn't you?"
He held her gently and for the first time in nearly twenty-three years he kissed her with all the love and quiet passion of all those missing years.
"The number of times I've said 'I wish I could put the clock back' and now you've made it so easy for me. Meryl, I too have never stopped loving you. When I ran away I was a boy, too frightened to accept the responsibility of marriage."
"I do understand Michael."
"Shall we go and tell them? Let's hope they will be as happy as we are."

Nick and Rosie drew apart as they reentered the room, a blush still suffusing Rosie's cheeks.
"Now would you like to hear our news?" Meryl said, linking her arm through Celleri's. "We thought we might join you and make it a double ceremony."
Rosie gasped. "You mean you want to marry each other now?"
"That would be the general idea," Meryl replied. "Mothers and fathers are usually married you know. We've both been in love with the memory of each other over these years and we are still in love now; it would seem the sensible thing to do."

"I think that's a marvellous plan. Congratulations to you both," Nick said. "I'm so pleased for you. Don't you think it's a super idea Rosie?"
"Yes," she answered hesitantly. "I'm so glad you have found each other after all those years. But it has come as a bit of a shock. I think it'll be so much nicer to have two parents."
"By the way Nick, would your parents be able to come to your wedding?" Meryl asked. "We could always accommodate them at the hotel."
"That's very kind of you to offer your help, but both my parents died some years ago while I was still in the South African army."
"Oh, I am sorry Nick."
"They were caught up in crossfire by marauding blacks looking for trouble. My younger brother and his family look after the farm back home now and I don't think he would want to drop things there to come to my wedding."
"Why don't you ask him?" Meryl said.
"No, I don't think so. There was some family friction when my parents died. He thought I should have been at home looking after things rather than away in the army. He's a really nice guy though; you'll love him Rosie."
"If he's anything like you, I'm sure I will," Rosie added.

The two couples spent a happy day around the bungalow, comfortable in each other's presence, each getting to know more and more about themselves. Love spread through the group, Meryl for Michael and he for her and Nick and Rosie flourished with their new parents.
Driving back to London, Nick turned to Rosie. "You know Rosie, we're very fortunate having two loving parents. They were so pleased with our news."
"Oh they were. And it's super they're going to get married too. It's wonderful to think their love is so strong after such a long time. I hope you'll love me as much Nick when we're that age."
"I think I will Rosie. In fact I'm sure I will. I can't see why not."

CHAPTER FORTY-TWO

It was dark when they pulled up outside the flat in London. They had eyes only for each other and neither saw the black Mercedes parked nearby. They went up in the lift and while Nick searched for his keys, two tall Middle Eastern men descended from the floor

above. Nick and Rosie took little notice of them until one grabbed Rosie as he passed. The other, built like an athlete, stepped quickly between them and Nick.
"Mr Royle?" His voice was gutteral and coarse. As Nick didn't answer, he asked again, "Mr Royle?"
"Who wants to know?" Nick advanced towards the man who held Rosie. His guard positioned himself between them.
"Mr Royle. Please don't cause any trouble. I am instructed to take you to my master now, tonight. I was told not to take no for an answer." He clenched his fists as he said, "I don't want to cause any pain or damage to either of you, so please come with us now. My master wants to talk to you urgently."
"Don't argue with them Nick; let's do as they ask. The sooner we go with them, the sooner we'll be back," Rosie squeaked nervously.
"No one makes me do anything I don't want to do Rosie and I don't want to go anywhere with these punks now or ever." As he was speaking he was slowly moving towards the man who had been doing all the talking. His hand flashed; he struck him so quickly, no one saw the movement, least of all the Arab who crumpled in a heap, soundlessly. He didn't make a move. Nick's gaze took in the other man, now looking apprehensively at his companion on the floor. He slackened his grip on Rosie, preparing to protect himself from Nick's attack. As he did so, Rosie brought her elbow back suddenly and forcefully, striking her captor in the solar plexus, driving the breath out of him, doubling him up. As he bent forwards, she kneed him in the groin and stood to one side as he fell to the floor.
"Well done Rosie; I couldn't have done it better. I suppose these two are emissaries from the sheikh. I'll put them in the lift to the basement."
"Is yours dead?" Rosie asked, an anxious look on her face. "That was some blow. I didn't even see it, it was all over so quickly."
"He'll be all right in an hour or so. He'll ache all over then," Nick chuckled. "I haven't used that move for ages. It's hard lines for anyone being on the receiving end of that. It's a hell of a punch."
"You must teach it to me," Rosie said.
"Seeing you in action, I think you'll be a good pupil," Nick laughed.

As they had been talking, Nick had dragged the two men into the lift and when he pressed the button for the basement, the doors closed and took them quickly downwards.
"Right then, where were we?"

"You were about to carry me over the threshold weren't you?"
"Well something like that," Nick replied, grabbing Rosie playfully and lifting her effortlessly into his arms as he opened the door and carried her into the flat.
"That was some day wasn't it?" Nick remarked.
"It certainly was. I am so pleased Mum and Mr Celleri have got together. I know they'll be happy."
"How d'you feel about a double wedding Rosie? Will it spoil it for you?"
"No, of course not; I couldn't be more pleased for them."
"I thought you might have preferred to have stayed with your Mum tonight, rather than come back with me to London? Don't you women have lots to do preparing for a wedding?"
"Hey, aren't you glad I've come back with you? I want to be with you Nick and help you with your work if you'll let me."
"And you can, I expect. But we can talk about that again; right now I have something else in mind."
"Oh you have, have you? And what may that be young sir?" Nick covered her mouth with his. Their kiss was long and passionate. The bedroom door shut quietly behind them.

CHAPTER FORTY-THREE

They both left early the following morning for the office, but this time they did notice the black Mercedes parked across the road.
"He's a stubborn old man that sheikh. I would have thought he would have got the message by now."
They drove quickly to the works and to Nick's annoyance, the Mercedes trailed them all the way.
"Damn, I wish he'd learn I'm not interested in his proposition."
Once inside, they locked the doors firmly behind them. Sly was already there, working at his bench.
"Morning Baas; how are you Rosie?"
"I'm very well Sly, thank you."
Nick walked over to the window and opened the slats of the venetian blind to look into the street below. He was in time to see the Merc draw away and leave.
"What d'you think Sly? We had another visit from the sheikh's men last night. When Rosie and I got back from her Mum's, these two thugs of his were waiting for us on the stairs. I had to tell them once again I wasn't interested in his offer, but they didn't seem to understand English; quite stupid really. After all, there were two of us; more than

enough to deal with the two of them. You should have seen Rosie, Sly; she was superb. The poor chap didn't stand a chance; she hit him so hard, he just crumpled up; folded in half."
"I would have liked to have seen that," Sly said.
"That was their car outside when we arrived. It's just moved off. Let's hope that's an end to it."

Nick and Sly started the jobs they had to do while Rosie watched what they were doing, learning the way they worked. She was so interested in the whole process, the morning simply flew by. It was a little after eleven when they stopped for coffee and the bell rang.
"Who the devil can that be?" Nick asked. They viewed the doorway outside through the television camera poised above the entrance. Nick groaned when he saw on the screen their visitor was the sheikh, in person. Strangely, he had none of his bodyguards with him.
"I suppose we'd better talk to him," Nick grunted. "Cover this stuff up for the moment Sly. We'll keep him away from it in the small office."

Come in your Excellency. You are alone?"
"Yes, what I want to say to you is rather private, not for all to hear. It is difficult to get to speak to you Mr Royle. And did you have to be quite so rough with my men last night?"
"I'm not used to being threatened by anyone your Excellency and anyone who threatens Miss Haynes must be dealt with firmly. I'm sure you would agree."
"I expect they were heavy-handed; please accept my apologies. Now may we talk together?"
"I'd like my colleagues in on this conversation."
"That's up to you of course and in any case, I'm sure Miss Haynes would be very interested in what I have to say."

They entered the small office and Nick placed a chair for the sheikh's use, facing the window while he and Sly and Rosie sat in an arc in front of him.
"Mr Royle. Some time ago I asked you to purchase the diamond collection of my relative who is deeply in debt."
"Yes, I was flattered you should come to me, but pressure of work prevented my accepting your instructions. I wrote telling you this."
"However, in between whiles, a Mr and Mrs Regale, an American couple approached my relative, intending to buy the collection."
When Nick heard the sheikh speak of the Regales, he wondered just what the sheikh really knew and what was coming next.
"Is that so?" he said.

"Yes. He examined the collection and do you know what? After he referred to his notes, he said the most valuable diamond my relative was selling was not real, but a fake; it was artificial. Apparently he had all the specifications of the real diamond in his possession."

"All buyers would have that information. I have it and would have used it if I had acted for you. When spending that sort of money, the buyer has to take all the precautions possible."

"I see," he mused. "I didn't know that. Anyway, after leaving my relative, it would seem that Regale and his wife must have left for Spain." Nick tried hard to hide his concern.

"So? Why shouldn't he do that?" he asked.

"A good question Mr Royle. It would seem he knew the previous owner was a Count who lived in Barcelona and guessed he probably still had the stone. He arranged to meet the Count and somehow or other agreed to buy the diamond, probably at a discount price."

"I suppose if it's a hot stone as this diamond would be, the Count might agree to sell for less than it's really worth. But all he has to do is disclaim ownership now and there's nothing anyone can do."

"Someone with initiative might plan something to do."

"I don't understand what you're getting at," Nick said.

"Would you find it strange Mr Royle if I told you that having agreed to buy the diamond, Mr and Mrs Regale disappeared again? They never turned up to conclude the deal they had made."

"So they changed their minds; everyone is entitled to do that."

"Again, you're right. But I'm told he saw and examined the diamond and agreed this was the genuine stone. He agreed to buy it and then disappeared."

"I find all this disappearing very confusing," interjected Rosie.

"Have you thought that, rather than disappearing, the Count may have kidnapped the Regales and done away with them? If they were killed, no one else would know where the diamond was. The Count would be safe."

"Yes, I had thought of that. By the way, my relative also worked out the Count had the diamond. He called with his strong-arm men and threatened him. The Count didn't like it at all when his little finger was broken; he told my relative everything. How he had exchanged the diamond at the auction. How the Regales had come to see the stone and had offered to buy it and how they had gone. He showed him the stone, which was examined by my relative's adviser, a lapidary from one of the large London houses, who by the way, was also in my pay. What d'you think he recognised?"

"I have no idea," Nick answered.

"He recognised the diamond the Count showed him was a fake; a beautiful fake but a fake nevertheless."

"You mean the Count had been holding on to a fake diamond believing it to be the real thing? Did your adviser tell your relative it wasn't real?"

"No, he said it was a beautiful stone."

"But you said Regale had agreed it was the Geneva diamond."

"Yes; interesting isn't it?"

"I suppose Regale must have made a mistake; well, someone must have. But I'm not sure what all this has to do with us."

"Regale thought it was the real diamond. I believe Regale exchanged the stone himself for the fake. I think Regale has the real diamond now."

"That's a long shot," Nick said. To the others sitting around, he said, "What do you think of the sheikh's interpretation of what's gone on?"

"There seems to be a lot of fake diamonds floating around and good enough copies to mimic the real thing too it would seem," Rosie said. "I shouldn't have thought it would be an easy thing to steal a valuable diamond in front of its owner; he'd be watching it like a hawk."

"Perhaps; but if his attention was distracted, even for a moment, it might be possible for a clever person to make a switch," the sheikh responded.

"And then the stone has to got away. How big is this diamond anyway?" Rosie asked.

"You are a very clever young lady Miss Haynes. It is not so large that it presents an insurmountable problem."

"Well, I still don't see what it's got to do with us," Nick said.

"You disappoint me Mr Royle. Mr Royle, Royal, Regale. Are you saying there is no connection? Mr Nick Royle; Mr Mick Regale. Are you sure there is no association."

"Yes, I suppose they do sound similar now you've pointed it out, but you said they were American . . ."

"An easy accent to imitate," the sheikh interjected.

"You said they were a middle-aged couple."

"No Mr Royle. I didn't describe them at all." An uneasy quiet descended over them all in the room.

"Well I got the impression from what you said they were older, Nick said.

"So easy to look older than you really are; so difficult to look younger. But you are right. The Regales looked nothing like you two."

"I'm pleased to hear it."

"Nevertheless, I have a proposition to make to you. Firstly, buy my relative's collection and assume the fake stone he shows you is real.

Secondly, should you meet up with the Regales, offer them six million pounds sterling for the real diamond. Of course, I will expect you to verify it is the real thing. What do you have to say to that? Very fair?"
"It certainly is. Now all we have to do is find the Regales," Nick said.
"Somehow, I think you'll be able to do that fairly soon. When you've bought the collection, please let me know. My letters of credit from the bank for you are still valid though I think your commission on the transaction for the purchase of the diamond from Regale might be waived. Do you agree?"
"It all sounds very fair your Excellency. I will proceed as instructed."

They accompanied the sheikh to the door. "May I ask what you would have done if I had not agreed to act on your behalf?"
"My men would have kidnapped Miss Haynes and I would have threatened to admit her to my harem. Then you would never have seen her again, never. There is as well, a small hotel in the Home Counties owned by Miss Haynes' mother. She has an interesting guest staying with her at the moment; someone from America, recovering from burns. When I saw him briefly a few days ago, I must say I thought I had seen him before. Then I remembered he resembled the manager of the Green Baize casino I met in New York some months ago. But it couldn't have been him; he died of his burns in the casino fire, though I must say he did look very much like him. I said to myself, 'now what if they were one and the same person?' That would be very interesting to many people; the police, the hospital, the Mafia, yes, especially the Mafia." He paused. "If you comply with my request, then we can all go back to a normal way of life."
"I'm glad we've come to some accommodation your Excellency, because if you had carried out what you said you would do to Miss Haynes, I would have killed you."
The sheikh looked intently at Nick, who returned his gaze unflinchingly.
"I believe you would have tried," he said.

CHAPTER FORTY-FOUR

"Am I glad that interview is over," Rosie said. "I have a feeling he knew a lot more than he was letting on."
"Maybe, but he knew a devil of a lot anyway. You were quiet Sly; what did you think about all that?"

"Like Rosie, I think he probably knows everything. I expect he has eyes and ears in his relative's camp and knows all that is going on there. And money talks. It loosens many tongues and I expect he gets most of his information that way. And he's smart too. It's clear he's been thinking it out, step by step. What with the information he's receiving and his logical deduction, he was pretty close to the mark. I don't know if you agree but I don't think we've anything to lose if we do as he wants; it would finish that chapter off neatly. You could then think what you're going to do with all that money."
"We were talking that over with Rosie's parents."
"They've got together have they?"
"Well, getting together would be more correct. They think we should give it to charity."
"All of it? Remember charity begins at home," Sly remarked.
"Well most of it," Nick said.
"Once the deal with the sheikh is completed and the money is in the bank, then maybe we can plan some sort of trust or other and use the money that way."
"Sounds okay to me," Sly said.

"I suppose I'd better get back to the sheikh's relative who's selling the diamonds and try and fix a meeting. The sooner it's done the better now. I must say I'll be glad when the whole thing is over."
"Can I come along with you?" Rosie asked.
"I think it would be wiser not to, just in case he starts working things out like the old man. Then you know what would hit the fan."
"I don't think you should go there with Nick either, Rosie; it's far too risky," Sly said. "As you found out when you went as Mrs Regale, these Arabs are a queer lot. How much do you plan to offer him Nick?"
"We know most of the stones he's selling and what he paid for them, so it shouldn't be too difficult to fix a price."
"But what if he's put quite a different value on them? You've got problems then, even with the backing you've got."
"Well, I'll have to cross that bridge when I get there. At the moment, leaving out the Geneva diamond, the rest are worth about four million, give or take a few hundred thousand. If we are to consider the fake stone as real, as the sheikh instructed me, then the offer would be twelve million pounds. He'll probably argue the Geneva stone was nine million and will want to get that at least, but I'll beat him down quite easily I expect; anyway, I hope so."
"It seems silly offering him the full price for a fake stone," Rosie said.

"I agree; but the sheikh's instructions were to pay him the proper price."
"You've got to remember you're dealing with the world's experts at bartering; I should offer half the price you're prepared to pay to start with, because they'll certainly begin at some ridiculous figure," countered Sly.

Nick's call to the vendor of the stones produced a rapid response. "My master would be pleased to see you Mr Royle. Would two o'clock this afternoon be convenient? Yes? At his suite at the Ritz? Until then Mr Royle."
"Well that part was easy; now we'll just have to wait and see how it goes."

Nick was on time when he arrived at the Ritz and was received by the same minion who had welcomed him as Regale some weeks before. "So pleased you were able to come along this afternoon Mr Royle. My master is due to leave for his home in a day or so."
"I too have business commitments abroad soon, so I shall be glad to see this collection and decide whether the syndicate I represent will buy these stones. It's been quite a time getting an appointment to view them; you must have had a number of interested parties."
"Some it is true and offers have been made, but the collection is quite unique and worth a lot more than has been suggested."
"Maybe; but the world in recession hasn't got the cash to buy baubles."
"Baubles?" His voice was raised in anger. "Baubles? These are some of the best diamonds which have appeared on the international market for many years. Some of these stones are almost priceless."
"We'll see," Nick said as they entered the lift to ascend to the penthouse.

When the doors opened, the same search happened as before, but Nick made no complaint.
"Do you have to do that?" he asked.
"We think we should take all precautions necessary. Now then, sit here Mr Royle." Once more he sat at the low table in the centre of the room. From his case, he took out his notebook and his loupe.
"Ready when you are," he said, knowing the Arab hates to be rushed. The wooden casket was brought out and placed in the centre of the table. It was opened and the contents, in soft leather pouches, were spread over the table top.
"Go ahead Mr Royle. Examine the diamonds."

Nick undid the tie of the first sac and tipped the diamonds on to the soft cloth covering the table. The stones were relatively small ones, about five carats and looked perfect. They were marquise cut and Nick recognised them from his previous knowledge of the stones he had read about in sales' catalogues. They had once belonged to a countess of the Hapsburg family who, when she had fallen on bad times, had broken up her tiara and sold the diamonds. There were only ten stones left now and they were worth perhaps a half, maybe three quarters of a million pounds. Nick looked at them through his lens, confirming his initial opinion of their origin. He made a note in his book and reached for the next sac. When he tipped the diamonds out on to the cloth, he knew again these were stones from a necklace, broken down when some other Middle European royal family had hit rock bottom. They all had fine defects on the edges of the stones where the mounts had been attached and had produced a little wear over the years of their use. These stones were of lesser value but as there were thirty-six of them, their total value was probably close to a million pounds. Slowly Nick examined the contents of all the leather bags in the box. Strangely, it was the last sac which contained the solitary Geneva diamond. He looked at it most carefully; Sly had done a good job making this. It certainly looked as beautiful as the real thing. He knew if he weighed it and measured it, it would not be the same data as those of the true diamond; but this time he wouldn't go through all that rigmarole. He would accept it at face value as he had been instructed to do.
"That's a beauty," he said. He turned to his book in which he had made his notes and added up the figures entered there. "For the whole collection as seen, I am able to offer you ten million pounds sterling."
"That's ridiculous Mr Royle; the large stone you looked at last was purchased two years ago for nine million pounds. The total value must exceed fifteen million."
Nick put his book and his loupe back in his case and closed it. He prepared to stand up. "I'm sorry to have wasted your time. There's no way this collection of diamonds, no matter how beautiful they are, is worth anything like the sum you suggest. If that is the figure you're looking for, then I'm afraid you'll have to look for another buyer; I'm not interested."

While Nick had been examining the diamonds the owner had come into the room. When he appreciated Nick might leave without buying the collection, he intervened. "As you are interested in the purchase of the complete collection, may I suggest the sum of thirteen million pounds would be fair?"

Nick turned to him. He was in the shadow so his face could not clearly be seen. "I gather you are the owner?" he said.
"Yes, they are mine; they are lovely and I'm sorry I have to sell them."
"Eleven million," Nick said.
"Twelve," replied the Arab.
"Eleven and a half is my final offer. I'm afraid that's as high as I'm permitted to go."
"Eleven and a half million pounds it is then." He advanced towards Nick, his hand extended. "You westerners rely on a handshake to confirm a deal I believe." Nick took his hand. It was limp and cold; it stimulated no confidence in Nick at all.
"May I give you my cheque now. I suggest it is taken to my bankers at once. They have been instructed to honour it immediately. I will remain with the stones and once the bank has confirmed the transaction is complete, I will be on my way. I hope you find that satisfactory?"
"Indeed, my agent will proceed at once. You will take coffee?" Remaining at the table with the diamonds, Nick nodded. "I'd be delighted," he said.

The ritual of drinking coffee was adhered to and it was a half an hour later, when the emissary returned, before Nick was able to get away and back to his office. The diamonds were placed in the vault, the safest place that Nick could use.
"You know Baas. I've been thinking. If someone should let the sheikh know you've got the diamonds here now, someone in the employ of his relative, yet paid by him, he could make it difficult. All he'd have to do is plan a raid or something on this place. And I believe Rosie is at risk until the whole thing is tied up. I think you should get these diamonds to the sheikh as soon as possible, even today."
"Well that should be possible. However, I would like to know that we'll be paid for the Geneva stone. I know what the sheikh agreed but I'd like to have the money in the bank. So firstly, I'll transfer six million pounds from the sheikh's account to ours. Once that's done, I'll deliver the whole collection to his hotel today. Will that make you happy?"
"It sure will Baas; but do it now. I've got a gut feeling, the longer the delay, the more likely something can go wrong."

Nick walked across to the telephone and dialled the bank.
"This Nicholas Royle speaking; may I be put through to the manager?"
There was a little delay before the operator indicated he'd been connected.

"Good afternoon Mr Royle. I hope the transaction we've just carried out was done to your satisfaction? Eleven and a half million pounds was transferred to the vendor's account."
"That's absolutely right. Now, I would like you to transfer to the account of Mr Michael Regale, six million pounds from the same account as paid the other sum. When that has been done, this particular deal will be completed."
"I'm sorry Mr Royle, that's not possible. As soon as the first transaction had been paid, the sheikh rang, making all other transfers of money void. I thought you would have known about it."
"So would I. Well, it's just as well I rang now or otherwise I might have been the loser of the six million pounds. Thank you for telling me."

"You were right Sly. There's going to be trouble. The sheikh has cancelled the funds. There is no money in the kitty to pay for Regale's Geneva diamond. He's hoping to get it for nothing. By the way, where is Rosie?"
"She went out shopping; said she'd be back about now," Sly said slowly straightening up. "All we need now is for him to try something with her."
"He'd better not even think about it. I will kill him if he hurts Rosie."
As he spoke, Nick's eyes flashed; no one could have doubted that he meant it.
"It wouldn't be in his best interest to hurt her, but he might hold her against her wishes for a while, just until you part with the diamond," Sly said.
"Well, there's nothing I can do for the time being; we've just got to wait until she gets back."

The minutes dragged by like hours. If Nick had looked at his watch once, he'd done it a dozen times, and it seemed an age before the bell rang and Nick saw it was Rosie at the door.
"Am I glad to see you," he said.
"And I've only been gone an hour or so to do some shopping," Rosie replied kissing him cheekily.
"I was rather afraid the sheikh might have decided to call my bluff and kidnap you," Nick explained. "He's blocked the account. I can't transfer the money to Regale. Until he pays up, we still have the diamond on our hands."
"I expect he's trying something on but I shouldn't worry; it will all become clear in a while," Sly guessed.
"Yes: but what's he up to? What's he doing? That's what I'd like to know."

Nick rang the sheikh at his hotel late in the afternoon.
"You asked me to let you know when I had obtained the collection of stones from your relative. The deal was concluded at about three and the bankers were asked to transfer eleven and a half million pounds to his account. I have confirmed that they have done so. Securicor will deliver the diamonds to your suite within the hour."
"Well done Mr Royle. I had expected to pay nearer thirteen million pounds for them. I am very pleased. Have you had any success in obtaining the stone Mr Regale has in his possession?"
"Not yet your Excellency. My agents have tracked him to New York. I am still waiting to know his address."
"Again, very good Mr Royle. Perhaps you'd let me know when that deal has been concluded as well?"
"Of course your Excellency. But I still have to find him and negotiate with him and persuade him somehow or other, to let me see it and then to part with it for six million pounds."
"Well, once it's done, let me know."
"One small thing your Excellency. The bank has told me the account I used is now frozen. If I found the Geneva diamond right now I couldn't buy it."
"Did I do that? How silly of me. I'll have to correct that won't I? I'll ring the bank in the morning."
"Why not now? It would seem the right thing to do," Nick retorted.

As he put the phone down, Nick murmured to his friends. "He's got something up his sleeve, I'm sure of it. But what? I'm no nearer to working it out."

CHAPTER FORTY-FIVE

Nick and Sly were working diligently at their benches the following morning, Nick preparing the first stone for laser treatment, while Sly was engrossed with the filling technique of the Yehuda method. Neither was aware of the other, they were so involved with the work they were doing. Rosie was spending an hour or so visiting her old friends near Bond Street and was expected at the office mid-morning. Nick had set the stone securely and using the control light, he had aligned the beam on the largest of the carbon flaws. He pulled the screen around his part of the bench so that Sly could continue his work while the laser was running, and warning Sly that he was about to start, he donned his protective goggles. The light, a pure light, did not refract into a spectrum, but spread brightly and uniformly as it hit the

screen. From time to time, Nick took his loupe and turning off the laser quickly, he examined the stone. It was some time before he changed the angle of entry of the beam and directed it on to another carbon defect. While that was working, he went around the screen to talk to Sly.
"That first one went very well. I can't see where it was at all now. If all the rest are done so easily, it will certainly be well worthwhile."
"I thought it would. This Yehuda method is much more tricky. It's easy enough to fill the crack but to do it completely and invisibly is fiddly to say the least. Still, I've been quite successful with this one so far."

They were both deeply preoccupied in their work when the door of the workshop suddenly crashed open noisily. They turned together to see the sheikh holding Rosie tightly, protected by two of his bodyguards. He walked into the room, dragging Rosie unwillingly behind him, her eyes averted from the laser working on Nick's bench.
"Ah, there you are Mr Royle; or is it Regale today? I see you are extremely busy. We met Miss Haynes outside so I thought I would escort her in to you rather than let her get lost. I hope I can persuade you to let me have the Geneva diamond as you call it, more cheaply than we contracted for. Perhaps I'll let my men free in your office to do a little damage first. As you watch them work, I'm sure you'll soon see things my way."
Nick had said nothing. He wanted the sheikh to come nearer to the bench and the laser, still working on the diamond in the clamp. He knew what he was going to do. When the sheikh and his guards were near enough, he'd fling back the protective cover over the source of the laser beam. If the sheikh was near enough, he would be blinded, perhaps permanently as well as his henchmen. If not blinded, then incapacitated for a time, long enough to sort them out. The sheikh continued his slow approach towards Nick and the bench, Rosie still trailing behind, her eyes tightly closed and her hand in front of her face.
"Good morning your Excellency. Not your usual way of entering I must say."
"I've come for the Geneva diamond," the sheikh snarled aggressively.
"I'm afraid the Geneva stone is not here. I haven't had the chance to ask Mr Regale yet. In any case, I doubt if he will part with it for the six million pounds you are offering. I'm not sure after this display whether I'll bother to ask him anyway."
"You've got my diamond; I know you have and I want it, now."

The sheikh had reached a position Nick thought would be effective. "Let me show you what I'm doing," he said, nonchalantly waving his arm in the direction of the laser. The sheikh's attention was drawn momentarily towards the machine. With a quick flip, the metal protective housing of the laser was opened and the intense laser rays radiated everywhere. The sheikh screamed with surprise as well as pain and so did both of his bodyguards, who, clutching their hands over their eyes, let Rosie free. She had kept her eyes closed. She turned and ran backwards, away from the light source while Nick replaced the cover and switched the power off.
"Are you all right Rosie," he asked anxiously.
"Yes, I kept my eyes closed. I knew you'd be using the laser."
"Good," he said to Rosie. Turning to the sheikh, he admonished him.
"You really should have taken precautions and worn eye protectors. The warning is outside the workshop; didn't you see it? If you've had a large dose, you may well be permanently blind; with a bit of luck though, it will be only conjunctivitis. Very sore of course and you won't know what long term damage you may have done to your eyes; you won't know that for years."
"Help us Royle. I wasn't being serious," the Arab whined.
"It's of no consequence now, your Excellency, our business is over. But I'll take you to the local hospital casualty department. They'll help you."

Dragging the sheikh and his guards behind him, Nick waved to the black Mercedes parked across the street. It pulled away from the kerb as soon as they all appeared on the pavement. Nick opened the rear doors and crammed the sheikh and his bodyguards on to the back seat of the car. The driver climbed out to assist. Pushing him out of the way, Nick took his place behind the wheel and slamming the door shut, he drove off to the local hospital, blue smoke billowing from the squealing tyres. When the porter approached him, telling him he couldn't park there, in front of the main entrance, Nick said, stressing the urgency of the situation, "His Excellency and his servants have had an accident. Take them to the eye ward quickly. They need urgent treatment; laser injuries to their eyes." Once that had been done, Nick was gone.

Nick left the sheikh's car there and walked slowly the mile or so back to the office. The sheikh's strong-arm men had done a good job, destroying the doorway where there was now a gaping hole, ragged and torn timbers holding together fragmenting plasterwork and broken bricks. It looked as if they had used a bomb to blast their way in. Security had gone by the board. There was no way they could continue their work there with all those valuable diamonds and other expensive equipment about with that huge gap in the wall. Nick was somewhat at a loss knowing what to do. He rang his insurers, more for advice than to make a claim. It would be difficult to complain a that a client had been cross enough to smash the door down, even though it was the truth. They listened sympathetically and within the hour, a repair team had arrived and shortly they began to take the rubble away. It seemed no time at all before the new wall had been constructed and the door frame built.

"Need a few guard dogs around tonight Guv," the foreman grinned. "Either that or fix yourself a bed here. Perhaps you'd better get yourself a dog as well to protect you."

"You're right," Nick agreed, as he turned to ring Securicor, a service he had used frequently in the past.

"I'm afraid I've had a little trouble in the workshop. Can you arrange guards and dogs to keep an eye on things tonight?" he asked the supervisor.

"Of course, Mr Royle; no problem."

"Many thanks," Nick answered.

By the time it was possible to leave the premises, guards had been placed in the office and workshop and Nick felt he had taken all the precautions he could. Tomorrow, the builders had arranged to hang a new and stronger door. Once that had been done, business would be as usual.

"What a day," he said to Rosie, as they left the office. "Who would have forecast this morning that all this would happen?"

"I warned you I thought he was a nasty piece of work, but I must say I didn't expect this. Let's hope he leaves us alone now; we can do without his patronage," Sly said.

"However, we've still got a diamond worth six million pounds plus on our hands. He knows it and as well, he knows about Rosie's father and her mother and where they're living. I think we've still got trouble; loads of it."

"Do you think we should warn Mum and Mr Celleri?" piped up Rosie.

"I don't think we'll worry your Mum and Dad just yet. The sheik is going to need all the help he can get while his eyes are worrisome to him. I must say I feel a bit sorry for him. I hope he won't be blind permanently. I think I'll call at the hospital later to see how he is."

All of them had their dark thoughts that night, yet during the evening, Nick and Rosie found time to call at the hospital looking after the Arab. He no longer looked a powerful force, wrapped up in bandages framing his hooked semitic nose and thick pointed grey beard, though, because of these features, he was instantly recognisable. He became aware of their presence as they approached his bed.

"Who is there?" he demanded.

"Well I don't suppose you'd expect it to be Nick Royle with Miss Haynes after your behaviour today. Why on earth did you have to break in the way you did? The door's nearly always open and all you had to do anyway was knock or ring the bell. Someone would have let you in."

The sheikh did not answer immediately. "I behaved badly today; I was a disgrace to my race," he said. "I thought I could bully you into giving me the diamond. You see Mr Royle, I know you are Regale."

"I don't believe you, your Excellency."

"When you first visited my relative as Regale, I had my men follow you both when you left the penthouse. You took many detours and many taxis and eventually they lost you near a block of apartments. But after the Regales had disappeared and they were still hunting around for them, they recognised the two of you coming out of the same building and as my agents said, 'You were both looking very pleased with yourselves'." Nick looked across at Rosie with amazement.

"At the time, the significance of that was not apparent. But then, other things began to occur, especially your unexpected Spanish trip. I know the Regales went to Monte Carlo via Spain and that they flew back in a private aircraft. One thing the pilot remembered in his drowsy state was Miss Haynes calling Mr Regale, Nick. He said you covered it up by using your assumed name Mick Regale, but it stuck in his mind."

"All rather circumstantial evidence I would think," Nick said, a hint of uncertainty in his voice.

"Maybe Mr Royle, maybe."

"Well, we came to see how you are. You've been on my mind since all this happened. What has the doctor said?"

"Before the bandages were applied I was beginning to see faintly again; not clearly, but I could make things out. It would appear the laser has damaged the outer part of the retina, I think the doctor called it and I may never see with that part properly again, but he hopes the central vision will be unaffected."

"I do hope so. I felt very guilty when I did what I did, but very threatened as well."

"Don't blame yourself Mr Royle; you did what you felt you had to do.

I have been told I shall remain bandaged for a day or two and then hopefully I shall be all right. It was thoughtful of you to care. When I'm out of here, I will have the six million pounds in cash delivered to you. Perhaps you will let me call on you respectfully next time? You see, I still want to acquire that diamond. I'm counting on you."
"Next time, try telephoning first your Excellency. We both look forward to your complete recovery. We shall leave you now. Good night."
The sheikh extended his hand towards Nick's voice. "Good night Mr Royle and thank you again for coming."

"He really was well informed wasn't he? There didn't seem to be a thing he didn't know," Rosie said in amazement.
"He must have spies around all over the place. That's what wealth can do. He didn't seem such a bad lot tonight. I expect he's been very frightened by what happened."
"Anyway, enough of him for tonight. He won't be able to know what's going to go on in your flat for the next few hours, will he?" Rosie asked, mischief written all over her face.
"I certainly hope not," Nick replied.

CHAPTER FORTY-SIX

Back at the office the next morning, while the builders were busy fitting a new door, Nick and Sly were at their particular places at the bench, each engrossed in his task. Outside, the Mercedes which had so often been the harbinger of bad news, drew up. Two Arabs, servants of the sheikh climbed out and opening the boot, they each lifted out a large leather case. The cases were heavy and they struggled with them up to Nick's office. One of them had been delegated spokesman.
"We have been instructed to deliver these cases to you. Our master wishes to receive the merchandise as soon as you obtain it."
"What's inside the cases?" demanded Nick.
"We do not know; we assumed it was money," the Arab replied.

Nick lifted one of the cases on to a space on the bench top. It was unlocked and when he lifted the lid, there were bundles of fifty pound notes, each bundle of two hundred was worth ten thousand pounds. In each case, there were three hundred bundles; in the two cases, there was six million pounds.
"Phew; I've never seen anything like it before," he said. "I guess the

Geneva diamond is the sheikh's now. What say we let these two emissaries take it to him now; it would save us the effort."
"And if they disappear with the diamond, we'll still owe the sheikh six million pounds. With all due respect to these men, I think you should deliver the stone yourself Nick," Rosie said, smiling towards the Arabs.
"Perhaps you're right. I'll get it out of the vault and take it personally to his suite. I expect he's back at the hotel now." Turning to the Arabs, he asked, "Is your master still in hospital or is he back in his hotel suite?"
"He came out of hospital this morning," the spokesman said.
"Tell your master I'll be calling on him in a short while with the merchandise."

They salaamed and left, backing out of the workshop respectfully, murmuring they would tell their master what had been said.
"I was thinking Rosie, perhaps you'd come along with me. You can so conveniently carry the diamond in the locket around your neck. It's still unlikely anyone would suspect that."
"That's fine. I'd quite like to see where the old devil hangs out."
"That's not the way to talk about one of our major customers albeit he is an old devil," Nick joked. "I'll go and get the diamond and then we can get on our way."

Down in the basement of the workshop, the smooth steel front of the vault faced Nick at the foot of the stairs. The container part was buried in concrete taking up most of the side wall of the cellar. It looked impregnable and it would probably have taken a fair amount of explosive to have destroyed it. When it was built, it had been the best Nick could afford. He tapped the combination in to the dial and spinning the handle, he eased the massive door ajar. As it swung open, a light switched on automatically inside the vault, illuminating the shelves of steel boxes on either side. The fronts of the boxes were protected further by thin steel rods which slotted inside rings on their fronts. It would have been impossible to open a box without first being able to unbolt the rod and slide it out from its place on the shelf. Nick knew which box contained the Geneva diamond and the gem was in his pocket, inside its leather sac within minutes. Reversing the process, the contents were protected once again and the heavy vault door swung back into place. Back upstairs in the workshop, Nick tipped the diamond on to the table top and while Rosie put it into the glass locket, Nick put one of the larger, but poorer quality Russian stones in the sack. It was a stone of little more than industrial quality. He tightened the draw-string and put the sack into his inside pocket. Now all precautions had been taken, they could make their way to the sheikh's lair.

The sheikh was resting when they arrived at his suite, but he rose to greet them, dark glasses shading his eyes.
"How are you today Your Excellency?" Nick asked. "Is your vision better?"
"I've been lucky. Apparently very little vision has been lost. Have you brought the diamond?" the sheikh asked greedily.
"But of course. If I'm Regale, I must have had it all the time."
"Yes. May I see it?"
Nick removed the locket from around Rosie's neck and gently tipped the stone from its hiding place on to the sheikh's open palm. Imediately, the fire of the diamond was released. Tongues of flame flashed around the room, gasps of awe and perhaps fear murmured from all their lips. Reverentially, the sheikh whispered, "It's mine. That wastrel of a nephew has it no more. And all for nothing."
"Did you say something I should have heard?" Nick asked the sheikh.
Grinning, he said, "No, I don't think so Mr Royle."

The business with the sheikh done, Nick and Rosie returned to the office. Sly was still working at his bench, quietly, systematically repairing nature's defects in the diamonds she had produced. There was no sign of the money.
"I've put it all in the vault. I've never seen that much cash before."
"Nor have I Sly, but it's too late to get it round to the bank today. It'll have to be our first job in the morning," Nick said.

Nick and Sly struggled down the stairs and on to the pavement with the heavy leather cases containing the six million pounds the sheikh had paid in cash for the Geneva diamond. With equal difficulty, they lifted them into the boot of Nick's car.
"Perhaps you'd better come too Sly. I'll never manage them myself the other end, they're much too awkward for me alone."
"Sure thing Baas. I'll lock up first." He disappeared up the stairs to ensure everything was safe. Millions of pounds worth of diamonds were lying around in the office and workshop, easy pickings for an opportunist thief.
"Where's Rosie this morning?" he asked when he got back.
"Gone window shopping for a wedding dress I believe. Do you know Sly, I've been so lucky finding her. She's all I would ever want in a woman."

"It's a pity she hasn't any sisters, you could have pointed them this way," he said jokingly. "I know you'll be very happy together; I can feel it in my bones."
"And we've got to respect the old man's bones, haven't we?" Nick laughed.
"You can mock, but you know it's true."

They arrived at the bank during a busy period and there was some difficulty finding a parking space.
"Out you get Sly. Ask the doorman if there's any easier parking around the back. It would be safer too."
Sly jumped out with all the speed his injured leg would allow and dashed up to the doorman outside the bank. "Excuse me. We've got a very large amount of money in cash in the boot of the car to deposit. Is there any way we can get the car closer?" Sly asked.
"First turning on the left Guv," the man said. "It'll bring you round the back where all the security vans unload. I'll meet you there."
Nick drove around the corner to an alley where the rear door of the bank opened. The large feeding chute, into which the boxes of money were to be tipped, was closed now by a stout metal plate. The commissionaire appeared and opening the security screen, he indicated to Nick where the cases of money should be emptied, into a tunnel which ended deep inside the bank. Nick and Sly heaved again and the cases disappeared.
"Let's go and talk to the manager now; see if he can arrange some sort of anonymous trust fund."
"If it's the same to you Baas, I'll leave it to you. I'm in a delicate place with one of those repairs. I'll take the car back if that's all right."
"Okay Sly. See you back at the office."

Inside the bank, Nick waited for the manager to appear; many minutes went by. Nick looked at his watch. It had been nearly twenty minutes since he had tipped the cases containing the cash down the chute. Could they be counting it all before talking to him? No, they weighed money now, even paper money. There were so many other jobs waiting to be done in the workshop. He stood up and approached one of the personal bankers in the foyer.
"Excuse me," he said. "I deposited a large amount of money in the safe at the back of the bank a little while ago. I had arranged to speak with the manager before I went. Could you see if he's likely to be free shortly?"
"Can you wait a moment sir? I'll enquire what's keeping him."
There were several minutes more delay before the manager came out to

Nick. He looked harrassed. "Mr Royle, I'm so sorry to have kept you waiting. Would you mind coming into my office for a moment?"
Nick followed him across the bank and the manager held the door open for him as he entered the room. Three men were inside already. Two of them stood up as he came through the door and though Nick was well over six feet tall, these men seemed to dwarf him. The third was a smaller man, with fair sandy hair combed backwards from a prominent brow and his skin was sallow as if it rarely saw the light. Bushy eyebrows shaded piercing pale blue eyes, rimmed with metal-framed spectacles. When he looked at Nick, he felt his innermost thoughts were being read. He remained seated.
"Mr Royle, these men are police officers. I've had to ask them to come in. I hope you don't mind their being here."
"Police? No, of course not."
"It was you who deposited six million pounds through the security hatch a short while ago, wasn't it?" the manager asked Nick.
"That's right. Two large leather cases containing that much money as far as I know. I hadn't counted it."
"May I ask you how you obtained such a large amount of cash? You see, it's much more than we have here at any time in the bank. We don't have many depositers leaving that sort of money with us."
"You will remember the sheikh with whom I've been doing some business recently, cancelled a banker's draft for six million pounds?"
"Yes, I remember."
"He wanted a diamond I was selling, but wasn't prepared to pay for it. He wanted to try and get it for nothing. He thought he could trick me into parting with the gem; that's why he cancelled that draft."
"Continue Mr Royle."
"He hoped I would deliver the diamond to him before the money had been transferred into my account. When he found I had checked, he was more than a little upset."
"I see."
"He sent his men to threaten me first and then he came himself, suggesting he would kidnap a good friend of mine if I didn't do as he asked."
"Good Lord. Can you prove all this Mr Royle?"
"Yes, I can. Then later, when he forcibly entered my workshop a few days ago, he sustained laser injuries to his eyes which necessitated his urgent admission to hospital."
"You were using a laser at the time?" It was the third policeman who now took over the questioning.
"Yes. Fortunately his injuries were not serious but while I visited him in hospital, he intimated he still wanted to buy the diamond. Yesterday,

his henchmen delivered the cases of money which we then brought along here for safe keeping."

"Is that the whole story Mr Royle?"

"Yes," Nick replied.

"And where is the diamond now?"

"The sheikh has it. I delivered it to him yesterday afternoon, after the money had been received."

"Did it ever cross your mind to ask where all that money had come from? How it was possible to pay six million pounds in cash for the diamond?" the policeman asked.

"No, it didn't. I know the sheikh spends much of his time in casinos and gambles heavily. I supposed he kept a large amount of ready money for his expenses there," Nick replied.

"Why didn't you deposit the money at the bank yesterday rather than risk keeping it on your premises overnight?"

"It was late in the afternoon when the money arrived and both my colleague and I were busy with jobs we had started. We just didn't have the time."

"Will the sheikh confirm your story Mr Royle?"

"I don't see why not. That's exactly what happened."

"Where is he staying?"

"At the Dorchester, in the penthouse suite."

"Perhaps you'd come along with us Mr Royle."

"If I have to, but I've an enormous amount of work waiting to be done."

"If we go now we shouldn't be too long. Would you come along too Mr Brown?" the policeman asked the bank manager.

"Yes, if you think it necessary, though I've never met the sheikh. All our business has been done by letter or 'phone."

"Come along anyway. You may be able to help."

"Can you tell me why you want me to accompany you to the sheikh's apartment? I really do have loads of work to do," Nick said.

"Mr Royle. You deposited six million pounds of largely counterfeit money at the bank. Now I would agree that would be a dumb thing to do if you knew it was funny money, but nevertheless, it was you who had it in your possession. That's a serious offence Mr Royle. It's our job to find out where it came from. At the moment, you're our only suspect."

"You mean he's tricked me. I might have guessed he'd have the last laugh."

"What do you mean?" the policeman asked.

"If the money is counterfeit, the old devil has got the diamond for nothing after all; and furthermore, he's landed me right in the mire. I

can tell you now, he's unlikely to admit he's done anything wrong."
"Maybe you're right sir. If that's the case Mr Royle, you've got problems."

Nick's mind was racing as they rushed through the London traffic to the sheikh's hotel. He knew the sheikh would deny everything he'd told the police and doubted whether they would believe Sly's or Rosie's confirmation of his story. And it was imperative no one should talk about the Spanish connection; that would really cause problems. He sighed. Perhaps he was worrying unnecessarily; maybe the sheikh would have a simple explanation for all that had happened though Nick couldn't think of any way out.

They all crowded into the tiny lift which took them to the top floor. As the lift door opened into the sheikh's apartments, there was that heavy perfumed atmosphere characteristic of the Middle East. But the place was empty. Just as the bedouin could up tents and leave an oasis in the desert, quickly, in the middle of the night, leaving little trace of his presence, so the sheikh had left the penthouse suite in the Dorchester. The only memory he had left there was the heady perfume which lingered.

"Looks as if the bird has flown," the police officer said. "While it does nothing to confirm your story, it does seem to make it more likely." He lifted the telephone and called reception.
"Can you tell me where the last occupant of the penthouse suite is now?" he asked.
"His Excellency left in the early hours of the morning," reception answered. "I assume he left for his home country. You might try his consulate."
"Thank you." He dialled again, this time speaking to someone at immigration. After a few moments he said, "the sheikh and his entourage left in his private plane some hours ago. I would guess he's somewhere over northern Europe right now, flying south. Well, Mr Royle. You'll have to come down to the station with us while we make some more enquiries. You're not out of the wood yet I'm afraid and I'm sorry, the money you deposited is confiscated. Let's hope it's tax deductable," he added lightly.
"Can I tell my friends what has happened?"
"You're allowed a phone call if you wish," the officer said.

Nick rang the office and explained to Sly that he was at Bow Street police station. "I think Rosie had better stay away for the moment. They say they have to make their enquiries. I've no idea what that means nor how long it's likely to take. Look after her Sly."

At the police station Nick was treated as if he had been found guilty of some heinous crime. His finger prints were recorded and those photographs known as mug-shots taken and his watch and the contents of his pocket emptied into a paper bag. When all the details had been taken down, his belt and tie were taken as well before he was locked in a cell on his own to await the return of the police whom he had met at the bank. The door slammed shut; it had a fatalistic sound; a release from reality. The place smelled of disinfectant, vaguely masking that of alcohol and vomit. Nick looked around him, loathing any contact with the place. The yellow painted walls were crudely scratched in places by previous occupants, who like Nick, had endless time on their hands. The underlying nauseous green paint showed through;the whole place was soul-destroyingly, mind-bogglingly boring.

Nick had no idea how long he had been kept there before the short policeman, who had done all the talking previously, returned.
"It's about time someone came," Nick remarked, jumping up as soon as he recognised his visitor.
"Mr Royle. I am a senior officer in the fraud squad," he said, waving some form of identity in front of Nick's face. "You were in possession of a huge amount of counterfeit money and it was only right we should try to find out how you came by it and whether you were telling me the truth. If we had been unable to confirm any of your story, you would have been charged with possession and I would have thrown the book at you. A place like this may then have been your permanent home for a long time." He paused, letting his words sink in. Nick waited anxiously for what he was going to say next. "As it is, we went over the penthouse apartment with a fine tooth comb and found some good quality paper which looks as if it is the sort the notes were printed on. We realise of course, you may have left it there to implicate the sheikh."
"But that's not possible if he left early this morning," Nick said.
"Well, if not you, then one of your friends could have."
"But none of us had any idea the sheikh was going to leave."
"That's what you say and I'm inclined to believe you. I believe too the paper may have been left there deliberately for us to find. Then, though you were implicated, it would have been unlikely that you were guilty of the offence."
"You mean the sheikh may have been trying to protect me?"

"It looks rather like that."
"The old devil. But why does he do it? He must be as rich as Croesus," Nick asked.
"He gets his highs on gambling, chancing his arm. As you say, he doesn't need the money; it's the con that gives him the thrill."
"Yes, I can understand that," Nick replied somewhat guiltily.
"We've been investigating the odd fake fifty pound note which has been turning up all over the place especially at centres of gambling, casinos, the races and suchlike for some time," the policeman said.
"I see," Nick said.
"And there has been some evidence of a Middle East connection. We believe that notes printed out there somewhere are being imported into this country, perhaps in the diplomatic bag, for sale and distribution in the underworld here."
Nick said nothing. He felt relieved.
"Oh, by the way. The doorman at the Dorchester was tipped by the sheikh after he had helped with all his luggage. He was given two fifty pound notes, both as dud as yours; the same printing as yours. He's been much more descriptive of the sheikh and what he'll do to him should he show his face there again."
He smiled. His was quite a boyish face when he smiled. Nick wondered at the change in appearance with his change in mood.
"I'm glad you're not the guilty party Mr Royle," he said. "But I'm disappointed we didn't catch the sheikh. If you had deposited the money the night before, we'd have got him."
"I'm sorry too," Nick added. "If you think I'm not guilty now, does that mean I can go?"
"Yes, you can go. That's a lot of money for your company to lose Mr Royle. Can you afford to take the loss?"
"We're going to have to," Nick replied. "Fortunately, we've entered into a large contract with a Russian source of gems recently. The Russkies need the hard currency urgently and so we've been able to buy at very reasonable prices which will allow a healthy profit margin. Our bankers will have to wait for repayment of capital, but as long as the interest is paid off, I'm sure our credit will remain good. It would have been horrendous if you'd arrested me and charged me, keeping me in custody. As long as I'm working I can help to clear up the debts we've got."
"A very philosophical view Mr Royle. Not many would be so sanguine. I'm sorry that this has happened."
"By the way; you implied earlier that some of the money deposited was genuine. I suppose I'll be able to use that?"
"I don't know Mr Royle; I'll have to take advice, but I don't see why

not." All Nick wanted to do now was to get back to the office and confide in the others. Whatever they let the police know, their trip to Barcelona must not be mentioned. Anything, but that.

CHAPTER FORTY-SEVEN

It was very late in the evening by the time Nick returned to the workshop. Sly was still there, working away at the Yehuda treatment on a diamond.

"You've been a time," Sly said. "I was getting anxious. Rosie's worried sick. It was all I could do to persuade her to go back to the apartment. She kept wanting to go down to the police station."

"I'm glad she didn't do that." He paused as he rethought what had happened during the last few hours.

"That old devil of a sheikh well and truly conned us, paying us off with counterfeit money. We carried out our scam successfully only to be cheated by him. A lot of the notes in those cases were duds; funny money. I've been all this time talking with the fraud squad, trying to persuade them I knew nothing about it."

Sly's grin cracked his face. "Just think how we struggled lifting those cases and all for nothing. Did you tell the police the money came from the sheikh?"

"Of course I did. So they said, 'what say we go and ask him?' And what do we find when we get there? The cupboard was bare; he'd gone with all his entourage. The only thing to link him with the penthouse suite was the perfume of Arabia. He's certainly had the last laugh, the old villain."

Sly grinned again. "I told you he was dangerous. We'll just have to write it off to experience."

"We don't want too many deals like that or we'll go bust. Let's call it a day Sly. You must be whacked and I know I won't be able to concentrate on anything right now."

Nick and Sly were wrapped up in their work when the bell rang the following morning and the two policemen from the fraud squad appeared on the television screen of the front door.

"That's all we need right now," Nick said. Nick released the electronic lock, calling for the two men to open the door and come upstairs. He watched them as they followed his instructions. He met them at the entrance.

"Come in," he said, inviting them into the workplace. "This is my partner," he said, waving his arm in Sly's direction.

"Hi there. What a pleasant working place you have," one of them said.
"Thank you."
"What d'you do here exactly?"
"Together, we run a business, importing and preparing diamonds mainly for resale, usually to the trade. We carry out some mounting for private sale, but that is a very limited part of our business. We certainly have nothing to do with printing money, real or fake." He smiled as he spoke about printing money, but their faces remained dead-pan.
"We need to take a complete statement from you Mr Royle and from your partner if he was present when the sheikh visited you."
"Of course. And while you're taking statements, you might like to speak to the firm of builders which has just completed the repairs to the damage done by the sheikh when he came last."
"You didn't tell us about any damage to your property."
"No? Well, when the sheikh called on us last a few days ago, he destroyed the doorway. That had to be repaired quickly for security reasons. The builders finished it yesterday."
"You and the sheikh didn't get on too well it would seem?" the police asked.
"It was a complicated relationship. He wanted something he thought an unworthy relative of his owned. When he found out he didn't have it, he expected me to find it and obtain it for him. Once I'd done that, he wanted to welch on the deal and get the stone from me for nothing. In fact, that's what he has done by paying for the diamond with counterfeit money."
"What do you plan to do now?" Nick was asked.
"There's not a lot I can do at the moment. It's largely my word against his and he's a very rich and powerful man to oppose, perhaps with diplomatic immunity. Furthermore, he's somewhere over there and I'm here. Still I'll bide my time."
"That sounds rather like a threat."
"Not really; maybe he'll need my services on another occasion; I can wait."
"Can we take a look around? We have to make sure you don't have a printing press on the premises," the other policeman said, sounding just a little more friendly than his colleague.
"Be my guest," Nick said cooperatively.

When they had completed their search the two policeman had coffee with Nick and Sly, meticulously taking down their statements in long hand.
"Well there's nothing more we have to do here," one of them said. "We have to ask you both to surrender your passports for the time being.

I'm sure you'll be off the hook pretty soon. Our boss is fairly certain the Arab is the one he wants. But while he's still looking into it, we're to instruct you not to stray too far from home."
"I'll be glad when he tells us he believes everything we've told him."
"It won't be long sir, I'm sure. We'll be off now. Thanks for the coffee." They were gone.

It was much later in the day when the chief of the fraud squad himself called at Nick's office.
"I thought I'd let you know that we've been talking to Interpol. It would seem that some other European countries have been troubled with the appearance of counterfeit money in large amounts over the last year or two. I'm sure you'll be pleased to know their enquiries have suggested a Middle Eastern source, rather as ours have."
"I'm glad to hear it," Nick said. "Does that mean we're no longer your favourite suspects?"
The policeman smiled. "I don't think I ever thought you really were involved. Mind you, I had to go through all the motions. Maybe you were implicated. But I must say you'd have to be a real fool to have deposited at one go all that forged money in the bank. They would have been sure to have recogised it."
"That's what I said all along," Nick said.
"Still, people do silly things, hoping to get away with it just because it's so unlikely. Here're your passports back. I don't think I need to restrict your movements and I suppose you may want them for your business."
"And I'm to be married shortly. We haven't planned our honeymoon yet but I'm sure we'll be off abroad somewhere."
"Just as well we've got it all sorted out in time then. Best of luck." With a wave of his hand, he was gone.

"That's a weight off my shoulders," Nick said. "I thought that would be hanging over our heads for some time; what a relief."
"Now why don't you go and tell Rosie the good news. She was pretty upset, thinking her husband-to-be might be locked away before the wedding." Sly grinned at his attempt to be flippant.
"Okay Sly, I'll be off. Thanks."

As he opened up the flat he could hear Rosie moving about inside, humming quietly as she prepared a meal for them both, a focus of domesticity.
"Rosie, have I got some news for you?"
She came through into the hall, her hair slightly awry, a small splodge

of dough on the tip of her nose and an early blush spreading over her face. Her hands were dusty with flour and held well away from her apron.
"And pray tell me young sir what is this news of such great import that it drags me away from preparing the meal for my lover's arrival?" she asked cocquettishly.
"Rosie, they have returned our passports. We are no longer suspects. They are pretty certain the sheikh is an international crook, passing off counterfeit money in many other countries as well as Britain. Anyway, we're off the hook; we can plan our wedding and honeymoon without any worries now."
"Oh Nick, that's wonderful. I was speaking to Mum today and we wondered whether we can arrange something for a month's time. What d'you think?"
"That's fine with me. Have they been able to arrange a church service?"
"No Nick, it'll have to be in a registrar's office I'm afraid, but you don't really mind, do you?"
"No Darling, of course not. I've told you I just want us to be married."
"Oh Nick Royle, I'm such a lucky girl." She kissed him gently on the lips. The small splodge of dough was now squashed on to Nick's cheek. As they separated, she laughed wickedly, reaching for the handkerchief in his top pocket to wipe it away.
"Where would you like to go on your honeymoon? Now my passport has been returned we can plan to go anywhere. I had been concerned the authorities would have held on to it. That would have been a problem."
"Let's have a look around tomorrow Nick. With only a month there mayn't be as much choice as we'd like. Do you have any preference?"
"I've never been to the Seychelles. I understand it's very beautiful there. There's a hotel I've heard about, which has cottages right down on the beach of brilliant white sand. It sounds wonderful"
"Oh Nick, I can't wait."

CHAPTER FORTY-EIGHT

Sammy and Elizabeth arrived from New York two days before the weddings were due to occur. Since they had received their invitation, everything else had had to be sidetracked, much to Sammy's irritation, while they concentrated on their preparations. Sammy had to have a new suit. Elizabeth said so.

"You can't go to a wedding in England looking like that. You need a nice subdued pinstripe grey, the sort of suit Nick would wear," Elizabeth had said. "We'll go this afternoon and choose something for you and then you can come across to Bloomingdales and help me with my outfit."
"It's supposed to be a pleasure going to a wedding," Sammy groaned. "I've got loads of suits in my closet, enough for dozens of weddings. I don't really need another one do I?"
Elizabeth withered him with a stare. "You're coming with me to buy a proper suit this afternoon and that's that."

With bad grace, Sammy went with Elizabeth uptown in the early afternoon. It was not easy to find something that Elizabeth thought Sammy would look smart in, but eventually they did find just the thing she had in mind. Despite his protestations, he had to agree it was just right for an English wedding. Mind you, he hastened to add, he wouldn't be seen dead in it for his everyday work in New York. No one would recognise him. And with even worse grace, he accompanied Elizabeth across town to Bloomingdales. Despite the recession it was a busy store that afternoon and it was some time before they found the floor they wanted and then something that Elizabeth liked. Like many women choosing something special, she saw an outfit she fancied almost as soon as she entered the department. But it was necessary to see many more and try them all on, only to find it was that which she had seen first was what she ultimately chose. Sammy was bored out of his mind. He tried to maintain some enthusiasm, but it was impossible after the umpteenth collection was tried on. Even the assistant was beginning to look a little weary. But choose they did and when at home they packed ready to leave, even Sammy had to admit that Elizabeth had been right; they wouldn't shame Nick or Rosie on their very special day. They'd look the part.

Their preparations for the wedding had been recognised by one of the Mafia button men and their conversations about the wedding had been eavesdropped and eventually relayed to Celleri's don out on Staten Island.
'A wedding uh? Must be between Celleri's pretty little pup and that Englishman, the one that was doing business with the Jew, Goldstein. I'd sure like to louse that up somehow. Serve them all right.' He chewed it over for a day or so.
'Perhaps I could knock off Goldstein? Now that would give me some pleasure, but it wouldn't really do much good. What about killing the girl? Had the chance once before; should have done it then. No. What

about wasting the Limey? There'd be no wedding then.' The more he thought about it, the more he liked it. 'Yeah, that's a swell idea. After all, if he hadn't come to the States then, none of these bum deals would have happened.' He paused. 'It would mean going over there. Bit tricky trying to kill someone in England but not impossible. Who shall I send? Ain't got no one I can rely on to do a real neat job. Maybe I'll go and do it. Bit rusty but I guess I could if I tried. Yeah, I feel like a trip. Make it a working holiday.'

Through his agents scattered in the many businesses in which he had a finger, the don found out all the travelling details the Goldsteins had made to get to England. He reserved a seat on the same flight, where he could keep an eye on his target. He knew if he followed them closely, they would lead him to Nick.

Nick and Rosie met Sammy and Elizabeth at Heathrow. They were all so thrilled to see each other again, it was a noisy gathering and it was sometime before Nick was able to get them and all their luggage into the car and drive them to Meryl's place in the Home Counties. Celleri's don was among those passengers on that flight and he watched carefully to see what was happening. When they left, he followed them all the way to the hotel. Now he knew where they were all likely to be for the time being.

Meryl had never met Sammy and Elizabeth before of course but she laid on the very best accommodation that was possible for them. She made them very comfortable in the best suite in the hotel. That evening they all joined together for dinner, Meryl and Michael, Sammy and Elizabeth and Sly, Nick and Rosie. Sammy and Michael had a lot to reminisce over since those weeks Celleri had been nursed to full health again at Sammy's home. The two men were now firm friends. Once coffee had been served, Sammy turned to Celleri.
"What d'you think would happen if the mob knew you were here?"
"I hate to think. I wouldn't give much for my chances."
"Don't spoil the evening with such talk," Rosie said. "There's no way that evil man can know you're alive now. He was there at your funeral. I saw him there."
"Don't ever underestimate the Mafia, Rosie. They have eyes and ears everywhere. In shops and stores, in transport, in just about everything you use regularly in life. They put snippets of information together and always report back to someone higher up the chain of command. I know, I've been part of that chain for years."

"You're worrying me now," Sammy said. "What say they know about our trip? If they can put two and two together as you say they can, then they're sure to have worked out why we're here."
"I had thought about such a possibilty," Celleri said. "I too am on the lookout for trouble all the time. I've too much to lose now Meryl and I have found one another again. I can't let that happen."

Two very different weddings took place at the registrar's office on that Friday, late in October. Miss Meryl Haynes married her childhood sweetheart, Mr Michael Chaney, recently returned from America, where he had been living for the last few years. Meryl looked stunning in a two-piece outfit in eau-de-nil and looked far too young to be the mother of the other bride, Rosie. Michael overcame his stoop and the skilful effort of his coiffeur concealed the ravages of the fire on his head. That day, he looked very much the senior figure and the head of the family.

But nothing could detract anything from Rosie. She looked simply beautiful in a pale ivory creation, softened with a hint of cream, with a mist of tulle and a large brimmed hat which matched the colour of the dress exactly. Her long shapely legs were sheathed in the finest denier hose, also in the palest of shades and her complexion matched her clothes perfectly. And beneath the brim of her hat, her wayward sovereign coloured locks threatened to spill on to her shoulder; but who cared? They were so magnificent. Nick, so tall and elegant stood alongside Rosie. What a handsome couple they made.

One other lonely figure had witnessed them leaving the registar's office from across the road. His heart, so full of hate, had leapt when he watched the tall, yet slightly stooped man escort his bride into the waiting limousine. Despite the changes caused by the burns, he knew that man instantly. That man was Celleri, his capo, the man who in his eyes had been responsible for the fire in the casino, his casino. He knew then the man he had to kill was Celleri. He was his enemy.

The formalities over, they all returned to Meryl's hotel where a reception had been arranged for them. Sly had been Nick's best man and he had agreed to act for Michael too. His speech was short and to the point, much to Nick's relief, but it was enough to round off the day for the newly-weds. Meryl and Michael planned to stay in England, taking a short break in the Lake District, where neither of them had been before. Later, on their return, Michael would have to start thinking how he was going to occupy his time. He wasn't trained to be anything other than the manager of a casino but hopefully, there'd be something he could help with. And Meryl too wondered what part her new husband might play in the running of the hotel. Strangely, she had never thought she might wish to delegate the responsibility of the running of the hotel to anyone, least of all to a husband. But so much had happened in the last few weeks. She had wanted it to happen. No one had pushed her into doing anything she hadn't wanted to do. She knew exactly what was going to happen from the first moment Michael had returned to her life. She had loved him all these years, no one could change that. Now he had come back and she wanted him to stay. And that meant marriage together. And Michael had wanted it too; she was sure of that.

And Michael did want to be with Meryl. He could only have dreamed in the past she would take him back after all that time apart and that disastrous running away. Now all those 'if onlys' gained perspective. She had still loved him and now they were married. They were together. Though Meryl had been thoughtful and kindly and so very helpful in Michael's recovery and rehabilitation, their physical relationship had not progressed. Michael was prepared to wait until Meryl made a move; he feared being rebuffed. After all, he had been celibate all these years and he had been the guilty party, running away. Maybe it would never happen; if that were the case, he could accept it. The point was they were together again and happy. That was all that really mattered.

CHAPTER FORTY-NINE

Nick and Rosie had booked their honeymoon in the Seychelles. They spent their first night as man and wife in the bridal suite in Meryl's hotel, as the flight from Heathrow left on Saturday in the afternoon. Nick had reserved a cottage on the beach at the Fisherman's Cove Hotel on the southern end of the Beau Vallon bay, overlooking the west of the island. It was in the cool pre-dawn when they arrived, jet-lagged and tired at the Victoria airport at Mahé. They were taken to their granite-walled cottage, the roofs thatched with palm fronds, the windows opening directly on to the patio and the beach, cooled by the sea breezes. The sand was a brilliant white, formed from the offshore coral reefs and the dark green tropical forest flowed down to the water's edge from the granite peaks towering inland. It was magical.

"Nick, it's simply wonderful; it's so breathtakingly beautiful," Rosie

whispered as she turned to him on the patio. "Oh, I'm so in love with you. Wasn't it lucky we met and fell in love?"
"It is beautiful isn't it? I had been told about this hotel but I would never have thought it could have been so lovely. And to be able to share it with you my love, makes it all the more marvellous." Their two heads came together to seal their love for one another.

Back in Britain, Michael and Meryl had left for the Lakes on the Saturday morning, Meryl driving her old Volkswagen, much to Michael's pleasure. He hated driving on the left hand side of the road; when he had tried, they both had a feeling of impending disaster, so it was left to Meryl to get them there. With eyes for one another only, neither of them was aware of a hire car driven by a solitary figure which followed them northwards.

They stopped for lunch in a road-side pub somewhere north of Birmingham, leaving their pursuer enough time to have a good look at their car. It took him no time at all to remove the front off-side hub cap and loosen the wheel nuts until they were hardly holding the wheel on. He hoped that once they started off, the movement of the steering wheel would detach the bolts completely. If they were going fast enough, they would veer into the pathway of oncoming traffic and, boom! What he had planned would have been achieved. He smiled to himself. It would look natural. No one would question why it had happened. Poor maintenance. It was foolproof.

When Meryl and Michael came out of the restaurant, the don watched them from the safety of the hire car. He saw Meryl switch on the ignition and the car slowly moved off. He tracked them again, a few hundred yards behind and he felt happier still when they took the exit from the roundabout which would lead them on to the motorway. They'd be travelling faster there and the accident he had planned would more likely be disastrous. The thought of the tragedy which was going to happen bouyed him up. He was elated. He started to whistle quietly to himself. They were accelerating; good, the faster the better. The miles went by.
'Strange. I would have anticipated that wheel dropping off by now' Fifty miles on, the car was still travelling northwards towards the lakes. 'Damn them. Damn, damn, damn. It's not going to happen.'

What the don didn't know was that Volkswagen cars are almost indestructible. Though the don had loosened the four nuts of the wheel, one of them had been left slightly tighter than the others. That was enough to keep the wheel on the front of the car. It was only when they slowed down and turned into the hotel where they were going to stay, the bolt gave up the ghost. The nut sheared off the hub and the wheel dropped off. The car gave an ominous tilt to the right and jerked to a sudden stop as the steering bushes hit the ground. Had they been going fast, they probably would have rolled over into the path of any traffic about. Michael got out with Meryl and inspected the damage. It didn't look too bad. If he jacked up the front end, he would be able to reattach the wheel. He levered off the cap only to find the nuts free. He frowned. Could this have happened normally? He took off the hub cap on the other side; the nuts were all firmly secured. He checked the rear wheels; they too were tight; he couldn't loosen them. And yet the wheel that had come off had four loose nuts. He was suspicious. He looked around, but he didn't see the car parked in the lay-by three hundred yards away. He didn't see his don, but he was a worried man.

Michael bolted the wheel back in place and the car limped slowly onto the hotel forecourt. He lifted out the luggage and escorted Meryl into reception. He signed the register as Mr and Mrs Michael Chaney for the first time and collecting the key, they were taken to their room for their first night away together. The door closed gently behind the porter who had helped with their luggage. Michael turned towards Meryl, a blush spreading over his face, his arms outstretched. Meryl approached him shyly, her face reddening too, just as his had done.

"We'll make it succeed Michael. We'll just have to take it slowly."

Michael enveloped her in his arms. "I love you Meryl. I couldn't have dreamed of this moment in my wildest dreams. What happens, will."

He kissed her gently, aware of deep fine sensations inside him. Meryl too recognised a warmness and moistness where there had been nothing like that for years; for more than twenty-four years in fact.

Later, Michael returned to reception and telephoned the RAC. He told them what had happened and asked them to call as soon as they could. Fortunately, they were not far away and were soon at the hotel carpark.

"Could those bolts have loosened themselves on their own?" he asked the serviceman.

"I wouldn't have thought so," he said. "Perhaps they weren't tightened up properly after servicing, but I don't really think that's likely."

"You mean they must have been loosened deliberately."

The RAC man looked at Celleri searchingly., "Do you think that's a possibility?" he asked.

"No, I wouldn't have thought so, but if there's no other explanation, surely that must be the case?" Michael said.
"I wouldn't know," the RAC man responded. But Michael knew deep down the explanation must be that the wheel nuts had been tampered with deliberately. If that were the case, the only man who wanted to kill him and have the courage to and was evil enough to carry it out, was his don. But where was he now? Was he close by or still some way off? Michael began to fear for Meryl's safety. In fact, for the safety of the two of them.

"What did the RAC man say," Meryl asked as soon as he came back into their room.
"I'm not really sure," Michael replied. "He finds it difficult to believe the wheel nuts could loosen themselves. He thinks they may have been interfered with by someone."
Meryl turned sharply towards him. "Do you think it's them?" she whispered. "How could they know where you are? Oh Michael, I'm frightened."
"Now don't get upset, we aren't sure what has happened yet. Perhaps the nuts did undo themselves; perhaps they hadn't been tightened properly. In the morning we'll get the garage to check the steering. We'll make sure it's all right. We'll ask them then."
He tried to look reassuring but it was hard to hide his feelings. He knew deep down the wheel had been tampered with; but by whom?

Their first night together was tense with the worry about what had happened to their car hanging over them. They lay together in each other's arms, each gaining support and comfort from the other. They kissed and fondled one another, learning again the love that close contact alone can bring. They fell asleep like that, exhausted by the stresses of the day, soothed and calmed by the presence of the other.

After breakfast, they drove the car carefully to the local garage only to learn that the steering arm had been cracked in the accident and any further driving would be hazardous. They heard from the mechanic that, in his view, anyone who had left the wheel nuts so loose that they could work undone, ought to be shot.
"Criminal," he said.
"But if they had all been properly tightened after the previous service, to find them undone now means that they must have been loosened deliberately?" Celleri asked.
"I suppose so. But who would do a daft thing like that? You could have been killed if the wheel had fallen off on the motorway."

"And perhaps that's exactly what was planned to have happened," Michael said as he turned to Meryl. "I'll bet someone tampered with the wheel while we had lunch yesterday. And I bet he's here somewhere watching what's going on." Both of them looked around, hoping to catch a glimpse of their adversary, but neither saw the shadowy figure afar off.
"Can we hire another car from you while you're repairing this one?" Michael asked the garage owner.
"Of course, take your choice," he said, waving towards a fleet of parked cars. "They're all for hire."

The don had had an uncomfortable night in a smaller hotel on the outskirts of the village chosen by Michael and Meryl. He was cross with himself; his efforts had failed. His sleep had been fitful, leaving him tired and irritable when he had risen early in the morning to follow the newly-weds. He had seen them visit the garage and watched them choose another car for their holiday. He knew he had to try and kill them again; he had to. But how was he to do it, having failed at his first attempt? He wasn't so sure this time. He had none of his men with him, men who would have killed without a second thought. He had no weapons he could use. He had to rely on a fatal accident to succeed. But how? He couldn't undo wheel nuts again; that had failed anyway. He began to wonder if it was going to be too difficult to carry out. There had to be a way.

He watched them drive away. Let them get on with their holiday and relax. It would be easier to do something when their guard was down, unsuspecting. It would give him time to think. He drove to their hotel.
"Do you have accommodation?" he asked, trying to hide his coarse American accent as much as he could, but without much success.
"We do sir. How long are you planning to stay?" the receptionist asked.
"Maybe two or three days. Just long enough to have a look around your beautiful countryside."
"It is lovely here isn't it, especially when the weather is as nice as it is at the moment. Will you fill in the card please? Then sign the register and the porter can take you to your room." As the don bent forward to sign the book he looked to see who had arrived yesterday. Mr and Mrs Michael Chaney. Chaney; no Celleri. Nobody else had signed the book yesterday. He began to perspire. Had he made a mistake? Perhaps this guy wasn't his capo, Celleri. But it was, it was him. He was sure.

The room he had been given was on the same floor as the Chaney's. It was all now beginning to fit in place. He knew what he was going to do, if not today, then tomorrow.

The don had his meals sent up to him that day. He knew he couldn't risk recognition in the dining room and the following morning he was in a position to see Meryl and Michael leave for their tour around the countryside. He waited until the maid had cleared their room before he left his to pick the lock and gain entry. It was easy. This hotel had locks that were ancient before the last war and it took him no time getting in. He worked quickly. He didn't mind which of them died, the man or the woman, it made no difference to him. Revenge was all he could think about at that moment. He unscrewed the light switch, joining a wire from the live pole to the metal surround. Now, as soon as the switch was turned on, the surround would become live and administer an electric shock, hopefully fatal to whoever was touching it. With a bit of luck, the other party, if in close contact with the person switching on the light, would be electrocuted too. He smiled to himself. Now to do the same thing to some of the other light switches, just in case they didn't use that one. And finally, he went into the bathroom and ran a thin wire from the live switch of the shaver plug to the chromium plated taps in the wash basin. He had now covered all eventualities. All he had to do was wait. Locking the door, he returned to his own room and lying on the bed, he debated whether he should leave now or later, when it was all over.
"I'd better see it through," he murmured to himself.

He must have dropped off to sleep. There was a scream and a loud bang outside in the corridor. He roused himself. He looked at his watch; it was a little after three, too soon for his victims to be back. Opening his door, he peered along the pasageway. The door to their room was open and the black-stockinged legs of the chambermaid lying on the floor stuck out into the hall. It must have been her scream he had heard and the bang was her falling. He felt sick as he went back into his room quickly.
"Damn them. Why the hell didn't they come back in time." The fact that someone else had died didn't worry him at all. To him life was cheap, anyone's life that is, other than his.

Rushing feet could be heard along the corridor outside his door. He could hear someone say she was dead and another saying

nothing should be touched and yet another saying they should get a doctor and the police. Now was definitely the time to keep his head down. Some time must have passed before there was a timid knock on his door.
"Pardon me sir," the hotel manager said, "but did you hear anything untoward this afternoon?"
"I've been resting," he said. "I thought I heard a shout some time ago but nothing else; I guess I must have dropped off to sleep again. Why, has something happened?"
"I'm afraid one of our maids has been electrocuted from a light switch. Would you mind if we had a look at your lights to make sure they're all right while we're here?"
"Sure, I don't mind. Take a look around."

They found his switches were all in good working order and after their check, they excused themselves. But the corridor was a hive of activity that afternoon with plain-clothed policeman examining the Chaney's room carefully. Naturally, they found the other dangerous lights and the wire in the bathroom, all of which could have killed anyone who came into contact with them. Fingerprints were taken from the metal plate around the switch and the officer commented enthusiastically on the quality of the records he obtained. The don began to wish he'd taken more care in his preparations. Perhaps he shouldn't stay around for the investigations. Perhaps he should get away while the going seemed to be good.

While he was deliberating what to do, the Chaneys returned to the hotel. The police were still there and wanted to question them urgently. It was absurd to think that they would have wired up the room in this dangerous way but the enquiries had to be made.
"Did you have anything to do with this wiring?" they were asked.
"Of course not," both of them answered in unison.
"Then you're lucky to be alive and that poor girl has died in your place," the policeman said. "Someone must have been trying to kill you."
"I believe you're right," Michael answered. "I think I should tell you now that the wheel nuts of the car we were driving yesterday were deliberately loosened and a minor accident occurred at the entrance to this hotel's driveway. If we had been driving quickly, then I think we would both have been killed."
"You mean someone's trying to kill you? Where is the car now?"
"It's having the repairs done in the local garage."

"Why wasn't this reported at once?" the more senior of the police asked.
"It was very difficult to know what had happened exactly. I suggest you talk to the mechanic in the garage. He can tell you what he said to us, that in his view, the bolts were undone by someone."
"And now someone has wired your electric light switches in an attempt to kill you. Do you know anyone who would want to do that to you?"

Michael knew very well someone who would have enormous pleasure doing that. His don. But there was no way he could tell the police that, if for no other reason than he wasn't Michael Chaney; he was Celleri, someone whom the New York authority considered was dead and buried. And furthermore, the insurers of the Bellevue Hospital had paid out a vast sum in damages upon his abduction from their hospital and his subsequent death. No, it wouldn't be easy to assume his correct identity and tell his complicated story to the British police. Much rather they tried to work it out for themselves.

The don wasted no time hanging around the hotel now his scheme had failed. He paid his bill and left before anyone should associate him with the peculiar goings-on of the day before. He had to get away, right away. Back to the States in fact and quickly.

The police, however, continued their painstaking investigations but the fingerprints they found matched Meryl's and Michael's only.
"Reception has told us the man who was staying in the adjacent room has left rather suddenly. Do you think he may have been the one who fiddled with your light switches? Had you met this man?"
"We wouldn't know who was in this room," Michael said.
"That's right," the receptionist confirmed. "The occupant of this room arrived in the late morning, after Mr and Mrs Chaney had left for the day. They couldn't have met the man who was here."
"Is that right Mr Chaney?" the policeman leading the investigation asked.
"Yes, we left shortly after breakfast, about half past nine, I would say. We didn't arrive back here until after five in the evening."
"What was this man like?" the police asked the receptionist.
"He was a big man, American, though he seemed to be hiding his accent."
She pushed the register towards the policeman, pointing out the signature. Michael strained his neck to see. A, and a scribble and Bar

and the rest was unreadable. Michael knew it at once. It was the signature of Angelo Bargello, his don. He had made no attempt to conceal his identity. He hadn't needed to. If he had been successful, there would have been nothing to have connected him with their deaths. No one would have questioned who he was. But now that he hadn't been successful, and had left the hotel rather than sweat it out, he was on the run.
'Let's hope he's on his way back to the States,' Michael thought.

The don realised he had signed the hotel register in his own name and that his flight from the hotel might make him look guilty. Unless he got to the airport quickly and was lucky enough to get a seat on a plane to the States immediately, he felt he may have been in trouble with the British police; big trouble. He pointed his car southwards on the motorway and ignoring the speed limit, he raced towards the nearest and largest airport in the north of England, Manchester. Somewhere north of his destination, while still on the motorway, travelling at about eighty-five miles an hour in the outside lane, feeling the exhilaration of fast driving, he thought he recognised the blue flashing light of a police car following about half a mile behind. He knew he couldn't afford to be arrested. He pushed his foot to the floor of the car and his speed surged upwards, the speedometer needle flickering just over the hundred mark. If he could keep this up as far as the next exit, he thought he could probably avoid being caught by the police when he left the motorway.

It was then a stone, probably thrown up by another car, hit the windscreen. It shattered into a myriad pieces; at once, all forward vision disappeared. The don panicked. He was driving fast, something he wasn't used to doing, on the wrong side of the road for him, in a strange car. He jerked the wheel suddenly as the windscreen became opaque and trod heavily on the brake. The car slewed across the road, while he struggled with the steering. It was no use. As the car started to roll he screamed, but it went over and over. The roof caved in on the first impact, like the top of an egg being tapped in an egg-cup. It ripped off at one side, the torn metal following the twisting car in a grotesque dance and the next time the car rolled, it was the don's unprotected head which took the direct blow. His skull cracked wide open, like a coconut struck with a machete and with each further turn of the car, his now inert head was damaged more and more. The car came to a halt three or four hundred yards along the road, where it struck the crash barrier.

It was upright. The don was dead and unrecognisable; an anonymous corpse, still strapped into the driving seat, his face hideously injured by the accident.

The police were on the scene within a few minutes. The young officer gagged as he looked at the mutilated head. His partner threw a blanket over it to hide the gruesome sight, while he telephoned for a mortuary wagon, assistance in clearing the road of debris and the removal of the wrecked car. In fact, to clear the world of the mortal remains of the don.

The news that an American who had been staying at the hotel had been involved in a dreadful road accident and had been killed instantly, spread like wildfire. When Meryl and Celleri heard, it was as if a great weight had been lifted from them; the only thing that could have spoiled the rest of their lives was over at last; the threat to their very existence had gone. Celleri's don was dead. They walked on air. They could hardly contain themselves awaiting Rosie's and Nick's return.

Two weeks later when they came home from their honeymoon, Meryl and Celleri were there at Heathrow to welcome them. Their joy hearing the news was apparent.
"It's a dreadful thing to say, but how marvellous he's dead. What a relief it must be to you both, in fact to all of us. We'll just have to celebrate this," Nick said. They all agreed enthusiastically; after all, Celleri's don, the man who could have ruined their lives, was dead.